MARK OF ORION

GUARDIANS OF ORION BOOK ONE

S. L. RICHARDSON

S. L. Richardson

www.slrichardson.com

Available in these formats:

ISBN: 978-1-7340644-0-7 (eBook)

ISBN: 978-1-7340644-1-4 (Paperback)

Cover Design: Natalie Narbonne at Original Book Cover Design - www.originalbookcoverdesign.com

Book Formatting: Haunted Unicorn Publishing

Editing: Alexandra Ott

Published by Flasheila Press | Friendswood, Texas

❀ Created with Vellum

For my family, who's undying love and support gave me the courage to write this book
For our Lord, who makes all things possible

PROLOGUE
DARK PRINCE

Humans...

They made killing easy.

Delightful.

So absorbed with themselves, they never looked into the darkened corners, sure their childhood monsters weren't lurking, eager for their next victim.

But they were.

He and his accomplices blended into the shadows across the street from the church. His fingers tapped a wicked metal blade not of this world resting on his hip. Anticipation hummed through him, hungry for his sinister plan's fruition.

The nun emerged from the church. Its brick front and looming tower with large wooden double doors dwarfed her. The somber habit hid her body, her hair under the black veil. But the unshapely garment couldn't conceal her ancient cursed lineage from his infernal senses.

The moonless night was crisp. Leaves swirled on a soft breeze down the deserted street, carrying her scent where he lay in wait. He closed his eyes and inhaled deeply.

So fresh.

So naïve.

So pure.

As soon as he opened them, his seething rage clouded his vision. His hate for the nun was as pure as her vocation. She represented everything he despised, yet she possessed what he desperately needed... her soul.

The nun took a few steps but paused. She twisted, her eyes scanning the shadowy street behind her. She peered in his direction as if she sensed something hidden in the shadows. He pressed deeper into the blackness. Hunting the prey was as delicious as catching it. He would stretch this cat-and-mouse game out longer. Feeding off her fear excited him, but time didn't warrant such a decadent luxury.

The nun hurried down the sidewalk, risking a hasty glance over her shoulder. She headed for the lone car in the vacated parking lot, keys jingling in her grip. He sneered, propelling himself out of the shadows.

It was deathly quiet as he started across the street. Just how he liked it. His three accomplices materialized out of the shadows and followed him. His black blood pounded, intoxicated by the promise of her dormant ancient soul.

Her car's remote chirped, piercing the still night. She reached for the handle but stiffened. She spun, and her face paled. A sharp gasp escaped when she saw what bore down upon her. She scanned the lot, glancing back at the church, but the icy mask of terror froze on her face. There was nowhere to run. Nowhere to hide.

She pressed backward against the car door as they surrounded her. Her chest heaved as her eyes scoured his high forehead, sharp nose, and chiseled jaw. They darted over his black leather clothing and widened when they found his sword dangling from his hip. The scar across his left cheek lifted as he leered at her. Recognition tightened her features while her lips worked in silent movement. He couldn't detect her mumblings, but he didn't care.

His deep voice spoke, void of emotion. "Crying out for God? Begging Him to save you? You'll understand soon. He never comes."

She's mine tonight... including her soul.

But the murmurings continued. Her doe brown eyes gaped at him, yet something else flared within.

Peace.

His hot hand slapped her face, snapping her head back. Now she turned and faced him with horror and pain. Her shaking hand covered her bright red cheek.

That's more like it.

He pressed closer, suppressing the urge to strike again.

"Anne, do you know who I am?"

Her throat convulsed as her parted lips trembled.

"Yes. Mother Superior warned me of you. You're a Prince from Hell." Her hand trailed down her cheek and smeared the blood leaking from the corner of her mouth. "You can kill me, but I'm not afraid." Her other hand clasped the wooden crucifix, with a silver metal figure of Jesus on it, dangling from her neck by a long leather cord. "My heavenly Father awaits me."

A low rumbling started in his chest as a hideous smile stretched across his white marble-like face. The three Fallen behind him joined in with their cackles of laughter. The Prince shook his head, snickering at her bold statement.

"So stupid in your blind faith."

He seized the fist clutching her crucifix, engulfing it. He squeezed, pressing the crucifix into her delicate palm. She whimpered as blood trickled down her wrist.

"Let's play a game. You know who I am, but do you know who you are... what's entombed within you?"

Confusion and desperation alternated on her face. No recognition in her eyes this time, only useless tears. The Prince was correct. Only he knew the aged secret.

Prying her fingers open, he tore the bloody crucifix from her maimed hand and yanked. He sneered as he flung the object of his repulsion to the ground.

"Those wretched nuns never told you, did they? Cold jealousy hidden under all their righteousness sealed their withered lips. Even better."

"God will still forgive you. It's never too late–" she stammered between her shallow breaths.

His maniacal laughter echoed through the night air. "I have no interest in your God's forgiveness. He doesn't frighten me." He lifted his brow as he scanned the starless night. "Looks like He hasn't heard your sobs. It's too late, anyway."

A bright, hot light exploded between them. Another flash threw him from the nun. Anne gazed at the brilliant light. An exuberant smile spread across her awed face.

A magnificent creature glowed within the light. The angel stood tall in her pure white armor, except for a red-hilted sword strapped to the red belt around her hips. Her large, luminous white wings extended behind her, each feather catching the breeze. Long silver hair enveloped her like an aura, and her crimson eyes sparkled. The angel drew her blade and stood ready for battle.

"So, your mighty protector arrives. A little late, aren't you?" The Prince glared at her in open mockery. "Did we catch you lounging in the clouds adoring your Maker?"

"What brings you out of your fire pit, Prince? You never leave your hovel. You always send your Fallen to do your dirty work." She cocked her head. "Something must have changed. Need some fresh air?" She lifted her brow, matching his mockery.

The Prince waved his hand, dismissing her.

"This air is too cool for my taste. But, yes, there's been a significant change... my future."

At once, the three Fallens' black wings swept out from behind them, sending ash and smoke into the air, covering their quick movements. The angel raised her weapon while her other hand sought the nun. But she was too late. The nun raced toward the protection of the church. Two Fallen gave chase; their red pupils, encased in obsidian eyes, flared with hate as their hyena-like cackles filled the air.

"You can't fight us all." He laid his black-veined hand on the sword's hilt.

The remaining Fallen lunged at the angel from her right. She swung her sword with both hands, striking across its neck. The head stayed in place for a moment, then tumbled, silencing its shrieks of outrage. His body and putrid black blood changed to ash, disappearing with the breeze.

The Prince fumed at his Fallen's demise. He reached for the angel, but she pumped her wings and took flight for the Fallen closing in on the nun. The Prince also gave chase. He must stop the angel and the nun from getting inside the church, evading his destiny.

"Grab her!" The Prince snarled as he pursued them.

"Get inside the church, Anne!" The angel dived to intercept the Fallen.

Anne glanced up but stumbled as her foot caught the habit's hem.

"Meira help me!" Anne scrambled up, calling out to the angel.

The Fallen screeched as they drew closer. Anne lost her footing again when she glanced back at her pursuers.

Foolish girl doesn't have a chance.

The Prince concentrated on the angel. He targeted her back and tackled her mid-air. The collision sent them spiraling to the ground, cracking the concrete.

They surged to their feet, readying their weapons. The Prince paced around his enemy.

"Do you actually want to battle me? Leave now and let me have your precious charge. Stay and fight for her, you die, and she's still mine. Your choice."

Meira swung the sword in a wide arc, striking his side armor. He twirled and attacked, cutting his sword down on her shoulder. The heavy blow found a crease in her armor, slicing her, spraying her silver blood into the night. She cried out, falling to one knee.

The Prince rushed her. He swung across again, but she tucked and rolled away. She pushed up to her feet in a combat stance, meeting his next advance. They attacked each other, their swords a clash of matching blows and hostility.

She thrust forward, missing her mark. The Prince seized the opportunity and landed a strike to her hand. Her blade, freed from her grip, clanged, hitting the concrete. She shouted out, diving for her weapon, but he snatched it away.

"You've lost your sword, angel. That's a shame." He shoved it into his belt. "I enjoyed our fight. Got my blood pumping for the kill." He continued circling her as she picked herself up, challenging him. Her angelic powers healed her wounds, but she was left defenseless.

"Meira," he taunted, "I warned you that you were no match for me. None of you pathetic heavenly beings can match my powers."

"You disgust me!" she spewed in his face. "How dare you crawl out of your fetid pit to kill a nun!"

"You think it's just your nun I want? Your thoughts are so small." His wicked grin mirrored all the loathing he had for her and her kind. "My plan is just beginning, but you'll never see it."

The Prince charged. Meira spun away, surprising him with her speed. Her powerful wings lifted her up, and she slammed her boots against his chest. He fell back but snatched her boot, pulling her down with him. She landed on top of him, driving her fist into his mouth. His tongue flicked across his lip, tasting blood. His fist shot out and landed on her jaw, knocking her off of him.

She darted away, but he was right behind her. She spun and raised her hand. A red bolt exploded from her hand and soared at him as she took flight. He jumped, but it struck his leg, catapulting him backward. His armor absorbed the energy before he even took flight.

How dare she!

The Prince fired a swirling ball of energy from his hand, striking her wing. She shrieked as it knocked her out of the sky. She landed with a thud, and another crack split beneath her.

Even though her strength tested him, the thrill of their battle fanned his want, his need to kill. He came down next to her and gave her side a vicious kick. She raised her hands again, but he pulled out her sword. He slashed across her wrists. Silver blood sprayed as her hands toppled to the ground. He shifted and stabbed the top of her wounded wing, pinning it to the ground. Tremendous satisfaction spiked through him as he twisted the sword, separating her wing. Her screams were music to his ears. He removed the sword and dragged her up by her hair, his face inches from hers as her broken wing fell uselessly at her side.

"When will you learn these humans aren't worth fighting for? All they do is sin time and time again, not even asking for your help. Ungrateful filth. If you were my guardian angel, I'd call for you so I could watch your exquisite agony while I commit my heinous sins."

His arm snaked around her, trapping her struggling body against his.

"I have an offer for you. Come back with me, and I'll let Anne go."

Her chest heaved, pain and hatred boiling in her eyes. "I'd never go with you and neither will Anne. She's taken her vows. You lose." She panted in his face, her wrists sealed by her healing powers.

"We'll see about that." He scoffed at her arrogance while shuffling footsteps drew near. The two Fallen stopped behind the Prince. Anne's voice warbled as she spoke.

"Our Father, who art in Heaven..."

One Fallen grabbed Anne's hair and jerked her head back. He unsheathed his twisted dagger, pressing it against her neck.

"Say that prayer one more time, and I'll cut off your head." His spittle sprayed her face, silencing her words.

"Last chance." The Prince's lips pressed to Meira's hair, awaiting her answer.

She angled her head, the breeze lifting her long silver hair. At that moment, he hoped she'd agree to his preposterous offer. He wanted this pure creature for himself, for his pleasure.

"Never!" Her eyes went flat and lip curled, revulsion exuded from her.

His eyes narrowed. She'd regret her decision, but he'd enjoy watching her pay for it.

"No matter, I still have a use for you."

His fingers clamped around the angel's jaw, pressing deep into her skin. She grunted against him.

"Anne, do you love your guardian angel?" the Prince asked.

She nodded as tears streaked down her face. "With all my heart." Her body shook as her cries got louder.

"Do you love her more than yourself?"

Anne looked stunned, but her adoration for Meira glowed when she looked at her.

"Don't answer that, Anne! Don't listen to him!" Meira shook her head. "He's a liar!"

Meira looked back at the Prince. Silver tears fell down her translucent cheeks.

"Please, leave her alone. Set her free!" she pleaded. "She's an innocent."

"Never." A smile emerged when she bucked against him.

"I insist you answer me, Anne. Do you love her more than yourself?"

"Yes, I'm nothing compared to her."

The Prince's devious smile spread. He motioned to a Fallen. The Prince shoved Meira to the ground. She tried to flee, but the Fallen slammed his boot on her broken wing.

"Hold your dagger to the angel. Cut her head off if she moves." The Fallen seized her around the neck. He gnashed his teeth in her ear as he pressed the blade under her chin.

"Not too tight; we wouldn't want Meira to miss this," the Prince chided as he strode over to the nun.

His nostrils flared, inhaling the stink of fear rolling off of Anne in waves. Fear was the ultimate control, and control was the ultimate power. He had both. She recoiled as his black-veined hand grazed her swollen cheek. Her terrified eyes darted between him and Meira.

"If you care for your guardian angel, you can spare her. You just have to do one simple, unselfish act for her." The Prince grinned down at her.

Hope reflected in Anne's eyes. That was what he needed to see... what he craved. Give them hope, and they were putty in his hands. He stroked her hair like he was calming a frightened animal while blocking her view.

"Anything." Her voice quivered.

"Give her to me," the Prince said to the Fallen holding her, who bowed as he released her.

The Prince moved his hands and cupped her face. He brushed his thumb over her bruised lips and the cleft in her chin. She shivered at his touch. He engulfed her with his sinister presence, overwhelming her with his power.

"I'll take your life now, but it's your soul I want." She sought to pull away, horror frozen on her face, but his grasp only tightened.

"If you want her life spared, you will release your soul to me. If you do not, I will take her back to Hell with me and do with her what I will. The last thing you'll see before I choke the life out of you will be her disappearing into the portal. All because of you." Anne closed her eyes, body quaking in defeat.

Meira's wails of anguish increased behind them.

"Give me your answer, Anne."

She opened her eyes, her face pale and clammy, yet the words didn't come. Her doll-like eyes stared back at him. He gave her a hard shake, snapping her head.

"Now, before I change my mind!"

"Yes." She sobbed, sagging under the weight of her looming sacrifice.

His arm dropped around her waist. He drew the knife out of the sheath. Panic seized Anne, but he thrust the knife up under her rib cage. Her lifeblood oozed over his hand as he deepened the blade into her heart. A depraved thrill shot through him as the life in her eyes began to fade.

The Prince flung his head back and howled into the night sky. Her warm blood spurted down his arm and flowed over his stomach, soaking through his tunic. Her blood mingled with his tainted skin. The disguise disintegrated. A new, pure Fallen form emerged in front of the dying nun. Thick, ribbed horns erupted from the sides of his head. Spiked claws extended from his nails, penetrating the nun's waist. His scorching black armor burned her dying flesh. The pungent smell drove him into a frenzy.

"Come to me!" He beckoned the ancient soul.

He laid her down and covered her body with his own. As the fire spread, his mouth crushed hers in a macabre kiss.

He willed the soul with his evil essence to free itself from the flesh and come into him. A renewed fire entered his mouth but didn't burn. It spread like a light, a sensation awakening his every fiber. It consumed him, entwining in every part of his body as the damned and ancient collided and melded into one. A feral cry erupted until the metamorphosis ended and a new entity awakened.

Perfect.

Powerful.

Invincible.

The Earth and Heavens would be his to rule. A war would rage like no other, and nothing stood in his way. Not the Celestial Hosts, or God Himself.

He rose from the nun's ashes, swirling as they drifted away. He towered in his armor, glowing with an evil radiance. His massive wings of black translucent feathers were more like shavings of metal. Touching them, he reveled in their deadly beauty.

We are one.

Tortured cries penetrated his ears. He whipped around, insulted by her tirade. Time had grown short, but he had one last desire. Striding to Meira, he grabbed her by the neck. Long claws cut into her as he hauled her up, leaving her feet dangling.

"This is your God's doing! Outnumbered, we fought your kind, but He drove us out of Heaven like we were nothing, meaningless. He left us to survive underground among the fire, lava, and rock. And for what? Because we wouldn't serve his newest creation. No more! It's our turn to rule and decimate man!"

"You'll never win." Meira gasped against his closing grasp. "You aren't a god and never will be!"

The Prince presented his knife, still dripping with the nun's blood.

"But I did win. A simple lie to the nun, and I got what I wanted: her soul. Perfect, is it not?" His hollow voice taunted her as he returned the blade into its sheath. "You should have taken my offer."

He plunged a spiked claw into her chest. Her eyes widened at the sudden intrusion, her sharp scream assaulting his ears as he yanked out her heart. The Prince's eyes rolled back as he relished Meira's silver blood spraying over him, emptying her essence, killing her.

He flung her broken body to the ground, a heap of white feathers and armor, her silver blood pooled around her.

The Prince turned to the Fallen, whose crazed excitement glowed in their eyes.

"Come, we must leave now. The archangels will be here soon. They'll have heard Meira's death cry."

The Prince tossed her heart, which splattered as it landed in her glistening life blood.

The Prince reclaimed control of his current form. He must return to Hell in his old, molten armor. No one could discover his transformation. He would preserve that for later when he began his war.

They approached the shadows from which they had appeared. The Prince raised his hand, signaling the portal. It crackled with electric sparks as it spread, Hell's blackness beckoning them. Heat from his world blasted the cold night air. The Fallen entered first, swallowed up by the pitch-dark abyss. The Prince took a final glance behind him. The night sky opened up with white lights, like shooting stars, as warrior angels rained down.

He smiled, vindication surged through him when the angels discovered Meira. The Prince laughed at their worthless cries as he walked inside the portal. He shifted and faced his nemesis, who flew through the twilight aimed for the entrance. The electric web had almost closed when the champion angel with blue-tipped wings reached it. His sword lifted high; a war cry hurled from his lips.

"You're too late, Michael, but we'll meet again." The portal sizzled closed before Michael could strike his faceless enemy.

Heat engulfed the Prince.

He welcomed it.

No one could stop him now.

Not the other princes.

Not even Lucifer.

Soon he would reign over it all.

And his kingdom would have no end.

CHAPTER ONE
OLIVIA

2 :58
Tick-tick

Olivia glanced at the black-rimmed clock above the classroom whiteboard. The second hand moved like a minute hand. She slumped against the slatted plastic chair, bashing her knee under the small wooden desk. Instead of kicking the desk, she cursed the cramped seating. Her friend, Alisha sat in the front row. Shiny ebony curls bunched between her fingers as she rested her head on her cocked arm. Olivia smirked, knowing she wasn't the only person ready for the class to end.

Last class of the day before holiday recess began.

Hallelujah.

The glossy page of her thick textbook with minuscule words and dated pictures annoyed her. The page's corner creased over the same historical figure whose condescending face lorded from one of many posters tacked on dreary beige walls. Ms. Thomas paced the speckled tile and droned on about studying Napoleon after the break. But Olivia couldn't concentrate on her monotone voice. She liked school, even history, but a break from the routine sounded glorious. She twirled her purple pen between her fingers, chancing another glimpse at the time.

2:59.

The incessant ticking grew louder in her head. She sighed, knowing her internal clock ticked for more than school. Christmas loomed on the horizon. The most hated day of her life. Her holiday remembrances weren't like idyllic TV shows of a sleepy family opening presents wrapped in festive paper and bows. The shouts of glee for a treasured gift or powdered-donut-covered fingers reaching under the fragrant pine tree for the last hidden package.

No.

Sharp twisting pain and an endless void of sadness haunted her memories. A cherub little girl dressed in pink jammies adorned with snowflakes, watched her dad walk out the door. Gone. Never to come back. Skipped out on the happiest day of the year.

Jerk.

She set the pen on the scratched desktop. Worn pages fluttered as she closed the textbook with a thump. Her hand sought the unzipped gray backpack sagging against the desk's metal leg. She froze as her name punched a hole through her troubled memories.

Uh oh.

"Olivia? Did you hear the question?" Ms. Thomas quipped, resting her hands on her hips.

RING... RING.

3:00.

Saved by the bell.

"Miss Drake, stay after class, please."

Maybe not.

At once, books slammed closed and chairs banged against desks as students scrambled out of their seats. Excited voices, mixed with a few raised eyebrows, scurried by her, funneling out the exit. Olivia shoved her textbook into her overstuffed backpack and hefted it onto her shoulder. She slipped on a friendly face and approached her teacher's tidy desk, crammed in the corner.

"Yes?" Olivia asked.

Ms. Thomas waited with her thin arms folded, a bony hip jutting out. Her critical eyes narrowed behind tortoise-shell glasses; her lips pinched together in a sour expression. Olivia tilted her face, returning her stare.

Ms. Thomas cocked her head. "I've noticed you've developed a habit of checking the time and not paying attention. Something going on you'd care to share?"

Yes... your class makes my ears bleed.

Can't repeat that.

Olivia readjusted her heavy load, clearing her throat.

"There's no problem. I work at Cuppa Joe's, and my shift starts right after school. My boss wants me to beat the rush, so I get antsy sometimes."

"I appreciate your work ethic, but your employer should under-stand education comes first." Ms. Thomas's glare didn't waver. Olivia ran an uneasy hand through her long dark-blond hair, stopping to tuck a strand behind her ear. Her finger grazed over three small pierced earrings in her right lobe. She twisted the dainty silver drag-onfly before her hand fell.

"I'll pass that along." Olivia shifted her feet. "Can I go now? I don't want to be late."

Ms. Thomas exhaled, puffing out her cheeks. Her lean form folded into the black office chair, springs squeaking as she leaned back. "Yes, you may leave. But I hope you come back ready to pay attention in class... not the clock. You're a good student, but next time I catch you daydreaming, you'll be very late for work."

Olivia nodded and turned before she got caught rolling her eyes. Ms. Thomas's stare in the middle of her back gave it a weird itchy sensation. She hurried out, ready to put the curious episode behind her. The bustle in the corridor was a welcome reprieve from her teacher's misguided scrutiny.

Alisha materialized beside her and bumped her hip. She greeted Olivia with a white, toothy smile. Her tawny brown eyes sparkled against her rich dark skin.

"What was that all about? Are you busted or what?"

"No, I'm not busted, but thanks for the positive thoughts." Olivia grinned and hip bumped her back. "Essentially, she told me to quit daydreaming. But it was weird... like she was digging for something more."

"Phish... That's nothing. Doesn't she know having history last period is the worst?" They both chuckled as they walked down the emptying hallway. Fluorescent lights cast a dull glow over the litter-strewn concrete floors. The walls congested with rows of beat-up lockers. But it didn't dampen the air of excitement for holiday recess. Lingering students laughed and waved to passing friends making their way for the double doors to the student parking area.

Alisha glanced over before skirting around a hulking glass trophy case. "Girl, I miss you on the soccer team. How's your knee feeling? Please tell me our star d-back will be at spring training."

"Probably not. It still hurts and aches after work. The doctor said no soccer or running to help it heal. If it doesn't, surgery could be next, and I don't want that. Besides, senior year is flying by, and I have decisions to make about college."

"Like what?"

"Like, should I go now or stay home for a year? I could save more money... help my mom out with expenses." She shook her head. "It's complicated."

"Hmm, sounds to me you're thinking more about your mom than your future. You can't worry about her forever. Besides, college will be so much fun. I, for one, am so over this place." Alisha smirked, batting her hand at the school.

"Me too." They stopped at Olivia's locker. The pack slipped off, landing with a thud. "I know what you're saying. It's exactly what my mom says, too, but it's easier said than done. I'll decide by the end of the break."

"Good! Maybe we can be roommates."

Whether Olivia was ready for that wild ride, she didn't know, but it gave her heart a warm squeeze.

"And I miss playing soccer... bad... and the girls, too." A lump stuck in her throat as she turned the combination lock. Alisha surprised her with a big hug. Her clean linen scent wafted around Olivia.

"Let's get together during the time off and hang out." Alisha gave her an extra squeeze.

"I'd like that. Come by Joe's. Coffee's on me." She stepped away, pleased she had a fun night out in her future.

"Won't say no to that." Alisha's elbow nudged her. "Hey, look, it's your fine neighbor." She leaned in and whispered, "I'll come over late one night and we'll go peek in his window."

"Stop... that's wrong on so many levels." Olivia bit her bottom lip, stifling her laughter while she piled books in her unadorned locker.

"Not from where I stand. Hey, see you later." Alisha flashed a wicked grin as her long strides gobbled up the hallway.

"Bye." Olivia turned and saw Zach. Butterflies fluttered as she picked up her lightened pack. His shirt pulled tight over his tapered back when he opened his locker. He kept his dark brown hair cropped close on the sides, but longer on top, with a tousled look. He twisted and caught her eye before she could turn away. Bright emerald eyes pinned her as a grin tugged at his mouth's corners. She cringed inside but held his playful gaze even as a heat crept up her neck.

Busted.

He lifted his chin at her. Olivia returned with a hesitant smile, but it felt more like a grimace. Horrified, she spun away before her rising flush embarrassed her even more. She hurried down the hallway, hoping to blend in with the stragglers and disguise her hasty retreat. She mentally gave herself a palm-smack, irritated by how flustered she got whenever she saw him. Playing sports made her comfortable with guys, but he knotted her up like the necklaces at the bottom of her jewelry box.

Zach Paxton.

Mr. Tall, Dark and Handsome graced Las Vegas with his presence when he'd moved here over the summer. He'd been all the rage when school started but kept the fawning girls at bay. Even worse, he lived at the end of her street, compelling her to glance over when she drove past. Once, he was washing his truck and waved for her to stop. But she panicked and zoomed home, pretending she hadn't seen him. She'd parked and banged her head on the seat rest for being so awkward.

Coward.

Olivia pushed the exit door and headed for her car. She squinted against the bright sunshine as the brisk breeze cooled her blushing face. The Vegas skyline came into view, jutting up from the desert valley. Massive steel hotels, with their dazzling designs, vied for their piece of the glamorous Las Vegas Strip. Homes stretched out from the Strip like a sea of terra cotta tiled roofs with a smattering of greenery, creeping up the base of the barren mountains enclosing the intimate valley.

Even though she tried, Olivia couldn't understand why people came to gamble away their hard-earned cash. Mom once said it was because people dreamed of living outside their ordinary world, even if only for a weekend. She called Vegas the Adult Disneyland. Olivia shuddered at their foolishness, but the tourists' money provided for Mom's job at a glitzy casino's marquee show. She'd started after Dad left. How could a man do that... leave his family to make it on their own?

So selfish...

She spied her used SUV parked next to a new crossover. Years of harsh desert sun had faded the green paint, leaving it lackluster compared to the polished red car. She scoffed, pinning the new ride for an early Christmas gift. The hinges creaked when she opened the door, throwing her pack on the passenger's seat. She slid into the worn gray cloth seats, sighing in relief. As soon as the truck rumbled to life, music piped through the new car stereo she'd bought as a birthday present to herself. It wasn't the prettiest car on the road, but she loved that it was hers.

Gunning it for work, she shoved thoughts of Zach and Christmas aside. Instead, she drummed her thumbs on the steering wheel and belted out the tune blasting around her. Enjoying the music eased her tension until she drove past Joe's packed parking lot and saw her boss waiting by the back door.

CUPPA JOE'S large red script logo adorned the facade of a new strip mall facing the corner of a busy intersection. It had opened over the summer and soon built up a loyal clientele. High school kids hit the drive-thru before class yearning for morning caffeine and returned for their afternoon fix. Other customers brought their laptops or books, popped in their earphones, and settled in for uninterrupted time. Olivia adored coffee and needed a job, so she applied. She started on the first day of business and had loved it ever since.

Unless her boss stood at the back door.

She parked and snatched her gear from the back seat, racing for the door while tying the apron around her waist. She stopped, pushing her hair out of her face, and found Joe's hazel eyes squinting at her.

"You're late." Her boss's tall, lean frame blocked the doorway as he held a plastic trash bag. His shaggy chestnut hair hooked behind his ears, revealing small gold hoops piercing each lobe. Joe wore a coffee logo T-shirt and skinny jeans, looking much like a customer, except for the brown apron tied low on his hips. When he hefted the garbage into the pungent dumpster, it exposed a tribal tattoo winding around his bicep.

"I know. I'm sorry. My teacher wanted me to stay after class." She pressed her lips tight, exhaling through her nose.

His hands settled on his hips. "Why? Something happen at school?" As his eyebrows drew together, he examined her from head to toe.

This tone of concern surprised her. Joe was a nice guy and didn't pry into her world, keeping most of their conversations about work. She liked that he respected her space. Why the change?

"My teacher noticed how I kept checking the time. She wanted an explanation, so I said I had a tyrant boss who doesn't appreciate it when I'm late."

"Why–" His jaw dropped.

"I am just kidding." She nudged his arm. "Thought it was easier than explaining how bored I am in her class. By the way, she told me to pass along that my education is more important than my job."

"Noted, but next time throw someone else under the bus." Joe's lips twitched. He leaned closer. "You sure that's it?"

"All good." She tipped her head toward the shop's door. "I better go break Callie."

Even though he nodded and opened the door, his furrowed brow remained in place.

The sounds of murmuring mixed with coffee beans grinding greeted her. She inhaled the rich aroma. It was as stimulating as if she had sipped a cup of cappuccino herself. Waning sunlight filtered through the floor-to-ceiling windows lining the front of the cafe. She walked past the chest-high walls on each side of the hallway. Game rooms were behind the walls. There were gathering areas with charge zones for electronics and gaming consoles hooked up to big-screen TVs.

"Do you do anything but play this game, Ryan?" An irritated voice drifted over the wall.

"Not my problem you guys suck. Are you going to play again or whine, Ethan?" Ryan's condescension hung in the air.

Olivia spied Ryan's copper hair when his pudgy body stood. Ethan and his buddy got up from the oversized tan couch, tossing their controllers on the cup-ring-stained wooden table. Ryan bumped Ethan's shoulder as they walked past him.

"Quitter."

Ethan shoved him, knocking him back a few steps. Ryan lunged forward, grabbing a handful of Ethan's shirt.

"Hey, knock it off! No fighting, you two." Joe slammed his fist on the wall, startling a few kids.

Ryan let go, snickering as he plopped back on the couch. Ethan glared at him as they stalked out of the game room. Ryan stared around the room. "Who's next?" A few boys shrugged and snagged the controllers.

Olivia ignored the boys and entered the main shop, the heartbeat of

Cuppa Joe's. She swung right and shoved open the waist-high door, stepping behind the long counter. The space was narrow but efficient, while the front L-shaped counter gleamed with burnished steel and glass cases. She stashed her purse inside one of the cabinets lining the back wall. Above, a chalkboard covered the entire wall. The menu items were written in white chalk; the words flowed in a scrolling script. She washed her hands in the sink next to a shelf stocked with specialty beans, to-go mugs, and gear with mottoes like: *Cuppa Joes: Rise and Grind; Life happens~ Coffee helps;* and her favorite, *Adulting begins after Coffee.*

"Enjoy." Callie placed a big chocolate cookie into an eager outstretched palm. Neat rows of cookies, brownies, and cupcakes enticed patrons with a perfect match for a cup of java.

The teenager took a bite and walked toward the simple steel bar-like counters facing the front windows. Kids lounged on barstools gabbing while their phones charged next to them. A couple sat in colorful chairs across from each other at one table. A sagging love seat and two stuffed loungers covered in bright gypsy fabric softened the opposite wall. Another pair cuddled on a gray sofa. Her blond bob fell over her face when she drifted over, whispering in his ear. His mischievous grin grew as his letterman jacket stretched while pulling her closer.

"Hey." The cash register dinged as Callie finished ringing up a purchase.

"Hi. How was your day?" Olivia asked.

Callie's jet-black hair swung in a ponytail, showing off her sharp cheekbones, pointed jaw, and crystal-blue eyes. Her shoulders sagged when she rested her hip against the counter. Black yoga pants and a small work shirt enhanced her petite shape.

"Holiday shoppers kept the drive-thru busy, and kids piled in right on cue." She pushed off, untying her apron. "I better get going. I have to pick up Chloe from preschool." Chloe was her two-year-old daughter, who mirrored her mom in attitude and all.

Olivia raised her hand, not letting her off the hook. "Okay, but what about you? Any news?"

When Callie exhaled, tears glistened, threatening to fall as she hugged herself.

"Divorce papers are final. It's such a relief, but overwhelming thinking about how I will juggle work, classes, and Chloe on my own." She shook her head, staring over Olivia's shoulder. "I also don't like how he rolled over at the end, considering his endless tirades on never letting me or Chloe go. Makes me nervous."

She scrubbed her arms, then swiped at her tears. "But we're free now, and he's not worth my time or tears." A spark lit in her eyes as her jaw set with determination.

"Now that's what I want to hear!" Olivia gave her a big hug. Since she understood the difficult road of a single parent, she promised to do whatever she could to support them.

"So glad you're rid of that psycho. You know I'm here to help, right?"

When Callie pulled away, she planted a quick kiss on her cheek. "I do. You've been so awesome through all this... watching Chloe... listening to me rant... like the kid sister I never had." They both chuckled, but Callie turned serious. "Thank you, Olivia."

"Anytime."

"Can you come in an hour early tomorrow? I have a test I need to cram for on Monday."

"Sure." Olivia nodded and waved bye. Since her social calendar was a big fat zero, she might as well make a few extra bucks.

"Great. Have a good night." Callie walked away from the counter, waving at Joe as she made her way to the back exit. He nodded, but his eyes lingered on the hallway. When the rear door clicked closed, he returned to wiping the empty tables.

Interesting.

A steady flow of customers kept Olivia busy for the next few hours. The front door bells jingled. Sergio strutted in with his big lopsided smile, showing off the cleft in his chin. A mop of thick, straight black hair tumbled over his forehead. His wiry body weaved through the tables, turning a few girls' heads along the way. Jake followed him in but headed for the game room.

"Hey. Want a coffee?" Olivia returned an easy smile back at her best friend.

"Nah. Jake and I were hanging out and he decided he wants to try out a new video game he's thinking about for Christmas. Thought I'd ride with him and say hi before Manny picks me up. My big bro got a new hot rod and wants to show it off." Concern clouded his golden-rimmed brown eyes. "How are you doing?"

"You're the third person to ask me that today." She huffed, glancing at Joe. "I'm fine... I guess. Although, I'm thrilled for the break from school." Olivia pulled an elastic band from her pocket. She smoothed her hair back, securing it into a messy bun.

"Thought school would never end." He reached up and wiggled her knotted mass. "Your hair is getting long. Ready for a change?"

Her mouth opened, but the sharp reply dissolved on her tongue. Instead, she shifted away before he noticed the painful jolt of an old memory.

"Hey, I'm sorry, Olivia." He caught her arm before she could walk away. "It's an awful time of the year for you. I wish you had good memories of Christmas, not sucky ones filled with your dad." She wanted to pull away, but he leaned in, not letting her run away.

"Keep your hair long because you love it, not because your dad did," he pleaded with her.

"That's not why—"

"You were only five, Olivia. Whatever happened wasn't your fault. Let go and move on with your life."

She bit her bottom lip. "Easy for you to say. You have an amazing family. And I have moved on, but sometimes those flashbacks catch me by surprise and take hold... and I've trimmed my hair." Sergio rolled his eyes, making her smile. "Besides, my hair *is* what *I* like most about me. I'm not keeping it long because my dad liked it." She narrowed her eyes, daring him to disagree.

"Well, personally, I think your eyes are the best." His playful smile beamed as he batted his eyes at her. She snickered, nudging his arm.

"Thanks for the pep talk. I needed it."

"I get you, girl." He winked, pushing away from the counter.

"Best feature, huh?" She fluttered her eyelids like butterfly wings. He threw up his hands in feigned defeat.

"Moment's gone." They both chuckled, easing the knot in her belly. Even though she knew Sergio was right, a few memories had deep, painful roots.

Amy sauntered up behind Sergio. Her yellow polka-dotted cup's handle dangled from her finger while interest bloomed across her face.

"I'm going back to check up on Jake. See ya." When Amy stepped in his way, he walked around her, oblivious to her blatant tactic. She and Olivia both watched him disappear into the game room.

"He got a girlfriend?" Amy cocked her head, handing Olivia her cup.

"No, Amy. He says he's too maxed out with school for dating. What can I get you?" Olivia didn't mask her impatience, grabbing the cup.

"Skinny vanilla latte."

Olivia placed the cup under the coffee machine. She inhaled the earthy smell of the ground beans as she pulled the shot of espresso.

Amy peered at the game room with a gleam in her eyes. "Hum, have to work on that," she mumbled. Olivia frowned as the whirr of the froth machine ended. Vanilla-scented steam rose as she added the frothy milk. When she lifted the cup, the door jingled, signaling another arrival. She peeked up and gasped.

What's he doing here?

The hot liquid sloshed over the edge. As Olivia stifled her yelp, the cup tipped and spilled, running like a river over her hand and onto the counter. Her seared hand shook as she watched it go from pink to an angry red, clanking on the counter as she almost dropped it.

"Hey!" Amy hopped backward, avoiding the splatter. Olivia's cheeks felt as scorched as her burn. She snagged a towel, ignoring the rush of pain and embarrassment.

"Give me the rag."

Olivia's stomach dropped when she looked up at the emerald eyes that belonged to only one guy.

Zach.

CHAPTER TWO
OLIVIA

"Ouch! Are you okay?" Amy grimaced at Olivia's burn.

Fourth time... argh.

Already embarrassed, Olivia relinquished the cloth to Zach and hurried to the sink. She sighed as cool running spray soothed the angry splotch. She scooped a handful of water with her other hand and took a sip. What was it about this guy that flustered her? Besides the obvious fact he was cute, it was more than just his good looks. It was an instant pull to him that excited yet angered her because she had no control over it. She knew what happened when someone had an emotional hold over another person. They hurt you, crushed you, changed your life forever. Olivia had no intention of letting it happen to her... ever. Before she made a bigger fool of herself, she needed to reel in her emotions.

Good luck with that.

"Yeah, no worries. Sorry I spilled your drink. Let me make you a fresh one."

She shut the water off, patting it dry with a towel. It felt raw, but no signs of blisters. She took extra care folding the cloth, giving her another moment to collect herself. She turned and faced the stares of Zach and Amy, one concerned and one apathetic.

"Perfect. And I'll make a new friend." Amy shifted her attention to Zach. She flipped her hair in front of her, mirroring a cascading blond waterfall. But Zach's gaze held little interest. Even as Olivia worked on the latte, her curiosity dictated a few stolen glances.

"Hi. I'm Amy. Haven't I seen you at school?" Amy turned on a megawatt smile, offering her hand.

"Zach. Yep, we moved here a few months ago." He shook her hand but stepped backward.

She perked up on her tiptoes. "Hey, I'll show you my favorite places around town during the break. It'll be—"

"My folks have made family plans, so–"

How pathetic. Olivia stifled a snort.

"Here you go." Amy reached out, not taking her eyes off of Zach. It took all of Olivia's willpower not to drop the cup. But she'd just have to clean up the mess, keeping Amy at the counter even longer.

"Thanks." Amy took a sip but didn't leave. "We could—" But she didn't finish, because Zach turned his back on her and faced Olivia, kicking her pulse up a notch. Amy closed her mouth, forming a pout.

"Maybe you should have your burn looked at?" His grin showed off a dimple in his right cheek.

This guy is trouble.

"Uhhhh, no... it's fine." She wiped her sweaty palms on her apron. "But thanks." When she glimpsed her hands shaking, she snatched another towel and wiped the espresso machine to hide her body's betrayal.

"Hope to bump into you again." Amy brushed her fingertips against his forearm. Her smile slipped as Zach nodded, holding Olivia's gaze. Amy took off in a huff, but not before she gave Olivia a scathing glare.

Whatever...

Zach surprised her when he reached across the counter and placed his hand over hers. His long fingers encircled her wrist and tugged it toward him. Although she pulled back, he didn't let go.

"I need to look for myself." His determined eyes held hers, drawing her closer until she was precariously near him.

Lord, a girl could lose herself in those emerald pools.

Heart hammering, she broke eye contact and peered at her fair-skinned hand being examined inside his tan one. A strand of his hair spilled forward as he scrutinized her injury, turning it toward the light. "Olivia, right?" She nodded, cringing at her moist palm inside his warm touch. But he didn't seem to notice as his thumb skimmed over the red skin, creating a tingling sensation not stimulated by the wound. "I'm Zach."

"Yeah, I overheard. What..." She tugged again. "Are you a boy scout or a doctor-in-training?" She shifted her weight as a tingle zipped up her arm. "Really... it's fine." He smiled as he stole a sidelong glance.

"The skin will be tender, but it won't blister." When he released it, she tucked both hands into her apron pocket. "And yes, I'm an Eagle Scout."

Cute and a do-gooder... Too good to be true.

Run away while there's still a chance.

"How 'bout that." She smiled, struggling to sound nonchalant as she waved at the machinery. "Can I make you a cup of coffee?"

He scanned the wall behind her. His brow scrunched as he pointed at the chalkboard.

"That's quite a list of drink options, but I just drink black coffee."

And a no-frills kinda guy... figures.

"Sure, I can do that." She pointed to the shelves on the next wall. "Choose a mug, and I'll fill it with coffee."

"That's a cool idea." He walked over and faced three long shelves stocked with eclectic mugs. He slipped his hands into his pockets, taking his time exploring his choices. Olivia watched with interest. To her, each mug told a story and gave a peek into the customer's personality when they singled it out. After considering a few, he stretched to the top shelf and picked a speckled gray enamel mug with a glazed black handle. The corners of her lips twitched. She had always imagined a dusty cowboy at campfire after a long day on the trail enjoying his hot coffee from that mug.

Eagle Scout with a dash of cowboy... gulp.

He strode over, handing her the modest mug. "Here you go."

She tilted her head, filling it with rich dark brew. "Why this one?"

"I don't know." Rocking back on his feet, a smile appeared. "I like how it's different from the others... Uncomplicated in look and unassuming by nature. I guess that's what attracts me." A darker green flashed in his eyes as he lifted his brow. "Which mug would you pick?"

A warmth spread across Olivia's chest. She got the distinct impression he was comparing her to his cup choice, an insult to most girls. But his straightforward response exposed how he dug deeper, past the superficial to what lay beneath the surface. Just as she did. A customer showed up behind Zach, saving her from stammering out her reply.

"Sorry, how much do I owe you?" He reached for his wallet, giving his head a brief shake.

"On the house." She shooed him away with a wave of her hands. "For checking me out... I mean my burn."

Face-palm...

"You're welcome." He chuckled as he raised his mug to her. Her heart did a flip, while her hands wanted to strangle herself.

Yep, I'm in big trouble.

He stepped aside and took a sip. "Mmm, that's good." He spotted an empty stool by the windows. Hooking his trail boot on the stool's leg, he had another sip while looking out the window. She wondered what he was thinking as she accepted a frilly cup from an animated girl talking into her sparkled-pink phone.

Angry shouts rose from the game room. Heads turned; cups paused mid-air. Olivia did a double-take when a copper-haired boy and a black-haired boy, locked together, stumbled into view. They wrestled while moving into the center of the shop. Chairs scraped, and nervous chatter grew as people cleared a path for the scuffling boys, not wanting to become part of the melee. A few guys tried to separate them, but haymakers flew as they each grappled for the upper hand.

"No one beats me. No one!" Ryan fought against the arms trying to hold him back.

"It's just a stupid game!" Sergio shoved Ryan's heaving chest.

Ryan grabbed Sergio's shirt and rammed him against a table, but he lost his footing, falling sideways, bringing Sergio with him. Sergio's shirt ripped as they crashed to the floor in front of Zach. Olivia couldn't see Ryan, but Sergio had his fist raised high, a snarl on his face.

Joe pressed his way through the crowd. "Stop fighting! Hey!"

Shocked, Olivia charged out from behind the counter to break up the fight, only to find Joe and Zach had separated them. Joe hauled Ryan up off the floor while Zach helped Sergio. He put himself between the pair. Ryan's face was as red as his hair, baring his teeth as if he'd loved to take a bite out of Sergio.

"Get out! I've had it with you. And don't come back here again!" The muscles twitched in Joe's jaw as he pointed to the door.

Ryan yanked his arms out of the restraining grips, sneering at the crowd. "Don't worry. I won't be back to play with this bunch of losers." He swiped at the blood trickling from his lip.

But something else caught Olivia's attention. Out of the corner of her eye, a dark shape materialized. Olivia stilled as the shadow emerged behind the crowd and floated toward Ryan. She blinked a few times as dread prickled at the base of her spine. As much as her brain wanted to believe it was Ryan's shadow, her eyes told her otherwise. A body of thick dark smoke with wispy arms and legs came to a stop and hovered near him.

"We're not finished here, *amigo.*" Ryan pointed at Sergio. Before Sergio could reply, he straightened his shirt and shoved open the front door, disappearing into the dusky night.

Olivia's heart slammed against her chest as she scanned the room. But everyone had returned to the business of sipping coffee while gossiping in hushed tones. Everyone but Zach and Sergio. Frozen in their spots, faces bunched with confusion, they stared at the same smoky figure.

Olivia jumped when it turned and confronted her. A shapeless void, except for two white eye sockets aimed only at her. She lifted trembling fingertips to her lips, gasping, backing up until a table hit the back of her legs. She was trapped, it rushed her like a powerful wind. The stink of smoke invaded her and burned her eyes, choking her as it shifted around her. Feelings of suffocation, and intense inspection, consumed her as bile rose, terrified by the invasion.

Trapped by evil.

"You can see me?" Its deep, hollow voice brought goosebumps to her flesh. Tendrils of smoke wrapped around her like vines, pulling her deeper inside its smoky mass. She gagged, her senses overwhelmed.

"Humans can't do this. Only if I want to show myself can they see me."

Olivia's body shuddered, terror clawing at her to run. Her pulse quickened. A scream was trapped in her throat. Evil engulfed her, threatening to swallow her, and she had no way to stop it. The hot, thick haze couldn't thaw the frozen pit growing inside as it dominated her. She winced as the skin on her right collarbone flared in pain as if it had seared her with a branding iron.

Its hot, ragged breathing assaulted her ear. It sniffed her hair as tendrils slithered around her neck. "You don't carry the stench of an angel."

What is happening to me?

Her breaths turned shallow. Too blinded by the smoke to find Zach or Sergio, she clung to the hope that they saw her.

"Let me go!" She sobbed as she struggled, but the tendrils grew tighter, sealing her inside its sinister presence.

"Who are you? What powers do you possess that you can see me?" It boomed inside her head. The more it talked, the more agitated it grew. The smoke began to whirl around them. "Can it be true? Could you be one of the ancient ones sent to destroy us? Answer me!"

"Help me!" Her cry was hoarse from her raw throat, scorched by smoke. The world faded around the edges as her vision tunneled and her coughing increased.

"I'm taking you back to Berith. He'll unearth your secrets."

No... please.

"Get away from her!" Zach and Sergio shouted. But they sounded distant and muffled. Their frantic hands sought her through the blackness, working to tear her free. The presence shrieked against their intrusion. It shot out a force, knocking them back.

"What? You can see me too?" Outrage vibrated in its roar. "This is impossible!"

The smoke dissipated; the room shifted back into view. Olivia recoiled as it morphed into a solid shape. Something more menacing and sinister arose from the smoke. A bald demon with marble-white skin. Irises were blood red, floating in black eyes, emanating with hate. Small round horns jutted from each temple, pointing forward, threatening to jab whoever got too close. His barrel chest rose above strong legs in a wide stance. From his belt hung a sword slashed in red and a matching dagger on the opposite hip. Clothed in black leather, his horrid transformation was complete.

The boys jumped in front of Olivia. She clung to the backs of their shirts. Icy terror leached through her as large bat-like wings snapped out behind him. Another scream bubbled, but fear clamped her throat shut. Although people moved around the room, no one paid the trio any attention. It was as if the demon ensnared them in a bubble of invisibility, blocking outside sound while warping the room and its occupants.

"Step away from her or die. I don't care." His wicked sneer tightened on his vicious face. "Because she's coming with me."

The demon lunged, arms raised, but the shop's lights cut out, plunging them into darkness. Startled gasps erupted, but for Olivia, it was much worse. The demon melted into obscurity. She scoured the shop, desperate to find his gleaming red eyes before it snatched her away. But a howl pierced the air. Sounds of scuffling and grunts came from where the demon had stood. Steel clashed against steel. A battle mounted, rising above them, hurtling throughout the shop.

Who is attacking it?

Freed for the moment, the boys pushed Olivia to the ground. They found themselves hunched under the counter, backs to the wall. Olivia prayed for protection against the unseen battle raging above them.

"We have to get out of here!" Zach's ragged breathing was hot against her cheek.

"The front door... on my right." Sergio crawled away, but Olivia feared the demon's reemergence. Panic seized her jerking limbs, hindering her efforts to escape.

"Move it!" Sergio urged ahead of her.

"I'm trying!" she yelled, willing her body into motion.

"Come on, Olivia," Zach pleaded and pushed her forward. An enraged cry split the air, galvanizing her body. She lurched forward, straining against her paralyzing terror.

An explosion of blinding lights ripped the trapped scream from her throat. She fell on her back, throwing her hands up to protect herself. Strong fingers wrapping around her arms released a surge of primal survival. She fought with her fists and feet, terrified he'd drag her away. She lashed out again, her fist glancing off of a scratchy chin.

"Olivia... Olivia. Hey... it's Joe." He shook her as he dodged her elbow. "Easy now."

Her eyes focused, chest heaving as she sought to catch her breath. Joe bent over her, his hazel eyes filled with concern. The boys stood on each side of her, wide-eyed as they scanned the room.

"Hey, what's wrong?" A half-smile tugged at his lips. "That afraid of the dark, are you?"

But Olivia only half-heard him as he helped her to stand. She hunted for the demon, afraid it still lurked in the corners, waiting to strike. But it had disappeared. Normalcy flowed around the room where a thing of her nightmares had just terrorized her. She spied a black oily puddle as the stench of sulfur burned her nostrils. Ashes floated to the floor. The inky pool's edges collapsed in on itself until it disappeared, leaving the tile clean of any black liquid.

"Are you okay, Liv?" Zach whispered against her hair. She nodded, but she knew she would never be the same. Her eyes darted between Zach and Sergio. They were both pale, a sweaty sheen covering their faces. The room buzzed with excited talk, a few patrons lined up for coffee refills. Joe patted her shoulders and then hustled behind the counter.

"What— what was that?" Sergio ran his fingers through his hair, scanning the room again. "It wanted to take Olivia."

"I don't know." Zach shook his head and brought a finger over his mouth. "But we're the only ones who saw it. I don't get it."

Even though her tremors had subsided, the demon's intentions shocked her mind. It churned with the horrid possibilities of sickening outcomes. She stared at where the demon had besieged her with surreal questions, intent on making her his prisoner, while she feared her imminent death.

Where did it go?

Had the demon disappeared into a putrid puddle and a pile of ashes?

Who had fought it?

And why were they the only ones unlucky enough to see it?

As more questions bombarded her, fear spun a dreadful new reality. If she didn't get any answers soon, she'd never be safe again.

CHAPTER THREE
OLIVIA

Snickers from the crowd cut through the fog in Olivia's head. Reality struck as she understood how ridiculous they must look cowering on the floor. She winced, noticing the customers staring at her with amused curiosity. Why hadn't any of those mocking eyes encountered the demon? Answers eluded her, leaving her chilled and scared. Determined not to give the busybodies any more fodder, she turned around only to meet Zach and Sergio's worried gazes.

"Stop gawking at me, you're only making it worse." She glanced at the door, wishing she could slip through it and disappear.

"Way to knock us over, Olivia," Sergio spouted loud enough for everyone to hear. He slapped a grin on his pale face. Zach's laugh sounded like he had just sucked in a bug. Both boys looked as frazzled as she did as they searched the room. Some might assume the boys were embarrassed because of their nervous glances, but she wasn't the only one worried about the demon's return. What if he brought others back with him?

"I'll protect you from the dark," came a catcall from across the shop. The crowd's giggles rankled her nerves, but the talk changed to Ryan, replacing their interest in the quirky incident. Olivia detested the thought of being a part of the rumor mill. With any luck, the kids would forget this day before school started. But not her.

She took a deep breath while her trembling hand smoothed a wavy lock of hair that had been freed from her ponytail. Instead of standing there, she reached for the counter door. The skin on her upper chest still twinged when she pushed it open. Could she have knocked into something when the lights went out? But her recall was fuzzy. Her clammy hands ran over her apron, checking for rips or snags. Everything was in place, except for her shattered psyche.

"I'll figure out what happened with the lights. Sorry it upset my best employee." Joe nudged her arm. "Why don't you grab a cookie and take a break. Fresh air will do you good. I got this." His head nodded toward the back door. This softer side of Joe was getting weird. She felt a twinge of guilt that he thought the lights going out made her react like a scared rabbit.

"Thanks. I can't believe I hit the floor like that. Sugar would do me some good." She cracked a smile as her shaky legs headed for the bakery case. Deciding her favorite cookie was in order, she snagged a triple chocolate chunk. Joe had coffee orders lined up, giving her pause, but he waved her away. Zach and Sergio stood huddled together as she peered over the case.

"I'll go outside with you," said Sergio.

"Me too." Sergio looked at Zach, but he looked at her, ignoring Sergio's irritation.

Her eyebrows lifted at Sergio and Zach's possessive behavior. The last thing she needed from them was some idiotic notion that she would fall apart because of this. She was scared, but she wasn't a flake. She rolled her eyes and took two more cookies.

"Look, we need to talk about what happened," she whispered as they came closer. "I'm going out back. You two leave through the front and meet me there, okay?" Both nodded and turned their separate ways. She walked out from behind the counter, holding her head high as she passed through the crowd. When she shoved the back door open, she heard the front door bells jingle.

Olivia paused, relishing the fresh air washing over her. She drew her first real deep breath since the fight between Ryan and Sergio. Her head swirled with questions, but no answers. That didn't sit well with her. Olivia prided herself in solving her own problems. She always dug until she found an explanation. This incident was no different. A slight shiver snaked down her spine. They needed answers, and fast. Because her life, and the boys' lives, depended on it.

EXPOSED. That was her, standing alone under the door's spotlight, like bait for the predator. Goosebumps rippled over her skin as she searched beyond the edges of the light into the parking lot. But smoke and shadows danced the same in the dark.

What if it's hiding by my car?

Her shoulders relaxed when she spied the boys turning the corner. She took a bite of her cookie. Chocolate and sugar exploded in her dry mouth. She hoped the sugar would give her a much-needed kick.

The boys emerged from the light's fringe. Zach assessed her from head to toe. "Good."

"What?" Olivia took another bite, glancing down making sure she hadn't missed something. She handed them each a cookie. Sergio ate half of his in one bite.

"Your color looks better, and you've stopped shaking." Zach nodded with satisfaction and took his own giant bite.

"Well, I'm glad my recovery meets your approval." It came out sharper than she'd intended, but her emotions were still riding a roller coaster. And for some inexplicable reason, this guy got under her skin. "Need to check my hand again, too?"

His face turned to stone. "Wow. Sorry I said anything. I'll just go—"

She threw up her arms in exasperation. Her feelings may be a hot mess, but she didn't want him to leave.

"Wait, I'm sorry. I'm fried, that's all. That... that demon wanted to take me away, and I'm sure it wasn't someplace fun. And no one else saw it, only us, and..." Her eyes pleaded with him. "What if it comes back?" The thought made her stomach churn. She tossed her half-eaten cookie in the dumpster.

Zach's body relaxed. "There was no way we'd let him take you."

"You can't say that. You both came to my rescue in there, but it may not be so easy next time." She swallowed the lump in throat. Tears welled, threatening to fall and shatter what little composure she had left. "It terrifies me to think what would have happened if you two hadn't–"

"It's over now," Zach said as he leaned closer. "No one is taking you anywhere."

She only nodded, not sharing his certainty.

"Where did it come from? One minute, that jerk sent me crashing to the ground, and then the next minute, the demon was staring at Olivia." Sergio shuttered. "I've never been so freaked out."

"I find it incredible that no one else saw it besides us. How could that be?" Zach started pacing, running his fingers through his hair. "And where did it go?"

Zach and Sergio tossed out the same questions she struggled to answer. Anxiety rattled her nerves.

"Wait. Stop for just a minute. We have the same questions but zero answers. Maybe if we write them down, we can figure out where to start..." She trailed off as the boys looked at her as if she'd lost her mind.

"We'll need more than pen and paper to figure this out," Sergio quipped as his brow scrunched. "We'll need weapons and a priest–"

"Massive weapons... Did you see that ax hanging from his hip?" Zach shook his head.

"Okay, you guys are not helping my stress level. We don't have any weapons, and we don't know how to kill it." Olivia crossed her arms. "We can think of other options." She looked over at Sergio, who was rubbing the top of his chest.

"What's wrong? Did you hurt your shoulder?"

"No, but that jerk landed on top of me. Why fight over a game?" He rotated his shoulders backward. Olivia startled when she glimpsed raised black dots against his caramel skin.

"Hey, what's that?" When she pointed below his collarbone, Sergio pulled the torn piece to the side.

"That's weird. It wasn't there before the fight." He touched the exposed marks. "Ow! It's tender. I guess I landed on something."

Zach and Olivia moved in for a closer look. Olivia's finger grazed over the raised black dots. There were seven. Three offset on top, three below in a diagonal line, and two equal distance from each other on the bottom. They were smaller than the size of her fist. She'd never seen them before on Sergio. They'd been friends since middle school and had spent many summers by the pool.

Zach studied the spots but shrugged. "It looks familiar, but I can't place it." Olivia nodded, but then remembered how her chest ached. She pulled back the collar of her t-shirt to take a quick peek. She gasped, releasing the shirt like it bit her. Zach also glanced inside his shirt. He looked back with wide eyes.

"What?" Sergio's eyes darted between their stunned faces. Zach and Olivia pulled their collars down. Where nothing had been before, the same seven dots marked their skin. Olivia's mind went blank.

This is impossible...

"I don't understand." Sergio rubbed his eyes with his fists. "This is too much, man. I've gotta go. Manny will be here soon." Sergio turned and ran, swallowed up by the darkness.

"Sergio... wait!" Zach lurched forward, but Olivia grabbed his arm.

"Let him go. He just needs some space. Besides, if Manny is waiting, we don't want to raise any suspicions with him." Her heart skipped when she saw her shadow. But the demon wasn't a shadow. It was a smoky, vile horror that wanted to steal her away.

Zach faced her, scrutinizing her again, not intimidated by her long-standing walls. An unwanted warmth spread across her chest. Even though she hated to admit it, his presence eased her tension.

"I don't blame him. This has blown up our worlds." He stepped closer, bringing a wave of body heat with him. She shivered. Had she been cold, or was she responding to his closeness? The last thing she needed was to deal with these rising feelings for him. She hugged herself, needing a barrier between them.

"Are you chilly? I'm surprised you aren't in shock after what took place." He lifted his hand and tucked a stray lock of hair behind her ear. Her pulse kicked up a notch. She wished, for just a silly second, he would hold her and tell her that everything would return to normal.

So much for my walls up.

"You were brave in there. Fighting Joe like that when you thought it was the demon. His face was priceless." He grinned at her, but she grimaced.

"I guess I owe him an apology."

"I bet he's fine." Zach's face turned serious. "We'll figure this out together. I promise. I don't know where that... that demon came from or how these marks appeared. But we'll sort this out. Do you trust me?"

She pulled back, thrown off by his question. Trust was something only her mom and Sergio had earned. Could she trust someone else? This handsome stranger now entangled in her life by incredible circumstances? She turned away, but his hands wrapped around her arms, keeping her in place. His tall frame bent over and looked her in the eyes. "Olivia, you can trust me. It's how we can get through this *together*. And we are in it *together*."

She fought against the wave of panic shooting through her body. He didn't understand what he asked of her. But for the first time in a long time, she wanted to jump off the cliff and trust his words. That terrified her almost as much as the demon.

"But I don't even know you, so..." She threaded her fingers through her hair in frustration. "It's been a long day. I— I just need some thinking space." Her eyes pleaded with him as she stepped back.

"Okay. I understand." But disappointment tinted his words. "It's too much to ask right now." He looked at the ground, rubbing the back of his neck.

"I need to get back to work." But exhaustion swamped her as the sugar and adrenaline were long gone. The last thing she wanted was to return to work. But she needed to face down her fears. Her cold fingers reached for the door handle.

"Hey," Zach called out. She stopped and looked back.

"Be careful, Liv. Everything as we know it has changed." He then slid into the shadows and walked away.

Night came early in the wintertime desert. Vulnerability overcame her as she was left alone in the isolating darkness. She jerked the door open, wanting the walls of the shop between her and the unknown.

Stepping into the glare of the overhead lights, she knew Zach was right. Nothing would ever be the same again. How could it when evil, strange marks and Zach shook up her world like a toddler with a snow globe?

OLIVIA HELD her composure as Joe gave her a once-over when she returned. He must have liked what he saw, because he said nothing more. That worked for her, since she didn't want to rehash it either. The rhythm of work and chores helped settle her mind. Only once did the hair lift from the back of her neck. She spun around, but nothing lurked, just a few customers working on their laptops while Joe swept the floor. A nagging sensation that she wasn't alone kept her stomach in knots and her senses on high alert.

Thankful it was closing time, she put away the clean mugs. She paused as she realized she held the one Zach had chosen. Her thumb ran over its smooth lip. Had it only been a few hours since he'd walked into the shop? It seemed longer than that since the demon had catapulted their lives into a horrifying unknown. She sighed, placing the cup back on the top shelf.

Joe peeked out from his office. "I'm almost done. Why don't you take a token and go play an arcade game while you wait?"

"Thanks." She smiled before he ducked behind the door.

Olivia loved the old arcade games in the coffee shop. Pac-man, Frogger and Defender lined the far wall next to the game room. The tall, black, bulky consoles were state-of-the art not too long ago. But now the games were simpler in design and play compared to their current high-tech counterparts. But that simplicity was part of the appeal for her, and Defender was always her game of choice.

Tossing her apron on the counter, she pulled out a worn cigar box full of silver tokens. She took one and hurried to the three machines, each designed with their own colorful logos. The middle console had DEFENDER splashed across the top. It had a space hero, planets and stars covering the black frame in bright colors of yellow, orange, and red. On the console, the colorful knob and white buttons had most of the paint worn away from years of use.

She slipped the token into the slot, bringing the game to life. A small blue spaceship appeared in the center of the screen. Soon alien ships began descending to the surface to capture the humanoids. Her fingers tapped hard on the thrust and fire buttons, moving her ship across the planet, shooting her enemy with a white laser beam. A smile stretched across her face as more alien ships swarmed, trying to destroy her spaceship. She shoved the knob up and down, avoiding their kamikaze attacks, exhilarated by blowing them to bits.

Just as she'd made it to the next level, a low ringing started in her ears. The floor tilted. She clutched the machine's sides, steadying herself. The simple game she'd been playing faded from view. She frowned, her eyelids fluttering as a different scene came to life, but not of this world.

Olivia faced a barren wasteland with a smoky mist hovering above the surface. She wore a silver armor bodysuit, but it was sleek, not cumbersome. Her long ponytail whipped in the wind. The dust stung her face as an unknown, rancid smell assaulted her. She held a shiny gold sword high, astride a magical beast that blurred at the edges of her vision.

A massive horde of black-armored bodies emerged from the mist. Some flew on black wings while others rode rabid, monstrous beasts. They rushed closer. A different bold color ingrained each black armor, matching their glowing swords. But no beauty glistened in the color's vibrance. It pulsed with a malevolence reflective of the demonic intent. The earth vibrated beneath her while their shrieks split the air.

Her heart pumped in a frantic tempo; blood pounded in her ears. She let out her war cry filled with boldness and outrage, ready to confront this evil propelling towards her. No longer was Olivia playing an arcade game. As the mounting collision grew imminent, she knew she must somehow be *in* the game— very much a part of the unfathomable battle.

The beast beneath her started galloping, its muscles rippling against her thighs. It thundered towards the demons, who darkened the horizon as they raced over the vacant terrain. But she wasn't the only one charging for battle. She looked over her shoulder, fearing she was being surrounded. Her breath seized when she saw the army of angels spread around her. Glorious and mighty in their white armor, flashing swords and powerful feathered wings, all a kaleidoscope of vibrant colors. Male and female angels soared above, while others rode fantastic animals, the likes of which she could have never imagined. Fearlessness embodied them as they confronted the horde of evil almost upon them. She turned back, no longer fearing her fate. The angels' battle cries roared in defiance and vengeance. A demon bared down on her, its orange eyes ablaze. The orange in its armor flowed like lava. It sneered at her, lowering its weapon—

"Olivia, Olivia!" her name called out by a familiar voice, but it sounded muffled and distant. It tugged at her, pulling her from the battle and transporting her back to the coffee shop. Strong hands shook her shoulders, continuing to call her name.

"Olivia... Hey..." The urgency in his voice rose. Her body felt weightless, trapped between two worlds.

She blinked a few more times, trying to focus on the fading battlefield. The roar in her ears diminished. But the battle no longer played before her. Instead it was replaced by a flashing *Game Over* on a black screen, the opposing starships frozen in place. Her breaths came out in sharp gasps as she tried to adjust to her surroundings. Did she just witness herself about to wage war, or had the stress from earlier caused her to daydream of being a fearless warrior? Even though it made no sense to her, the experience was real. She'd been in that battle.

Olivia paused before she let her hands slide away from the console, not ready to surrender her surreal vision for the surrounding reality. But she knew who had called her. The new voice in her life. She turned and braced herself against the console. Once again, she looked into emerald eyes searching hers for answers she didn't have.

"Hi, Zach."

CHAPTER FOUR

OLIVIA

O livia hated feeling vulnerable. That uncertain, exposed, life-off-kilter sensation she swore to never let happen again since that devastating Christmas morning. She prided herself on controlling her environment, like a fighter pilot commanding a powerful jet.

But ever since the demon attack, she had lost control. And like a pilot trapped in an airplane spiraling to Earth, she was a victim of external forces with no option to eject. This couldn't be her new normal. She and the pilot would suffer similar fates; they'd never survive.

"Didn't you hear me calling you?" Zach asked. He waved at the arcade game. "You were holding on for dear life with this far-off look... like you were on another planet. What gives?"

She stepped out of his grasp and walked toward the counter. Her legs moved like jelly, but she needed space from Zach. She wouldn't tell him what took place in the game. For one, she wasn't sure about the vision, let alone how she would try to explain it. She turned around and faced him. Steeling herself against his intrusive stare, she lifted her chin and crossed her arms.

"I was playing Defender and got light-headed, so I held onto the sides. My ears were ringing. I guess that's why I didn't answer you,"

Olivia said. At least that much was true. "It's been a long day. I just need to go home." Her shoulders sagged, like the weight of the world had just slammed down on her. She held her ground against his probing gaze, irritated he gauged her every word.

"Ready to close shop?" Joe asked. His body stiffened when he saw Zach. He came over and stood next to Olivia, putting a protective hand on her shoulder. She scrunched up her face. Her head swiveled up to her boss, thrown off by his treatment of her today.

"Didn't hear you come in?" The accusation in his Joe's voice surprised Olivia.

Zach returned his pointed stare. "I came by to see how she was doing. Thought we might get a bite to eat..." Zach's voice trailed off when she walked away.

"Thanks. But like I said, I want to go home."

"All right. Can I at least walk you to your car?" Zach asked.

Does he ever let up?

She sighed, remembering her paranoid thoughts of the demon in her car. Zach walking with her was a good idea, but she wouldn't share that with him.

"Sure... fine." She yanked her purse strap over her shoulder. "Good night, Joe." She raised her hand in a half-hearted wave.

"Night."

Zach and Olivia walked out the back door while Joe locked up the shop. They turned and waved again in the awkward silence. Joe headed for his truck while they went to her car. Joe slowed as he drove by and gave them one last glance. His eyes lingered on Zach until he pulled away. Since when did Joe decide he was her big brother?

Whatever. Too tired to care.

"So why are you here?" She scowled as she faced Zach. "Did something happen?" Her mouth went dry. She couldn't take much more upheaval.

"Have you talked to Sergio since he left?"

Olivia's stomach dropped. She'd been so absorbed with work and her thoughts she hadn't texted him.

"No. I can't believe I didn't text him." She bit her lip while checking her phone. No text from him either. Her pulse quickened as she typed the message. "Nothing yet. Maybe he shut off his phone."

Come on, Sergio.

"I'm sure he's fine. Listen, the three of us need to meet tomorrow morning. I have a theory about the marks. Can we come to your house around nine?" Excitement gleamed in his eyes, awaiting her answer.

"Okay, but tell me." She gripped his arm. "Help me understand what took place. Anything." If Zach had an angle or an idea, he needed to tell her. Now.

"It's better if I show you my theory with Sergio. It's easier that way, I swear. You just keep texting Sergio and tell him our plan."

She narrowed her eyes. "You mean your plan."

Zach didn't reply, instead handing her his phone. "Put your number in and text me his answer," he said. She did as he asked and handed it back. Their hands touched, startling her when he took her hand in his.

"We'll figure this out. We can do this." Giving her a reassuring squeeze, he backed away. "Night, Liv."

She placed a fist on her hip. "Why do you call me that? Everyone calls me Olivia." It bugged her, but she didn't know why.

He chuckled as he reached out for a strand of hair, rubbing it between his fingers. "Good. I like that I'm the only one. Keep it that way." His face turned serious as he looked away. When his eyes locked on hers, they had an intensity that made her want to duck and hide.

"You are one of a kind." He stepped closer; his woody scent wrapped around her. "Besides, Liv is a spunky name, and you are definitely spunky." His smile lit up, showing off his dimple cutting deep into his right cheek.

A little piece of her heart melted, but she couldn't get caught up in her feelings for him. Instead, she punched his arm. "That's right, and don't you forget it." He raised his hands in feigned defense, and they both laughed. The laughter helped loosen the knots in her stomach.

"Good night, Zach. Thanks for checking on me." She opened the car door and slipped behind the wheel.

"See you in the morning." He closed her door, then strode away. She followed him in the rear-view mirror as his long strides carried him out of sight.

Her phone dinged. Finally, Sergio texted her.

"Sorry I ran out on you today. Jerk move. Are you okay?"

She shook her head and typed her reply.

"Tired and still a little scared. Be at my house tomorrow at nine. Zach has a theory about the marks."

"Okay. Don't know him, Olivia. Play it cool."

Great. Olivia leaned back against the headrest. She didn't need Sergio pulling this male-macho thing. All three of them were involved. They couldn't waste time or energy on petty stuff.

"Don't look for trouble. See you mañana."

She got a thumbs up in reply. Good.

She headed home, eager to put distance between her and the coffee shop. A sudden thought struck Olivia. Another hurdle lay in wait between her and her bed.

Mom.

Please be in her bedroom.

Please be asleep.

Please.

THE QUIET STREET was as sleepy as its residents, but Olivia's senses were wide awake. She pulled into the short driveway of their two-story stucco home. They built the houses on tiny lots with desert and rock landscaping. There wasn't much difference between her house and the neighbors except various shades of tan exteriors.

Mom always left the porch light on for her. Before, she'd taken for granted being able to see the wrought-iron bench with cheerful red pillows and the blinking Christmas lights framing the picture window. Now, she sent a silent thanks as she searched deep into the shadows between her and the house. But nothing shifted inside them. A shadow moved across the living room. She paused, keys in hand. Mom must be up waiting up for her... if it was her.

Jeez... Was she schizoid? Had she just not wanted her mom in bed?

She slammed her car door and made a mad dash for the porch. She pressed the remote. The car's beep cut the silence. Her heart pounded as she stumbled through the front door. She shut it, locked the deadbolt and sagged against the solid door.

"Hi, honey." Her mom, Stella, stood in the sunken living room to her right. The neutral walls created the perfect backdrop for the bright throw pillows, eclectic wall art and a Turkish rug adorning the tiled floor. In the corner, a Christmas tree twinkled with small colored lights. Ornaments that Olivia had made in school or her mom had bought hung from each fragrant branch. Three furry red stockings hung from the fireplace. "Olivia," "Mom," and "Thunder" were written in red glitter on the white fur tops. Olivia had gotten used to her mom's insistence that the house be decked out for Christmas. She'd long ago stopped fighting it. Not worth the battle.

"Hi there. Did the boogeyman chase you in here?"

Little does she know...

She smiled as she climbed the two steps to the foyer with arms opened wide. Stella was a hugger, and she was coming in hot tonight. She gathered Olivia up in a big hug and kissed her on the cheek.

Olivia returned the hug. Strength, reassurance and love filled the embrace. She melted into her mom, soaking up what she so freely gave.

Mom unwrapped her arms, giving her daughter a hard stare with amber-colored eyes. Her mouth turned down as her head cocked to one side. Olivia had inherited her mom's wavy hair, but Mom's was dark brown with sun-kissed highlights.

"Have a tough day? I saved you dinner if you're hungry." Mom's eyes roamed over Olivia as she waited for an answer.

"That sounds great. Thanks." Olivia followed her mom's willowy frame, dumping her gear at the staircase in front of her. Mom stepped into the den with a dancer's grace. She turned right into a small, efficient kitchen with a breakfast nook nestled beyond it.

"Did you make minestrone? It smells amazing!" Olivia's stomach growled as she inhaled the spicy, fragrant aroma.

"Yep. Your favorite, with fresh crusty bread."

Olivia plopped on the counter barstool with her back to the den. Mom ladled a steaming helping into an oversized red bowl, grated fresh parmesan on top, and placed it in front of her. Olivia grabbed a spoon and scooped up a bite. Melted cheese hung over the edges as she blew on it. She dared a small slurp, trying not to burn her tongue. The hot soup spread its warmth on the way down, chasing the chill from her bones. She slathered the bread with butter and dunked it into the soup.

"It's delicious. Thanks." She buttered another slice. "You on tonight?"

"No, but I go in for tomorrow and Sunday's show." Mom sat on the barstool next to her. "You didn't answer me about your day, honey." Her husky voice had a way of lulling Olivia to spill her guts. Mom tucked a stray strand of hair behind Olivia's ear, the bangles on her wrist clinking against each other. "Are you okay? You look a little pale." She laid her hand on Olivia's forehead.

Understatement of the world.

Olivia took another bite, trying to ward off her mom's inquiring mind. She couldn't share what had happened today. How did one start a conversation like that? *Hi, Mom. A demon attacked me, and I had a vision I was in an epic battle between good and evil.* That wouldn't go over well.

"How about I make you a nighttime herbal tea from the dried herbs I picked this morning–"

"I'm fine. Just a long week with finals, and the coffee shop was slammed tonight."

Her mom nodded, settling onto the barstool.

That was easy.

Olivia had a sneaking suspicion the other shoe was about to drop.

They sat in silence except for the spoon clinking against the soup bowl. Done with her last bite, Olivia headed for the dishwasher.

If I can get out of here...

Mom cleared her throat. "It's a week till Christmas. I was wondering if you had a wish list this year."

There it was. The elephant in the room. Mom sat ramrod straight, but not because of her perfect dancer posture. This was an age-old argument. Olivia closed her eyes, trying to tamp down the instant flare of her temper. She had to hand it to her mom. Every year, even though she knew she was on thin ice, she asked that same question. Olivia slammed the dishwasher door closed and crossed her arms in front of her, planting her hip against the counter.

"I don't have a list, Mom," she huffed. "Just like last year and every year since I was five. It isn't a day of celebration for me. It's a day of misery."

Maybe it was the exhaustion, but she couldn't stop her torrent of words or the hot tears burning in her eyes.

"He left us. I came downstairs in time to hear him say goodbye. It didn't matter that you were begging and crying. Or telling him there had to be another way. No. He just shook his head and backed up from you until he hit the front door." Anger and hurt strangled her voice as the tears spilled onto her cheeks.

Mom moved around the counter, but Olivia raised her hands. "No. Hugs will not make this better."

Her mom stopped and dropped her arms. "Honey, please, I'm so sorry... Don't—" Her chin quivered as a finger swiped away a tear.

"He looked up and saw me. His mouth moved, but nothing came out. He just stared, frozen for a moment. I remember thinking that Daddy needed to shave before he gave me my morning kisses. What an odd thing to remember." Olivia's throat convulsed. "But I can still see him like it was yesterday. Then he finally spoke. He said, *Olivia, I love you.* He then pressed his lips together, grabbed his bag and walked out the door." She wept for that little girl. Her hand clutched her chest. The painful memory ripped open, fresh and sickening. "That's not love, Mom. That feels like hate."

"Don't think that, honey. One day you'll understand." Mom's words rushed out, trying to cover up the harshness. "I promise. It will make sense... please—"

"How can you say that to me? It will never make sense!" Olivia's face flushed in an explosion of anger.

Olivia shoved herself off the counter, done with this argument. She loved her mom but couldn't understand why she always said these same words. A sudden sadness enveloped Olivia. Would there forever be this chasm between them that neither one could cross?

"Here's my Christmas wish. I hope I never see him again. Never."

Olivia turned and ran up the staircase. Her mom's soft sob chased her up the stairs. Even though she'd waited a long time to get those painful words off her chest, she didn't feel better. It was worse. She'd kicked her mom when she was in pain too. They only had each other. She should turn and go back downstairs, but she opened her bedroom door instead.

Flipping on the light, she closed her door and sagged against it. Her fist pounded against her thigh, lamenting her tears. Done with this day, she pushed off and headed to her bathroom. She needed the hot shower to burn away the memories of the past and today.

The hot water stung her face. Her cool tears mingled with the spray. Too tired to stand, she sank to the bottom. Wrapping her arms around her knees, she laid her closed eyes against her kneecaps. She imagined she was under a waterfall far from here, not here facing unknown fears and her tragic past. The heat soothed her, and the sobs faded. Hot water turned cold, forcing her back to her numb reality. But she made promises to herself as she shut off the water.

She would not be weak, she would not be a victim, and she would get her answers.

The shower had worked its magic, but the ache behind her eyes foretold a headache greeting her in the morning. She climbed into bed, bone-tired, eyelids swollen from crying. The smell of lavender drifted from her pillow. As she snuggled into the sheets, Mom's bedroom door clicked shut. Their usual good night wishes were a bridge too far tonight.

I love you, Mom.

Her eyes fluttered closed as sleep beckoned her. But turmoil stirred beneath the surface. She clutched the sheet under her chin. Her heart hammered as she erased the demon's face floating behind her eyelids. She turned on her internal DJ, hoping the music's lyrics would chase away her fears of the demon snatching her while she slept.

CHAPTER FIVE
OLIVIA

O livia woke with a start, her heart pounding. Entangled in the damp sheets, she pushed the matted hair from her face. She closed her eyes, trying to hold on to the last remnant of her fading dream. The demon's face morphed into her father's in a room full of smoke. The sound of her screams still echoed in her ears. Her dad walked toward her in the demon's body, arms outstretched, saying, *I love you, Olivia.* Her sword gleamed in her right hand. She rushed at him, screaming, but her words slipped away with the rest of the dream.

Jeez, no wonder she had woken up.

She lay there trying to calm her heart and erase the effects of the dream. The smell of bacon replaced the smoke she swore still lingered in her nostrils. A cabinet shut, followed by the sound of running water. She craved the coffee being made, but the bacon's aroma got her out of bed. Grabbing her phone from the nightstand, she checked for messages. No new ones from Zach or Sergio, but it was already 8:10. A gray blur jumped from under the comforter, landing with a thump.

"Sorry, Thunder. Come here, kit kitty." He looked up at Olivia with his bushy gray tail swishing. He jumped onto her lap, nudging her chin in full purr. She stroked his back as he arched in pleasure.

"Did you have a good prowl last night?" He nudged her face with his head, then jumped off her lap into the warm sheets. She smiled at the cat as he gazed back with his light-green eyes half-open. He spent the nights outside and the days asleep on her bed. Mom let him in her room after retrieving him from the porch along with the newspaper.

She dressed in yoga pants and her favorite soccer hoodie and left her room. Pausing at the staircase, she heard '80s music and the sounds of a whisk slapping against a bowl. The sizzling bacon made her mouth water. Mom was pulling out all the stops for breakfast. Olivia's tension eased as she made her way downstairs.

"Hi, Mom."

The whisk stopped as Mom glanced over her shoulder. Deep creases lined her face and puffy eyelids accentuated heartbroken eyes. Her face fell as she set down the bowl. She skirted the counter and gathered Olivia up in a big hug they both needed.

"Olivia—"

"Mom—"

"I'm sorry..."

"Not your fault..."

They both laughed and hugged even harder.

"I'm so sorry I got so mad last night." Olivia sighed. "I don't know why I said all those horrible words. Christmas isn't any easier for you than for me. We remember him through different lenses."

Mom kissed her cheek. "You're right. Even though it's the day your dad left, it's still the day Jesus was born. We must celebrate this day even when we are suffering. That's what I celebrate, along with the gift of my daughter." She walked back to the bowl and began whisking. "You'll find your reasons, too."

Olivia grabbed a strip of hot bacon and took a bite. The crispy crunch of the salty goodness filled her mouth. She pondered her words while she chewed. Her mom was right about Christmas. They attended church when their schedules allowed. Olivia had always been a believer. But her dad had tinted her lens for so long. How did she even begin to put his memory behind her?

She shook her head. "You hate bacon, Mom." Olivia ate the last bite and snatched another slice.

"But you don't." She gave Olivia a hip bump when she reached the stove. "Thought you might like it, since you had a rough day yesterday."

She poured the pancake batter on the hot skillet into four neat circles. They bubbled around the edges, making Olivia's stomach growl in anticipation.

"Thank you, Mom... for everything." Her tears welled as the bacon stuck in her throat.

"You're welcome... for everything." Mom gave Olivia another hip bump. "Get yourself a cup of coffee. It's ready."

Olivia loved her coffee strong and sweet, so she added two packets of sugar and savored her first sip. She watched Mom over the lip of her coffee cup. She wore what Olivia called her "witchy woman" clothes, but now it was called the "boho" look. How the flowing sleeves on her dark robe didn't catch fire or have the batter on them amazed Olivia. But her mom's movements were elegant and precise from decades of dance training. She sat at the same place where she had eaten dinner last night, like revisiting the scene of the crime.

"Here ya go." Mom placed a plate in front of Olivia full of pancakes and bacon, with syrup overflowing over everything.

"This is perfect." Olivia dug in with a fork, the syrup running over the stacks. She stabbed the next bite, its savory decadence the best way to start the day.

"Any plans today besides work?" Mom asked as she wiped down the granite countertop. Olivia kept her head down, deciding how to best answer the question.

"Sergio and Zach are coming over at nine," she mumbled, shoving in another bite of pancake. Her mom turned with a raised eyebrow.

"Who's Zach?"

"He's the new kid who moved in on our street over the summer. We have a science project due after the break, and we want to get a head start. And I work this afternoon." She hated not telling her mom the whole truth, but she needed more information before she attempted that conversation.

"Sounds like a full day. I'll be at work, so heat the minestrone for dinner. I'm headed off to barre class and errands. So, I'll see you later." She kissed Olivia's forehead. It relieved Olivia to see the worry lines from earlier fade.

"Love you, sweetie."

"Love you too, Mom. And thanks again for breakfast. It hit the spot."

Mom headed for the stairs. Olivia got up and put her plate in the dishwasher. She checked the clock. She'd better hurry, because Zach and Sergio would be here soon.

———

THE HOT SHOWER cleared away the last remnants of her dream. She hustled downstairs, hoping to enjoy another cup of coffee, but she could hear the boys bickering on the porch before they even rang the doorbell. She opened the door and smiled. Zach had his finger poised to push the doorbell and a fast food bag in the other hand.

"She loves my mom's breakfast tacos. She won't touch that junk." Sergio glared at him with a brown bag of his own, waving it in front of Zach's face.

The boys turned at the same time. They both cringed at being caught arguing over their food bags.

It was Olivia's turn to raise an eyebrow, putting her hands on her hips.

"Hola! Mom made you your favorite breakfast tacos." The spicy aroma wafted across to her as Sergio handed her the bag.

Sergio bent over and picked up Thunder before he escaped out the front door. "Hello, Thunder, it's nice to see you too." Thunder purred in his arms as Sergio stroked his back. Both sets of eyes narrowed on Zach.

"Hi. I brought breakfast sandwiches." Zach handed the greasy bag to her and scanned her face when he walked by. She hooked her damp hair behind one ear.

"Thanks, guys, but Mom made me breakfast. You're welcome to eat if you're hungry." Olivia swore they both were crestfallen when they stepped inside the foyer. She closed the door behind them. She didn't have time for their games.

Zach tried to pet Thunder, but he jumped out of Sergio's arms, scooting away.

"Looks like Thunder doesn't like you," Sergio snickered.

"I'm sure he smells my big black dog," Zach said as he leaned toward Sergio.

Olivia's sharp whistle made their heads swivel. "You two, knock off this bickering. We have more important issues than arguing over cats and sandwiches. I don't know why you guys irritate each other and, honestly, I don't care. I do care about demons and threats about being dragged away by one. So, can you please put aside whatever you think about each other and focus?"

Zach turned to Sergio. Something unspoken passed between them. Sergio shrugged and walked away, leaving Zach to follow him into the den. Olivia shook her head.

That won't last...

"Sit down, and I'll get my laptop." She plopped the food onto the coffee table. The boys sat on opposite couches and ate in silence. She raced up and down the stairs, joining them in the den.

She sat down and glanced over her open laptop. Sergio's leg bounced up and down while Zach hunched over his, his hands dangling between his legs. Both looked anxious as they waited for her laptop to boot up. Her hands trembled as she entered her password.

"Hey, I think we should just forget about what happened yester-day," Sergio blurted, jumping out of his seat. "It was just this freaky thing, and I don't think we should try to figure it out. That was Diablo stuff, man, and I want no part of it!" He made the sign of the cross and paced around the den.

Olivia and Zach exchanged glances. Zach hung his head. He then sprang up and walked over to Sergio. Zach grabbed Sergio's arm, but Sergio yanked it away.

"Don't touch me." Sergio leaned forward and pointed into Zach's face. "Listen, I'm only here because of her, not you. I don't care what you think happened or any of your ideas. I want nothing to do with demons."

"Oh, I get it. You think you're the only one scared?" Zach sneered at him. "Well, guess what? So are we!"

They stood toe-to-toe with clenched fists. Zach was a good head taller, leaving Sergio staring up at his angry face.

"What happened yesterday terrified me! I couldn't sleep last night because I kept seeing that hideous face. I was worried that somehow it might have found one of you and that you wouldn't be here today." Zach's face flushed. "But I won't run and hide. I'm not going to live afraid of my own shadow."

Olivia jumped off the couch and moved between them. She put a hand on each chest, feeling their pounding hearts.

"Please stop this. We can't fight," Olivia pleaded. "We have to stay and work it out together. Whatever is going on, it includes all three of us. Which means we have to stick together." She looked hard at each of them. "Please," she whispered.

Zach ran his fingers through his dark hair. "That's what I want, too," he said with a sigh.

Olivia turned to her best friend, grabbing his hand and giving it a squeeze. Sergio's black eyes held so much confusion and apprehension.

"We are in this together."

He closed his eyes. His throat worked up and down, and he released a huge sigh, ruffling her hair. When he opened his eyes back up, Olivia saw his resignation.

"All right, I'm in."

His eyes met Zach's. Sergio stood straighter, offering his hand. After a moment, Zach accepted the handshake. Thankful some tension had left, Olivia sat back down with a sigh of relief. They plopped onto the couch.

Maybe now we can start digging...

"We don't know where it came from or why it left. But we can agree it's not of this world."

"That's an understatement," mumbled Sergio. They nodded in agreement.

"I want to research images on the internet. Maybe I can find a match. This has to have happened to someone else."

"That's it? That's your plan? You can search all you want, but I don't think a demon gets its photo taken," Sergio snorted.

Olivia raised an eyebrow, secretly wanting to strangle him. "It's a good place to start. If you have a–"

Zach leaned forward. "Wait. What I couldn't get out of my mind was the raised black marks we each have on our chest. Mine aren't as dark as they were, but they're raised."

"I noticed that too," she said.

"So did I." Sergio rubbed the area like he was trying to erase his mark.

"When I got home, I drew the spots on a piece of paper." Zach reached into his back pocket, unfolded the paper, and smoothed it out on the coffee table. Olivia and Sergio leaned closer.

Olivia tilted head, but she couldn't find any pattern to the dots.

Sergio flopped back against the couch. "I only see seven dots."

Try as she might, nothing clicked. Zach laughed and nudged Sergio's knee.

"You guys need to get outside more. It's the constellation of Orion. I'm positive."

"What?" Olivia turned the paper so that it faced her. Sergio lurched forward for a second look.

"What makes you think that?" Sergio asked. "I could be anything... random pattern. Why are you so sure?"

"When I went camping with my scouting troop–"

"You're a boy scout!" Sergio pointed at Zach, covering his mouth with a hand. "That makes so much sense. You're so straight-laced–"

"Stop being a jerk, Sergio. I think he's right. I can see it now." She reached for her laptop and entered *Orion*. The images of the constellation popped on her screen. "Come here."

The boys got up and stood behind her. She scrolled through the images of Orion in the night sky. While most pictures were only of the constellation, a telescope had captured its colorful nebula.

"This is the closest match." Olivia scrolled back to an image at the top of her screen. It was a simple image, but a line connected the dots, creating an hourglass stick figure. She pointed at the middle three stars. "These stars make up his belt. It says it's named after Orion, a hunter in Greek mythology."

"Cool. I like that it stands for a hunter because I feel more like the prey." Sergio nudged Olivia as she nodded in agreement.

"I need a pen," Zach said.

Olivia pulled one out of the coffee table drawer. Zach took it and connected the dots. When he finished, there was no doubt it was Orion.

"Why would Orion be on us?" Olivia said.

"I've got no idea. But we'll find out more tonight." Zach stood and gathered his paper.

"What do you mean?" Sergio's voice squeaked. "What happens tonight?"

"We're going to Red Rock Canyon to check out Orion away from Vegas's bright lights," Zach said. "We need to check it out ourselves and see what happens." They were quiet for a minute.

"You mean, if we attract any demons."

"This is a bad idea." Sergio rubbed his eyes. "We're asking for trouble. Big trouble."

"You got a better idea?" Zach challenged him, crossing his arms.

Sergio shook his head and glanced over at Olivia.

"Are you going up the mountain?" Sergio asked.

"We have to go. We can't just wait for another attack. So, yeah... I'm in." She rubbed the goosebumps rising on her arms.

"Fine," Sergio grumbled.

"Great. You guys keep searching the internet, but I've got to run. I promised my little sister I'd take her present shopping. Meet at my house at eight tonight. We'll take my truck," Zach said. "Don't be late."

"Sure. Don't want to be late for my date with a demon," Sergio said with a smirk.

Olivia waved and watched Zach leave. A shiver went through her body as she wondered if that would indeed be their fate.

CHAPTER SIX
OLIVIA

Olivia caught her reflection in the kitchen window as she rinsed her soup bowl. She looked into the darkness beyond, wishing the night air would whisper who might wait for her on the mountain. Her day at work had passed with no unwelcome visitors. It didn't stop her from being on edge. She'd messed up drink orders and jumped when someone called her name. Her stomach was in knots about going to Red Rock tonight. Part of her prayed they'd find answers, but the other part worried that demons would confront them. Their trip was risky, but they had to take the chance.

She felt a bump against her calf. She let out a startled cry and jumped away, wild-eyed, expecting to see a demon ready to grab her. Instead, Thunder arched against her, weaving his way between her legs.

"You scared me, cat. Are you hungry?" She walked to the pantry, trying not to trip over the cat.

"All right, all right," she mumbled, opening the pantry door. She grabbed the cat food and went to the laundry room. She poured the kibble in his continuous feeder sitting on top of the dryer. Thunder jumped up and nudged her with his nose while the food filled the bowl. Smiling, she ran her hand over his soft fur as he attacked his food.

Olivia left Thunder purring over his food. She ran up the stairs two at a time to grab her gear from her room. Stepping inside, she grabbed her backpack. Her pack bounced when she tossed it on the bed. She opened it, checking the contents: flashlight, notebook, pen, water and a scarf. Satisfied she had what she needed, she zipped it closed.

After grabbing her hiking boots from her closet, she sat in her desk's chair. She shoved her feet into the boots, lacing them up tight. A flash of white caught her eye on her desk. She plucked the feather out of the cluttered mason jar and ran her thumb and forefinger over the smooth sides. It was the most beautiful feather she'd ever seen. Over a foot long, it was strong yet supple, tickling her finger as she moved across the edges. The white iridescent color had a glowing effect. She twirled it between her fingers, remembering when she had opened her eyes that fateful Christmas morning and gasped. A chubby hand reached over and plucked it up, glistening against her tan pillowcase. The wispy ends fluttered with the overhead fan's gentle rotation. It still lay on her bed when she'd returned to her room, devastated by her dad's abandonment. Putting the feather under her pillow, she had cried herself asleep. She tossed it back in the jar along with the painful memory.

Backpack over her shoulder, she raced downstairs. She grabbed the silver thermos of coffee and headed out the door before she lost her nerve.

"Hey."

She shrieked, jumped back and swung the thermos before she recognized his voice. He ducked with a raised hand, avoiding the silver blur.

"Wow. Is that how you greet everyone who comes to your door?" Zach smiled under the porch light. "You have a mean hay-maker."

"You scared me." She hoped he missed the flush of her cheeks. "I wasn't expecting you."

"I should have texted. I thought I'd come and get you so you didn't have to walk alone." His hands slid into his front pockets.

In the dark... nice thinking.

"I've been on edge all day. Almost kicked my cat tonight when he bumped my leg." Nervous laughter escaped her as she turned and locked the front door, hearing the bolt click into place. They stepped out into the dark night and headed for his house.

"So, what's in your weapon?" Zach nodded at the thermos.

"Coffee. Might be chilly on the mountain, so I thought we'd enjoy something hot."

"Good idea. You could always use that thermos as a weapon if we meet up with any demons." His try at humor fell flat with Olivia.

"If any show up, this thermos won't help." Her stomach rolled as she imaged facing a demon with only a thermos. Zach's full-sized navy-blue Chevy truck was just ahead, parked on the curb. The truck wasn't a new model, but it shined under the street light.

"Nice truck." Olivia tapped the back bumper.

"Thanks." He sounded a little embarrassed. "It was my dad's until he handed me the keys this summer. Anyway, Sergio asked if we could pick him up at his house."

He led her to the passenger side, opening the door for her. She jumped in, acting like it happened all the time. She settled into the seat as she busied herself by checking out the gray interior. Not a speck of dust lay on the dash, and a pleasant pine scent filled the cab.

She watched Zach walk around the hood to his door. Dressed in black, he walked with a confidence she didn't see in many guys her age. Her heart fluttered, her sweaty hands folded in her lap as he jumped into his seat. His presence filled the cab along with the smell of Irish Spring and leather. She leaned against her door, over-whelmed by him. Zach turned to her, his eyes bright in the darkness.

"I promise I don't bite." Keys jingling in his hand, he started the truck.

"Well, that's a relief, because I have enough to worry about."

He grinned, exposing his white teeth. "How do we get to Sergio's?"

"Turn right at the end of our street." She averted her eyes and stared through the windshield.

Classic rock pumped through the speakers. Olivia gave clipped directions while she pushed away a vision of Zach's white teeth nipping at her neck.

OLIVIA POINTED out Sergio's house as they approached it. He pulled up in front of the ranch-style home and parked his truck.

"There he is," Olivia said.

Sergio's dark form emerged from the porch and ran down the path. He reached the back door of the truck as a car rumbled down the street. Sergio stopped, shook his head, and shoved his hands into his jean pockets. The car pulled up in front of Zach's truck, blinding them with its headlights. The muscle car's engine cut off, returning quiet to the street. A figure got out from the driver's side. He closed the car door and approached the truck.

Standing between the headlights was Manny, Sergio's older brother. He had the same coloring and features as his younger brother, but there was a hardness to him that made most wary. His frame was wiry and his bearing alert. The girls loved him, though. He had the bad-boy down to a T. Sergio met his brother near the truck's hood. As they talked, Manny kept glancing between the truck and Sergio.

"Who is that? He doesn't look happy about something." Zach's hands squeezed the steering wheel.

"That's Manny, Sergio's older brother. He's nice to me, but I don't know him that well." She shrugged. "He doesn't live at home. But Sergio idolizes him."

As if on cue, Manny came over to Olivia's window. He motioned for her to roll down the window. She pushed down the window button and faced him with a smile. Manny's musky aftershave drifted inside, but his handsome face didn't return her smile. He was all business.

"Hi, Manny." She tried to sound cheerful, but he stayed stone-faced. Sergio was mouthing something behind Manny's back, but she couldn't make it out.

"How are you?" She got no reply as his eyes locked onto Zach.

"This is Zach," she offered, pointing to him. "He moved onto my street this summer."

Zach reached across and offered his hand. Manny looked at the hand and then back to Zach. While keeping his hand and eye contact steady, Zach's smile slipped. Manny finally reached in and gave his hand a firm shake.

"Hello, Olivia... Zach." He nodded in Zach's direction. "What's this I hear you about guys going to Red Rock?" Manny hung his arms over the window, sticking his head inside the cab. His sharp eyes scanned both their features and the truck's interior.

"We have a science project due when we get back from break." Olivia shrugged. Sergio's eyes were big, and he was nodding up and down. "We need to observe the stars away from the city lights, so we figured Red Rock is the best place to check it out."

Manny stepped away and opened the back-passenger door. He rummaged under the back seat and pulled back the pockets behind the front seats. The cabin light illuminated a tattoo on his forearm of a tiger holding a knife between its teeth, peeking out from his pushed-up sleeve. The tiger shifted along his lean muscles, appearing to prowl down his arm.

Zach turned around and flung his arm on the seat rest. "There's no beer, if that's what you're looking for." Zach clenched his jaw as Manny returned his stare.

Manny grabbed the thermos, removed the lid and took a whiff. "I don't know you, gringo, so I'll look all I want." He screwed back on the cap. "I watch out for my familia." His voice was low and threatening. Satisfied, he backed out, not breaking eye contact with Zach.

"Don't you forget that." Manny pointed at Zach. A low groan escaped from Sergio, but he stood up straight when Manny turned to him.

"Not too late. Makes Mama worry." Manny gave Sergio a brotherly punch in the arm as he walked by, sending Sergio back a step.

"Fine," Sergio said. He jumped in the back, threw his backpack across the bench seat, and slammed the door shut. The sound resounded in the quiet neighborhood, causing the dog next door to bark. Manny swaggered over to his car and opened his passenger door. Out stepped a dark-haired beauty. Manny smiled at her and then glanced at the truck. Olivia thought she saw a curtain move as they walked arm-in-arm to the front door. Zach scoffed and started the truck.

"Wow," Zach said. "That was over-the-top."

"I know. I'm so over him treating me like I'm still ten." Sergio punched the back of the front seat. "But he won't listen to me. Instead, he talks about protecting familia, and I'll understand when I'm older. I'm seventeen! Then he warns me to keep out of trouble... going to college. Blah blah blah! I'm sick of it!"

"I guess that's what big brothers do," Olivia said. "He means well and loves you or he wouldn't be so protective."

Sergio rolled his eyes at her and stared out the window.

"Turns out he's been going through my stuff. He found my ripped shirt and laid into me about fighting. Now he's on high alert." Sergio's bitter snort echoed off his window.

Olivia turned and squeezed Sergio's knee, hoping to reassure him. He responded with a weak smile. Zach pulled away from the curb, another old metal song filled the silence.

A curtain from Sergio's house peeked open, a hidden set of eyes following them until the truck turned the corner.

CHAPTER SEVEN
OLIVIA

No one spoke during the drive, letting the rock music fill the void. The run-in with Manny didn't help the tension emanating from Zach and Sergio, crashing on Olivia like a wave pounding the shore. She was thankful for their solitude. Olivia didn't want to speculate on different scenarios. She needed to calm her racing mind and frayed nerves and ready herself for any possibility the night might bring.

The edges of the suburban neighborhood, along with the lights of Las Vegas, faded behind them, turning the landscape dark outside her window. The night sky was clear of clouds. Bright stars twinkled, inviting her to search for their prize: Orion.

Olivia stole a glance at Zach. One hand gripped the steering wheel while the other tapped his thigh along with the music. But his lips were set in a firm line as he gazed out the windshield.

"Penny for your thoughts?" Zach startled her. He gave her a quick reassuring smile, one of those that said *trust me, I've got this.* She looked away where the scant scenery was safer than looking at Zach.

"Um... just thinking about how we'll find Orion." She closed her eyes and gave herself a mental shake. "I mean, where are we going?

No. Like... in the park, do you have a place in mind?" Sergio snickered from the back seat.

Zach will think I'm an idiot!

"It's called Calico Hills. It's not too far inside the gate on the scenic loop. There's an area of huge flat boulders where we can lie down and gaze up at the stars. I have flashlights if you need one. The walk is a piece of cake."

"I've been hiking there with friends. That's a good choice." Olivia nodded.

"Thanks, Boy Scout, but I brought a flashlight." Sergio tried to sound flippant, but Olivia caught the snide undertone he intended.

"Actually, I'm an Eagle Scout. If you want to be a jerk, you might as well have it right." Zach stared at Sergio in the rearview mirror.

"Whatever... Boy Scout." Sergio returned his gaze.

Olivia sighed and let it be. The gate was close. They could soon hike and work off their tension.

Zach turned right and stopped to pay the fee at the entry gate. They drove on the thirteen-mile one-way scenic drive that meandered through a section of Red Rock park. It disappointed Olivia she couldn't see the various layers of the red and tan sandstone hills. It amazed her how Las Vegas was a desert now, but millions of years ago this was all under the ocean. The sand dunes hardened over time, with iron oxide leaching into the sandstone, creating the stunning red rock structures. She made a promise to herself to come back during the day and soak up its splendor.

The truck wound its way along the narrow road. Zach pulled into a deserted parking lot and parked. Olivia unzipped her pack and grabbed the flashlight. Deciding she wanted her other hand free, she pulled out the scarf and notebook to make room for the thermos. She grabbed the pack and jumped out of the truck.

"The Vegas valley looks awesome from up here." Sergio pointed to a cut-out between the dark hills. Bright lights from the houses shone as if they reflected the stars on the valley floor.

"That's a cool view. Come on, it's this way." Zach turned, getting back to business.

A simple split-rail fence bordered the trail's entrance. Darkness loomed before them until the hilltops bordered the night sky. As her eyes adjusted to the dark, Olivia made out the jutting hills and the gigantic boulders lying at the bottom. They turned on the flashlights, and Olivia lost the hills in the bright beam.

They walked single-file with Zach taking the lead, then Olivia with Sergio behind her. Three flashlight beams bounced across the asphalt as they headed for the trail. Despite the chill in the air, dampness spread under Olivia's arms.

"The walk isn't too far. Just stay behind me." Zach's flashlight showed where the dirt trail started. He walked with caution along the path. The crunch of gravel under Olivia's shoes broke the quiet night. Her flashlight beam caught small bare bushes and tumbleweeds dotting the trail's edges as it sloped down before them. On the left, rocky terrain replaced the parking lot. On the right, a steep decline loomed like a gigantic dark abyss. Her heartbeat kicked up a notch. Olivia skirted the left side, not wanting to tumble over the dark, ominous edge.

"Here we go. Watch your step." Zach flashed his light in a wide arc in front of him. The path had stopped, and a large rock plateau took its place. "We can lie down here. It's a perfect view of the stars."

They stepped onto the plateau and found a level place in the middle to sit. The ominous darkness outside the beams pressed upon her, leaving her exposed to whatever moved beyond her vision. She swung her light, hoping that no eyes reflected back at her. Nothing peered back, but that didn't mean it wasn't there. Resigned, she sat on the dusty boulder.

"Anybody want some coffee?"

"No thanks. Maybe back at the truck." Zach shrugged off his pack. Sergio shook his head while he scanned the light's edge.

She lay against her backpack. The boys picked a place on either side of her.

"Turn off your lights." Zach's voice bounced off the red dirt hills surrounding them. Her heart skipped a beat when he cut out his light. She bit her lip as her thumb pressed the rubber button. She held her breath, waiting for her eyes to adjust. Olivia exhaled as the blanket of stars exploded above her.

"Very cool," Sergio said.

"It's beautiful, isn't it?" Zach whispered in her ear.

"Magnificent." A million stars lay on top of her, enveloping her in a twinkling cocoon. Her tension melted away, in awe of the magnitude and artistry of the universe before her. What would it be like to float among the stars, weightless in thought minuscule in its expanse?

Sergio sent out a low whistle. "God does great work."

"His universe humbles me every time I stare at the stars. I could stare at them all night. Have you found Orion yet?" Zach nudged her with his elbow.

She scanned the stars, then jabbed her finger toward the night sky. There was no mistaking the seven stars of the hunter outshining the other stars.

"It looks just like our marks, but mine doesn't feel different. Any change for you guys?" Olivia asked. She'd been hyper-aware of the mark all day, but it never tingled.

"Nope."

"Me neither."

Olivia sighed, dug out her phone, and took a picture of Orion in the night sky.

"This is a bust." Sergio jumped up. "Total waste of my time. I told you we should forget about the whole thing." He dusted himself off, pounding on his jeans.

"It wasn't a bust, Sergio." Olivia scrambled to her feet, grabbing her pack. "At least we're sure it's the shape of our marks and nothing happened when we looked at it at night. Gives us something to work with now."

"Whatever. None of it helps us. Let's go back." Sergio flipped on his light. "All this was for nothing and made matters worse for me. I now have Manny breathing down my neck." His light crisscrossed along the plateau onto the path, his frustrated stomps echoing up the hill.

Olivia looked at Zach. "Don't worry about what he said. I'm glad we came."

"Me too. We'd better go." He grabbed her hand, hurrying to catch up to Sergio.

They were near the top of the path when a low rumbling cut the quiet night. It rumbled louder the closer it got, and soon there was no mistaking the sound. Motorcycles were turning into the lot.

"Cut your lights!" Zach hissed. Blood pounded in Olivia's ears as they were plunged into darkness. Their gasoline exhaust mixed with the dry air. The engines stopped, but the male voices and raucous laughter were more ominous.

"Ouch!" Sergio stood in the hooded darkness, but Olivia could make out his hand clutching his shirt where the mark lay. The stinging sensation erupted on her mark. She pressed her hand against it, willing it to stop as her heartbeat thrashed beneath it.

A cold dread washed over Olivia. The last time this pain had happened, a demon tried to take her away. It was happening again, except now they were in the middle of nowhere with bikers standing between them and their escape.

THEY PRESSED their backs against the dirt bank, desperate to hide from the male voices above them. The mark on Olivia's chest throbbed, setting her heart beat racing.

Are the demons attached to the bikers or did they attract them?

Please, just go away...

"My mark is throbbing," Sergio whispered. "We have to get out of here."

She nodded, but Zach put his finger on his lips. Olivia's chest tightened as she scanned the surrounding darkness. The voices above grew louder. Olivia gripped her flashlight, hoping she didn't have to use it as a weapon.

"Nice truck. Anything inside the cab?" The low, raspy voice drifted above them.

"Can't tell. Windows are too dark, but nothing's in the truck's bed." The second male voice had a higher pitch. "Let's bust a window."

Zach punched his leg and looked ready to charge the hill, but Olivia grabbed his hand. She shook her head and pulled him close.

"You can't go up there. Just stay here until they leave," she whispered in his ear. Anger radiated from Zach, but he didn't move.

The shattering of glass made her stomach drop. "Hurry and get your skinny butt in there." Zach lurched forward. but Sergio and Olivia both pulled him back. Sergio whispered something in Zach's ear. A yelp and deep laughter rained down on them.

"Man, you're an idiot. What ya got there?"

The truck door opened, then slammed shut. "Nothing inside but a scarf."

Olivia's skinned crawled at the thought of this creep touching her scarf. She'd never wear it again.

"Let's wait for the chick to come back and have a little fun." His excited high-pitched voice made her stomach roll. Bile rose in Olivia's throat as she thought of what could happen if they found her.

"Nah. Let's get out of here." A fist smacked the hood. "We'll go up the road to the next parking lot and swing back later." He snickered, striking the hood again like an exclamation point. Olivia closed her eyes, praying for them and any demons that may have come with them to leave. The bike engines came alive, and soon their rumble faded from the lot.

Zach raced up the hill. Olivia and Sergio scrambled after him, but Zach was quicker. She turned on her flashlight but lost sight of him as he cleared the top of the hill. The mark's throb deepened. As she broke the top of the hill, her heart stopped, shocked at the sight before her.

"Olivia, don't move." Sergio stood frozen at the trail's entrance, clutching his shirt over the mark.

Two dark shadowy forms swirled around the truck. Their movements grew faster, rocking the truck back and forth. The springs squeaked, and the tires bounced against the force. A primal sound filled the air, the same screeching from the coffee shop.

Zach stood a few yards from the truck. He put his hands over his ears, stumbling backward. He turned to run but tripped over his feet.

Getting to his hands and knees, he stared back at his truck and froze as if mesmerized by the chaos engulfing it.

"Get away from the truck!" Olivia cried, holding her hands over her ears. She gaped as the circling grew faster and faster, becoming a single blur of darkness circling the truck.

"Come on, Zach!" Sergio waved his arms, but Zach stayed rooted to the spot.

She had to help Zach. She took a few steps, but her feet moved as if encased in cement blocks.

Come on, Drake! Move it!

She glanced between the truck and Zach. She pushed harder, fighting against her panic. Turbulent air blew around her, plastering her hair to her face. She lunged for him, grabbing his clammy hand. His raspy breath came in bursts.

"Zach, look at me... We have to move... Come on!" she yelled, tugging his hand.

"Okay... okay." He shook his head as if coming out of a fog. Sergio emerged and grabbed Zach's other arm, helping him to his feet. They scrambled away from the swirling vortex consuming the truck.

The screeching stopped, leaving blood pounding in her ears. Olivia looked behind her. Something more terrifying had replaced the black whirlwind.

Two large demons dressed in black stood by the truck. Huge coal-colored wings expanded behind them with sharp feathers that looked more like weapons than ones created for flight. The male demon wore similar clothes to the demon at the coffee shop. His red eyes glared at them, one small red horn sprouting from his forehead. A double-sided ax hung from his belt. He sneered, revealing black pointed teeth glistening with saliva.

The other demon was a female, with black skin and matching black shoulder-length hair ending in bright blue tips. Her tight, dark clothes accented her muscular frame. Ice-blue eyes glowed inside the black pools, and short spiral horns erupted above her ears. Two small swords with blue hilts hung from the curve of her hips.

They drew their weapons and moved away from each other. The

male demon slapped the side of the ax against his black-veined white hand. "What do we have here, Agora? Human trash looking at us?" He cocked his head and sniffed the air while moving toward them. "They smell and look human, but they must be angels in disguise if they can see us." He licked his lips as his shrewd red eyes examined them.

Olivia stood between Zach and Sergio. The familiar odor of smoke and oil assaulted her nostrils as the demons inched closer.

They'll kill us.

Lord, please help.

Olivia, Zach and Sergio formed their own circle, putting their backs to each other. "We have to get to the truck. It's our only way out of here," Zach whispered.

"There's no way." Sergio motioned to the dark hills. "We can try the path—"

"They don't look like angels to me, Orban." Her words were spoken like an evil caress. "Just filthy little humans for our amusement. Yet, I have a pull towards them... more of a connection. Do you feel a connection to me too?" Her cackle was a horrifying as her voice.

Connection to us?

"Yes. I sense it too, and I don't like it. Let's kill them now." Orban started toward them, raising his ax.

The female demon turned to Orban. "Wait! We need to know how—"

"Run!" Zach yelled.

He pushed Olivia and Sergio back toward the path. Olivia's legs pumped as her survival instinct hit high gear. Sergio closed in on the path's dark entrance first, with Olivia and Zach close behind him. Sergio chanted *run, run, run,* urging them.

Just a few more steps...

Maybe we can use the dark as cover... if I don't fall over the side.

The surrounding air began to swirl. Where once lay hills and skyline, it blurred into wisps of black smoke. The demons circled faster and faster. Maniacal laughter drowned out Olivia's screams. Evil, directed at them inside the vortex, taunted them at will.

Sergio clapped his hands over his ears. Zach grabbed Olivia and pulled her against him. Her mark burned as she coughed against the onslaught of smoke. The horrendous screeching and laughter pierced her eardrums.

Her mom's face floated in front of her. A sob broke from her wheezing chest. She couldn't leave her mom alone, abandoned again. Anger swelled inside of Olivia. She pushed herself away from Zach. Clenching her fists, she looked up into the sky, but swirling smoke obscured the blanket of stars. Olivia yelled into the black vortex, repeating one word. *"STOOOOOPPP!"* She packed up her welled-up terror and anger, releasing it into the vortex.

The swirling curtain began to slow and morph. The even turbulence of the circling smoke became the chaotic beating of wings, battering her with their heat. Ash fell, blinding her as she punched out at her enemy. A feather's ends caught her hair, yanking her scalp. She lifted her hand to protect herself. A sharp pain struck her hand as a feather slashed it. She swung her fist but connected with nothing but air.

The beating wings stopped, but Olivia stood alone. Orban had Zach pulled up against his chest with a large dagger held against his neck. Agora held Sergio up against her with sharp metal fingernails gripping the side of his neck. If she exerted more pressure, blood from his jugular would spray everywhere. The boys stared wide-eyed back at Olivia.

"Please don't hurt them." She felt nauseous, as their predicament had gone from horrifying to deadly. "What do you want? Please! We won't tell anyone what happened. I promise. Just let them go."

More laughter rumbled from the demons, their delight palpable. Hatred for them filled Olivia as she glimpsed horror and something worse—surrender—in the boys' eyes.

"We won't hurt you. Yet. You're coming with us. Berith must meet you first. He'll know what trickery you scum are using to see us. And then, after this delightful meeting, we'll decide how we want to kill you. Death may be quick or slow. Depends on my mood." Agora shrugged.

The boys struggled, but their captors tightened their grip. Sergio cried out as a trickle of blood fell from a nail prick on his neck.

Berith... That's the same name the demon said at the coffee shop.

"Who's Berith?" She'd never heard that name until yesterday, but she knew she didn't want to meet him.

"Berith. You don't know who Berith is?" Orban scoffed. "He's the—"

A sound, like a clap of thunder, came from above them. Olivia looked up as three bright lights fell from the sky. She didn't know what these lights were, but a glimmer of hope spread that help had arrived.

"Angels!" Orban and Agora turned their heads away, screaming, using the boys as shields. But it did little in hiding the large demons from the falling lights.

Huge, majestic white wings expanded from inside the lights. They landed near Olivia, transforming into something more magnificent than she ever could have imagined. Three angels glared at the demons. Standing in front was the largest angel. His shoulder-length golden hair framed sharp blue eyes, a square face and full lips set in determination. His bright white wings spread out behind his sleek sliver armor, but the last few rows of feathers shone in a magnificent shade of cobalt blue, like they were freshly dipped in vibrant paint.

"Michael," Orban seethed.

His two companions stood on each side of him. The other male had ebony skin, close-cut black curly hair and light purple eyes. His armor matched Michael's. A long silver sword with electric purple swirls hung from his side, and across his breastplate lay a strap of purple luminescent throwing stars.

The other angel was a female with short chestnut-brown hair spiked with flaming gold ends. Her upper lip lifted in a snarl on her fierce, heart-shaped face. She turned to Olivia, revealing three long scars running from her milky-white left eye and across her cheek. The other eye was a dazzling gold. She turned back, raising a flaming gold sword in front of her.

Michael nodded at Orban. "Let them go and you can crawl back into your pit." The demons glanced at each other, defiance gleaming in their eyes.

"Eliphaz," Michael called. "Get Olivia to your side."

Wait... How does he know my name?

Eliphaz grabbed her hand, never taking his eyes off the demons, and whisked her to his side with ease. His purple eyes flashed at her, flooding her with a reassuring calm. But the demons still held Zach and Sergio captive.

"They must be important for you to try to save them," Agora sneered. "I think you'll have to fight for them. Or maybe"–Sergio gasped as her claws dug into his neck–"I'll just rip his throat out." Her evil grin showed hideous black teeth.

"No!" Olivia strained against Eliphaz's grip. She looked up at the angel. "Help him before she kills him!"

"Zemira and Michael won't let that happen... and neither will I."

Time turned to slow motion as mind-numbing fear gripped Olivia. Agora looked ready to shred Sergio's neck, but a whooshing sound passed by her. Agora's right eye exploded into a cloud of black blood. Embedded in the mangled eye socket was a gold knife. Her hands flew to her injured eye, releasing Sergio from her grip. Her screams sent chills down Olivia's back.

"Run, Sergio!" Olivia shouted over the demon's shrills. Sergio scrambled away. His jerky movements sending him toward Zemira. Her wings gathered in Sergio, her hands wielding her sword.

"You'll pay for that!" Agora grabbed the knife and pulled it out, leaving the black hole oozing blood. Drawing her sword, Agora expanded her wings and flew at Zemira.

Orban shoved Zach to the ground. He turned to Eliphaz and threw the red dagger at him. The blade hit its mark, embedding in Eliphaz's upper chest. Silver fluid sprang from his wound, coursing over his armor. He fell to one knee and pulled the dagger out, throwing it aside. Olivia watched in disbelief as the bleeding slowed. Eliphaz unsheathed his sword, pushing Olivia behind him.

A war cry erupted from Orban. He raised his sword high and charged Michael.

"Leave. Now!" Eliphaz motioned toward the truck.

Olivia locked eyes with Zach, and they sprinted.

Zemira pushed Sergio in their direction. "Go! More might arrive!"

Agora landed in front of Zemira, but she was ready. A gold blur sliced across Agora's neck, spraying black blood as the demon's head tumbled to the ground. Her headless body crumpled in a heap, exploding into ash. Agora's sword melted into a black puddle and evaporated, leaving no trail of her evil existence.

Olivia yanked the door open and jumped into the seat. Sergio landed with a thud in the back seat. Zach started the truck and punched the engine. He turned the truck away from the battle and peeled out of the parking lot.

Sergio stared out the back window. "Go, go!" His fist slammed on the seat. "Get us out of here before they come after us!" Zach turned the wrong direction on the one-way road. He raced for the exit, putting distance between them and the parking lot.

Brisk air blasted through Olivia's busted window. She turned to watch the battle unfold behind her. Zemira and Eliphaz were in a ready stance scanning the lot, waiting for more demons. Orban swung his black sword at Michael, but it clashed against Michael's, creating a surge of blue electricity between the steel. Michael pushed against the swords sending Orban stumbling backward. Michael raised it high, in what Olivia hoped was a death blow for the demon. But she lost sight of the battle when Zach turned a corner.

Zach pounded on his steering wheel as his eyes darted to the rearview mirror. "Liv, you okay? Are you hurt?" She shook her head, not trusting herself to speak.

"Sergio?"

"No, man. I'm not okay! What was that?" His loud, high-pitch voice echoed inside the cab. He touched his neck, where the nail wounds had stopped bleeding. "Those were demons! Same as the coffee shop. I thought I was dead! If those angels hadn't shown up..." He covered his face with his hands, flopping his head against the back window.

"We're okay, Sergio. We made it!" Olivia glanced at Zach. His white-knuckled hand squeezed the steering wheel. He yanked it left, sending her careening into the passenger door.

She gathered her hair, fighting the turbulent air coming through the broken window. Olivia glanced out the back again but only dark terrain and stars remained. "They're not coming after us, Zach. Just take it easy and get us home."

He nodded, turning out of the park and onto the main road. He blasted the heater, but the air coming through the window was no match. But it didn't matter. Olivia was numb. Her mind spun with images of stars, demons, angels and blood slicks that evaporated into thin air. The what-ifs bombarded her, thinking about the different outcomes if the angels hadn't arrived.

Tonight's episode left her with more unthinkable questions holding more unimaginable answers about this nightmare. She rubbed her arms, fighting the icy chill settling into her bones and the reality staring her in the face.

Her life, and the world as she knew it, was forever and inexplicably changed.

CHAPTER EIGHT

ZACH

Zach's heart raced with the flush of adrenaline as he sped toward the city lights. He tried to swallow, but his mouth was bone dry. He lifted his fingers off the steering wheel. They shook in the dashboard's dim lighting. He ached for a hot shower to thaw his icy body and ease his pounding head. His mind flashed in terrifying slices of the demon's ambush in the parking lot.

The demons swirling in their smoky mist, terrorizing them with their laughter and threats of death.

Orban's dagger to his neck.

Angels... warriors... St Michael?

Sergio... metal nails... blood on his neck.

Olivia sat next to Zach, her freezing hand holding his in a tight grip. The wind howled through the broken window, forcing her shivering body against his. Olivia's mass of unruly hair hid her pale face and haunted eyes. Zach had seen nothing as fierce as when she yelled at the swirling demons. Then Orban had grabbed him...

No, don't go there.

He glanced in the rearview mirror at Sergio. He hadn't spoken a word since Zach turned onto the highway, escaping their nightmare at Red Rock. The dark red puncture wounds on his neck stood out as a reminder of how close death had come to Sergio. He had a distant stare that concerned Zach.

"Hey, man, how ya doing?"

Sergio remained silent.

"Hey, look at me."

Olivia turned and reached behind the seat, shaking his knee. He jumped at her touch. "We'll be home soon," she said.

He nodded but remained silent, leaning into the corner of the back seat.

"Talk to me. You can't go home this upset," Olivia said.

"What do you want me to say?" Sergio croaked. "That I'm glad that demon didn't rip out my throat?" His voice rose in anger. "That what happened was okay? I don't want to die, Olivia!" He pointed an accusing finger at her. "You should have listened to me. I wanted to leave it alone, but no. We had to go out there. And for what? To gaze at stars? We almost got killed!" He slammed his hands against the seat and yanked his jacket closer around him, glaring at both of them.

"I don't want this either, Sergio. I'm scared. We're all scared. But we made it, and we have to stick together. Please." Her voice pleaded with him.

Zach glanced over at her. Tears fell from her blue eyes. She looked back at Zach with fear and desperation.

"Just relax. You can't blame Olivia." Zach met Sergio's eyes in the rearview mirror. "None of us understand why these demons are out for us, but we can figure this out. We'll research more on the internet—"

"Internet!" Sergio exploded. "The internet won't help us! This is evil, man!" Sergio's outburst silenced them for a moment.

"What if we tell our parents?" Olivia said. "I don't want to scare my mom, but what if something happens when we're with our families or apart from each other? They could at least help us figure it out." Olivia looked between Zach and Sergio.

Zach wasn't sure he wanted to share this with his parents. His relationship with them was getting back on track. Tonight was so terrifying and unimaginable. How would they react? They might worry about him again. His stomach rolled at having to face their doubts. Or what if they assumed he'd taken drugs or been drinking? There must be another way than asking their parents for help, but an answer stayed out of reach.

Sergio shook his head. "Manny would flip out. And my parents? I don't know, Olivia."

Zach made the turn into Sergio's neighborhood, which was decorated with cheery Christmas lights and blow-up yard decorations. But as the neighbors slept in their cozy beds, evil had struck a few miles away. Peace and security were fleeting. Zach understood this first-hand after having a knife at his throat. He parked in front of Sergio's house.

"At least Manny's gone," Olivia said. "Zip up your jacket. It should hide your wounds in case someone is up waiting for you. If they are, tell them you feel sick."

He nodded and opened the door. He released a heavy sigh, peering back at them. "Thank you for... uh... not... not leaving me back there."

Before they could answer, he jumped out and ran to the front door. He sent a sly glance over his shoulder and stepped inside his house.

"I'm worried about him." Olivia ran her hands over her face. "I'm so tired and scared that I can't even think. What if–"

"Shh." He gathered her in for a hug. It felt so good having his arms around her, holding her close. She sagged against him. A surge of protectiveness swelled inside him. He didn't know how to kill a demon, but he'd do everything in his power to learn. For Olivia. For all of their sakes.

"Don't replay the memories and torture yourself with the *what if* game. It'll make it worse." He gave her one last squeeze and let go. "Let's get you home."

As Zach pulled away from the curb, a curtain floating closed caught his eye. If someone was up waiting for Sergio, Zach hoped he'd hold up under the pressure after the stress of their horrendous night.

ZACH WALKED Olivia to her front door. The glow from the Christmas tree lights filtered through the porch window, but nothing else stirred. The house key shook in Olivia's hand. She hesitated before inserting it into the deadbolt.

"Do you want me to go inside with you?" Zach touched her shoulder. "Just to make sure everything is okay?"

She closed her eyes, releasing a sigh. She turned and gazed back at him with blue eyes that caught his breath.

"Am I that obvious? That would be awesome. Thank you." She unlocked the door, and they stepped into the foyer. She flipped on the lights. A gray blur bounded up the living room steps. Olivia and Zach jumped away. Thunder's bushy tail slipped out the door. They shared nervous laughter as she closed the door.

"Jeez. Your cat scared me."

Olivia laughed again. He liked the sound of her laugh. It was deep and natural, not guarded or shrill. A warning bell went off in his head when he heard a fake laugh. Who wanted to be around someone who couldn't laugh?

Zach stepped in front of her. "Let me get the lights." He raised his flashlight, ready to use as a weapon if something jumped out. They checked the first and second floor, lighting up each room until the house was bright like the Christmas tree in her living room. Nothing out of place or hiding in the dark.

They made their way downstairs. "I don't think you've had any visitors." He inhaled and stepped into the foyer. "Besides, your house smells like cinnamon and apples, not smoke." He grinned at her. "You have a great house."

"Thanks. My mom loves to decorate, as you can tell." She waved her hand at the festive living room. Her face turned serious. "I'm better now that we checked the house. Besides, my mark doesn't hurt. At least that gives us a heads up to run for it."

"My mark hasn't hurt since we left the lot. I bet the demons attached themselves to the bikers, like it attached itself to Ryan. But that hideous female demon said she felt a connection. I wonder if it's because of our marks?"

She shrugged, rubbing her hands over her arms. "I was wondering the same thing. I still can't believe demons attacked us. And why can we see them? Anyway, Mom should be home from work soon. I'm exhausted. I just want a hot shower, and then I'm crawling into bed."

"Me too." He nodded, taking one last look at her. Color had returned to her cheeks, and her hands had stopped shaking. He reached up and took a piece of feather out of her hair. His fingers slid down the blond strand as the feather fell to the floor. He wanted to stay with her. But he was a walking zombie and desperately wanted to shower.

"Keep your cell with you in bed. Call me if something happens or you need me to come and stay with you. Promise?"

"I promise."

"You're a brave one, Liv. Sweet dreams." He leaned in and, on impulse, kissed her forehead.

Her forehead? Why didn't I kiss her cheek?

She grabbed his hand, surprise etched on her face. "Thank you for getting us home safe, Zach. And for... um—"

"No problem." He gave her hand a squeeze, not wanting to let go. "Good night." But he let his fingers fall away and left before he embarrassed himself further.

ZACH'S EYES FLEW OPEN, his body jolted awake. His bedroom was dark except for the thin beams of moonlight cutting between blinds. A static sound filled his ears.

I thought I turned the TV off...

He tried to sit up but couldn't move.

His heart jack-hammered as he lay on his back. His eyes grew wide as they strained to find what smashed his body against the mattress.

Nothing.

Just his sheet draped over his lower body.

He pushed against the pressure again, grimacing in his efforts.

Trapped. Held down by some kind of buzzing force field.

What is happening?

His mark burned...

Panic erupted, setting off every nerve ending like a firework blast.

The field suffocated him, like he was wrapped in cellophane and couldn't break free.

Something was in his room. He sensed it with every fiber of his being.

Hands grabbed his wrists at his sides. He screamed, but made no sound. He thrashed against whatever held him. It didn't work. He looked to his right and it stared at him. The hate from it rolled off in waves. Zach's throat ached from his screams, lost against the buzzing field. His body trembled, shattered with the realization he was helpless against the entity's grip.

A demon has found me.

The shadowy black figure crept over the bed. Zach commanded his body to buck, but it lay frozen, defenseless as the demon slid on top of him. The demon hovered inches over him. Electric pink eyes glared from the shadowy face above him.

No, please. NO! Get off of me!

His screams careened in his mind, reeling from the horror. His harsh breathing grew louder, mixing with the blood pounding in his ears.

The demon pressed its shadowy form against him. The pressure began at his legs and moved up his body, scorching every inch of skin along the way. Its hands released his wrists, tracing up his arms like a feathered caress. Wispy hands traveled over his shoulders while the static increased to a fevered pitch.

Oh God! Help me!

Demented laughter mingled with the buzzing. Everywhere the demon touched, it pushed him deeper into the mattress until he thought the mattress might swallow him. He was at its mercy, vulnerable to whatever it wanted to do. But he still struggled, moved, flailed, trying to fight back.

The demon's face consumed his vision. Black lips parted, exposing a sizzling, hot-pink tongue that whipped inside like a snake. The gaping hole grew wider until all he saw was the slithering tongue. The demon's hands reached Zach's neck. Its long fingers wrapped around it while its thumbs pressed against Zach's windpipe. The tongue flicked against his sealed lips, like a whip's first lick at bare skin.

Please stop... please...

Zach jack-knifed up. A scream tore free from his throat. His arms and legs thrashed, fighting to free himself from the demon. He scrambled out of bed. He lunged for the light switch and flipped it on. His fists were up, gasping for breath as he searched his room.

Nothing... except the pounding on his door.

He looked again, but everything was how it had been before he fell asleep. Except for the sheet, laying half on the floor. No demon lurked, waiting to strike. Zach's body shook, damp with sweat and rank with fear.

"Zach! Open up!" His mom pounded on the door again. The knob rattled as she tried to open it.

Zach rushed over, unlocked the door and threw it open. His mom stood wide-eyed, hand up, ready to pound on the door again. Her gray robe fell open, showing a wide stance, ready to kick in the door.

"Hey," he said.

"What's going on, Zach?" She pointed at his room.

He ran his fingers through his damp hair. "Just a nightmare. Sorry I woke you."

She let her hand fall, sighing in relief. "Must have been a whopper! Scared me to death when I heard you scream, but your dad didn't budge." She smiled, but concern clouded her eyes, a carbon copy of his own. She hooked her auburn hair behind her ears. "Since we're up, can I make you a midnight snack?" She tried to peek around him, but Zach moved the door, blocking her view.

Mom's mantra was that a sweet treat, a hot drink or comfort food fixed any problem. Most of the time, he'd have been glad to have her whip something up, knowing full well she loosened him up to get him to talk. But not tonight. Zach was too raw, and he sure didn't need his mom asking questions.

"Nah. But thanks, Mom." Zach hoped his smile appeased her. "I think I'll just go back to bed."

"Okay, if that sounds best." She stood on her tiptoes and kissed his cheek. "Love you, sweetie."

"Love you too." She walked the long hallway to her bedroom, glancing back and giving him a wave before closing her bedroom door behind her. He shut his door and rested his back against it, taking one last survey of his room.

Alone.

Thank goodness.

He sighed as he tried to piece together his night after coming home from Red Rock. His parents had been in bed when he got home. Thankful he didn't have to make small talk, he'd come upstairs, showered and crashed. Until the demon woke him.

Zach walked to his bathroom and splashed water on his face. He took a hard look at himself in the mirror. What reflected back wasn't a stranger. He'd seen this hollow face before, marred by a furrowed brow and dark circles under his eyes.

He hung his head and took a few deep breaths. His hand trembled as he touched his throat, which still ached from his silent screams. He shook his head. It'd been a stressful few days, full of weird and dark stuff.

His mark...

In the mirror, he found his mark of Orion. He placed his fingers over the seven spots, raised and sensitive to the touch. His stomach dropped as he looked back at himself in the mirror. The mark connected them to demons.

You don't know that for sure, Zach.

His palms smacked the bathroom counter. For the first time in his life, he glanced at his bedroom with fear and trepidation. How could he go to sleep knowing a demon might return?

Zach climbed back into bed, wide awake. He wanted to call Olivia, but that was a bad idea. No need to freak her out in the middle of the night. He could call Sergio, but Zach didn't think he'd want to hear from him either. As much as he wanted to share his ordeal, it would keep until morning.

Zach reached up to turn off his light but paused. He'd never had an issue with the dark before, but tonight changed that. His hand slipped back under the sheet and pulled it up to his chin. It was a false sense of security, hoping the sheet provided protection. Silly, he knew, since it didn't work the first time. But he kept it there, preferring it to exposing his skin to the open air.

His lamp was staying on tonight.

Maybe forever.

CHAPTER NINE
ZACH

The early-morning sun warmed Zach's face as he stretched his legs before his morning run. His black lab, Hank, sat beside him, wagging his tail while his nose twitched in the air. When Hank was younger, Zach ran him every day to burn off the dog's energy. Now seven, Hank only accompanied him on shorter runs.

Zach stepped off the curb and started a light jog. He needed to work out the tension stringing his body tight. He loved music but didn't run listening to it. He preferred the sound his running shoes made when they hit the ground. The slapping rhythm of his feet mixed with his breathing got him in a zone. Just him, the road, his thoughts... and sometimes Hank's tags clinking next him.

Zach tossed and turned after the demon in his room. His body wanted to sleep, but his brain kept churning. It didn't matter that the light drenched his room. He jumped at any small sound. When dawn's light came through his window, he gave up and decided on a run.

He increased the pace as his body started to relax. His mind went back to last night at Red Rock. The three of them needed to meet soon and make a plan. Now that the shock had worn off, they might remember something vital. The problem was, today was Christmas

Eve, and getting away from his family would be impossible. Zach let his thoughts churn as he left the neighborhood.

Sweat rolled between his shoulder blades by the end of the run. His long legs pumped as he sprinted down his street. He ran past Olivia's house, glimpsing Thunder perched on the porch railing. He hoped Olivia had gotten a better night's sleep than he did.

Olivia.

He remembered the first time he got a glimpse of her, driving on their street as his family unpacked the moving truck. She had driven by in her green SUV and grinned at him. He had smiled back, thinking she was cute, but didn't see her again. School started soon, and to his surprise, her locker was across the hallway from him. That was when he started to watch her. Her wave of long, dark blond hair swayed as she weaved her way through the hallway. He liked that her body had curves and how she walked with a confidence he recognized in athletes. But what stopped him in his tracks were her electric blue eyes, so bright it looked like a light shined on them. But it was more than the color. Her eyes held no pretense. It had been a gut punch last night when that openness was gone, replaced by fear and horror.

"Zach!"

His head twisted over his shoulder. She waved from her porch, then scooped up Thunder. He smiled, turning for her house. When he and Hank approached, the cat jumped out of her arms and darted through the crack left open in the front door. Zach guessed Thunder wasn't a fan of big black dogs. He stepped onto the porch and his pulsed jumped, but the run hadn't caused it.

"Hi. I came out to get Thunder and there you were, running by with your dog. What's his name?" Olivia smiled, pointing at his dog.

"Hank." The dog sat, panting with his tongue hanging out the side of his mouth. Olivia ruffled his thick neck fur. She got a big lick on her hand for a thank-you. She laughed, wiping her hand on her yoga pants. "He's so handsome."

"Yeah, he's an awesome dog and doesn't know a stranger." Zach patted the top of Hank's head.

Her brow creased as she scanned his face. "You don't look like you slept well." She wrapped her arms around her middle.

This wasn't the right time to tell her about his nocturnal visitor. "What, did my dark circles give me away?" He smirked. "Don't worry. It's hard to fall asleep with my brain working overtime. I needed a morning run to shake out the cobwebs."

"I miss running for that exact reason." Olivia pointed to her leg. "Hurt my knee playing soccer. I had to quit the team, but I hope it heals enough so I can enjoy runs again." Olivia sighed.

Zach stepped closer and placed a finger under her chin, tilting her head back. "How did you sleep? By the looks of your bed-head, you were out for the count." She laughed and slapped his hand away.

"I crashed, but woke up early this morning." She stepped back, rubbing her forehead. "So many questions kept swirling in my head. I decided to write them in a journal this morning to clarify my thoughts. We need to research demons and how they get here, how they kill people, and–"

"Whoa." He grabbed her arms, stopping her mid-stream. "Don't get yourself worked up. We'll figure out when the three of us can meet and talk about it. In the meantime, do your research and stay with your mom. Will you be at church today?"

She nodded.

"Good. No demons there."

She nodded again.

"Come on, that's supposed to be funny!"

Olivia chuckled and rolled her eyes. "I better go get ready."

"Yeah, I have to go tell my parents about the truck window first." He frowned as he looked at Hank, who was sprawled on the porch.

"What are you going to say? Will they be mad?"

"I hope not." He let out a deep breath. "I'll tell them we returned from our hike, and the window was smashed. The rest can wait till we have more answers."

"I'm sure it'll be fine." She nodded, biting her bottom lip.

He pulled on the leash and took a step backward. "See ya, Liv."

"Bye."

He heard her front door close as he jogged to his house. His stomach dropped when he saw his parents standing toe-to-toe by his truck, having an obvious disagreement.

Great...

Already arguing over him... again...

This had disaster written all over it.

HIS PARENTS HAD their hands on their hips, tracking him coming up the street. Zach stopped in front of the truck's hood. A scowl lined Dad's lean face, but Mom looked more worried than mad. Zach was as tall as his dad, but years in the Army had built up muscle and enhanced his sixth sense.

Dad closed the distance and pointed at the window. "You mind telling me what happened, Zach?" He shoved his big hands into his pockets. "Why did I have to find the busted window while getting the morning newspaper, instead of you telling me in person first? What happened last night? Huh?"

Already guilty...

The thin thread of trust snapped between them and fell away.

Mom came up and put her hand on his arm. "Matt, we were in bed when he got home. I'm sure his plan was to tell us this morning, right, honey?"

"Stop answering for him, Rachel. He's a big boy now. Well?" He stabbed a finger into Zach's chest. "That truck was in mint condition when I gave it to you. I expected more from you."

Zach's stomach clenched. His dad's temper hit him square in the chest, deflating him.

"This wasn't my fault." Zach threw his hands in the air and stepped back. "It happened last night at Red Rock. We parked and set out on a hike. When we got back, the window was smashed, but nothing was stolen. There were no other cars in the lot, and the guard shack was empty when we exited the park." He put his sweaty hands inside the hoodie pocket. "We didn't go anywhere but Red Rock. In fact, we can

go now, and I'll show you the broken glass, or you can ask my friends."
He glared at his dad. "Don't worry, no one got hurt."

This time.

His mom moved closer, reaching out her hand. "We know–"

Zach stepped away and shook his head. "When I got home, you
guys were in bed. I got up early, so I went for a run. I wanted to catch
you before you found it." He stared at his dad. "I thought by now I
would get the benefit of doubt, but I guess not. I'm sorry." Zach turned
and faced the garage as the flush crept up his face. "Don't worry, I'll
pay for it."

Zach walked away from his parents and their silent judgement.
Dad reached out to grab his arm, but Zach side-stepped and kept
walking. Dad's footsteps followed him to the garage door. Zach
punched in the code, and the metal door creaked as it opened. His
dad's hand didn't miss his arm this time, stopping him before he could
escape inside the garage.

"This isn't about who pays for the window. Look at me." Dad
tugged back, making Zach face him, but Zach glared at his dad with
hurt he couldn't disguise. Dad's shoulders fell, and he released a heavy
sigh. "When I came out and saw the window busted, I got upset. I go
to your room and you're not there. Your mom finds me and shares
that you woke up screaming last night. So yeah. I'm thinking there's
more going on that you're not telling us." He gave Zach's arm a quick
squeeze and let go. "You can understand, right?" Zach looked away
and kept quiet. "I'm glad you and your friends are okay."

Okay on the outside...

"Are you ever going to trust me again?" Zach's throat clogged with
emotion when he looked back. They stared at each other, silently
exchanging raw, painful memories that still hovered near the surface,
festering like a wound too deep to heal.

Why did I ask him that?

"Zach–"

"Never mind, Dad." Zach headed for the back wall of the garage.
Bins of tools and household items were stacked on tidy, organized
shelves.

"Come inside and let's eat breakfast." Mom laid her hand on his shoulder. His stomach churned. Food was the last thing it needed.

"I want to cover the window first. I'll come inside when I'm done." Zach pulled down a bin, not making eye contact. If he found disappointment shadowing them, it would crush him.

"Okay." The back door closed as he pulled opened the bin's lid. Through the haze of unshed tears, he searched for plastic wrap and duct tape. Not finding them, he slammed the lid back in place, hitting it once, and then he couldn't stop. His fist pounded away in his desperate need to batter back the memories and hurt haunting him, eating at his soul.

Push it deeper, Zach.

He stopped and hung his head while his chest heaved. Hank whined beside him, nudging his wet nose against Zach's hand while his tail wagged across the dusty concrete. Somehow, Hank knew when he was hurting. He crouched and rubbed between Hank's ears, leaning his forehead against his dog's big head.

"Thanks buddy. I'll be all right." Zach stood under the gaze of his soft brown eyes. Hank turned and laid on the floor with a big groan. Zach scoffed, not sure if the groan was because the run wore Hank out or because Hank was tired of hearing Zach lie to himself.

Zach opened more bins, rummaging for the supplies while he searched inside himself for more space to pack away his agonizing memories.

CHAPTER TEN
OLIVIA

O livia laid her purse and jacket over the den's sofa. Her stomach growled as she strolled to the fridge to prepare lunch. Grilled ham and cheese sounded wonderful, so she plucked out the ingredients and closed the door. She jumped at the sight of her mom standing behind the door, gazing at her with shielded eyes. Mom had been quiet during church. Olivia even nudged her a few times to get her attention, which was a role reversal for them.

"Want a sandwich?" Olivia waved the sandwich makings in front of her.

Mom shook her head but stood her ground while watching Olivia make her sandwich.

"What? You're being creepy." Olivia chuckled, trying to lighten the mood. When it didn't work, Olivia put the bread and butter knife on the counter and faced her. Olivia tilted her head, noting her mom's creased brow and lips pressed in an unfamiliar thin line. Mom walked to the den and sat on the couch.

"Come sit with me, please." She patted the spot next to her. With a twinge of apprehension, Olivia sat in the requested spot. She mimicked her mom's posture with her feet tucked behind her and an arm slung over the top of the couch. They had many relaxed and natural conversations sitting in these same spots, but now the under-currents ran tense and unsure. Olivia's stomach flipped, but it wasn't because she was hungry.

"What's wrong? You're scaring me." Olivia was unsure she wanted to hear the answer.

Mom took a deep breath and released a long sigh. "Olivia. I'm not sure where to start with this, but..." She ran a hand through her hair and flipped it off her neck. "I overheard your conversation this morning with Zach on the porch–"

"Mom–" Olivia jumped off the couch, staring incredulously back at her.

"Wait. I wasn't snooping. Thunder ran through the cracked door, so I got up to shut it."

Olivia turned away as a rush of heat swamped her.

Oh no! What if–

"I only caught the tail end, but it was enough to figure out something horrible is taking place and you need to tell me right now."

Olivia closed her eyes, a sinking sensation engulfed her.

"Mom, please, I can't–"

Mom pushed herself off the couch and faced her. "Olivia, I'm not asking, and I'm not kidding. If what I gathered was correct, you need to spill it." They stood a few feet apart, but their clash of wills had them toe-to-toe. How could Olivia even share these last few days, and was she ready to unpack her horrifying story? But Olivia could see it in her mom's eyes: she wasn't backing away from her demand.

She'll think I'm nuts... What if she doesn't believe me?

"Mom–"

She closed the gap, placing her hands on Olivia's arms and giving them a squeeze while her eyes responded with her. "Just let it out."

Olivia's throat constricted as unshed tears blurred her vision. They sat down on the couch and faced each other as Olivia worked up the courage to start her story.

"Okay. What I will tell you will sound frightening. But I swear, I'm not lying or exaggerating. When I start, I don't know if I'll be able to stop, so please, let me get it out before you ask questions... deal?"

"Deal," Mom whispered with a small, reassuring smile.

Olivia held on tight to her mom's hands, letting them be her anchor as the events of the last few days poured out of her. Mom started to interrupt a few times but kept her lips in a grim line. Olivia began with the fight in the coffee shop, how no one but the three of them saw the demon and how the marks appeared. Mom's face paled when Olivia showed her the Orion mark. Olivia's grip tightened as she shared the video game vision, how they discovered the mark was Orion and their encounters with the demons and angels at Red Rock.

"I can't believe what's happening to us." Olivia wiped away her tears when she finished her story.

Mom's warm hands caressed her face, her thumbs wiping away the last bit of moisture. Her unexpected reaction of silent acceptance stunned Olivia.

"I'm so sorry I wasn't there to protect you. You could have been–" Mom's face blanched as she bit her bottom lip.

"Mom, you couldn't have stopped any of this–"

Mom's fingers tightened around her face, silencing her next words.

"Olivia. Listen to me. Just... listen." She leaned closer. "This is dangerous and carries the potential risk of you getting hurt. We can't take any chances, so you need to stay home. You can't go anywhere. Promise me."

"Okay, Mom... um... That's a little extreme. Tell–"

"Look." Mom closed her worried eyes and took another deep breath. When they opened, composure had returned.

"Sorry, I didn't mean to scare you. I'm worried for you, and I want to keep you near as we figure out our next move. Let me call a friend of mine from our old church. He's dealt with the supernatural before and can give us much-needed direction."

"No, I don't want anyone else involved.... Mom–"

"Olivia, I trust this person, and we need guidance on how to keep you and your friends safe." Olivia nodded. What if it upset the boys, bringing a stranger into the equation? Her gut told her yes because they wanted to keep this hidden from their families, but she could only worry so much. Besides, Mom's plan had possibilities for answers they needed to figure out how to stay alive.

"You're right. Call your friend. Thank you for listening and for finding us help. I'm sorry this happened."

"You've got nothing to be sorry for, honey, because you didn't ask for this. I'll go make the call." Mom kissed her cheek and headed upstairs.

A huge weight lifted off Olivia's shoulders. She replayed the talk in her head, and a funny feeling nagged at her that her mom knew more than she showed. Although scared and worried, Mom didn't ask many questions or even consider her story far-fetched. Olivia always got grilled for details. Why not this time? And who was this friend? She didn't remember any demon chasers from their last church.

Stretching out, she laid her head on the couch pillow and closed her heavy eyelids, exhausted and numb from retelling the horrors of the last few days. Her lunch of grilled cheese was long forgotten in the talk of demons and angels.

OLIVIA WALKED to the den with Thunder in tow, who was purring with excitement. He had figured out long ago that the smell of popcorn meant a vacant, unmoving lap on the couch for a few hours. She nestled herself in the couch's corner and lifted the popcorn bowl just in time before Thunder claimed his spot, his large body spilling off her lap. She laid the bowl on the armrest, wondering what was taking her mom so long.

Mom had spent the entire afternoon upstairs, coming down to make dinner and then back to her room. Today's events had subdued their normal talkative dinner banter. Olivia waited for an update to their earlier conversation, but to her surprise, she never got one.

Just as well. Too exhausted by the whole thing.

Olivia's goal for tonight and Christmas morning was to ride out the time without conflict or revived painful memories. As much as Mom had tried to start a Christmas tradition such as presents or

Christmas PJs, Olivia wanted no part of it. They had one tradition: sharing a pasta dinner followed by one of their favorite chick flicks. This year was no different... or so she thought.

Olivia flipped through the movie channels. Salt and butter glistened on her fingers as she tossed a kernel into her mouth. She licked her fingers, eager for the two-hour escape from her current madness.

Mom entered the room with one hand behind her back. Olivia lifted an eyebrow when her mom stopped in front of her. Her arm came around, and a small package wrapped in shimmering silver paper tied with a purple ribbon lay in Mom's elegant hand.

Olivia sat up, tossing the remote and an irritated cat off her lap. "Mom, you know–"

Mom sat next to her, placing the present on Olivia's lap. "I've waited a long time to give you this gift." She reached out with both hands and cupped Olivia's face. "Please, take it, honey."

Olivia stared into her mom's soft eyes and knew she couldn't refuse. She gingerly picked up the box, examining it from different angles. "It's so pretty." She grinned at her Mom.

"Open it." Mom nudged her leg, grinning back at her.

Olivia held her breath as she pulled the tail of the delicate ribbon. Her mind raced at the possibilities of what her mom had waited so long to give her. She ran her finger under the tape and unwrapped the silver paper.

A simple, square antique velvet box rested in her hand. Olivia glanced at her mom, who sat with her hands clasped in her lap and anticipation gleaming in her eyes.

The box's hinges squeaked as Olivia lifted the lid. She gasped at the exquisite gift nestled inside the black velvet lining. An antique silver ring with a brilliant red stone. It gleamed with streaks of blue and purple as a faint orange glow radiated from within the stone. A delicate crown setting encased the stone on top of a wide scrolling band.

A single tear slipped down Olivia's cheek. "It's the most beautiful ring I've ever seen." She moved the box around, fascinated at how the stone changed colors as it hit the various angles of light.

"Put it on, sweetie," Mom said, her voice cracking.

Olivia hesitated, then slipped it onto her right middle finger. Its fit was perfect... like someone had made it for her.

They both giggled, delighted by the ring's colors dazzling on her finger.

"It's just mesmerizing. What type of stone is this?"

"The stone is a fire opal called Dragon's Breath," Mom said.

"That's a perfect name for it!" Olivia laughed in agreement.

Mom grabbed her hand. "This was my mother's ring. She gave it to me when I was your age. Legend says it will enhance intuition and help you to better trust yourself. The colors reveal the strength and energy of your inner fire." She turned serious as she gazed back at Olivia. "When you came into this world, I stopped wearing it and tucked it away until the time was right to pass it on to you. I ask you now to wear it, remembering what I said."

"I will.... I promise, Mom." Olivia sniffed. "Thank you," she whispered.

Olivia watched the orange glow grow inside the ring. "I wish I could meet her... Grandma." When Mom didn't reply, she glanced up at her.

A sadness flickered across Mom's face. "Maybe we will get to Ireland someday." Her smile didn't reach her eyes.

Olivia threw her arms around her. "Thank you so much, Mom." She gave her a big squeeze. "I love you."

"Love you, too." She untangled herself from Olivia and laughed. "Now, let's watch a movie." Mom leaned over, grabbing the remote.

Olivia didn't pay much attention to the movie. Instead, she got lost in the stone's vivid colors and the mysteries of the women who had worn it.

CHAPTER ELEVEN

SERGIO

E xhausted.

Sergio stepped into the steaming shower. The hot water's heat ran over his goosebump-riddled skin, reviving him since he hadn't slept last night. Sergio sighed as the spray pelted his face. Visions of the demons at Red Rock played like a movie loop in his head. He wanted to press the stop button, but it kept up its relentless repetition of last night.

Sergio's hand gripped the black armor, trying to pry her nails away from his neck.

He poured shampoo into his hand and lathered his hair, scrubbing hard, wishing it would erase the memories. White foam smelling of forest rolled over his face. His fingers searched the side of his neck, finding the small puncture wounds from the demon's sharp nails. It was tender, reminding him how close he'd been to death.

Dark mist surrounded him as ash fell upon him. Bile rose as fear surged through his body, smoke filling his senses.

He scrubbed his body red, wanting his skin free of any demon ash or smell.

Her nails pressed into his skin. He knew at any second, his blood would spurt from his neck, draining over him.

Sergio's fresh tears ran down his cheeks as dry sobs threatened to erupt. Could he ever forget last night?

Someone pounded on the bathroom door, jarring him from his memories.

"Hurry, mano. All the good deals will be gone," Manny yelled through the door.

"I'll be out in a minute." Sergio shut off the water, trying to calm his racing heart. Manny and he always shopped together on Christmas Eve. He looked forward to their tradition, but not today. Not after last night. Sergio didn't want Manny's critical eyes on him or more of his bulldog questioning.

Sergio toweled off and threw on his clothes. He glanced in the mirror, making sure the hoodie covered his puncture wounds. If he stayed on one side of Manny and kept his chin tucked, the wounds would stay hidden. If he snagged Mom's makeup...

"Let's go. You're pretty enough." Manny snickered through the door. "No time to pick up chicas today."

Sergio yanked open the door. "Give it a rest, Manny. You're pretty enough for both of us." Sergio darted past him, ignoring the smirk on Manny's face. He couldn't let him get under his skin today.

Just stay cool.

The hallway emptied into a large family room, expanding into a big, bright kitchen. Female voices mixed with laughter greeted him as he made his way to the fridge. The heavenly aroma of tamale makings filled his nostrils. A few of his mom's friends bustled around the kitchen. Blanca hand-mixed the masa in a large red bowl while Marisol scooped the tamale filling into three separate bowls. Six women sat at the family kitchen table, each building their tamales.

"Good morning, Mijo," his mom, Sofia, said from the table. Her large onyx-colored eyes found his while her hand reached for a corn husk. "You and Manny going shopping?" The corner of her eyes crinkled as her full lips stretched into a smile.

"Yep, I need to buy a few more gifts." He closed the fridge door. Nothing sounded good with his stomach still in knots. He walked over to the table and kissed her cheek. Mom spread a thin layer of masa over the husk and filled it with the spicy pork filling, smelling of red chili. She smiled back at him as she folded the bottom inside and rolled the husk together. She laid it on top of the tamales stacked on a big tray in the middle of the table. "Smells good, Mama."

He leaned over and kissed the soft brown cheek lifted up towards him. "Buenos dias, Abuela." His Grandma's short, spiked gray hair smelled of flowers. Her kind brown eyes reflected in her smile as she reached up and cupped his face.

"¡Mi nieto! ¿Como estás?" She searched his face, waiting for an answer, but he shuffled out of the way as the ladies brought more ingredients to the table.

"Él es muy bueno, Abuela." Manny waved his arm at Sergio as he headed toward the door. Sergio waved goodbye, following Manny.

"¡Adios!" A chorus of goodbyes rang out until Sergio shut the door.

"You're like trying to get Mama out of someplace," Manny said, thumping Sergio's chest.

"Whatever," Sergio mumbled as he climbed into the passenger seat. Manny's car roared to life. The houses became a blur as Manny maneuvered his way out of the neighborhood. Soon the streets grew hectic with people in a rush to get their last-minute shopping done.

"How did it go last night with your gringo friends?" Manny asked, stopping at a red light.

He looked at his brother's handsome profile and his muscular hand on the wheel. "Fine, no thanks to you. I don't know why you harassed my friends last night."

There goes my cool.

"I don't care what your friends think of me, except maybe the chica." Manny smirked. "She's hot. Is she available or does she only have eyes for... what's his name?"

Sergio glared at his brother as he gunned through the green light. He was trying to get under Sergio's skin, so he bit his tongue, not daring to speak his mind.

"Zach." Sergio shrugged deeper into the hoodie. "And leave Olivia alone. She's not like the girls you date."

Manny chuckled as he sped up onto the freeway. "Somebody got a crush–"

"Shut up. She is one of my best friends," he shot back. "I don't see her that way, so... just leave her alone." He sagged against his seat.

Manny remained quiet, but Sergio was sure this conversation wasn't over between them. The last thing he wanted was Manny's curiosity radar trained on him, Olivia or Zach. What happened last night had to stay their secret.

The sprawling mall came into sight when Manny exited the freeway. Sergio was thankful for the distraction he needed to get Manny off his back. Manny found a spot in the crowded parking lot. They got out of the car, but Manny cut him off by stepping in front of him.

"Manito, something is going on with you. I feel it." Manny grabbed Sergio by the scruff of his neck, pulling him closer. Sergio tried to look away, but Manny put his finger in front of his face. "You come to me first if you're in trouble."

"Manny–" Sergio said as he tried to pull away.

"Hey, listen to me. You come to me first." Manny released him and turned as he swaggered to the entrance. Sergio shoved his hands in his pockets, following him through the glass entrance doors. Manny couldn't fix Sergio's problems with a fistfight or tough talk. Although if anyone could kill a demon, it was Manny.

No.

Sergio couldn't risk his brother's life. For better or worse, he and his friends were on their own.

CHRISTMAS SHOPPERS JAMMED THE MALL, jostling for position inside and outside the stores. They crowded long tables of half-folded clothes while salespeople scrambled to restock more items or manage long checkout lines. It was chaos, and Manny loved it. He had once told Sergio he enjoyed the frantic atmosphere of people struggling to spot the dreaded last present. It put him in the Christmas spirit.

Sergio considered it nuts because he was here for the deals, not the manic hustle and bustle.

Manny whistled a Christmas tune while he considered the shirts on the circular rack. Sergio was uninspired and couldn't recall who he had left to buy for on his Christmas list.

Ah yes... Abuela.

A slight grin crossed his face as he thought of his Grandma Camilla. She was the gentlest, most loving person in his life. Her sharp eyes and quick tongue didn't tolerate any nonsense, but her rebukes were spoken with patience and care. None of his friends had their grandma living with them, but he enjoyed her and the special relationship they had formed.

For as long as he could remember, she had always worn a scarf. Rain or shine, one adorned her neck in various stylish knots. He headed to the scarf rack and inspected each one. He found a silky gray one with a watercolor pastel floral print. His fingers grazed across the delicate material, imagining it looped around her neck.

Perfect...

As he paid the cashier, he checked the store for Manny but didn't find him. His stomach growled in protest while a headache brewed behind his dry eyes. He pushed through the crowd; still no Manny.

Sergio pulled out his phone as a low ringing started in his ears. A flush crept up his face, and the room began to swim. He blinked as his eyesight narrowed. With no chair around, he leaned against the wall behind him, desperate for support. He gasped for air as the ringing grew louder. No longer did he see the store's racks of clothes or individuals lugging bags. Instead, he stared into darkness; an ominous canvas waiting for the artist's first strokes.

No. No. No.

He squeezed his eyes shut, not wanting the vision to come alive while he slumped to the floor. But it didn't matter. It came into focus like a film playing on his eyelids.

And he was the star.

Gasping...

Sweating...

Running... in the desert on a moonless night.

The flashlight beam bobbed over the dusty ground in front of him. Footsteps pounded near him, matching his beam of light in his peripheral vision. Something chased him in the blackness. Familiar noises of snarls and cackles sent chills up Sergio's spine as he urged his legs to race faster into the soundtrack of his nightmares. But a different scream pierced the air, one he never wanted to hear.

Olivia.

It echoed in his head as his legs burned and heart pounded. He had to make it to her... save her... from the demons.

"Olivia!" Sergio yelled. In the distance, a small red glow appeared. It spread, expanding into a wide circle, illuminating a broad form running toward the vibrant red ring suspended in the night. If the demon made it inside with Olivia, he would lose her forever.

Faster.

Almost there.

The horrendous smell assaulted him.

Smoke.

Ash.

Sharp feathered wings surrounded him, knocking him backward. He fought, but their frantic beating and suffocating ash pushed him to his knees. He threw his arm up to protect his head. Menacing laughter taunted him as he struggled to search past the wings for the red, glowing circle. When his burning eyes found it, to his horror, the red glow had grown narrower and then disappeared.

No! Olivia!

"Sergio! Sergio!" Manny shook him harder, then grabbed his jaw, giving it a rough squeeze. Sergio's vision faded as his brother's worried face filled his view.

"¡Manito! ¿Que pasa?" Manny cried. Sergio's senses came back along with his headache. His stomach knotted as the vision connection lingered.

What had happened to Olivia?

"I don't know. I was looking for you and–" Sergio stopped.

"You were yelling for Olivia. Is she here? Did something happen to her?" Manny asked, his face inches from Sergio's. Words escaped Sergio. How could he explain to Manny what he saw? He'd never believe him–

"Sergio! Talk to me!" Manny gave him another shake.

A small crowd had gathered around them. His face flushed as people whispered while others pointed at him. He licked the sweat off his upper lip. "She's fine. Get me out of here." Sergio croaked as he scrambled to his feet.

Manny gave the crowd a withering glance as they pushed through them. Sergio's legs wobbled, but he willed them to move while Manny grabbed their bags, leading him in angry silence out of the mall.

The blast of fresh outside air revived Sergio's battered senses and cleared his head. Manny opened the passenger door, letting Sergio slide onto the seat. Sergio stared out the windshield, watching his brother race around the car's hood, and got inside before he buckled. Manny grabbed the front of his sweatshirt, yanking Sergio toward him. Onyx eyes blazed at Sergio as Manny held them face-to-face.

"What happened to you!" Manny gave Sergio's hoodie an indignant shake. His brow frowned, but anger swelled in his words. "I go to the dressing room and come out to hear you yelling for Olivia. Not only yelling for her, but on the floor with your arms flailing around you."

"I'm so sorry, Manny." Sergio tried to pull away. "I don't know what happened–"

"Don't lie to me!" He shoved Sergio away, glaring at two teenagers peeking inside the windshield.

"I'm not lying. Come on... don't be mad at me." Sergio put his hand on Manny's arm, but Manny shrugged it off. "My ears started ringing, and I guess I passed out."

Manny looked him over and smirked.

"Seriously! I was texting you when it happened. I must have thought Olivia was here."

Manny shook his head, unimpressed by Sergio's explanation.

"I am sorry."

Neither spoke as a weighty silence remained in the car. When

Manny looked away, he smacked the steering wheel with the heel of his hand.

"I told you to come to me. You're not telling me the whole truth." He wagged his finger in Sergio's face. "You come clean soon, or I'll tell Mom and Dad about your fainting spell." Manny snorted.

"Don't do–"

"¡Callate!" Manny yelled, stabbing his finger into Sergio's face. Sergio's lips pressed together at his brother's silencing.

Manny drove out of the parking lot and headed home. His anger and disappointment were the last thing Sergio wanted, but no way could he confide in him what had occurred the last few days. More questions raced through his mind while nausea rolled as he recalled the vision. Could she be in physical danger or was the vision brought on by his stress? Dread of this unknown ate at him on the trip home. Manny stopped at the curb, but the car remained running.

"I'll see you tonight for midnight Mass," Manny said. His tone was detached as he stared out the front windshield.

"Manny, I–"

"Adios."

Sergio stepped out and shut the door. His brother drove away without a backward glance, leaving him to stare at the car until it disappeared around the corner.

Sergio trudged up the walkway and slipped through the front door, closing it with care behind him. The house was quieter, no longer crowded with the chatty women making tamales. Sergio sought his bedroom's solitude as he grappled with what had happened at the mall and how it fit into the last few days.

His feet dragged down the carpeted hallway, and he felt deflated like a day-old party balloon. His heart ached as he remembered how Manny didn't make eye contact during the drive home. Manny may ride him hard, but Sergio loved him and ached for his approval. He was everything Sergio wanted to be: confident, fearless, and not concerned with the opinions of others, all while breezing through college. Sergio strived to emulate him, but always came up lacking.

Muffled, elevated voices came from the bedroom next to his.

Abuela's soothing tone mingled with another occupant who moaned and cried.

Lucia.

Sergio's hand reached for Abuela's door but closed into a fist instead. He didn't have the energy to help with his twin sister, and he might make matters worse in his current state of mind. A twinge of guilt hit him, because it could have been him in the wheelchair instead of his sister. He forced the thought aside, having enough on his plate right now.

Better to let Abuela handle it.

He closed his bedroom door with a minimal clicking sound and flopped on his bed. He put a pillow over his head, hoping to shut out the harsh sounds inside his skull and from the bedroom next door.

CHAPTER TWELVE
OLIVIA

Olivia snuggled deeper under her comforter as dawn's light filtered through her window blinds. She loved lying half-awake in her bed, letting the lazy morning unwind around her. But as her fog lifted, dread pressed against her chest at the reality of her day, compelling her limbs to stay hidden under the blanket.

Christmas morning.

The day her entire world had shattered.

Would the pieces of her life ever fit back together? Or would there always be one piece missing, forever lost when Dad ripped it from her as he walked out the door?

She closed her eyes as the memories of the catastrophic day surfaced. Time had blurred while she'd cried, not recognizing how much had passed before Mom came upstairs after Dad left. She remembered the click of her bedroom door opening, but she had pretended to be asleep. The bed sagged at her feet when Mom sat, but she didn't wake her. Olivia sensed her gaze as her mom cried softly. But Olivia stayed still, smothered by her mom's sadness and by her own anger and painful confusion. Mom muffled a sob when she left her room, breaking something deep inside Olivia. A part of her was still frozen at that moment of heartbreak, preventing her pain from thawing and moving on with her life.

Olivia held on to a shameful anger against her mom for a while for letting him abandon them. Why didn't she fight harder to make him stay and face their problems? But she couldn't blame it all on Mom. Olivia came up lacking too. He didn't love either of them enough to want to stay.

Whatever.

Selfish jerk.

Mom tried to excuse his rejection of them, explaining that he wasn't happy with Mom and needed to find his purpose. It didn't matter why he left anymore. He had made his choice, and it left them to pick up the pieces, to build a life without him. And they had, and it was a good one.

But a part of her heart held a black hole of grief. It snuck up in unsuspecting moments, threatening to pull her inside; raw, hot and ready to devour her if she let it. But emotional survival had taught her to shove the pain behind a hidden door, tucking away the key, so the oppressive and excruciating pain didn't suck her into the black hole forever.

She opened her eyes and found the alluring white feather in the mason jar, its delicate ends dancing with an unseen partner. The soft, wispy movement soothed her frayed heart. Sometimes Olivia closed her eyes and pretended she had white wings made from her feather and could fly away and set herself free from her sadness, disappointment, and resentment. But reality always greeted Olivia like a slap in the face, leaving her to face the day, if for no other reason than because she loved her mom.

She sighed as an orange glint caught her attention. Her ring flashed in the morning light. She was still stunned Mom had given it to her. Resilience swelled in her. This day wasn't only focused on her pain, because it wasn't an easy day for Mom either.

She tossed back the covers and jumped out of bed. A pair of sweatpants and her favorite zip-up hoodie draped the back of her chair. She got dressed and left her bedroom. Olivia decided to return the favor and treat Mom to breakfast. Waffles sounded good as she dashed down the stairs. She hoped they had blueberries to mix in with them. Mom loved–

No, it can't be.

A single living room lamp cast a dim light on shadowy figures into the foyer. Olivia's world tilted as her brain tried to absorb what her eyes saw. Her hand clutched the stair rail as she took another step. Her stomach rolled; her ears rang as dizziness threatened to topple her. Bitter emotions swirled inside as she fought for control.

Mom stood with her profile to Olivia, her head back, hair twinkling with the reflection of Christmas tree lights. Tears tracked down her cheeks; her mouth was open in elation.

But it wasn't her mom who made Olivia vibrate with outrage.

Kneeling before her with his arms wrapped around her waist and face planted in her stomach was someone Olivia never wanted to see again. His shoulders shook with sobs muffled against her mom's robe.

No.

Hot tears filled her eyes as her chest tightened, making it hard to breathe.

He can't be here.

He's not welcome.

He left us.

Dad.

Mom's hands weaved into his thick brown hair, pushing his bearded face toward hers.

"Home." His dry sob escaped, gazing up at her.

"Home." She slipped her hands around his face.

Olivia's hands curled into fists as her mouth drew back in a sneer.

White-hot fury ripped through her. "What are you doing here? Get out!" Olivia vibrated as he turned his anguished face at her. "Get out!" she yelled louder, pointing to the door.

He rose, reaching for her. "Olivia–"

"No!" She stumbled back up a stair, the idea of him touching her repulsive. "How could you? No... you don't belong here. Never come back again!" she screamed with her fists clutched at her sides.

Olivia turned and rushed back up the stairs on wobbly legs. Her breathing was hard and her eyes were wild with panic as the key to the hidden door slipped into the slot, threatening to burst open the door she had vowed to keep locked.

"Wait–"

"Please come back–"

She slammed the door on their pleas. How could this be happening? Why, after twelve years, would he show up, and why today? She had to get out of here or suffocate under the pain infusing her every fiber. Locking her bedroom door, she grabbed her phone and started a text.

Zach

Ding, ding.

Zach opened one eye and peeked at his phone on the nightstand. His alarm clock illuminated 6:00.

In the morning?

Who texted him this early? Certainly not Santa.

He groaned, reaching for his phone.

Liv.

Are u awake? Need to leave house... Can I come see you?

Instantly awake, his mind created horrible scenarios of her in danger or worse, hurt.

Yes. Meet me on my porch. Demons?

No reply.

Please let her be okay.

He bolted out of bed, put on his sweatshirt and jeans, and dashed downstairs. His mind reeled as his heart pounded in his chest. He reached for the door–

"Where are you going?" his sister called from behind him.

He shifted and found Kaylee sitting in front of the Christmas tree with wrapped presents spread around her feet. Petite for a twelve-year-old, she wore Christmas pajamas with red slippers tucked under her knees. Mom's auburn-colored hair framed her sleepy face, but bright honey-colored eyes scanned Zach.

"It's Christmas morning! You can't go anywhere. Look, I found a present for you." She waved a wrapped green present in the air, making it rattle against the sides. "It's from Santa!" A full smile spread as she rolled her eyes.

"Are Mom and Dad up yet?" His eyes snapped back up the stairs.

"No, but I'm going up there soon to wake them. I'm dying to find out what this one is." She presented a small box, holding it as if it were the most precious object in the world.

"Kaylee, a friend just texted me. Something has come up, and she needs to stop by and talk. Can you please wait till I'm done before you wake them?"

"On Christmas? Who is it? A new girlfriend?" Her mischievous smile and teasing exaggeration of the word "girlfriend" had his eyes narrowing at her.

"No, just a friend." Zach grabbed the doorknob.

She stuck out her bottom lip, releasing an exaggerated sigh. "Fine, but I go first when we open presents."

"No problem." He hurried out the front door before her curiosity peppered him with any more questions.

Olivia

Olivia's hand shook while she held her phone. She took a deep breath, trying to calm her pounding heart as the memory of her parents clutching each other tore her apart. Her mind reeled, trying to fathom why he had returned home, but there was no way she could stomach his excuses, his lies, his fake love. Determined to leave before they ambushed her, she cracked the door and listened. No one stood outside, nor did she detect their voices.

It's now or never...

Please don't let them hear me...

Biting her lip, she rushed downstairs as quiet as possible. She hit the last step and lunged for the front door. Pain zipped through her knee as her hand closed around the front doorknob and turned. She pulled—

"Where are you going?" Mom asked quietly from the living room chair.

Startled, Olivia spun around and faced the woman who had betrayed her. "I'm going to Zach's." Her lips peeled back as she shook her head. "I can't be here. I can't even look at him... and you... you were holding him—"

"Wait a minute—"

"No, I'm not listening to you or him.... I have to get out of here.... I —" She tried to speak, but the words stuck in her throat. Her mom reached out, but Olivia pulled back in revulsion. "How could you let him touch you?"

"Let me explain—"

"Mom, I can't..."

Olivia opened the door and ran out into the dusky street. The brisk air hit her face, taking the last of her breath. Calling Sergio was her first impulse, but she knew their family Christmas morning started early. She had to leave her house before she exploded, so she took a chance and called Zach.

Please be out there, Zach.

A tall figure moved across the porch. Her heart fluttered, hurrying as fast as her bum knee took her, not stopping until she hurled herself into his waiting arms. A soft groan escaped him as he held her close, burying his face in her hair.

"Hey, are you hurt? Did you see a demon?" His breath was warm on her scalp as she leaned into his strong embrace.

She shook her head against his chest, unsure she could speak. Her throat raw and her body numb, she gripped the back of his shirt as she grappled for control. His hand skimmed over her hair and down her back.

"Liv—" he whispered. "What's happened?"

She sniffled, pulling back to look up at him. Zach's brow dipped, his eyes bright with concern.

"I'm so sorry. I didn't know where else to go–" Olivia whispered.

"It's okay, Liv." He ran his hands over her arms as she shivered. "Let's go sit in my truck. I'll turn on the heat while you talk." He took her hand and led the way. "Besides, my sister is probably peeking out the window, dying of curiosity." He smiled, nodding back at the house.

Olivia stopped in her tracks. "Oh no! Were you opening presents?" She tried to pull away. "I'm so–"

"No. Our parents are still asleep. It's all good."

They jumped inside and Zach started the truck, turning on the heat. The plastic taped to the broken window blurred his house. She turned and gazed at Zach with his arm draped over the steering wheel, she appreciated his patience while she found her voice.

She glanced out the front windshield, which faced her house. It looked so peaceful from the outside, but not anymore. Her hands clenched into fists.

"I came downstairs to make breakfast for my mom," she whispered. "And there he was... kneeling before my mom." Her mouth dried up at the memory.

"Who?"

Silence filled the truck. She looked back at her house. "My dad."

"What? I don't understand–"

She twisted her head to him. "He left us twelve years ago on Christmas morning. Poof. Never seen or heard from again." Her eyes narrowed, and she hated the tears filling them. She stabbed her finger at her house. "And then... this morning... he shows up out of the blue. And my mom..." She punched her leg with her fist. "...is holding him. I can't believe she did that!"

Fresh waves of anger and betrayal crashed through her. Zach grabbed her hands and pulled her over to him. She leaned into his open arms, needing the comfort he offered.

"Wow, " Zach said. "Must have been a huge shock."

She snorted against his chest.

Understatement of the world.

"Did you ask him why he was back?"

"No. I yelled at him to leave and then came to see you. I don't want to listen to his sob story. He needs to return to whatever rock he crawled out from under and leave us alone. We were fine without him." She pushed herself back, looking up at his handsome face. "But I doubt he'll turn around now, so what do I do?"

His reached over and twirled a small piece of her hair around his finger. He unraveled it and sighed as he tucked it behind her ear. "Somehow, some way, you gotta find the strength to walk back and face him because—"

"But I–"

"And you may not like this either, but, there's got to be a reason he's back, Liv."

She shut her mouth and looked away.

"And you need to find out why."

She shoved away from him. "That's easy for you to say. You don't understand, Zach. I hate him. I don't know if I can speak to him or even listen to him. He's just going to hurt us again."

"I'll go back with you if it'll help." She closed her eyes, running her hands over her thighs. She took a deep breath, trying to relieve the tightness in her chest.

"No, it's okay."

"Liv–"

"You're right. I need to get this over with, because the sooner I find out why he's here, the sooner he can leave." She sagged against the seat. "Thank you for talking to me... Jeez... On Christmas morning... I don't know what–"

He put his finger over her lips. "You're welcome."

Her heart raced as the shade of green in his eyes darkened as they gazed at her lips. Moving his finger away, he kissed her with a warmth and gentleness that surprised her, sending a sharp current through her body.

He pulled away and smiled. "For good luck."

"Yeah. I'll need it." Olivia cleared her throat and smiled back before she scrambled out of the truck. Her face flushed from both the kiss and the realization of confronting her dad for the first time since she was five. Could she set aside her anger long enough, or would she just blow up in his face? As she approached her house, she was still unsure, even as she licked her lips across where Zach had planted his good-luck kiss.

Olivia

The smell of coffee drifted to Olivia as she shut the front door. With her jaw set in a hard line, she strode to the den. When she'd gotten out of Zach's truck, his kiss had lifted her confidence to face her dad. Now the reality of confronting him made her want to vomit. Her parents both stood up from the couch, holding hands. Her anger rose at their blatant reunion. She, on the other hand, wanted to punch something. She crossed her arms and waited for the lies to begin.

Conner and Stella Drake. What a joke.

"Honey, I realize your dad's return is shock—"

"Mom. I just want to find out what he has to say, so he can take off again." Her eyes zeroed in on him. He was bigger, more muscular than she remembered. A full beard masked his angular jaw and his longer brown hair covered most of his ears. He dressed as if he lived on a mountain with his flannel shirt and boots. She hated the fact that the eyes staring back at her were the same color and shape as her own. He took a step toward her, but she held up her hand, irritated that a minuscule part of her wanted those unfamiliar arms around her. But she wasn't that five-year-old girl anymore.

"Livy, I surprised you coming home today and completely accept your anger and confusion. But I hope one day you and I can move past this and heal our relationship. I'm sorry—"

She stared at him in disbelief.

"You're kidding, right? You think you can just waltz back in here, throw out an *'I'm sorry'* and I'll welcome you back with open arms?" She jabbed her finger at him, her body vibrating at his audacity. "Well, you're mistaken."

"That's not what I thought—"

"I don't care what you *thought* would happen today, but let me tell

you what *did* happen twelve years ago. You left us! Never called, no
birthday card, no soccer games. Mom can easily forgive you, but I
never will. And never call me Livy again!" The pounding in her ears
increased as Mom, with her crestfallen face, moved toward her, but
Oliva shook her head. "Mom, please, no."

"Let her finish, Stella." His voice was hoarse as he reached for his
wife.

"No. This is my doing, Olivia," Mom said, hands clutched together
in front of her.

Olivia's jaw dropped, her hands fell to her sides. "What do you
mean, your doing?"

"Your dad returning. I contacted him and explained what
happened to you. I told him it was time now for him to come home."
She glanced over her shoulder. "So, he did."

Olivia stood dumbfounded as she processed her mom's revelation.
Her chest tightened as she wished the pieces of their betrayal hadn't
slipped together so easily.

"You contacted him.... You knew how to reach him? You've talked
to him?" The harsh accusation of her mom's betrayal punctuated
Olivia's shock with every word. "All this time?" she yelled.

And there stood her father. The man she had cherished as a child.
Why would he not want to talk to her too, and why did Mom go along
with it? They denied her this simple interaction, costing them nothing
but a few minutes of their precious time?

Any truth she had held dear just shattered.

Honesty.

"I could have talked to him?" she asked in disbelief, staring at her
parents, one an intruder, the other now a stranger. "You've both been
lying and keeping secrets from me for twelve years... twelve years!"
she yelled as a numbing cold penetrated her bones.

"We did it to protect you. To protect us," Dad said. "We had no
choice, Olivia."

Pain ripped through her like a bright light. "Oh, there's always a
choice, and you both made yours loud and clear. You chose yourselves

over me. You were supposed to love me, be here with me... not lie to me."

She stepped backward. "I'm done with this conversation. The two of you make me sick."

"Honey, please listen–" Mom reached a hand out for her.

"No, don't touch me. It's all been a lie... a selfish lie."

She ran upstairs and slammed the door. The white feather swayed when Olivia ran by and threw herself on her bed. Pain and betrayal poured out in sobs only her pillow absorbed. She lost track of time when her exhaustive crying turned into a disturbed sleep, dreaming of demons swarming while her parents clung to each other, absorbed with only themselves.

And of how a chaste kiss, tender and comforting by nature, might weaken her in spirit and open vulnerabilities she had fought against her whole life.

Or at what point during the night she jerked awake when the front door closed.

CHAPTER THIRTEEN
SERGIO

C hristmas morning at the Mendes house was always boisterous.
Sergio bent over laughing at the book Dad gave Manny on how
to understand women and their love languages. Manny's look of
horror was priceless as he mumbled something about knowing more
love languages than the author, but they chuckled when they gave
each other a big back-slapping hug.

Sergio looked at his gift pile and smiled. He got clothes and new
running shoes along with a video game he was dying to play. He
wouldn't let the fact that the last time he had played a video game he'd
gotten in a fight and seen a demon ruin his anticipation. It was
Christmas morning with his family, not the time to worry over those
events.

Mom elbowed him and nodded toward Abuela. Sergio's gift lay in
her lap while she opened the red wrapping paper with care. She lifted
the box top and pulled out the gray scarf. Her smile lit up her face as
her fingers rubbed the silky fabric.

"¡Es hermoso, Sergio!" Abuela tied it over the other scarf around
her neck. She stepped over the discarded wrapping paper and placed
her soft hands around Sergio's face, planting a big kiss on his forehead. "Gracias."

He smiled back at her with all his love brimming in his eyes. "De nada, Abuela. I thought it was beautiful too, and would look perfect on you. It does."

"Who's ready for breakfast?" Mom asked. Cheers resounded as they stood, stretching their backs.

"You know I'm ready, Sofia." Dad reached over and pulled her into his arms. She swatted his arm but returned his kiss as she welcomed his playful adoration.

"Gross," Sergio yelled.

"Get a room," yelled Manny.

"Javier" Mom swatted him again and wiggled out of his arms. She turned toward the kitchen, dodging the land mine of presents along the way.

"What?" He spread his arms out before him. "Can't a man show a little affection to his wife?"

"No!" The family called back in unison. Both of his hands shooed them away, causing more laughter to break out.

Javier made his way over to his mom. He bent over, kissing each cheek before wrapping his arms tight around her.

"Feliz Navidad," he said.

"Feliz Navidad, mi hijo," Abuela said, returning his hug.

"Merry Christmas, Papa," Lucia said. She leaned over the side of her wheelchair, holding her arms open for her dad. A fleece Christmas blanket draped over her thin legs, showing only her red sweatshirt with a kitten wearing a Santa hat. He hugged her, then held both of her hands as he spoke to her. The three of them laughed when she lifted her blinking Christmas tree necklace and swung her chin-length black hair, showing off her red glitter earrings.

Sergio came up next to her, kissing the top of her head. Her brown doe-shaped eyes found his as he rested a hand on her shoulder.

Could have been me.... Should have been me.

"Merry Christmas, Lucia," he said taking her hand in his. "Do you like the bracelet?" It was a leather band with her named stamped across it. She held out her arm, twisting her wrist back and forth as various chunky beads rattled against each other.

"I love it! It goes perfectly with the other ones you've given me."
Lucia kept her style simple with minimal makeup, but she liked jewelry... a lot.

"Breakfast is ready," Mom called, wiping her hands on her red apron.

Sergio slid into his seat at the dining table. "It smells delicious, Mama." His mouth watered as he loaded his plate. Once everyone got seated and their plates were filled, they glanced at each other, crossed themselves and bowed their heads. Dad started grace, and the rest of the family joined him.

"Amen," they said in unison, followed by the chatter and clanking of utensils on plates.

Sergio sighed as the spice of the chorizo and eggs hit his tongue. He tore off an edge of his flour tortilla and used it to pinch another scoop of eggs into his mouth. "This is so good, Mama!" he said with his mouth full; his next heaping bite of refried beans hovered near his lips.

"Eat up; there's more." She motioned to the kitchen stove full of covered pans.

"Sergio."

He looked up from his plate at his mom's voice.

"I have tamales for you to take to Olivia's later."

"Awesome! She loves your tamales. I'll go after breakfast."

Perfect.

He'd been trying to come up with an excuse to leave today, because he needed to tell her about the vision at the mall. She was the only one he trusted with this secret.

"I'll drive you over," Manny offered. Sergio nearly choked on his eggs.

"Uh... Thanks." Sergio's stomach knotted, his appetite for breakfast fading. The morning cheer continued for everyone but Sergio, who dreaded the drive to Olivia's house.

Once morning clean-up was over, they jumped in Manny's car. He hadn't mentioned the incident at the mall, but Sergio had felt Manny's stare during Mass and this morning. Sergio had ignored him, not wanting to broach the subject. But now, alone with him in the car, Manny could push him for more answers.

"Thanks for the shirt, mano. You know black is my favorite color." He winked at Sergio.

What's Manny up to?

Sergio's brow wrinkled. "You're welcome, and thanks for the video game." Sergio rubbed his hands against his jeans as silence fell between them. He sensed Manny wanted to say more, but Sergio diverted his gaze to out the passenger's window.

Please don't ask.

"You seem better than yesterday," Manny said, turning onto Olivia's street.

"Yeah. I got a good night's sleep."

Not...

"Uh... listen... about what happened at the mall." Manny pulled up to her house. Sergio looked back, finding eyes full of doubt and... sadness. "I was just hungry–"

"Stop it." Manny pointed his finger at him. Sergio closed his mouth and leaned against the door as Manny moved closer. "Your eyes were locked onto something, and it wasn't a rack of clothes or Olivia. You can lie to everyone else, but not to me." Manny waved his hand towards Olivia's house. "Go talk to your friend. Figure it out, and then you will tell me what really happened, mano. Or I tell Mom and Dad about the torn shirt and your... fainting spell." Manny scoffed as he sat back in his seat. "And soon."

Sergio jumped out of the car, slamming the car door. He didn't look back as the bag of tamales swung at his side. His stomach gurgled while his shaky finger pressed the doorbell.

Please let Olivia know what to do.

Olivia

The doorbell rang, but no way would she answer it. Let her parents get it. She planned to avoid her parents for as long as possible. The muffled voices drifted through her door, followed by footsteps on the stairs. She stood and braced herself, ready for their intrusion.

"Hey, it's me," Sergio said. Olivia opened the door and hugged him. He laughed. "I should bring tamales more often." She laughed, but didn't let go. Sergio understood the pain her father had caused. She was tired of wondering what to do while staring at her bedroom's four walls.

Zach had texted a few times, checking up on her, but she told him maybe later. She'd already dumped on him and didn't want him to think she was all drama. Especially after the kiss. The only bright spot in her day, except for Sergio's visit.

"What gives?" He pulled away; his eyes roamed over her face. "You've either been crying or barfing. Which is it?"

She smirked at him, shutting the door. The bed sagged as they sat next to each other. She fiddled with her hands in her lap, not knowing how to begin.

"You didn't see him downstairs? My dad showed up this morning." She sighed.

"What! No way! Why?" He jumped off the bed. "I can't believe it! Did you deck him?"

Yep. Nailed it...

"No, I wanted to, but all I could do was yell at him to leave. Then I ran upstairs because I couldn't stand looking at him."

He sat beside her while she spilled her guts about finding them in the foyer, their fight, and talking with Zach. But not the kiss. Sergio wouldn't like that at all. When she finished, her eyes ached, but she was too exhausted to cry. Instead, she leaned her head on his shoulder and let the silence fill the room.

"I still can't believe he's back. I thought he was gone for good when you never heard from him. That must have sucked to see them together, hugging like that. Why lie to you all this time?" Sergio asked.

She huffed as the hurt snaked to the surface. "Sucked doesn't even begin to describe it. I'm so confused and hurt by my mom. The thought of seeing or talking to him again makes me sick." She lifted her head and faced him. "What do I do?"

"Well, I hate to be the bearer of bad news, but you have to try again," he said.

"I don't know. I'm so crushed and overwhelmed, I'm not sure how I'll react when I see them again. This is such a disaster." She covered her face with her hands.

It'll be so horrible.... Is it worth it?

"Hey, look." Sergio pointed at the door. "Your mom called him. Is it because he knows something about this demon thing and can help us?"

"Ugh!" She walked to her window, crossing her arms. The bright blue winter sky was at odds with the dark, turbulent war churning inside her. She looked over her shoulder, and he shrugged at her.

"I'm sorry, Olivia. I don't like telling you to talk to your dad, but there may be no choice. You're a wreck about your parents, I get it, but you are so strong. Stronger than most people. You have the guts to face him head on and get answers we need. If he knows something, awesome!" Sergio did a fist pump. "If not, I guess we'll figure out our next move."

Her head fell forward in defeat. "Oh, man." She sighed and faced him. "I know you're right. I just hate it."

"Oh, mark the day and time." They both laughed as he got up and grabbed her hand, bringing her closer. He brought her hand up, examined the ring, and whistled. "Nice."

She pulled her hand away. "Mom gave it to me last night. I should have known she had an ulterior motive." She shook her head. "Hey, Merry Christmas! How was it?" She loved how Sergio's family was always so loving and open. Sometimes, a twinge of jealousy struck her, but his parents welcomed her as one of their own.

"Good," he said.

She cocked her head to the side. "Good? That's it?"

"Yeah. I got clothes and a few games. It was fine, low-key this year." He turned, looking at everything but her.

"And?" Olivia wasn't letting him off the hook.

He sat on the bed, staring at the floor.

Olivia's heart thudded as she sat next to him. "Hey, talk to me."

His face paled as he clasped his hands together.

"Yesterday, Manny and I went to the mall. I bought Abuela's present, and then everything got weird and... I think I had this vision." He shrugged.

Olivia's jaw dropped. "What did you see?"

"I was running through the desert at night... chasing something... something evil," Sergio said. Her hand covered her mouth. "It raced toward a red electric portal, but I was beaten back by wings of dark figures. The same as what happened to us at Red Rock. I didn't reach the portal before it closed." His eyes glazed over as his hands turned clammy.

"Is that it?" she asked.

He nodded. "Hmh."

Then look at me.

"Did Manny see you during your vision?"

"Yep. He found me flailing on the floor, shook me out of my trance, and hauled me out of there."

She moved closer, putting her arm around his shoulders. "Did you tell him what you saw?"

"No way. It was terrifying, and I had a hard time even comprehending what it meant. I didn't tell Manny I had a vision. He'd test for drugs." He scoffed. "Besides, Manny knows something's up and is forcing me to tell him soon, or he'll go to Mom and Dad about my torn shirt and the mall." He ran his hand through his thick hair and over the tender marks on his neck.

"So, will you talk to your parents?" he said, turning to her. "If your dad knows something—"

"Fine."

He frowned at her.

"I said fine. I'll find out what he knows so he can leave for good."

OLIVIA CLOSED the door behind Sergio. She leaned her forehead against it and closed her eyes. Could she put her anger aside and face their lies again? She bit her lip, dreading the meeting, but she had made a promise to Sergio. She prayed that when the pow-wow was finished, he'd leave as quickly as he'd appeared.

What if Mom wants him to stay?

Can't go there.

No voices emerged from the den as she approached. Her heart slammed; her palms were sweaty as she prepared herself to face him again when she turned the corner.

Mom sat alone on the couch with a blanket over her lap and a pile of shredded tissues lying on top. She turned toward Olivia with puffy, red eyes. Olivia could count on one hand the times she had seen her mom cry. Olivia's shoulders slumped in defeat. A team, the two of them united against the world. Olivia promised herself to remember this moment as she scanned the room and glanced into the kitchen.

"Where's Dad?" Olivia asked. "Why did he come back?" But she got no reply. "Mom?"

Mom ran her hands through her hair, blowing out a breath. "I told him he needed to leave to give you time to adjust to his coming home. He got a room at a hotel." She trailed off in a whisper. Emotions churned in her eyes as she gazed at Olivia. "There's so much to tell you. Things you need to learn about your past and your future. But it's happening too soon, too fast."

"What's happening too soon?" Olivia sat next to her. "I don't under-stand any of this." She threw her hands against her lap in disgust. "Please, Mom. I need to hear it from you, not him."

"Olivia—"

"Mom, when I see him, I see red. I can't listen through my anger and confusion—"

"I understand, but listen to me." She grabbed Olivia's arms and drew her closer. "What is happening to you with the demons, your father needs to explain. I can't do it."

"That makes no sense—"

"I can't. It's not my place. Please understand," Mom squeezed her arms. "Please."

Olivia didn't want to agree. She wanted answers now, but closed her eyes, remembering the promise she had made.

"Okay, but can he answer them soon?" Olivia said.

Mom nodded with a shaky smile. "Thank you," she whispered in her ear, giving her a hug.

"Will you at least answer one question?"

Mom stiffened at her request but nodded.

"Why did he leave us?"

Mom tried to pull away.

"I'm old enough to be told the truth." Olivia sat up straight, bracing herself for the answer she had always feared.

Was it me?

Olivia held her breath as she waited. Mom stared off into the distance, and for a moment, Olivia doubted she'd get a response.

Mom turned back with eyes full of sadness and pain. Panic shot adrenaline through Olivia's limbs. Maybe she didn't want to know anymore. Mom's chin quivered as Olivia watched a battle of emotion rage across her face. Acceptance won.

"All you need to know for now is–" Mom rubbed her forehead. "It wasn't your Dad's decision to leave. I asked him to leave."

This isn't happening...

"But you told me–" Her voice cracked as she fell back against the couch.

"I lied. Because the truth was too much for a five-year-old to bear." Her admission was a blow to Olivia's heart.

"And now what?" Olivia cast her mom in a new, unflattering light. "I'm old enough now for you to stop lying to me?"

Mom's breathing hitched as her fist pressed against her breastbone. "You're never old enough to learn the sins of your parents, the trials and heartbreak of their marriage, and the crushing sacrifices. But yes, the time has come. The time I've dreaded for you since the day you were born. The truth you'll learn from your dad. I hope one day you'll forgive me."

Mom got up and left the room, her footsteps heavy on the staircase. But Olivia let her go. Shattered on the inside, body hollow with numbness, she had no wish to move. Olivia's entire world was turned upside down by the admission of more deceit.

And to her horror, her dad might be the only source of truth.

CHAPTER FOURTEEN
DELILAH

A soft glow emanated from the airplane night-light in the bedroom's corner. The baby monitor on the white dresser gave exhausted parents a sense of security while they captured a few hours of precious sleep. But the unseen and unheard visitor approached the crib, her feet gliding over the floor. Delilah hovered next to the crib of a handsome baby boy, so small and precious, perfect in every detail. His innocent blue eyes peered at her, his chin quivering as he fussed, alone in his crib. Delilah ached to pick him up, hold him, ease his fears, but she couldn't. Instead, she hummed for his ears only, reassuring him he wasn't alone. Her large white wings stirred the air around his face like a delicate kiss. Her streaming red hair became a curtain surrounding his little body as she bent over him. His whimpering ceased, lulled by her soothing song. Delilah's bittersweet sigh fanned his serene face.

Oh, to have a child... his child.... Don't go there.

The eternal ache tore through her heart. She'd dared to dream of a baby similar to this one. His brown hair and blue eyes resembling...

Delilah bolted upright, startling the baby. Her vision tunneled to a distant home, one of joy and homecoming, forbidden by the vow he had made to her.

No. How can it be? Conner wouldn't dare risk it.

But there was their reunion playing out before her wide eyes. She trembled with outrage. He dared to break his oath. The baby whimpered, but it fell on deaf ears. She had to leave and see for herself as disbelief coursed through her. Nothing else mattered. Delilah left the room like a mist fading away in dawn's light.

DELILAH GAZED through the porch window. The Christmas tree was lit with colored lights, and the gold star at the top blinked as if it were a star in the night sky. As she drifted closer, her vision narrowed around him as his betrayal unraveled in front of her.

How dare he...

Conner had returned, not to Delilah, but to his wife. He kneeled before her, clutching Stella around her waist, tears streaming down his face. Her hands wound through his dark hair, gripping her closer to him. The look of sheer rapture on his face shot a spike of jealousy through her body. His lips repeated a word. What was it?

Home...

NO! This is not your home anymore! You promised!

Delilah backed away from the window. She glimpsed herself hovering in the window. Long red hair framed her face, flowing around her arms. Her large green almond-shaped eyes gleamed wildly while her hands fisted at her side.

Delilah turned, incapable of bearing their reunion of love and longing. Cold numbness enveloped her as she remembered how he'd gazed at her in the same manner. How Conner had wanted her, longed for her, lied for her, loved her. How could he break his vow? But his betrayal played out before Delilah's eyes. Did Conner assume she wouldn't remember his promise to stay away from his family forever, or did he assume time had let his vow fade away?

Absolutely not.

He's a liar, a deceiver.

Fury filled her.

Revenge filled her.

Vile emotions coursed, overtaking her.

Her large white wings lifted her into the morning sky, but a cavernous, malignant purpose consumed her.

He'd pay for his scathing treachery. Conner's consequences were simple. Delilah had sworn to him if he ever returned to his family, he'd lose everything he loved. Now, there was no turning back. Even if it damned her.

CHAPTER FIFTEEN
OLIVIA

O livia rubbed her dry eyes as she sat at the red light. Sleep had evaded her last night, plagued by continued dreams of demons and her dad intermingled with one another. She woke up unsettled, edgy and definitely not wanting to go to work. The headache that had nagged her the last few days throbbed behind her eyes.

It had been a tumultuous time for Olivia since seeing her Dad on Christmas morning. But the movie reel in her head kept playing while the festering chasm of pain gnawed inside her. Mom continued her silence and Olivia continued to wait.

The house had been quiet when she'd come downstairs this morning, but Mom left a note on the fridge.

Dad's coming over at 6 for dinner.

Love you,

Mom

So, tonight was the night.

Great.

As much as she wanted answers, cold fingers of dread squeezed her insides at having the confrontation. But she didn't have a choice. The only way forward was to hear Dad's story. Or, more likely, his excuses.

Olivia pulled into Cuppa Joe's parking lot. She didn't close tonight, so no excuse for missing dinner. Someone could be sick–

Stop it, Chicken Little. Just get it over with.

Fine.

ALL MORNING, the shop was busy with kids from school hanging out, showing off their new gadgets while others got their caffeine hit before shopping the after-Christmas sales. Olivia welcomed the busyness and the easy vibe of the coffee shop.

She was putting mugs away when the front door chimed. She turned around, wiping her hands on her apron, ready to greet the new customer. Her eyes locked on the pair of hooded eyes coming toward her.

What's he doing here?

Something about him was off as he stalked toward her. Shaky hands grabbed the counter edge not trusting herself not to throw the first thing her fingers grasped.

"Hi, Olivia," Dad said. "I need to talk to you. It's important." His pale face scanned the room. "In private."

For a split second, Olivia considered his request. "Please leave. I can't talk to you right now. I'm busy." Olivia turned her back on him, returning to her task. She grabbed a clean mug with her shaking hands. She refused to acknowledge him still standing at the counter.

"Olivia, please." His voice cracked. Her eyes darted over her shoulder as warning bells clanked in her head. "I need to tell you something."

"Can't it wait till tonight?" She turned, frowning at him.

"It's your mom."

From the corner of her eye, Olivia spotted Joe approaching. He stopped short, then moved next to Olivia.

"What about Mom?" Olivia cocked her head.

"Uhm...there's no easy way to say this. She's been in a car accident."

The cup slid from her hand, shattering on the tile floor. The roar in her ears drowned out the shop's noise. Her heart slammed as her panic surged.

She took a shaky step towards him. "Is she hurt? Where is she?"

"She's at the hospital. I'll take you."

Olivia's hands flew to her mouth, her wide eyes searched the face of the man she hadn't seen in twelve years.

This can't be happening.

"Is it bad?" Olivia's voice sounded shrill.

Dad's eyes glazed over as anger replaced his pain. "I know little. She was driving through an intersection and a guy ran a red light—"

"No!" She moaned, shaking her head.

Joe's arm encircled her as dizziness threatened to overtake her while her world ripped open. "Go to your mom," Joe said. She turned into his arms, needing his comfort. "I'm saying a prayer for her. Now go," Joe urged.

She nodded. "Thank you," she whispered as silent tears tracked down her face. Olivia grabbed her purse, digging for her keys. She headed toward the back door, but Dad stepped in front of her. "You can't drive. Let me take you."

"Don't you tell—" Her dad's face swam in front of her.

"Olivia," Joe's calm voice said behind her. "He's right. Go with him."

"Fine," she mumbled, walking past him and out the front door. The blast of cool air swept across her hot cheeks. She paused, not knowing which vehicle was his. A beep chirped from a souped-up truck. She didn't look at him as she climbed into the passenger's seat. His woodsy scent drifted to her as he started the engine.

Olivia's mind swirled with images of Mom hurt, or worse, dead. A sob escaped as the unthinkable gripped her. What if she lost her mom?

That can't happen. I can't lose her.

Olivia caught Dad's reflection in her window. She turned, examining his rugged profile, but his stony face gave nothing away.

"What else did they say?" Olivia asked.

He gave her a quick glance, worry etched on his face.

"Nothing." He blew out an exasperated breath. "They wouldn't tell me anything over the phone. So, I wanted to get you first, and then together go to the hospital."

"How did you know where I worked?"

He expertly weaved his way in and out of traffic. Olivia thought he didn't hear her as he honked at the slow car blocking his way.

"Mom keeps me updated about you." He gave her another quick glance before he sped down the highway.

"What do you mean, she updated you?" Olivia's brow scrunched.

An awkward silence permeated the truck. Olivia slipped puzzle pieces together but didn't like the picture it created.

"Well?" she asked, crossing her arms.

"This was going to be explained tonight, before–" Olivia watched his Adam's apple work up and down; his grip tightened on the steering wheel. "This will all make sense soon, honey. I promise."

"And that's supposed to make me feel better? Or just pacify me? I've grown up since you left us... well... left me." She huffed, but the pain in her chest spread. Something else occurred to Olivia as a big, white hospital loomed in front of them.

"Why did they call you instead of me?"

Did she want this answer?

He waited until he slammed the truck into park before answering her. His tall, muscular frame filled the cab while the sound of a siren wailed in the distance.

"I'm her point of contact in her wallet and phone." The tired lines around his mouth set in a grim line. His body was rigid, but his blue eyes were soft, as if knowing he was delivering her a blow.

Dawning came as a swift punch in the gut. "You've lived near us this whole time," she sneered.

He nodded, never taking his eyes off of hers.

A cold, hard rage exploded inside of her as the totality of her parents' betrayal became clear. She held on to the rage, preferring it over fear.

"I hate you."

She climbed out of the truck and slammed the door, not looking back.

Olivia's body vibrated as she stormed through the hospital doors, which hissed closed behind her. Dad's heavy footsteps followed but she didn't care.

She couldn't care.

If Olivia stopped to absorb what her dad had just shared, she'd stop functioning. She had to focus on Mom's accident. That was all that mattered right now.

She stopped at the front desk. An elderly lady volunteer greeted her with a smile. Her white name tag, pinned on her blue cardigan, had *Helen* stamped on it.

"Hi. How can I help you?" Helen inquired.

"My mom was in a car accident. Her name is Stella Drake," Olivia said. The hospital's disinfectant smell repulsed her. Her heart hammered as the volunteer scanned the computer screen, fingers clicking on the keyboard.

Please let Mom be okay.

"Your mom is still in surgery." Helen reached for the boxy, beige phone blinking with miniature red lights. "I'll inform Post-Op her family is here. You can wait over there." She pointed to the waiting area on her left. Helen grinned, deepening the lines around kind eyes. "I'll let you know if I hear any updates."

"Thank you," Olivia whispered. Her mind tortured her with images of her mom mangled in a car, or a surgeon in blood-smeared scrubs operating on her as she lay dying in a sterile surgery room. Olivia collapsed into a chair, covering her face with her hands. She stiffened when her dad sat next to her. His imposing figure sucked whatever air was left out of her lungs.

"She'll be fine, Olivia."

Her hands slid down her face, falling into her lap. He reached for her hand, but she snatched it aside. Why could she remember the warmth of his hand? Those hands now belonged to a stranger who would never provide her anything but pain.

"I promise," he said.

"You promise! You don't get to make promises to me anymore!" Olivia snapped, jumping out of the chair. "That privilege dried up when you walked out the door!" A few heads turned her way, but she didn't care.

"This. Is. All. Your. Fault." She stabbed her finger in his face with each bitter word. "You should have never come back. I will never forgive you... Ever!" She stormed away, not giving a flip about his reaction. Curious eyes tracked her as she sat down across the room. She pulled her knees up to her chest and laid her head against them. Tears flowed, and her anger seethed.

Time stood still in the waiting room as minutes turned into hours, leaving her raw from her rioting emotions, which only ratcheted up her fear. Olivia glanced over at her Dad. His broad shoulders slumped, and his head hung down.

Double doors glided open. A doctor in light blue scrubs with a white paper mask hanging from his neck stood at the entrance. His hands rested on his hips as he scanned the waiting area.

"Family for Stella Drake," he called out. Olivia raced over, stopping in front of him. The roar in Olivia's ears was deafening. She wrapped her arms around her waist, struggling to keep herself together.

Please be okay.... Please be okay.

His hazel eyes were grim behind his black-rimmed glasses. "I'm Dr. Wilson. I performed the surgery on your mom." He extended his hand for a shake, and Dad returned it.

"Hello, I'm Conner Drake, her husband. This is our daughter, Olivia. How is she?" he demanded.

"Would you like to sit down?" Dr. Wilson gestured to the chairs. Dread snaked up Olivia's spine as she followed them to a quiet corner. The blue vinyl chairs squeaked when they sat, as a monotone voice from overhead announced a code red.

"The accident caused internal and external injuries. A broken left rib punctured her lung, but we found the hole and repaired it during surgery. The accident broke her left wrist, which we pinned and set. Her left ankle was banged up, but no break." Dr. Wilson paused, releasing a heavy breath. "The most concerning injury is her head wound from the force of the collision to the driver's side of her car. There's swelling on the left side of the brain, but we relieved the pressure during surgery. She's out of surgery in a coma and en route to ICU, where we'll continue to monitor her progress."

Brain injury... coma... punctured lung.

"When can we see her?" Dad asked with strangled voice. His dark beard was severe against his pale skin; he gripped the armrests, knuckles white.

"Soon." Dr. Wilson stood up, but Olivia didn't trust her legs to stand. "I'll send a nurse to notify you. We'll run more tests and hope she shows improvement."

"Thank you," was all Olivia managed to say as the world spun around her.

Olivia sat in silence as fresh tears fell. She was paralyzed and couldn't think... couldn't process what had transpired. Two police officers emerged from the swoosh of the entry doors. They headed to the welcome desk and rested their hands on their utility belts. They murmured to Helen, and she pointed their way. Dad grabbed Olivia's hand and pulled her up next to him. She didn't pull away this time. His hand was the sole thing keeping her from doing a face plant.

The officers approached through her haze of tears. The warmth of Dad's firm grip clashed against her icy hand. For just a moment, she soaked up his heat, willing it to melt the block of ice embedded in her bones. Dread clung to her as the officers stopped in front of them.

"Are you the family of Stella Drake?" the older officer asked as their eyes roamed over them.

"Yes. I'm her husband, Conner Drake. Is this about the accident? We have no information. What can you tell us?"

"Not a lot," the younger officer answered. "What we can tell you is that she was traveling through a green light when she was broadsided on the driver's side by an SUV traveling at an excessive rate of speed, running a red light." The two officers glanced at each other. "We came to see how she was doing and to update you on the driver who hit her."

"What about the driver?" Dad demanded, squeezing Olivia's hand tighter.

"Indications are the young adult male was under the influence of drugs or alcohol," the younger officer replied.

Olivia gasped; her hand flew to mouth as an explosion of heat ripped through her. Dad's once-pale face turned red, a vein throbbing in his temple.

"And?" Dad urged.

"He died in the ER."

CHAPTER SIXTEEN
ZACH

A persistent ringing permeated Zach's heavy sleep. He didn't want to wake up, drained from his night of tossing and turning. His nap felt too brief as he grudgingly reached—

He couldn't move.

Frozen.

Anchored under the invisible field restraining him.

Oh, God... Not again...

Sweat broke out on Zach's back, trapped against the leather couch cushions. His heart slammed, begging his body to move. He'd been in this powerless position before, yet he fought back. The phone quit ringing, his lifeline now gone, alone in his home. The frantic, hissing voices took the place of the ringing phone. It was hard to make out any words, but their chaotic cries became intense, as if each were desperate to be heard.

More this time!

Zach's eyes searched the living room for any menacing, shadowy figures. Nothing but the afternoon sun streaming through the curtains. The sunlight a bright contrast to the darkness encompassing him.

Where is it?

Invisible hands raked over his body; grabbing, groping and tugging at him like each wanted a piece of his flesh. Zach screamed into the crushing field.

No... Let go.... Go away.... Please!

His pulse drummed an erratic rhythm. Panic seized him, helpless, as their hands kept up a frantic pace. Zach strained against the forces yanking at him, but their malicious intent wasn't deterred.

More whispers. "Want him.... Take him...."

His mark burned against his flesh.

You can't have me!

His body thrashed against the couch. A distraught grunt escaped his lips, now freed from his captors.

The demons, you mean.

He pressed down on his mark, trying to ease the burning sensation radiating from it. What was happening to him? No demon had come to his room since his first experience before Christmas. How ridiculous to have hoped the earlier episode had been a nightmare fraught from stress. But, now, during a nap? In the living room?

They could get to him anytime, anywhere... if he slept. Were they toying with him?

He jumped as his phone beeped. His sweaty hand snatched it off the coffee table.

Olivia.

My mom has been in a bad car accident. Can you get Sergio and come? I'm at Mercy. With my Dad. I'm scared.

Zach's breathing hitched. He understood Olivia's helplessness... the numbing fear. Knew first-hand how despair clung like a heavy cloak in a hospital waiting room and didn't want Olivia to go through it alone. Her dad's presence would only make her stress worse. He had to get to her.

Be there soon with Sergio. Hang in there, Liv.

His shaky legs stumbled to the front door as he shoved aside his hideous encounter.

ZACH AND SERGIO rushed through the hospital's automatic doors. Zach turned and found Olivia sitting alone in a chair against the back wall with her head down, face hidden by her tumbling hair. He tapped Sergio on the arm and headed her way. The harsh fluorescent lighting buzzed over the muted female voice speaking through the hospital intercom. He passed a young couple holding each other, crying, while a baby wailed against another woman in the far corner. Wisps of anxiety fluttered in his chest as he shut out his own traumatic memories of a hospital waiting room. His vision focused on Olivia, not himself.

Olivia glanced up, her eyelids puffy and red, her blue eyes brimming with fear. She jumped up and dashed toward them, lunging into their arms. Her wet tears dampened his shirt as she clung to them. Sergio and Zach exchanged concerned glances as they let her cry.

"Hey, Liv. What happened? Is your mom okay?" She shook her head into his shirt. Zach's brow furrowed as Sergio pulled Olivia out of the hug.

"Come on, let's go sit." Sergio led them back to her spot. They each held one of her hands while she filled them in on the accident.

"The doctor hasn't been back yet, so Dad left, searching for answers. His pacing was driving me crazy." Her voiced cracked. "I can't lose her. She can't die." Fresh tears welled, but her face and body stiffened. Zach followed her line of sight and spotted a tall, broad-shouldered man speaking to a nurse. His chiseled features and beard gave him a dangerous, ominous persona. He nodded at the nurse and stalked their way. Had to be Dad. Under his frown lay eyes that were a carbon copy of his daughter's.

Zach and Sergio stood up with Olivia. Dad's intense gaze summed them up from head to toe.

Pretty possessive for not having been around.

Her dad stopped in front of them and extended his large, tan hand. "I'm Conner Drake, Olivia's dad. You are?" His voice was scratchy and tired.

"This is Sergio, and I'm Zach." Zach's hand was engulfed like a warm mitt. Dad continued his examination of Zach, then acknowl-edged Sergio in the same uncomfortable way.

Dad's face softened when he turned to his daughter. "She's settled in ICU, so we can see her. She's still in a coma." Olivia covered her mouth, stifling a sob.

"Good. I need to see her." Her chin quivered as she pulled her keys out of her purse. "My car is still at work. Can you guys drive it over and drop it off for me?"

"No problem. Go be with your mom." Zach put them in his pocket.

"My family is praying for her. They send their love." Sergio hugged her.

She nodded against his chest. "Thanks for coming." She pulled away and waved at Zach before turning down the bleak corridor. The polished floors couldn't disguise the dull, throbbing pain she oozed with every step she took.

"I feel awful for Olivia," Sergio said. "I'd be out of my mind if my mom was in here. Hospitals are not for me."

Zach shoved his hands in his pockets. "I can't imagine it either, but she's a strong girl. Stronger than she realizes."

"Jeez, her dad's an intense dude." Sergio scoffed. "Strutting up to us like he wanted to peel back our skin with his laser vision and get a better look." They hurried out the doors and into the sunlight. Zach welcomed the much-needed fresh air. The disinfectant smell clung inside his nostrils.

"That's an understatement," Zach said. "And Olivia didn't seem fond of him either."

"Yeah, she's messed up about him." Sergio jumped into the passen-ger's seat. "I don't think she ever expected she'd see him again. And now with her mom in the hospital and everything else going on–" He paused, peering out the windshield. "A person can only handle so much."

"She's got us," Zach said as he started his truck.

But Sergio was right. She was scared about the demons, upset about her mom and angry that her dad was back. A heavy bucket of water for her to carry. He'd figure out a plan to help her. Whatever it took. Besides, it was simpler to think about her pain than his. Zach was a pro at burying his troubles and not dealing with them, except his nap still lingered, his flesh still tingled.

Nope. Not going there.

Too many present and past demons haunted Zach as he raced off to Cuppa Joe's.

CHAPTER SEVENTEEN
DELILAH

Delilah glided above the busy hospital corridor. Her long white seamless dress flowed behind her. Below, doctors and nurses moved in and out of rooms, checking on patients and conferring with family members. Running feet slapped against the glossy tile floors as a hospital team rushed into a patient's room, where a long, sharp tone emanated. But none of these rooms beckoned her.

She recognized the luminous orbs of the guardian angels next to those souls who had prayed for their help, for their comfort, for their intervention. Worried families in need of their spiritual support.

Other rooms were devoid of angels. Those patients chose not to appeal to their guardian angels, ignoring them as if they were only folklore from their childhood. Those rooms' occupants held no hope, only despair or anger. Or worse, apathy. They had no other place to turn except toward themselves and their fruitless endeavors to control their lives.

Still other rooms had a distinctive air; dark and malevolent, full of hate and misery. Those souls had turned entirely from God. They chose a life of unrepentant sin, corrupting their soul with their immoral behavior. Demons didn't sit with them as they suffered. They only arrived to claim their souls, dragging them into another realm, becoming eternal slaves of the Fallen Angels.

And Satan.

Or Lucifer, as he was called by all who knew him. All who fought him. All who still fought for the spiritual welfare of Man and for the welfare of angels themselves.

Delilah left those thoughts behind as she approached her destination. The room she sought because he was there with his wife.

Conner.

Tortured by Conner and Stella's reunion, driven by indignation and anger, she'd dared return to the house. When he wasn't there, she sought his essence and, to her delight, found him in the hospital with his wife. Could her dark secret wish for Stella to be out of his life have come true? She had to see for herself. Perhaps he could be hers again.

Afraid Conner might sense her, Delilah kept her distance, watching through the wall as she hovered at the hallway's ceiling. It was reckless, but dark, dormant fires rekindled inside her when she'd been close enough to touch him, a need for him to desire her with the same desperation he had for his wife.

But her worst fears played out before her. Conner's head lay in Stella's lap. His shoulders shuddered while his hand grasped hers. His thumb stroked Stella's hand in silent comfort as machines beeped; IV bags and tubes surrounded her still, pale body. Conner lifted his taut face, his profile a hue of sickly green against the small fluorescent light above her bed. Stella wasn't dead. Her soul was still present, as was her guardian angel next to her. Delilah shrank back, but she couldn't force herself to break away, even as the knife of jealousy twisted deeper.

Delilah lost track of how long she observed from above, transfixed by Conner. Memories of their past tormented her, but those days were gone, lost in Conner's betrayal. Conner didn't want or need her anymore. Instead, he cried over his pathetic wife. Her anger deepened, taking root, leeching into her heart and soul.

She'd kept his secrets as her part of their oath, but his betrayal no longer bound her. Did he assume she wouldn't act upon her promise and share his secrets?

A sense of powerful calm entered Stella's room as a large white orb with an electric blue hue materialized next to Conner. The orb continued to shift into an angel with exquisite blue-tipped white wings. His back was to Delilah, but she knew who had arrived.

Michael.

Conner's face bore such pain, but a glimmer of hope floated across it. Delilah took one last glance at Conner as her sinister resolve deepened. There'd be no turning back, but Delilah realized she didn't care anymore.

"Delilah."

Her name exploded inside her head. She gasped as Michael stood before her in all his glory. Delilah glanced away and willed her body to be calm, fearful he'd notice her churning emotions.

"What are you doing here?" Michael's accusation sounded like a father catching his child where she shouldn't be.

She swept her arm toward Stella's room. "I felt his pain, Michael. I know I shouldn't have come, but I had to see for myself that he wasn't hurt." She bent her head, hoping to hide the resentment burning in her eyes. "I was just leaving." She buried her clenched fists in the folds of her dress. "I'm sorry," she whispered, not trusting her voice.

His silence pressed against Delilah while her heartbeat pounded in her chest. Donning her serene facade, she hoped he believed her.

"I understand it's difficult for you—"

"Thank you, Michael. I'm glad he finds comfort in you." She smiled at him, making her tight face want to shatter into a million pieces. "I must return to my charge. Goodbye." She glided by him.

"Goodbye. And Delilah..." She paused, looking back at him. His strong jaw set, his stern blue eyes pierced her. "Don't seek him, or his family, ever again."

Delilah nodded at his veiled threat and left. Her dark anger propelled her through the hall, away from the source of her heartbreak, fueling her desperate departure to get far away from the room occupying the man she loved but was forbidden to have. Hot tears of luminous silver trailed down her face.

How dare Michael treat me that way? Ban me from Conner like I'm nothing? He'll pay too!

The night's desolate darkness greeted Delilah outside the hospital, matching her despondent frame of mind. She flew past cars scattered in the well-lit parking lot to its edge, where a small seating area lay nestled inside a circle of stark, barren trees. Delilah landed on the bench and let her emotions tear open under the evening sky. She cried as malicious words spilled out, lashing out at her newfound enemies. All the while, her plan percolated beneath the solitary canopy of trees. And it felt good. She'd have the last say and punish those who had hurt her, used her.

But her new charge's innocent face flashed before her. The sweet baby boy she'd help guide and protect during his lifetime. She dared not make the same mistakes as she did with Conner. Her heart lurched. What if he grew to reject Delilah too? Could she handle that rejection again?

No.

Delilah swiped at her tears, wiping them and the memories of her charge away like newfound dirt on her pristine dress.

Delilah froze. A swirl of frigid air crept around her. She frantically scanned the parking lot in search of what had found her alone. At first, Delilah thought it was the play of the overhead lights making the shadows shift. But the rolling mass of black smoke advanced toward her. She jerked up and readied herself with her only weapon. Palm out, she made a circle in front of her. A vibrating force field formed around her, giving her precious time to escape.

A dark figure materialized out of the smoke. He was tall and lean, dressed in black jeans and a faded black t-shirt with tattoos swirling up both arms. His platinum hair hung to his shoulders, framing the face of a young man, except for his evil eyes. Inside black pools lay a neon green iris with a bright green ring around it. Short black horns swept back from his temples, seemingly pointing at his black wings, which were covered in sharp crow-like feathers. His stark white skin glowed against the inky night's sky.

Panic seized Delilah. A Fallen, powerful enough to split her shield and easily kill her. She started fading into an orb–

"Delilah," he called out, reaching for her. "Stop! It's me, Zar. Remember?"

Her eyes grew wide as his husky voice sparked faint, ancient memories. Zar. A friend, an angel... until the Fall.

"Zar?" She studied him closer, searching for signs of the lost angel she had mourned. "What are you doing here? Why–"

"I saw you in there with Michael." He cocked his head back toward the hospital. "Sounded like nasty business." He put his hands in his pockets, but his eyes never left hers.

Anger shot through her. "Well, that's none of your business, and you need to go before I signal him here." Delilah's voice was full of bravado.

Zar watched her with guarded eyes, making no move against her. She should leave, but an impulsive curiosity got the best of her. Delilah's red hair spilled across her chin as she tilted her head sideways, examining him. "Why do you dare approach me? We are enemies now."

He took a tentative step closer. Fear prickled at her neck. He was too close for Delilah's comfort. "When you two were talking, I saw how upset you were. But that clod didn't even notice your anger or sense your pain. I understand your emotions. Helpless, with no control. I remember that's how I–"

"Don't you compare yourself to me! We have nothing in common anymore! You left—"

"I hate Michael, too." His voice, so deep in understanding and unafraid to speak his truth, wrapped around her like an embrace. "He's one of the reasons why I left." His admission stunned Delilah. Angels and man loved and admired Michael.

"I thought–"

"Lucifer promised us a different world. Something better than simply adoring an Almighty and his heinous creation. Free–"

"Stop! I won't listen to your hateful words." She turned her back on him, afraid he'd find what lurked inside her. The ugly dark part that wanted his life. Did Zar find what he craved in Lucifer's promises? Was he free to do as he wanted, love who he wanted, be who he wanted to be?

An eerie quiet settled among the trees.

"I'll be here tomorrow at this time if you wish to know more."

She turned, but he was already gone, leaving behind a small wisp of smoke and a dare she just might take.

CHAPTER EIGHTEEN
OLIVIA

T he dawn cast a glow through the white metal blinds in Mom's drab hospital room. Olivia leaned her head against the chair, wishing the morning rays would wrap around her and chase her chills away. The scratchy blanket covering her did little to ease her shivers. Olivia's eyes raked over her mom's still body, closed eyes on her mom's bandaged, pale face, trapped inside the metal side rails of her sterile hospital bed. The various beeping monitors, blood pressure cuff and IV lines were all periphery.

Mom... Please wake up....

Mom... I love you.

She shifted her stiff body on the worn-out vinyl recliner, lying parallel to the bed. Olivia linked their hands, her ring reflecting its rich hues. She had prayed during the night for Mom's healing and hoped its blue glow illuminated the inner strength she required. She curled deeper into the blanket as another shiver sliced through her.

"You're going to be good as new, Mom," Olivia whispered, squeezing her hand. "I'm right here. Just wake up, and we can go home." Her throat closed, but she promised herself she wouldn't cry anymore. Olivia wanted to radiate her optimism, not her fears. Still, Mom's eyelids stayed closed.

She stiffened at the soft click of the door. She dreaded that it was either her Dad or the doctors, suspecting neither of them brought great news. Dad entered the room quietly for such a big man. He carried two coffees with a white paper sack swinging from one hand.

"Good morning." He held out a to-go coffee cup, nodding to her. "Black with two sweeteners." The rich aroma filled her senses as she reached for the cup with the familiar logo.

"Thanks." Olivia took the first delightful sip, letting the hot liquid roll over her tongue and down her throat. She closed her eyes, giving thanks to the coffee gods. "That's excellent."

A small smile cracked on his tired face. "Figured only Cuppa Joe's would do." He took a sip in appreciation. Opening the white bag, he plucked out a brown iced danish. "Joe said bear claws were your favorite, so–"

"That's nice, but I'm really not hungry." She peeked over the cup's lid.

Dad raised the danish toward Olivia. "We've been here for three days, and you've hardly eaten. She will wake up soon, and we'll need our strength to take care of her." He wagged it toward her again. "Please, for your mom."

She sighed, taking the danish. "For Mom." She looked him square in the eye. "But don't use that guilt thing again." She took a small bite, trying to hide her pleasure at the tasty explosion of sugar and cinnamon in her mouth.

Dad threw up his hands in self-defense, leaning back into the beige recliner. He dug out the other danish and took a big bite. She watched him through her eyelashes as she had another sip of coffee. Dad had dark circles under his eyes, and a pale pallor still lurked under his tanned skin. His damp hair and fresh woodsy scent drifted over her. Olivia took another bite, embarrassed by the fact that she looked like a critter Thunder had dragged around all night. A shower...

His voice startled her. "Do you think we can try to find some kind of truce, Olivia?" He rubbed his hands against his thighs. "We could let your mom's recovery become our common ground and set aside the other things between us." Hopeful eyes of the brightest blue implored her to say yes, but laced inside lay the same fear, sadness and heartache she'd spied in her own eyes earlier. She hated to admit it, but she would require help with Mom. Unfortunately for Olivia, Dad may be the only one who could do this, whether she liked it or not.

Olivia nibbled on the end of the danish, but it dried up like dust in her mouth. She set it on the bedside table. "All right. On one condition." She narrowed her eyes at him. "That you don't use it as an opportunity to ask me questions about my life. We only talk about Mom and her recovery." She lifted her chin and crossed her arms, daring him to push back.

"Deal," Dad said. Relief flooded his face as he reached across Mom.

"Deal." His huge hand engulfed hers. Heat traveled up Olivia's arm. A part of her craved his warmth, needed his warmth, but the door swung open, breaking the spell. Olivia released his hand, palm still tingling. Dad stood and greeted the doctor.

"Morning, Dr. Wilson."

The doctor nodded to both of them and mumbled "Morning" as he poured over Mom's chart. "The good news is her injuries continue to improve. Her lung function is good, and no sign of infection or pneumonia. Blood work and vitals are within normal ranges. We've done extremities tests, and her responses are positive." He glanced at each of them before his eyes flickered over the bed.

Olivia's chest tightened in anticipation of his next words. "The swelling to her brain is improving, but the brain takes time to heal. We won't know the extent of her brain injury until she awakens. And I can't give you an answer when that will be. We'll keep monitoring her until then." He closed her chart and tucked it under his arm. "I'll be back tomorrow morning unless something changes."

He made to leave, but Dad stepped in front of him. "Thank you for what you've done."

Dr. Wilson gazed at Mom. "I see this tragedy too often. Families destroyed and lives lost because of doped up or drunk drivers." His bitter words hung in the air. "I'll do everything I can to get your mom back." He stepped around Dad and slipped out the door. The incessant beeping of the monitors confirmed the long road in front of them.

"We're here, Mom. I'm not going anywhere." Olivia squeezed Mom's hand. She startled as Dad's hand covered both of them.

"I'm not going anywhere either, Olivia."

Olivia didn't look up but forced a small smile. His easy words sounded so honest, but they didn't penetrate the locked door of her heart.

CHAPTER NINETEEN
ZACH

Zach ran through the arid desert on a moonless night. Darkness enveloped him, but Liv's screams filled the vast night air. Chills ran down Zach's spine as he raced toward her desperate cries. He saw a red glow in the distance–

I'm not dreaming anymore.... The demon is in my room....

A part of Zach sensed it was coming before it hit him. A sensation of being caught in a wave, the energy crashing over him, trapping him in the paralyzed nightmare. Shadows loomed in the corners under the room's dim light. Zach panicked when he discovered his smoky nemesis crouched low at the foot of his bed. Electric hot-pink eyes sizzled, locking with his.

Zach thrashed. His breathing quickened, but the invisible force didn't budge. His terrified screams reverberated against his smashed face. A peal of husky feminine laughter drowned out his screams as the figure slithered over the end of the bed, beginning its slow move over Zach's body. The field between them didn't protect him from its malicious intent or the helpless horror gripping him.

"Don't fight me, Zach. You've tried before, and it's useless." The demon's hollow voice ricocheted in his head. "You are mine."

No. No. No....

Zach kept screaming, thrashing, fighting against this paralyzing evil, but its laughter only grew more excited.

"Have you liked my visits so far? They excited me. You'll get used to them... You might even grow to enjoy our time together."

Its husky promise repulsed him, pushing him to fight harder, dig deeper for a way to repel the evil seeking him.

"You'll prefer this shape."

It moved closer to his face, making his flesh quiver. His last vestige of escape disappeared when the smoky shape took form. Where once smoke surrounded him, a black translucent gown flowed as long, dark hair with pink strands floated around her caramel face like she was floating in calm water. But her eyes were not calm. They held something deeper and more sinister. They held desire. The shape of a woman now hovered over his vulnerable, trapped body. She began her torturous descent, pushing him into the mattress. She smelled of heat and smoke, gagging him, solidifying his complete terror. His mark throbbed as her long-fingered hands glided over his chest until they stilled at his hips. He bucked against it, trapped in the mattress's coffin. Her excited moans were all he could hear, her malicious eyes all he could see while her wicked fingers sought his body.

Stop it... Get off me! Get—

Flattened against Zach, she lowered her open mouth. A hot-pink tongue slithered out, flicking his cheeks and neck with a wet slap. Nausea built as her tongue circled his closed mouth, seeking entrance.

"Open up, or I'll pry it open." Her sharp fingernails dug into his hips as he clamped his lips together.

Her hands left his hips, her fingernails nails scurrying up his chest like pinching crabs—

"What is this?" the demon demanded.

An angry, irritated screech pierced his ears as she lifted her dark form, no longer suffocating him. She jumped next to the bed and crouched low, sniffing the air. Her vibrant pink irises glowed as she reached for the wicked silver blade on her hip. Her jet-black bat wings surrounded him, squelching any hopes of escape if he freed himself.

"I have to kill you now. You can't share my visits. Too bad. We would have had so much fun." She sounded like a petulant child not getting her way.

She raised high the deadly blade, hot-pink sparks igniting at the point. His struggles froze, as it descended toward his chest. Zach squeezed his eyes shut. His body braced for the invasion of the knife. His horrified scream muffled against the unrelenting force field while his heart pounded its last beat—

Her earsplitting howl echoed as the world around him exploded into cascading oil and black dust. His thrashing body, now free, rolled off the bed, taking the blanket with him, landing on the floor chest-first. A set of hands touched his back. He rolled over swinging.

"Get away from me!"

"Zach!"

He froze as the voice registered.

"Mom!" Zach's high-pitched cry was full of relief and surprise.

She fell to her knees, eyes wide as she grabbed Zach's face.

"Mom," Zach croaked as he pulled her into a desperate hug. He didn't realize he was crying until he felt the moisture against her hair. Mom's hands ran up and down his sweat-soaked shirt. He released his pent-up emotions into their embrace. Mom absorbed his tears, never wavering or prodding. When Zach's body stopped shaking, his tears exhausted, she pulled away.

"What happened?" When he didn't answer, Mom shook him. "Zach, talk to me."

Her worried face, inches from his, prompted him to tell her. It didn't matter if she thought he was crazy; maybe he was. But he was too scared to face it alone.

"I've been having nightmares—well—" Zach scrubbed his face in frustration. "Not really nightmares. More like a visitor." Mom went still, her face a mask of deadly calm. His hands clutched the bedcovers over his legs.

Please believe me.

The words tumbled out of him. "It holds me down in this weird force field as it touches my skin. No matter how hard I fight, I can't move. Then it touches me... climbs on top of me. And I can't stop it."

Zach's throat was raw; his head pounded. He stared at his mom, trying to gauge her reaction, but her face remained calm. He pointed at the bed. "Tonight, I discovered it was a demon woman, and I thought... it was—"

"Shh. It's okay." She tried to soothe him; her grip tightened on his arms.

"No! It's not okay! Something stopped her because she had this... this knife. And she raised it, saying she had to kill me." Renewed panic flared as the terrifying words kept spilling out. "And then she howled and turned to dust and oil—" He glanced at the covers, but nothing covered them. Zach's shoulders slumped; his head fell forward.

Was he crazy? Was he only dreaming?

"It's gone and it won't be back." His mom spoke in quiet confidence he couldn't mimic.

"How can you be sure?" Zach's chest still ached from fear, the memory of the hovering knife too fresh to ignore. A silver glint caught his eyes, peeking out from a far corner under the tangled covers. Zach's vision, still hazy from tears, squinted to get a better look.

Mom pulled him up, guiding him to the door. "Let's go downstairs. I bet a sugary snack will do you good. I, for one, could use a scoop of mint chocolate chip. We'll talk more." He was still numb as she hustled him out of his room.

Zach checked over his shoulder, scanning for what had caught his eye as his mom rambled off his ice cream options. But he couldn't find it. He stumbled downstairs, glancing at his mom, who was now sure two scoops were in order. Zach plopped onto the barstool at the kitchen counter, tracking his mom's movements.

His fog slowly lifted as he watched his mom scoop the ice cream. She placed the bowl of heaping green ice cream in front of him.

"Thanks." He took a small bite. The sugary mix of mint and chocolate fell flat on his sore mouth as a thought occurred to him.

Why did she come into my room? How did she hear me?

"Man, this hits the spot." Mom said with a wide grin as she gobbled up another spoonful. Her bright green eyes looked between him and the bowl. "Come on, sweetie. It's your favorite."

Two things became clear as Zach twirled the spoon in the melted green mound. First, what happened tonight wasn't a dream. Second, he was sure his Mom knew more, because if he wasn't mistaken, a knife's tip was sticking out from under the blanket's corner. And it wasn't his.

"I'm not hungry, Mom. I just want to take a shower." He pushed the bowl away as he stood up. Mom came around the counter. His arms wrapped around her, feeling a little embarrassed by his breakdown. "Thanks for... you know."

"No worries, but you can have dish duty tomorrow to thank me," she said, trying to keep it light.

A door closed quietly upstairs. Not surprising someone was up with the racket he'd made. Taking the stairs two at a time, he rushed into his room. Zach grabbed the covers and shook them, waiting for something to fall out. He threw the covers on his bed, checking the floor and under the furniture.

Nothing.

Zach had seen something. He was sure of it. So, where did it go? He kicked the bed and headed for the shower. The hot spray doused him as he inhaled the fragrant soap lathering in his hands, replacing the lingering odor of smoke. He considered his options. Ignore his mom and pretend tonight didn't happen? But that would be futile. Or he'd wait until she brought up last night to prod him with questions. He'd be ready with a few questions of his own for her.

Did you come into my room with a knife and kill a demon?

Do you see demons too?

That should turn the tables... if she told the truth.

CHAPTER TWENTY
SERGIO

The house was quiet as Sergio closed his bedroom door. He was off to visit Olivia at the hospital. The past week had been a nightmare for him, but Olivia had a double-whammy with her dad's return and mom's accident. She was struggling but holding it together, and he admired her for it. Whenever Lucia became ill or went into the hospital, Olivia was always there to make him laugh, let him rant, or unload his guilty feelings. This was his chance to return the favor.

Sergio headed for the kitchen and poured himself a glass of orange juice. He glanced up, startled to see Abuela sitting with her legs criss-crossed and her eyes closed. A rosary of worn wooden beads lay across her petite lap. Her thumb rubbed over the bead while her lips moved silently in the age-old prayer. Abuela's fingers slipped over to the next bead, breathing softly while she continued the rosary.

Sergio absorbed her peaceful look as a sense of calm fell over him. Her eyes flew open, and looked at him. He choked and sputtered orange juice on the counter.

"Buenos dias, mijo." Abuela smiled. "Come sit with me." She patted the seat next to her. He finished his drink and wiped up the spill, then came around the counter and sat down, causing the cushion to sag.

"Buenos dias, Abuela." He leaned over and kissed her cheek. Her smile crinkled the lines around her eyes. She turned and cupped his cheeks, holding his face close.

Her eyes scrutinized every inch of his face, making him squirm. She smiled even bigger but let him go. "You look tired. Something's keeping you up at night. ¿Que pasa?"

Don't get on her radar...

"I'm worried about Olivia, that's all. She texts me at night while she's with her mom. She unloads... Not a lot I can do." He shrugged, looking over her shoulder.

"How's her mom?" she asked as her soft hand found his.

"Still the same. Scary that she hasn't come out of the coma. Manny is picking me up to take me over there. Olivia's trying to be strong, but–" He sighed with a heavy heart for his friend.

"I'm praying for her." She lifted the rosary from her lap. "She'll wake up soon. Have faith." She sought his eyes again. "I'm proud of how you're supporting your friend. Olivia's a special girl."

Sergio nodded in agreement. "We've been friends for so long, she's like a sister. It kills me to see her carrying this pain, and I feel so help-less! I want to do more, but..."

She gave his hand a vigorous shake. "Just be present for her. That's all she needs. That's true friendship."

Now a little embarrassed, he scanned the living room. "Where's everybody?"

"Your mama is at the grocery store, and Lucia and Papa are at the physical therapist."

Sergio's shoelaces became his object of interest. "How's Lucia doing?"

"She's recovered well from her hospital stay.... No signs of infec-tion." She leaned over, demanding his attention. "Lucia's in a good place. She's back at school and getting her strength back. She's happy to be back home with the familia. Maybe you two can watch a movie together later?"

Sergio's nodded, but his reply was interrupted by Manny strutting through the front door. He came over and kissed Abuela's cheek. "Hola."

He nudged Sergio on his shoulder. "Ready?"

"Yep." Sergio moved off the couch, waving as he left.

"Tell Olivia hello," Abuela called. Her eyes tracked him until he closed the front door.

IT SURPRISED Sergio when Manny drove into a parking spot instead of dropping him off at the entrance. They hated hospitals. Lucia's hospital stays had left both of them uneasy and weary of suffering that happened inside of it. It was heartbreaking to watch a loved one in pain, mentally and physically exhausting to be helpless.

So why is Manny here?

Manny didn't say a word as he followed Sergio to the room. But under Manny's cool appearance, his vigilant eyes didn't miss a thing. Manny was here for a reason. Was it to check out Olivia's dad or Olivia? No telling or asking, because Manny did exactly what he wanted to do and his reasons were his own.

Sergio stopped in front of the room. He knocked, then opened the door. Olivia, her dad and Zach crowded the twin bed as machines beeped in the background. Olivia jumped up and gave Sergio a big hug. He and Zach exchanged a glance. Zach frowned as he looked back at the bed. Olivia's dad stood and smiled, but it didn't reach his tired eyes. Olivia kept an arm around Sergio, facing her Dad.

"This is Sergio's brother, Manny." The handshake was brief, interrupted by Olivia giving Manny a quick hug. He returned it with a gentle pat on the back. "I'm sorry about your mom," Manny whispered. "If there's anything you need, you contact me. Sergio will give you my number."

So, this is about Olivia... but why?

"That's sweet of you. Thank you."

Manny nodded but didn't step away, instead his keen eyes roamed her face, unsettling Sergio.

"How is she?" Sergio asked, putting a possessive arm around her shoulder.

Olivia shrugged, worry clouding her eyes as she looked at her mom. "No real change. Her injuries are healing, but we're just waiting for her to wake up from the coma. Thank you for being here." Her chin quivered. She looked so fragile, unlike the girl he knew. Olivia didn't deserve this. The same weighted-down helpless feeling he had for Lucia settled over him.

"Your mom will wake up soon, and you'll be celebrating the New Year with her," Sergio said.

Her brow creased, but her eyes widened as she grabbed his arm. "I didn't realize today was New Year's Eve. The days just melt away in here."

"It's okay, Liv. There will be lots to celebrate when she gets home," Zach said.

"I hope so. I wish Mom would just open her eyes. Even for a minute..." Olivia's voice trailed off, leaving behind an unsettling quiet. All heads turned to the bed, thinking what no one wanted to say.

But what if she doesn't?

Manny stealthily moved around to the other side of the bed, giving Zach a chin nod as he passed. He leaned over and whispered something in her mom's ear. They could have heard a pin drop as their ears perked up, desperate to pick up any word Manny muttered, but to no avail. Manny stood, squeezed her mom's hand, and walked back to Olivia. His face was a mask, but his eyes were gentle.

"She'll be awake soon. Adios, bella chica." Manny's eyes lingered on Olivia before he turned and nodded to the room's occupants. He walked out as quietly as he had entered.

Beautiful girl! What!

Three sets of eyes glared at the closed door, but Olivia only paid attention to her mom.

"What was that about?" Zach rasped in Sergio's ear.

"I don't know." Sergio narrowed his eyes. "But I'll find out."

CHAPTER TWENTY-ONE
OLIVIA

Olivia laughed as Sergio shared Manny's reaction to his dad's gift on Christmas morning. It struck her she hadn't laughed since her mom's accident.

"And then he mumbled something about writing his own book." Sergio smirked.

Zach scoffed. "I bet he could."

"But we don't need it!" A smile spread across Sergio's face as he held up his hand.

Zach gave it a high five. "You know it."

A warmth spread across Olivia. What a refreshing change to see, joking instead of arguing. Hopefully, their friendship would continue to develop. She needed them on the same side while they figured out their connection between the demons and their marks of Orion.

Olivia glanced at Dad brushing Mom's hair. He had held true to his word and hadn't pried into her life. She was getting used to him being here, but she caught him a few times looking at her with more to say. Instead, he'd get up and leave or give her a quick smile and turn away.

"Liv," Zach said, breaking her out of her thoughts. "Why don't we take you home? You can catch a quick nap, shower or whatever. I'm sure your crazy cat misses you, too." The guys broke out into a snicker.

"You think it's crazy because it doesn't like you, Boy Scout," Sergio snarked, elbowing him.

When was the last time she'd gone home? A few days ago?

Olivia looked at her mom. "I don't want to miss..."

Sergio leaned over and sniffed her hair. She slapped his arm, but his brown eyes twinkled at her.

"Go home and take a break," Dad urged. "I'll call with any changes."

She didn't want him taking control, but the thought of a hot shower and fresh clothes beckoned her. And she missed her crazy cat, she acknowledged with a smile.

"All right, but I'll be back in a few hours." She stood and stretched.

Dad laid the brush on the nightstand and nodded. He came around to her but stopped, putting his hands in his pockets.

"See you then." He smiled, but something else burned in his eyes.

Not now...

"Bye." She swung toward the door, but her shoulders sagged as she glanced back at her dad. "Um... thanks for being here–"

"Wouldn't be any other place."

She left without comment, unsettled by his statement. He'd been other places for most of her life, so it felt cheap. But if he were to remain here, how would she move past these hardened roadblocks of distrust and betrayal?

The burden of it pressed down on her on the drive home.

Olivia exhaled as she slipped the key into the front door's lock. Her home was her sanctuary, but she didn't realize how much until she faced being here without mom. They were a team, and this was their home base. She stepped through the doorway with Zach and Sergio behind her, mentally ticking off the items she wanted to bring back...

Olivia stopped short in the foyer, the boys running into her.

Someone's been here.

"Hey–" Sergio said.

"Shh..." Olivia whispered, putting her finger to her lips.

The inside air had a chill, but not because the house was cold. It was an icy current, like treading water in the warm lake as a tendril of frigid water weaved between the legs. The hair lifted on the back of her neck. Holding her breath, she searched every corner, but discovered nothing. Filtered light fell through the windows, casting long shadows. Her fingers fumbled on the wall for the light switch. She flipped it on, but the light did little to ease the house's eerie stillness.

Someone had been here. She knew it, felt it with every tissue in her body.

But were they still here?

She gasped when she spotted what she'd been seeking. A picture frame face-down on the entry table.

"What?" Zach whispered.

Her hand shook as she reached over and lifted it. Staring back at her through shards of broken glass was a black-and-white photograph of her and Mom. The once joyful picture shifted into one of foreboding. She scanned the shelves, discovering more frames faced down too.

Olivia strained to pick up any sound over the pounding rush of blood in her ears. She glanced back at the startled boys, showing them the frame. Sergio paled, while Zach's eyes narrowed as he scanned the room.

Nothing. Not a sound.

She placed her hand over her mark, but it didn't throb. Zach and Sergio did the same and shook their heads.

They must be gone...

"Where's Thunder?" whispered Sergio.

Olivia gripped the shirt over her heart. Thunder always greeted her at the door. He didn't hide from her. Where could he be? She dashed toward the kitchen. The boys followed, leaving the front door open. A lingering odor hit her as she rounded the corner.

Sulfur.

Same as the coffee shop and Red Rock.

"That smells like demons," Sergio hissed, his breathing ragged. He stepped back toward the open door. "We've gotta get out—"

A thud came from upstairs. A startled cry escaped Olivia as their heads snapped up to the ceiling.

Fearing for Thunder, Olivia bolted for the staircase. Not heeding the boys' cries, she darted up the stairs, but nothing met her on the landing. The bedroom doors were shut. Except hers.

Run!

Her heart slammed inside her chest as she stepped closer. The small gap was enough for Thunder to get inside her room.

Meow.

His muffled cry came from within. She started toward it, but Zach pulled her back.

"No, it's too dangerous. It could be a trap," Zach pleaded as he tried to pull her downstairs.

She yanked her arm away and rushed through the door. The dark room ignited her panic. Olivia ignored the odor and the clanging in her brain to run.

Meow.

She turned to the closed closet. Zach and Sergio stood at the doorway.

"Thunder," she whispered.

He pawed against the inside of the closet door as his meowing grew more insistent.

Olivia's sweaty hand settled over the knob and twisted. She flung wide the door, jumping back. Her startled cry filled the bedroom as a gray streak leaped out and jumped on her bed. His ears were tucked back and his tail swished furiously, while his narrowed green eyes peered at her, issuing a guttural growl.

"Hey, kit-kitty!" She plopped on her bed. He hopped into her lap, rubbing his body against her.

Four sets of eyes looked into the shadowy abyss of the closet.

Zach reached over and hit the closet light switch. It lit up, revealing only a row of shoes and hanging clothes.

"It's gone," Sergio said, hope filling his voice.

Olivia froze. "Look!"

The jar holding her white feather was not alone. A familiar long crow feather was positioned in front of it. She pushed Thunder off her lap. Her hand shook as she slowly withdrew it, showing Zach and Sergio. Zach took the feather from her and twirled between his fingers. Sergio ran his finger across the edges. Ash dropped from the sides, drifting to the carpet.

"It's been in my house, my room." Olivia was stunned. Zach stopped twirling it as she gazed at the feather.

"And it wanted you to know, too. But why?" Zach whispered.

Olivia rubbed her hands over her face. "I'll shower and then go back to the hospital." She stared at the boys, hoping they understood. "I need to talk to my dad. Either he did this when he was mad at me or... or..." She swallowed. "A demon found my home."

Silence settled upon them. Sergio looked back toward the closet.

"A demon would have stayed and hurt me, or dragged me back to Berith. So, I don't think it's a demon. If my Dad returned because of them, he might have assumed placing a feather in my room might scare me into being more compliant with his plan. Whatever that is." Olivia bit her fingernail. "My dad did this, and it's time I find out why."

She walked by them without them speaking a word. Zach and Sergio watched her until she shut the bathroom door.

Olivia threw back the shower curtain and shoved the nozzle toward hot. She peeled off her dirty clothes, tossed them in the corner and stepped into the shower, sighing as the hot water slid over her tired, tense body. She smacked the shower wall with her hand. Dad was a part this chaos. She needed to find out why... and now.

CHAPTER TWENTY-TWO
DELILAH

Delilah tapped her toe while she waited on the same park bench where she'd met Zar every day since he first approached her. She told herself she wouldn't return. It was too dangerous. She was an angel, he a demon. They were at war with each other. Dare she trust Zar? But no matter how many scenarios Delilah devised for not meeting him, the temptation to hear his story was too much to resist. When Conner, his family, or Michael came to mind, a cold hatred overtook her, blinding her to everything else except...

Revenge.

Ultimately, Delilah met Zar the following evening, driven by those dark, exhilarating emotions, but she was wary he might set a trap or fill her with lies, leaving her to figure out fact from fiction. He might even kill her. It was what he did, and the cruel joke would be on her. Delilah deserved death with these sinful thoughts consuming her. But she put her fears aside. Consequences be damned.

She had twisted herself up so tight for their first meeting that she jumped when she saw his shadow moving toward her. Zar looked just as surprised that she was there. She had her force field up, heart pounding in her chest, when he stopped in front of her. But Zar didn't threaten her. Instead, he asked questions about her and the confrontation with Michael. She gave partial answers concerning Conner, not wanting to reveal too much of her story. When she tried to turn the subject to him, he turned silent, was elusive, or ended their time with a promise for more tomorrow.

She'd grown impatient with him for answers to the questions he was evading. Delilah paced the secluded ground, her nerves stretched thin. Zar snuck up from behind, touching her shoulder.

"No force field tonight?"

She turned, meeting his neon-green eyes, which held a flicker of hope.

Shocked by her carelessness, she pushed past him, needing distance between them. "You kept me waiting for so long, I was getting ready to leave." She cringed at how feebly it rang.

"Or are you trusting me?" Zar tossed back at her.

Was she?

"Don't flatter yourself." Delilah rolled her eyes as she sat on the bench. She crossed her arms, raising her stubborn chin. "Where were you?"

She caught the gleam in his eyes. "I went on a mission."

She lifted an eyebrow. "What mission?"

"I may have gone to the Drakes' house and caused a little mischief." He grinned, rubbing his hands together.

"What! You'll ruin—" Delilah cried, jumping off the bench.

"It's no big deal! I just flipped a few picture frames and shoved the nasty cat, who tried to bite me, in the closet. That feline would give our demon cats a run for their money." Zar smirked. "And I left her a present too perfect to ignore." His face brimmed with mischievous excitement, yet his stance was cavalier. He made a nonchalant shrug. "It was fun."

Delilah paced, running her hands through her red locks. Dread filled her as she imagined the type of "present" he had left.

If Conner thinks she had anything to do with it...

"What present did you leave?" Her voice stretched tight.

"It was quite genius, actually. I added a black feather next to a white feather that looked so lonely in a pathetic little jar on her desk."

He reached out and touched her wing. "It looked familiar, so I picked it up and sniffed it. Could it be yours, by chance?"

She closed her eyes and sighed, slapping his hand away.

Well, no turning back now.

Zar snorted in dismay. "I don't understand why you're pissed. In fact, I expected you to be thrilled that I messed with her." He put his hands on his hips and walked away. "Whatever," he mumbled.

"It's time we have a serious talk. You set wheels in motion, but I guess it's for the best." Delilah walked up to him. He loomed over her, his dark wings blocking her view of the parking lot. A strange excitement zipped through her as she ignored her surroundings and saw only him. He became a pawn for her plan and her new life.

"I know what I want to accomplish, but the question is, can you help me?"

His eyes turned flat, his body taut, leaning toward her. Delilah knew she was playing a treacherous game. Her eyes slid over the two deadly knives dangling from his hips. The silver pommels each had a large green jewel encased at the end. They gleamed with a promise of a quick death.

"What exactly do you surmise I can help you with?" Zar's cold, lethal voice sent a shiver through her spine.

"I want revenge, plain and simple." Delilah stared back at the hospital, imagining Conner clinging to his wife. It was like a knife filleted her heart open, forever releasing her feelings of betrayal and desire for revenge. "I want to destroy Conner and his family." She looked back at Zar. "I want to destroy Michael." She paused, wondering if she could speak the words playing in her mind... and own them. "I want to be free."

A stunned silence settled, her harsh, ugly words hanging between them. But Delilah felt no remorse or even evil. Instead, she was relieved, cloaked in a peaceful calm from having uttered the dark truth she'd been dying to declare out loud.

"Afraid you missed your chance, Delilah. There was only one way to be set free, and that happened when we left Heaven. You can hurt Connor and his family... that's easy. I'll help you fulfill that wish." Zar scoffed, shaking his head. "But Michael and true freedom? That's a pipe dream."

Driven by her new sense of purpose, Delilah stepped closer to Zar. His smell of smoke didn't repulse her anymore; it only added fire to the growing flame burning inside her. A sly smile slid across her lips as she rose on her tiptoes, whispering, "I have a secret."

Zar's eyes ignited, either from her words or her breath floating across his face. "I do love a naughty secret," he whispered back, trailing a finger across her cheek.

Zar's touch sent a tingle through her, awakening sensations she'd long considered lost. He met her gaze with dangerous curiosity while his body signaled that Delilah might need her force field against him.

"What if I told you"–she leaned up, lips so close they could touch–"I can get my freedom and give Lucifer what he desires... to destroy Heaven." A raw power inside her vibrated, demanding a channel and gratification at all costs.

His brows furrowed while his tongue skimmed over his bottom lip. "I'd say you're mad, but I'm very intrigued." Zar grabbed a strand of her hair, tugging playfully. "Tell me more."

She smiled, her face lighting up with her newfound confidence. She cocked her head as a breeze rustled her silky hair. Zar's sharp intake of breath confirmed that her beauty magnified in this moment of power and control.

Oh, yeah... I could get used to this.

"Maybe tomorrow... or the next day." She took a few hurried steps back, transforming into an orb. "Until then..."

"Hey!" Zar reached out, irritated surprise etched on his face, but she'd vanished.

Holding all the cards, and all the power.

CHAPTER TWENTY-THREE
OLIVIA

Fresh clothes and a hot shower did little to change Olivia's disposition. She was pissed, exhausted, and sick of being kept in the dark by her parents. Coming home to broken frames was a scary invasion of her home, a place she'd always felt safe. Finding Thunder locked in her closet made her furious. But the black feather lying in the jar, a sinister yet seemingly innocent addition, was meant to send her a dire warning. She understood the intended message.

We're watching you, we can get to you, and there's nothing you can do to stop us.

Wrong.

But who did this?

She ran the scenarios in her head while Zach and Sergio drove her back to the hospital. Did a stranger break into their house? No. The feather ruled that out.

Did her father go home and do those things to mess with her because he wanted to frighten her? She didn't think so. Her dad was too concerned about Mom and trying to bridge a relationship with Olivia. Even though Olivia wanted it to be him, it didn't make sense for him to sabotage what he wanted: his family back together.

There was only one answer.

Demons.

Zach dropped her off at the entrance. "I'll call you later. Good luck."

She nodded. "Thank you." She waved as the truck drove away.

The hospital doors whooshed open, accosting her with pine-scented ammonia. She ignored the smell and headed for her mom's room. Her long hair fanned out behind her as her shoes slapped against the floor.

A nurse stopped short, coming out of a room. Her medical tray vibrated, knocking over a few empty cups. "Hey," the nurse called, but Olivia charged past, mumbling apologies. She set her mind to one thing: Mom's room and the answers behind it.

She opened the door.

And froze.

Dad didn't stop what he was doing. In fact, he didn't even acknowledge her. His large frame leaned over the foot of the bed with the blanket pulled back, exposing Mom's bare feet. He held a long, thin needle between his fingers, twisting into her big toe. Olivia gasped as she looked at Mom's head. On her scalp were more hideous thin needles, protruding like she was a voodoo doll. Olivia's eyes narrowed, looking back at Dad as her upper lip peeled back. He glanced at her, continuing to twist the needle.

"What are you doing to her!" Olivia rushed over to push him away, but it was like trying to move a mountain. "You're hurting her... Get away from her!" She slapped his arm.

"Olivia, stop!" He stepped back and grabbed both of her hands, dragging her away from the bed. "I'm not harming her. It's acupuncture. I am just trying to help her!"

She tried to yank her arms free, but he didn't let go. She looked back at the needles covering Mom, livid at him for attempting such a thing. "I don't care what you assume will help!" She struggled more, her heart racing in her fight to free herself. "Let me go!"

She stumbled back when he released her. He rubbed the back of his neck as his eyes examined the places the long needles nestled like slim spikes aimed at Mom's broken body.

"How did you learn acupuncture?" She fumed at his audacity, horrified at the sight of the needles protruding from Mom.

He scrubbed his face and ran his thick fingers through his hair. "I learned things when I was younger... and..." He shrugged. "While I was away."

"Away?" She sneered at him. Something snapped inside, her face flushing with the bolt of emotion. "You make it sound like you were on vacation or a long sabbatical becoming oh-so-wise and worldly." She scoffed, turning her back on him. Olivia took her mom's hand, rubbing it between hers, trying to warm up it.

"We weren't on vacation learning new things." Her tone scathed at him. "We didn't run away from our problems. Mom and I stood our ground, holding it together, while you were"—she looked over her shoulder with frosty blue eyes—"away."

"Olivia—"

"Take these awful needles out right now. You had no right to do this with asking me first." She kept her back to him as angry tears threatened to fall. He began to slowly untwist the delicate needles. He placed them inside a long, thin wooden box on the metal nightstand.

"Just to clarify something, I don't need your permission to take care of my wife. I asked the doctor, and he was on board." Dad closed the box lid, the click echoing in the heated silence. "You may not enjoy hearing this, but I'm back to stay." His voice rose with each syllable. "And you know what? She's happy about it too, kiddo, so you"—he jabbed a finger at her—"better get on board with the reality of what's happening."

"Reality? You're going to lecture me on reality when all you do is keep me away from reality! Keep me safe in a make-believe bubble because you and Mom don't think I can handle the truth. Well, I'm sick of it!" She released Mom's hand and faced the man who had caused her years of pain.

"Our plan was to lay it all out for you the night of her accident so you could understand why I had to leave and what is ahead—"

"Right... Why don't I trust that? Something else would have sprung up, an excuse why you couldn't be honest and stand before me like a man." Olivia's chest heaved as her bitter words spewed, fueled by the force of her locked door bursting like a dam, no longer holding back her tormented emotions. "The only reason you returned is because she called you, not because you chose to come home. So, don't talk about this new reality, because you don't even know what reality is!" Olivia jabbed her finger back at him.

Dad's face flushed as his jaw twitched, but she couldn't read his hooded eyes. "I'm sorry you feel that way. I hope when you learn the truth, you'll understand better."

Olivia rolled her eyes. "The only truth I'll accept is what Mom tells me. You've got no credibility with me. For all I know, you'll leave us again if things get too tough or you realize you don't love us... or me... after all." A heavy silence settled in the room.

There... She set it free. The opened door has emptied, now merely a void for his lies to fill it again.

"Is that what you think? That I don't love you?" His voice was low and hoarse. Color, a moment ago vivid on his face, drained as he shook his head in disbelief. "I love you and your mom... more than you will ever know," he whispered as he dropped back against the chair.

It stunned her that she had spoken her worst fear to him. But letting out those words, locked away for so long, was freeing. She was the brave one for telling the truth and facing reality, not him. She didn't care about his hurt, only her hunger for answers. It gave her the courage to ask more questions. The silence stretched, except for the faint beeping of the machines and the roar inside Olivia's head.

"I honestly don't care anymore why Mom told you to leave or why you did. Those years are lost, and you don't get them back. I need to ask you questions, and I need real answers."

He looked up at her and nodded, still looking shell-shocked.

"No more lies or trying to protect me."

"All right."

Here I go...

"Did you come into our home, break glass picture frames and leave behind a black feather in my room?"

He leaped out of the chair, bearing down on her with intense blue eyes. "What do you mean a black feather?" he asked, with such ferocity that she stepped back.

"A long black crow feather covered with a little ash." She flipped her hair to the side, putting her hands on her hips. "Some other kinda black feather I should know about too?"

Dad's lips stretched into a thin line. She could almost hear him counting to three. She didn't care. Maybe he'd count to a hundred and then leave. With surprising speed, he came around to Olivia's side of the bed, stopping in front of her. The anger rolled off of him, but something else filled his eyes.

Fear.

"I didn't leave a black feather in your room." Dad pronounced each word like chimes striking at midnight. "I haven't been back to the house since I left a week ago." He rubbed his jaw as pained eyes gazed at her. "It was most likely a... um... demon."

Now it was her turn to be shocked. Even though a part of her knew this was the answer, to have it said out loud brought home how much danger they faced. Her next question was lost in her tongue-tied mouth. She swallowed hard, battling back the trembling growing in her bones.

"Olivia... " He put his hands on her arms. "Your mom called me because your time is now here." She scrunched up her face, doubt swimming through her. "Your whole life is going to change, and it's because of me."

"And me," Mom whispered. Olivia thought it was a figment of her imagination, but she turned and met the most wonderful pair of soft brown eyes.

"Mom!"

"Stella!"

Laughter and chaos erupted. Relief, mixed with Dad's comments, had her body shaking.

A teardrop fell on her Mom's cheek when Olivia bent over and kissed her. "Hi, Mom," she whispered against her pale face. "I'm so glad you're awake. How are you doing?"

"Hey, Stel," Dad said from above her. Mom's eyes darted above

Olivia's head as her tears trickled from the corners of her eyes, trailing to the white pillow.

"I love you both so much," Mom said in a dry, hoarse voice. She grew agitated as she tried to speak. "The two boys in the car... that hit me... how–" Olivia barely heard her words.

Olivia and Dad's eyes locked for a moment. "Honey, there was only one boy-–"

"No!" She shook her head. "Two. I'm sure." The machines beeped quicker as she became more upset.

"Mom, it's okay.... Just please... relax." Olivia tried to soothe her, stroking her hand.

A nurse rushed in and paused when she spotted her awake. "Yes!" She made a fist pump and exited. The room became crowded as a doctor and two nurses returned. Olivia released her Mom's hand, backing away. She watched them check the machines and ask her mom questions, but she soon slipped back asleep.

"This is an excellent sign." The nurse smiled at her as they left the room. Olivia could only nod. Claustrophobia crept inside her, smothered by her overwhelmed emotions.

"I need some air." Olivia stumbled into the corridor before her dad replied. Her feet moved from the room while her mind grappled with the thoughts raging inside her.

Mom was awake, but she saw two boys in the car?

Did Dad truly love her, or was he just playing her?

How did he know a demon left the black feather?

How was Olivia's life going to change so drastically because of both her parents?

Olivia was running by the time she exited the hospital's automatic doors. Her legs pumped, even as a sharp pain shot through her bum knee. She continued through the parking lot, not heeding a car's horn blast or the squeal of its tires. She pushed until she tumbled onto a park bench across the lot. Olivia closed her eyes, welcoming the sun's warmth on her face. She leaned back, breathing in deep to loosen her anxiety.

Her eyes shot open as a swirl of icy air crept over her. Goosebumps raised on her skin as she sensed someone watching her. The wisp of air circled around her, leaving a trail of shivers. She peeked over her shoulder but spotted only trees. Her mark throbbed, igniting her to jump off the bench. She bolted for the entrance doors, all the while feeling an itch in the middle of her back. It wasn't until she was inside that the throbbing ebbed.

Had a demon been hiding in the woods, waiting for her?

Was this how she'd live her life, waiting for her mark to throb and then run for her life?

No. She couldn't endure like that.

And didn't plan to.

CHAPTER TWENTY-FOUR
ZAR

W hat a delightful surprise it was when Olivia ran out of the hospital like she was being chased by the Devil himself. Zar chuckled at his own joke as he watched, with great anticipation, her heading straight for him. Her hair fluttered behind her, and, good, she was crying.

Oh, a perfect new victim.

A thrill of excitement pulsed through him. She sat on the bench. Her anger, her sadness, and her hatred hit him like a drug. Olivia's misery was his delight; her hatred was his love.

He sneered at her back, hoping his visit to her house had helped fan the flames of these magnificent, tumultuous emotions. Zar slipped closer, wanting to absorb her misery. He knew the moment she sensed him when she straightened and peeked over her shoulder. He chuckled at her brave face, but her wide eyes gave her away. When she searched the trees, he was sure Olivia saw him, but she took off for the hospital. His eyes bore into her back the whole way until the doors closed behind her.

Olivia intrigued him, but the force driving Delilah to seek revenge on this family was eating him alive with profound curiosity. If Delilah didn't share her reasonings soon, Zar would make Olivia his next project and find out for himself.

He rolled his shoulders, eager for Delilah's arrival.

Delilah.

He was playing with fire, and he knew it. Something, buried deep inside of him, held on tight to the memories of Delilah before the Fall. When he closed his eyes, it came flooding back. Laughter and pleasure in her sparkling eyes and a vibrant smile when she looked at him. He fell in love with her the moment he saw her. But it was not to be. A stab of envy found its target when he remembered her choice to devote herself to God. Too naïve to understand the consequences.

Freedom.

She didn't listen to him, denied the Fallen. She stood with God as war raged in Heaven. He almost traded his freedom for her, but she didn't know that. The pull of Lucifer's world overruled his desire to stay. As did his hatred for humans.

Serve mankind and the Son of Man?

Never.

It had been a shock when he had seen Delilah at the hospital, but it ignited an internal turmoil. Should he destroy her or approach her? It was a battle fought then, and every time they met.

What happened to Delilah, the enticing angel of his memories, to cause her to burn with revenge? He didn't know yet, but turning an angel from the light to the dark would make Lucifer ecstatic and get Zar one step closer to his inner circle.

And now she promised to share her secret with him. But when? This tested a patience he didn't possess. But if it could bring destruction to Michael and those sanctimonious angels and also give Delilah the freedom to be with him again? He must wait. A wicked grin stretched across his tense face as he fantasized of obliterating the angels from Heaven. Yes, he could delay a little longer.

Humans.

He pounded the tree with his fist.

He hated them most of all.

So weak, so easy to manipulate. Why did God love such a flawed creature more than his first creation, his angels?

It gave Zar pure pleasure every time he took a soul to Hell and away from Heaven.

Like the latest one.

Bobby.

The stupid rich kid had it all. But he was bored, isolated, feeling like his parents didn't love or understand him. Always wanting more.

Whatever.

Ripe pickings for Zar. Pleasure cooled his hot blood as the power of the memory washed over him.

Zar had picked Bobby out at high school. Sulky, bitter, indulged. Zar's whispers had planted ideas of booze and then drugs as a way to escape. He fanned the flames of depression and loneliness while coaxing insecurities and self-hatred, which kept Bobby from seeking friends and family. Zar showed himself to Bobby, who reveled in having a demon confidant. Zar had pushed Bobby until he lost control and didn't care about anything anymore.

That was where Bobby was when his SUV slammed into the other car crossing the intersection.

High, angry, and hollow.

Zar reveled in the brutal impact. The quick scream, the last second squealing of tires, then the crunching of metal against metal. And the horrified face turning the moment before impact. The woman saw Zar, for an instant, before he left the wreckage. He snickered, remembering he almost waved at her.

Imagine the sweet surprise when he recognized her lovely face, beaming from the pictures tucked inside shiny black frames.

Stella Drake.

He laughed at the delicious coincidence of it all.

Finally, it was going his way. Zar wanted more than harvesting one soul at a time for Lucifer. He had bigger ideas. He wanted to lead the Fallen, along with the army of the Damned, and destroy Heaven and Earth.

It might come true, thanks to the beguiling and scorned angel materializing before him.

CHAPTER TWENTY-FIVE
OLIVIA

O livia woke with a start, curled up in the vinyl chair next to her mom's hospital bed. The magazine she'd been pretending to read slipped from her lap, falling open onto the floor. Whatever had chased her in her dreams melted away, and she had no interest in dredging it up to the surface. Day had faded into night in the small, stark room, except for the fluorescent bar above Mom's bed casting a yellow glare. Mom looked fragile under the sickly glow, but she was as strong as they come.

But also full of tightly held secrets.

Olivia pushed it aside, not wanting to dwell on why Mom had betrayed Olivia's trust. There must be a good reason... she hoped.

Mom's awake.

Olivia closed her eyes, thankful for having her prayers answered. The doctor had said Mom had a few more days here and then could go home.

Home.

What would that mean for them?

Dad was stroking Mom's cheek when Olivia had returned from the park a few hours ago. Her heart had squeezed at their obvious love. They whispered while exchanging a deep love language only they understood. Olivia hung back by the door, composing herself before she intruded. Nothing ruined a moment faster than demon talk. Besides, after Dad's reaction to the feather, she couldn't imagine his freak-out if she told them about the encounter at the park. She didn't want to upset Mom either, so she decided to keep quiet.

Mom had fallen back asleep soon after Olivia's return. Dad left moments later, mumbling something about errands as he darted out of the room. The chair across the bed was still vacant, signaling he hadn't returned.

"Olivia," Mom whispered. Olivia's heart leapt to her throat as she leaned over Mom. She kissed her cheek, smoothing away a few strands of hair from her mom's face.

"Hi Mom," Olivia whispered with a smile. "How ya doing? You want an ice chip?" Mom nodded and sighed when Olivia slipped the ice into her mouth. "I can get you a cup of soup or–"

"I'm fine, sweetie." She reached up and stroked Olivia's hair. "How are you doing? Dad said you hardly left."

"I couldn't leave you. I kept praying for you to wake up and come back to me. The thought of losing you–"

"Sshhh... I'm not going anywhere." Her grin creased the corners of her eyes. "I'm so sorry–"

"Mom, please stop. None of this was your fault. We'll be home soon, and you'll be back, good as new." Olivia wasn't sure if she was saying this for her mom's benefit or her own.

Mom's eyes swept the room. "Dad?"

"He left a little while ago." Olivia shrugged, glancing at the door.

Mom's soft brown eyes pleaded with her. "Please don't be mad at him. It's not all his fault." Her eyelids grew heavy.

"Mom, please. Just rest. We can talk later."

But Mom shook her head. "You have a destiny, Olivia, that only you and a few others can carry out." A tear glistened on the edge of her eyelash. "Your burden and your blessing," Mom whispered as she drifted off.

"Mom–" But the door opened, leaving the rest of the sentence lost on her tongue. Dad stood in the doorframe, dwarfing it with his wide shoulders and restrained intensity. Two long strides brought him to the bedside, causing Olivia to sit back. In a fluid movement, he kissed Mom gently on the lips, but her lips didn't return the affection. Dad sighed as he sank into the chair, the worn vinyl creaking.

"Were you and Mom talking?" He motioned toward Mom with his chin. Olivia couldn't read his eyes in the poorly lit room, but his body language screamed that his walls were up. But his closed demeanor didn't intimidate Olivia.

Your burden and your blessing.

"Mom asked me not to be mad or blame only you... like I can stop that," she said flippantly. "She also told me I had a destiny. Care to elaborate?"

Dad sat like a stone wall, unmoved by her barbs. "Your mom may not realize what she's saying right now. Let's wait till we get her home. Here isn't the time or place."

She fumed as he again refused to tell the truth. Had he already forgotten their argument from a few hours ago? "Dodging the question once again. You're unbelievable. I'll take Mom's words over yours any day." She crossed her arms and looked away. The sight of him made her want to scream.

"Go home, Olivia. I went by the house–"

"Why?"

"I needed to check it out for myself. It's safe now to go home. I have people watching the house–"

"What people–"

"Will you stop fighting me, for just once!" Dad said between gritted teeth. He leaned his head back, rubbing his temples. She was fighting him, and not sorry one second for it. Olivia's eyes narrowed as she skimmed her father's face. Tired, drawn, yet still handsome under it all. And untrustworthy.

She leaned over and kissed her Mom's forehead. Standing up, she gathered her purse from the nightstand. "Until you are honest with me, I've got no reason to trust you or listen to you."

"Olivia–"

She held up her hand and started for the door, surprised he had stopped talking. She paused as her hand closed around the door handle. "How do I know the house is safe? Should I look for someone or a car parked out front?"

"You'll never see them, but they're there," he said.

She smirked. "Perfect. More mystery." She yanked open the door, not looking back.

A chair clattered across the floor inside Mom's room.

Good.

I'm not the only one who wants to punch something.

Each step she took away from the room brought exhaustion, stress, and more anger. She had an overwhelming ache to curl up with Thunder and get a day's worth of sleep. The problem was that her turbulent and frightening dreams chased her while she slept. She wondered if she'd ever have a peaceful night's rest again.

Not when Mom drops bombs, like I have a destiny.

Let's just add that information to the equation.... Rude.

Olivia

On autopilot the whole drive home, Olivia was stunned when she parked in her driveway. The porch light cast a dim glow, making it difficult to scour the hedges or homes nearby. The deep shadows revved up her imagination, but she shoved them aside. Those images wouldn't help her get to the front door. Relying upon her dormant mark, she mustered up the courage and got out of her car. Keys in hand, she ran to the porch.

"Liv."

A startled scream escaped as she turned and swung out automatically with her fist, too late in recognizing his voice. She rolled her eyes as a smile crept across her face.

"Jeez, Zach! Why are you always sneaking up on me?"

His smile grew as he held up a brown paper bag with grease spots on the bottom. The enticing smell of cheeseburgers reached her nose, making Olivia's stomach growl.

"Why are you always throwing haymakers at me?" Mischief played in his eyes as he wagged the bag in front of her. "I thought you saw me walking down the street. I brought you some comfort food: cheese-burgers and fries."

"What if I'm a vegetarian?" she asked, knowing she'd devour the burger on sight.

"Then I guess it's burgers for me and fries for you."

She chuckled as she unlocked the door.

"Wait..." He brushed in front of her. Olivia caught sight of a leather knife holder clipped at the waist of his jeans.

"That's new. Where did you get it?"

"It's a hunting knife my parents gave me when I made Eagle Scout. I thought I'd wear it." He tapped the knife. Confidence rang in his voice. "I told my parents I was staying here tonight so you wouldn't be alone." His tense body dared her to say no, but then he cleared his voice. "Unless you don't want . . ." His voice trailed off, his hand paused on the door handle.

The air between them stirred, butterflies fluttering in her stom-ach. A gentle warmth flushed through her, realizing Zach stood beside her at the cost of his own safety. Knowing he shared her burden lifted a weight off her shoulders and bolstered her fledgling confidence.

"Thank you, Zach," she whispered, at a loss to say more.

She let him lead the way.

Zach

After Zach had dropped Olivia off at the hospital, he'd been distracted and on edge. Later, he went to her house and peeked through the porch window. Everything looked like they'd left it. The ever-present desert dust drifted through beams of sunlight until it settled, adding a layer on the untouched objects. The vacant house stood waiting for the owners to return and breathe life back into it. An uneasiness raised the hairs on his neck, but his mark didn't throb.

Even though he didn't see anyone around the house, a sense of being followed plagued him as he walked home.

Now the same eerie feeling he'd had earlier washed over him as he stepped into Olivia's foyer. He put his finger to his lips, looking back at her. Her eyes widened as she scanned the room. "I think someone is watching us," he whispered.

Olivia gave an exasperated sigh, shutting the door. She walked past him, snatched the bag of burgers out of his hand, and made her way to the kitchen. "Dad said he has *people* guarding the house." She flipped on the overhead light and dug into the bag. "Maybe that's it." She shook her head.

Thunder jumped off the den couch, scampering over to Zach. He rubbed against Zach's leg, arching his back, his loud purr rumbling. Zach bent over, scratching the scruff of his neck.

"Hey, look at that!" Olivia said, taking a bite of her burger.

"Yeah, it's crazy. I thought Thunder would never come to me after meeting Hank. I guess his experience in your closet changed his attitude." Zach chuckled. He could have sworn the cat winked at him before dashing off to demand the same attention from Olivia. She met Thunder at the pantry and grabbed his food. They left the kitchen, but she returned soon leaving Thunder to feast.

They stood in the kitchen in silence, devouring the greasy meal. Zach glanced at her, pleased she was eating, but she didn't seem to taste it. She had dark circles under her eyes and stared off into space as she mechanically put fries in her mouth.

Man, she looks drained.

Zach lamented the heartache she'd suffered and the stress lining her furrowed brow. But Olivia was tough, tougher than him, truth be told. But he detected the vulnerability etched in her eyes when she thought no one was looking. He didn't know how or why their futures were linked, but he was ready to face it head-on. For her, yes. But he needed to find himself again, or the person he was a year ago would never surface again from the abyss of cowardice and shame.

"Penny for your thoughts?" His voice echoed around the kitchen. He wadded up his burger wrapper and tossed it in the bag. Her blue eyes carried the weight of the world as she bit her thumbnail. He suppressed the urge to hug her, sliding his hands into his jean pockets.

"On the positive side, my mom woke up today." She grinned up at him.

"Thank God! That's awesome, Liv. How is she?"

"She doesn't stay awake long, and I think she's still kinda fuzzy. She said she saw two guys in the car that hit her, but there was only one. Hopefully, her memory will clear up soon." She hesitated, rubbing her hands together.

"And the negative side?" Zach prompted her.

"When Mom woke up, Dad and I were arguing. He told me the black feather was from a demon and that my life was going to change."

Zach's stomach dropped.

"He said this was his fault, and then Mom said it was her fault too. We were so excited when she woke up, I asked no more questions. My parents have secrets involving me, but they won't share them. I have this nagging fear everything will come tumbling down around us." Her voice caught as she turned away.

"Me too, but we're still here and we'll survive this... together."

She turned back with a sudden intensity. "You don't understand. Mom also said I have a destiny. My burden and my blessing, she called it. She said I'd share this with a few others. I think she means you and Sergio."

Something inside Zach knew what she said was true, but there were too many blank spots. Olivia had handed him another strange puzzle piece, and no matter how many ways Zach tried putting them together, the ends never fit. Did their parents hold the answers?

"I need to tell you something that happened to me."

Olivia's body jerked off the counter. "Are you okay? What–"

"I'm fine... I guess." He gave her a roguish grin. "Look at the time." He nodded toward the glowing green numbers on the microwave.

"11:07." Olivia cocked her head back at him.

"It's almost New Year's Day, silly." Zach chuckled.

Olivia smacked her forehead with her palm. "I have lost total track of time."

"It's been crazy, Liv." Zach pulled his hand from his pocket, reaching for her hand. "The fireworks will go off soon. Is there any place we can watch them? I'll fill you in while we wait."

"There's a balcony off my mom's bedroom with a perfect view of the valley. Come on." She gave him a big smile, clasped his hand, and led Zach upstairs.

Olivia grabbed two fuzzy fleece blankets from the upstairs hall closet. She glanced at the empty bed before opening the sliding glass door leading to the wrought-iron balcony. Thunder ran up behind them and jumped on the bed, padding the fluffy comforter with his giant paws. Fresh, brisk air rushed into the dark room, sweeping out the stale bedroom air.

The valley stretched beyond the balcony. Grids of street lights surrounded the dazzling neon lights of the Las Vegas Strip. Zach could only imagine the riot of people from all over the world crammed together to celebrate the New Year, hoping to escape the baggage of the past year and start fresh with a year that had yet to disappoint.

Two over-sized canvas lounge chairs, a small metal table, and two tall, broadleaf plants on each end decorated the balcony. They settled into the chairs, wrapping themselves in the blankets. Zach sensed Olivia was giving him time as they stared out into the valley. He exhaled deeply and let the words tumble out. Her hand materialized out of the blanket, reaching across and entwining with his.

Zach told her about the demon who had terrorized him twice while he slept and how, on the third time, its intentions became obvious. He shared his suspicions that his mom killed the demon. Olivia never interrupted, absorbing the story until he finished.

"I'm so sorry this happened to you. It makes me sick to think how it almost killed you! And all that time, you never said a word while you supported me, letting me lean on you. You're a strong guy, Zach Paxton." Her grasp tightened as she leaned closer. "This has to stop. Have you asked your mom more yet?"

Zach's thumb rubbed across her hand. She had no idea how much her words meant to him. He was so thankful she understood. "No.

She's been busy or out of the house, and this morning she took off on short notice to visit my aunt." He shrugged. "It'll wait until she gets back." He tugged on her hand. "Come here, Liv."

Olivia hesitated for a moment.

"I won't bite," he promised, smiling at her.

"You keep telling me that." Olivia giggled.

Sighing, she climbed over and brought the blanket with her. He chuckled as they both struggled to get comfortable. He lay on his back while she curled up against his side. He decided not to give her grief about her blanket, secretly hoping she wanted to share his. Olivia had many emotional layers he had to carefully peel back, or she'd throw up her walls. His heart skipped a beat as he gazed at her blue eyes, full lips and messy hair, framing a face that was never too far from his thoughts. Something clicked deep inside him, knowing their paths had merged into one.

"Stop staring at me." She nudged him in the ribs. He let out a big groan, making her laugh. But her face turned serious. "I wonder what the new year will bring us? For the first time, I'm scared about what the future holds."

Neighbors yelled the countdown to midnight from the street. "We'll get through this together. I promise." Zach tucked a stray strand of hair behind her ear. His hand continued through the silky mass. Fireworks exploded, lighting up the sky, displaying their colored light show across her face. He wasn't sure if the booms he heard were from the fireworks or the pounding in his ears. They both laughed into the night sky, and for a moment, forgot about the fears plaguing them.

"Happy New Year, Liv."

"Happy New Year."

He leaned down and paused close to her lips. She lifted her head as their eyes locked, then fluttered her eyes closed as his lips touched hers. Olivia's soft lips were warm and inviting. Her arm encircled his neck, bringing him closer, deepening the kiss. His fingers touched the back of her neck, sliding up and entwining in her hair. Zach's face flushed as his body awakened, ached, wanting more, but now wasn't the time. Life was moving too fast, which meant they had to move slow. But he'd take all she offered in the kiss, returning it twofold.

Salsa music played, breaking the moment. Olivia's arm slid down from his neck.

"My cell," she said with a nervous laugh. Zach reluctantly released her hair, letting his hand skim over her back. He kept his other arm wrapped around her, wanting to keep her close.

"Sergio sent a text. He wants to see us tomorrow. Says he has something important to tell us."

"Did he say what it's about?" Zach asked.

"No, just urgent." She sounded anxious, her body stiff against his.

"Whatever's up, he's not hurt. So let's just relax and enjoy the fireworks." Zach nuzzled the top of her head. "We'll watch a movie and then fall asleep, okay?"

Olivia nodded, wrapping her arm around his chest. Zach made a few resolutions as the fireworks lit up the sky in its frenzied finale.

He'd stay strong for Liv, no matter the cost to him.

He wouldn't repeat the mistakes from his past and have another friend die in front him.

CHAPTER TWENTY-SIX
SERGIO

Sergio needed to see Olivia.

He slipped out the front door and headed down the tranquil street. The unassuming peace, with its gentle morning light, conflicted with Sergio's turbulent and gloomy emotions. The brisk breeze ruffled his thick hair, sending a shiver through his body as the events of last night played over again in his mind, pushing him toward Olivia. He'd buried his head under his pillow last night, trying to muffle the hideous cries that served as a backdrop for the vision haunting him. He was grumpy and on edge. Talking to Olivia was the only way to ease his mind. Sergio set off at a jog, needing to loosen up his body and run off his nervous energy.

Sergio's heavy breathing mingled in his mind with the incessant mournful wails of Hell he had heard in his vision as he approached her house. Low morning sun cast long shadows across the stucco like tendrils crawling up the side. Sergio stumbled as he neared the porch, greeted by an uneasy sensation of eyes tracking his progress. His pace quickened, matching his frantic heartbeat. He leaped over the porch steps and pounded on her front door, sneaking a peek over his shoulder. A bright silver light flashed in corner of his eye. His stomach jumped to his throat. He jerked on the handle as a silent scream readied on his lips. The door cracked open, but he pushed his way through, panicked to reach safety.

"Dude, what's your problem?" Zach rubbed his shoulder where the door had hit him. Sergio slammed the door shut and leaned his back against it.

"Shut up, Boy Scout. Something's out there. It watched me the whole way, and then a bright light flashed."

Zach scrambled to the window, scanning the porch. He grabbed his sweatshirt off the couch and pulled it over his head.

"Nothing's out there now. Besides, it was probably whoever Olivia's dad sent to watch the house. Maybe they took a picture of you." Sergio didn't think so but wouldn't argue with him. Zach's scenario sounded better than a demon lurking in the shadows. Sergio followed Zach to the kitchen and plopped onto the bar stool.

"Well, that's rude. They better not hand that photo out to the ladies." They chuckled, but Sergio ran his damp hands over his pants. "Still felt creepy. Olivia sleep?" Zach nodded, rubbing the back of his neck as he watched the coffee brew.

"She finally conked out around two. You're here early." Zach opened the cabinet and grabbed three coffee cups.

"I really–"

"Morning, Sergio." Olivia rounded the corner, her sleepy face brightened with a smile. She accepted the coffee mug, inhaling its rich aroma. Her eyes cut back to Sergio as she took her first sip. "What happened? I've been worried ever since you sent that text last night."

Sergio stared at the two people who had been at the center of his life the last few weeks. He wondered if they were as scared and confused as he was. Something dangerous was ensnaring them in a terrifying web. Sergio's anxiety bubbled to the surface with the events of the last few days.

"I need to tell you something. It may sound crazy, but it's been happening since the demon at the coffee shop." Olivia and Zach glanced at each other. She reached over, laying her hand on top of his tan fist. "I had another vision."

"Another?" Zach's eyebrows shot up as he zeroed in on Sergio.

"Trust us when we say we won't think you are crazy," she said.

Zach leaned back against the counter's edge. "Spill it."

And so he did.

Sergio's voice was calm yet distant as he retold the vision at the mall, still keeping Olivia's name out of it. Zach's face paled and his posture got rigid, but he didn't interrupt him. Sergio hesitated, letting the latest vision take hold. He needed to get this out before he lost his nerve.

"I had it again a few nights ago." He sipped his coffee, hoping the hot liquid would melt the pit of ice in his stomach.

"But last night, during the fireworks show ..." Sergio swallowed. "I had another vision, but this one was totally different. It was like... I left my body or something." He shook his head, closing his eyes, trying to recapture the feeling. "I was flying... away from my body, but I still saw myself sitting in the driveway, waiting for the fireworks to start."

"Out-of-body experience," Olivia whispered.

Sergio nodded, afraid to say those words. "I was pulled, like there was a rope around my waist, flying through a tunnel. No lights, just dark, and then, I'm somewhere else." He paused and looked up at the tense, expectant faces of his friends.

"I was in a massive, dark stone room surrounded by arched floor-to-ceiling windows, glowing with bright pulsating colors. I was... floating on the ceiling above a huge man wearing a black, sleek body suit... light armor. His dark hair was slicked back, glistening like a black wet rock with big horns." Sergio swallowed again, trying to work up some spit. "They were jutting up from the sides of his head, ending in a sharp point. He strutted in front of the windows. He must have been in a tower. But all his attention was focused on what was happening outside." His voice was hoarse from his dry throat. "I could see a dark rocky landscape outside the windows. I didn't get a good look, except for the different brightly colored areas. It looked like bowls of boiling Easter egg colors had spilled, running rivers of lava, dumping into a black moat swirling around the tower." Sergio's shoulders slumped. "I don't know.... It all happened so fast."

Sergio licked his lips. The tang of salt hit his tongue. "But the sounds. I'll never forget the sounds," he whispered. "It was awful." His hands shook as he covered his ears, wanting to shut out their echoes. "There was wailing, groaning, cries of pain mixed with screams of terror." He didn't know he was rocking until Olivia's arms wrapped around him. "And this man. He loved it! Then six massive black wings sprang out from his back. He lifted his arms and laughed.... He welcomes the screams... feeding off them." Sergio grew quiet, fear knotting his guts. "And then his head snapped up to the ceiling. His face... oh man... his eyes. His face was cold, hard, like his white marble skin barely covered his skull. The whites of his eyes were red, but the pupils were black, alive with flames. And I swear, I thought he saw me or sensed me, but he took off down a circular stone staircase in the middle of the room, winding into a dark abyss, still laughing as he disappeared into the darkness." Sergio's voice caught on a sob lodged in his throat. "And then I was back into my body like that." He snapped his fingers. "And fireworks going off overhead."

"It's okay, Sergio," Olivia whispered, running her hand over his damp back. "You're safe and here now."

"We aren't safe. Don't you understand?" His eyes pleaded with them as his voice rose. "It was him."

"Who?" Zach croaked.

"Who else!" Sergio exploded, shoving himself away from them. "The Devil... Satan... Diablo... whatever you want to call him."

They both froze.

"It was him, and he was looking into Hell."

CHAPTER TWENTY-SEVEN
OLIVIA

M om sighed as she settled down in her bed, nestling between the sheets. She closed her eyes, inhaling the fluffy pillow. "Smells like lavender. I've missed my bed." She sighed. "I've about had it with the stink of disinfectant."

Olivia's heart swelled, thrilled Mom was finally home. It had only been a few days since she had first woken up, but it seemed like a lifetime. After Sergio had shared his vision, Olivia had had a difficult time relaxing. She jumped when Thunder leaped out of his hiding places or when she saw a bright light in the corner of her eye. It didn't seem menacing, just something else she had no control over.

On the positive side, she was back to work. Joe wanted her to take more time off, but she begged him to let her come back. She needed the distraction from her parents and the demon nightmare. Joe gave in, but she only worked during busy hours and never by herself, which was great.

And Zach's kiss. That definitely gave her something to think about.

"Take a nap, and then it's time for lunch. How about a short stroll after that?"

"I'd love that, honey." Mom's eyes fluttered closed as Olivia shut the door. She took the stairs two at a time, only to find her dad in the foyer, clutching a black duffel bag.

She crossed her arms, pausing at the bottom stair. "Will your *friends* still be lurking around now that you'll be staying here?"

The bag landed with a heavy thud. He walked past her toward the kitchen. She followed his ramrod-straight back. "No, but you're welcome." He poured himself a steaming cup of coffee, eyeing it instead of her.

Fine.

They'd been taking turns staying at the hospital, seeing each other in passing. It was like sailing by a colossal iceberg: cold and foreboding. Dad had grown more mysterious since she told him about the demon in their home. Olivia caught him whispering on the phone a few times, but he'd hang up when he noticed her. She also had caught a hint of an exotic smoke odor on him yesterday. It added another level of mystery to who he was.

"Mom's asleep, and I'm working a few hours at the coffee shop. I told Mom after she ate lunch she could go on a walk."

"I got it." Dad turned, wary eyes glancing at her over the brim of the coffee cup. "Yeah, on that note. Um... Mom always enjoyed camping. She asked if we could go for a few days to get away. I made arraignments for the fifth and sixth. Get those days off, okay?"

Olivia's mouth fell open. "What? Mom didn't mention this to me. Is this the best time for her to be away? What if she—"

"I asked the doctor. He said as long as she rests, the change of scenery and fresh air will do her good. I have a large fifth-wheeler, and we're just camping over at Valley of Fire." His eyes never wavered.

Olivia contemplated his demand. Her stomach twisted as she remembered that the last time she'd been to the Valley of Fire was before he left. A seed of anxiety rose as she tried to shut out a distant memory of her laughter while she climbed the rocky, red hillside with her parents.

Camping in his trailer... ugh.

"It'll be good for her... for all of us." His blue eyes continued to pin her, daring her to say no.

I doubt that.

"Okay, but on one condition. No more excuses. You tell me the truth." She defiantly lifted her chin and met his glare with the same intensity.

"You'll know everything by the time we leave. It's time." Dad's ominous prediction left her with a pit in her stomach.

"Deal," she muttered, stalking out of the kitchen. She was geared up to face her burden, but camping with Dad sure didn't sound like a blessing

---

Delilah

Olivia slammed the front door as she left her house. She unknowingly headed straight for Delilah with the same determined stride and blazing blue eyes of her father. Delilah knew precisely what it was like to have Conner's angry blue eyes bore into her. Excitement surged through Delilah as Olivia passed by, jumped into her SUV, and drove off, never looking back.

Looks like all is not well in paradise.

Good. I'm ready for a fight.

Delilah faced Conner's back when she materialized in the kitchen. An electric thrill tingled through her as his closeness ignited the craving she struggled so fiercely to deny herself. He stiffened and slowly turned to face her. Delilah delighted in the flurry of emotion on his face. Surprise turned to anger, and the betrayal of a dormant attraction flared in his eyes.

"What are you doing here?" His voice was a guttural growl.

"I could ask you the same thing." She rejoiced in Conner's war with himself. His hands grasped the edge of the counter. "You were never to return home."

"Well, the situation changed, Delilah, when demons attacked my daughter, invaded our home, and possibly caused my wife's accident." A vein throbbed in his temple. "Do you know anything about that?"

Delilah's energy ratcheted up a notch. Zar had told her of his coming here, but was he also responsible for these other events?

What have you been up to, Zar?

"I don't know what you're talking about," she taunted, licking her lips.

Conner moved with a speed that startled her. He snatched her arms and shook her. "Liar," he sneered, inches from her face. Delilah could disappear, but even his rough hands felt better than the hollow ache in her chest. "You're at the bottom of this."

Delilah remained silent. Instead, she radiated warmth and passion, letting it do the talking. She bombarded Conner with her memories of them together, hoping to spark the yearning he held deep inside. Conner shoved her away like she'd scorched his hands.

"Don't do that, Delilah. It doesn't work on me anymore." But she'd seen his eyes dilate before he refused himself the pleasure of remembering what they'd shared.

"Now who's the liar?" Delilah hissed, taking a step toward him. "You can't deny your feelings for me, no matter how hard you try. Your body betrays you, Conner. I see it in your eyes, feel the vibration in your body." She laced her words with her own escalating hunger, pushing him to face the truth.

"You mistake my repulsion for desire. My momentary weakness with you has long since been buried. My wife and daughter are all that I love, not you."

"You don't mean that. Come back to me. It's not too late. What we have is eternal—"

"What we *had* wasn't real and will damn me for eternity." Conner's words might as well have been a slap across her face.

They challenged each other in silence as their battle of wills searched for a stronghold. Conner turned in disgust, striding into the den.

"What do you want, Delilah?" He sighed, hands resting on his hips.

Delilah rushed to him, driven by disbelief, stunned by his words, and shredded by his brutality.

"I'll never touch you again, Delilah. You disgust me."

She stopped. White-hot rage burst inside her, inflaming her heavenly body, enlarging her as she hovered over him. Delilah's huge white wings brushed the walls while her hair fanned out in a sea of red. She punched the air. An invisible force slammed Conner against the wall. He collapsed to the floor, then rolled to his feet. He yanked a dagger from under his pant leg. Its silver blade gleamed with a blue electric current coursing from tip to hilt.

Delilah's hollow laugh echoed in the den. "I'm not afraid of your demon blade." She returned to her earthly size, glowing with ethereal beauty while she stepped toward him. "Besides, you won't kill me. You're bound to protect angels, not to destroy them."

Conner's body shook, his breathing harsh as he fought for control. "Leave my family alone." Conner raised the blade. "I'll break my vow to protect them."

"You put your family in danger when you returned. You broke your vow to me. And I swore to you that if you ever came back, you'd leave me no choice but to share your secret. You should have chosen to love me instead of them." She took another step closer, daring him to make a move. "But that's done now. You've chosen your path, and now I'm choosing mine!" She spat at him.

As her fateful words spilled out, Delilah embraced the power and control pulsating within her, shedding the final layer of her past self. This was what she wanted... her true ambition.

"You can't do this, Delilah! You're risking everything... everyone!" Conner fell forward on his knees. His eyes begged her to understand. "For what?" His hand struck his chest. "You can't still want me? We can never be together."

Delilah stared at him, seized by a cold loathing and something new. *Revulsion.*

This handsome, dynamic man, whom she'd once loved so desperately, she'd been willing to give up divinity. Now, he was powerless, so human, groveling at her feet, begging for her mercy.

"You're right." She cocked her head, examining him through this fresh, enlightened lens. "I don't want you anymore. I want something far better than you. Freedom and power, the likes of which you will never understand. And I'll destroy you with it." Delilah's vengeful promise hung in the air like a thick, stagnant fog. Her hand circled in front of her as she prepared to leave. "Goodbye, Conner."

His gut-wrenching *NO* boomed as he launched himself, blade slashing, at Delilah's fading form. A malicious thrill whipped through her, as his pathetic wife stood in the foyer, her face pale and glistening with a thin sheen of sweat. Delilah threw her head back in laughter as Stella fainted, hitting the floor with a thud.

Goodbye, paradise.

Zar

Delilah's tirade unfolded in front of Zar. He secretly watched, mesmerized by her fearless beauty, framed perfectly through the kitchen window. A gamut of emotions coursed through him: fury, confusion and, yes, admiration.

Delilah had missed their last few meetings, leaving him frantic to find her. He drove himself crazy imagining what fantastic secrets she'd tell him. Tantalizing fantasies of holding a dagger to her throat, forcing her to spill her secrets, became too much to ignore. Visions of slashing his demonic blade through her delicate white neck, her cool silver blood cascading over his hands, killing her while her shocked eyes stared back at him. But it was too soon. He couldn't kill her just yet. Zar still needed her, and a deeper, darker part of him wanted her. These conflicting desires entwined into a braided rope, tying a noose around his arrogant neck. Would Delilah strangle him with it, or would he end up hanging himself?

Did it matter?

The goon angels weren't lurking around the house anymore, so Zar took the chance that she might be drawn here like a moth to a flame. And sure enough, he'd found her, glorious in her dark rage, yet malicious in her white purity. Delilah played this human, Conner, like a master puppeteer. Zar tucked away the revelation, realizing he might be next if he wasn't careful.

Secrets.

Love.

Hate.

Revenge.

Death.

They sang to his dark soul like the screams of the damned.

Zar feasted his eyes on Conner leaping at Delilah, his blade swinging down, striking nothing but her faded body. The raw, desperate hate of the moment was like giving water to a dying man. It quenched Zar's thirst but left him aching for more. That Delilah was the one inflicting this chaotic pain shifted something in him. Something profound. Something he didn't know he still possessed.

The desire for her to be only his.

And he'd crush the man she'd once loved.

Conner turned and rushed to his wife, who was lying in a heap. He pulled her onto his lap, pushing her hair from her face. Zar sneered at them, communing with Delilah's laughter, reveling in their agony.

Zar pulled away from the house, determined to find Delilah. He coveted her dark secrets more than ever. They held the key to fulfilling Zar's self-proclaimed destiny of residing inside Lucifer's inner circle. But first, Delilah must divulge her secrets.

And then become his.

CHAPTER TWENTY-EIGHT
OLIVIA

O livia relaxed next to her mom on the dusty metal bench at the campsite. She swatted the red dirt off her sneakers, knowing it was a losing battle. The sun warmed her face as she scanned the desolate, wide-open scenery of red sandstone hills dotted with barren desert bushes and scrub trees. Settled at the bottom of the small, rugged mountains lay boulders and jagged fallen rocks tamed by Mother Nature. If Mars had vegetation, this vast red landscape would be its twin.

Distant memories of a time when her family had camped here when she was a little girl haunted her. Olivia closed her eyes, letting the pictures play across her eyelids like fragments of a film. They'd hiked the red trails searching for the perfect souvenir rock while chasing a pale striped lizard before it darted into a hidden crack. Dad gave her a piggyback ride in the afternoon, when she was too worn out to take another step. She remembered the warm scent of his neck as her arms locked tight around him. Mom laughing at Dad as he proudly held up the hot dogs he burned in the open campfire. He'd cut up the shriveled black pieces, feeding them to the ground squirrels loitering around the campsite.

She sighed at a memory so vivid, it caused her mouth to water.

Her first gooey s'more had melted against her tongue, to her delight. When night had fallen, Dad lifted her into his arms when she could no longer fight the sleep brought on by the hypnotic campfire flames dancing and kissed her forehead. Her parents' murmurings and stolen laughter were her lullaby. She hadn't wanted the day to end. Even at a young age, Olivia had known they'd shared something special. She woke up wrapped in her mom's arms. Dad's playful whistle and the smell of bacon had enticed her out into the morning sunlight.

Olivia opened her eyes as the memories shifted into something more painful and familiar.

Dad walking out the door.

Olivia watched him toss split wood from the truck's bed. He moved with efficiency; his muscles worked fluidly under his shirt as another log flew over the side. The hour-long ride this morning had been uneventful while Mom slept. A few errant glances in the rear-view mirror spoke volumes; his blue eyes sent a message of unease mixed with sadness.

Mom nudged Olivia. Her cheeks, rosy from the cool air, spotted her pale face. Olivia squeezed her hand, blessed by her smile.

"Doing okay?"

Mom nodded as her smile stretched across her face. "Feels great to get away from the city and breathe fresh air."

"I guess so, but you should be in bed, not camping." Olivia's brow furrowed as her eyes cut back to her dad. "We're too far away from your doc–"

"Please stop worrying." Mom patted Olivia's bobbing leg. "Relax and enjoy the fresh air."

Mom rested her head on Olivia's shoulder as they both watched Dad jump out of the back of the bed. Red dust puffed around his boots before settling back to the hard soil.

"Need any help?" Olivia called out, feeling antsy. His aviator sunglasses hid his eyes as he looked back over his shoulder.

"Sure. Help me pull this stuff out?" He lifted a compartment door on the trailer's side, revealing chairs and supplies.

"Looks like you've done this a few times," Olivia said, coming up beside him. She pulled out a camp chair, leaning it against the trailer.

He stood and slapped the trailer's side, beaming with pride. "This here thirty-footer has been my home for many years."

"Why?" Olivia cocked her head, never having pictured him living in a trailer.

He wiped his forearm across his damp forehead, glancing back at Mom. "Easier to move around in this. I love the outdoors, so I'd fish and camp—"

"And learn things," Olivia said, trying to keep her bitter tone at bay.

"Yeah, I guess I did. Had a lot of time to think about the past and the future." Unspoken words separated them. Olivia yanked out another chair and flung it to the ground at Dad's feet.

"Can I have a glass of water, please?" Mom called out. Dad moved so fast, Olivia wasn't sure he hadn't jumped out of his boots.

She continued unpacking the supplies until the low rumble of a truck engine cut the silence. She raised her hand, blocking out the bright sun hanging in the cloudless blue sky. Squinting into the horizon, she saw a truck pulling a camper lumbering along the long dirt road, winding through the campground. A red plume of dust trailed behind it, agitating her and the peaceful scenery. She recognized the van, pulling a pop-up trailer, that followed not far behind it. As the rising red dust clouds got closer, she sensed that trouble was brewing. Her brain grappled with what she was looking at and its meaning. She stormed over to her parents, pointing sideways to the approaching vehicles.

It couldn't be....

"What's going on? Why didn't you tell me—" The dirt crunching beneath the tires pulling into the adjacent campsite drowned out her question. A door opened, and a confused face emerged, letting her know she wasn't the only one in the dark.

Olivia raced over, met halfway... by Zach.

He snatched his sunglasses off his face, jolting her with angry green eyes. "What is going on?" Zach demanded.

Olivia shrugged. "No idea."

"Well, the party's complete now, 'cause Sergio's family is pulling up too." Sergio's dad backed the pop-up into the spot next to Zach's. Sergio jumped out of the van before it stopped.

"What—" Sergio asked.

"No idea," Zach and Olivia said in unison.

"But I assume we'll finally get the answers we've been waiting for," Zach said.

"From our parents?" Sergio's voice squeaked.

Zach's mom, Rachel, approached and tossed a water bottle at both of them. "Up for a hike?" She didn't stick around for their reply as she walked by them, heading for the hills. The trio gaped at each other.

Javier, Sergio's dad, nudged his shoulder. "Let's go." He followed Rachel up the trail. Olivia turned to discover her dad waiting behind them. He raised his arm toward the hill, eyes still shielded by his sunglasses.

Olivia bit her tongue, not uttering a word. Instead, she hustled up the trail, hoping answers would be revealed in the red hillsides.

CHAPTER TWENTY-NINE
OLIVIA

The six of them settled into a deep, red-skinned cave nestled in the hillside, carved out from millions of years of unforgiving water and ruthless winds. Its smooth walls lifted to a high ceiling. The dusty cave had little light except for stray sun rays streaking through the arched entrance.

Goosebumps raised on Olivia's arms when she spotted the faint hieroglyphics carved into the sandstone walls. Who had been here before her? Indians writing a tale to their gods, revealing secrets of a dark past and changed futures? A foreboding chill ran up her spine. Would her story be left for others to find?

Olivia, Zach, and Sergio sat across from her dad, Rachel, and Javier. Nobody spoke on the short hike, not even when they stopped at the cave's entrance. By the time Olivia sat on the sandy red ground, a cold sweat had broken out across her brow. Knowing answers were coming filled her with excitement and dread. Her life-changing moment was at hand. Was Olivia ready for the consequences?

Your blessing and your burden.

Dad's deep sigh echoed off the red storyboard walls. Olivia's heart pounded. Her nerves stretched tight in anticipation. The parents' looks were as intimidating as the watchful carved-out eyes of the ancient figures surrounding them.

"I know you have lots of questions about recent events, and I'll answer many of them today," Dad said. "Others you'll find out for yourselves later. So, I'll give it to you straight and ask that you let me finish before asking questions. Okay?"

The trio nodded. Olivia rubbed her throbbing knee, fighting the sensation of the cave walls pressing upon her.

"It starts with a story you've all heard. A tale from the beginning of time... and the beginning of mankind." His low, deep voice urged Olivia closer, listening intently to his every word. "When God formed the universe, He created a hierarchy of angels to love and serve Him in the heavens. God also devised them to guard and guide another creation. This creation was mankind."

Dad leaned forward, resting his elbows on his knees.

"And like mankind, angels were given free will. And like us, God tested them. He showed the angels mankind and their place on Earth, and Jesus, the Incarnation of the Son of God. When God revealed to the angels their role, to serve man and Jesus, Lucifer rebelled. He was the highest angel, of supreme intelligence. But this trial of humility and obedience repulsed Lucifer. He decided he would be subject to no one. So, in his pride, Lucifer rejected God and rebelled against Him. There was an immense and terrifying war among the angels. St. Michael and others fought and won the battle against Lucifer and those who joined him. There was no place in Heaven for this new evil, so they were cast out, never to return. The Fallen's angry cries were heard until they were lost forever in the abyss. After God and the angels cast the Fallen out of Heaven, a huge vortex of darkness, called the Mar of Sin, was left swirling at the edge of Heaven's floor."

Olivia waited with bated breath.

What does this have to do with me?

In the fading light, Dad had a faraway look, like he was reliving the moment himself.

"But during the battle, three angels who got caught up in the melee of war realized they didn't want to separate themselves from God

They wanted to adore Him and all He created. Unbeknownst to Lucifer, they fled to God as the battle raged, begging for His forgiveness and vowing to serve Him in any capacity He would allow. In His infinite love, He forgave them, but not without consequence for their initial complete rejection."

The hairs on Olivia's arms rose as she hung on his every word.

"God let the chasm, this evil abyss, stay open in Heaven as a reminder to the angels of their free will. If they chose, any angel could still follow Lucifer through the Mar of Sin. But leaving the portal open was dangerous and kept secret. If Lucifer and his army of Fallen found out about the Mar of Sin and discovered the way through the hidden portal, they could storm Heaven and wage a second war."

"So, He appointed these three angels as guardians of the Mar of Sin... this secret portal between Heaven and Hell. God showed them the secrets of how to find the opening and how to close it forever if Lucifer should discover it. The three angels also became warriors on Earth, protecting the secret at all costs and pursuing and killing any Fallen seeking the soul of man. But this heavenly guardianship came at a huge cost. They, too, would leave Heaven, but must live on Earth. They kept their angelic gifts, but were doomed to live a mortal life in a mortal body, having their wings separated from them."

Dad's last words were a mere whisper as the sheer agony of the moment was absorbed. His eyes were bright, his jaw set as he examined the trio. Blood pounded in Olivia's head as her dad's eyes settled on her.

"The three angels accepted God's command to serve as guardians of the Mar of Sin. They wanted to serve God and protect all from evil."

Dad paused and sat up straight. "You are descendants of these three angels, and now it's your turn to heed the call."

Olivia sat in dazed silence as she tried to comprehend her dad's words. "What call?" Olivia croaked, her mind reeling from the story.

"The guardianship of the Mar of Sin."

Total silence encapsulated the cave as all three of them grappled with this revelation. But when Sergio jumped up, chaos erupted.

"Descendants of angels?" Sergio yelled. "What—"

"How do we guard a chasm in Heaven?" Zach yelled, his arms flying up from his sides.

The boys peppered their parents with questions, their disjointed voices ricocheting around the cave like an errant bullet.

But Olivia didn't speak a word. She rose, her body shaking with each step she took toward her dad. He stood before she stopped in front him. The sharp crack of her slap echoed off the walls, cutting through the turmoil. Olivia's hand stung as the red mark bloomed on her dad's cheek.

"Is this why you left us? So you could play hero for God? Their parents didn't leave; why did you?" Olivia cried. Her voice ached with heartbreak and disbelief. But the horror of slapping her dad didn't stop her bubbling rage.

Dad's stunned eyes stared into hers, not moving a muscle. "I left because it was the only way to protect you and Mom." His throat convulsed as he formed his next words. "And still guard the Mar of Sin." Olivia shoved his chest, crying out in frustration as she turned to walk away, but strong hands yanked her back.

"Do you think I wanted to leave you and Mom and that I didn't miss you every day? Do you think I asked for this any more than you right now?" He struck his fist against his chest. "But I honored the promise I made to my fellow guardians and God, to give my life to protect Heaven and mankind from evil. This..." Dad pulled off his shirt and pointed at his upper chest. Olivia gasped, recognizing the mark as the same one on her chest. He took her hand and placed it over his mark. "This is bigger than our lives here on Earth, Olivia. We can try to run, hide, blame, or even deny this destiny. But if we do, evil wins. And that can never happen... no matter the cost." Dad's chest heaved.

"Never," Rachel proclaimed.

"Not on my watch." Javier's voice was deadly calm.

Olivia's hand smoldered against Dad's mark as tears of frustration ran down her face. When he released her hand, she stepped away. Could she be a part of something that had ripped her family apart?

Could she trust Dad's impassioned words and this fantastical story of good and evil?

Rachel and Javier took off their shirts and placed their children's hands against their marks.

"You killed that demon in my room, didn't you?" Zach asked his mom, staring at her in awe.

"I did." She said with a trace of a smile on her lips. Strength and a touch of sadness radiated from her when she touched Zach's cheek. "And you will, too. All of you." Her hand fell as she stepped back.

"Why do we have the mark?" Sergio asked as his hand moved away from the distinct black dots on his dad's muscular chest.

"There is much to learn about the mark and how to use it, mijo," Javier replied. "But for now, it's the constellation of Orion."

"We figured that out a few weeks ago, but why?" Sergio pushed his dad for more answers.

"This mark serves as a link between you and the Fallen. Use it wisely, and it will help you track them. Used unwisely, they can find you."

The trio glanced at each other.

Dad bent over and retrieved three flashlights from his backpack. He handed them to Olivia. "We know we've given you a lot to process and understand you've got more questions for us. You'll learn more tonight. We'll leave you alone to talk."

"Why?" Zach asked.

"Because after tonight, there's no turning back." Rachel glanced at them. "Tonight, each of you will take the vow to protect the Mar of Sin and fight evil. You can't know anything more before you take your oath. You each have to make a choice. Serve in trust and obedience and put your old life behind you, or deny your destiny."

"Has anyone ever said no?" Olivia asked.

"Some took longer than others, but none have said no. But that's your choice if you so choose," Dad replied.

The parents walked away, leaving them in the dark. Their flash-lights shone on an outside world that had irrevocably altered. Olivia turned on her flashlight, needing illumination in the cave, and in her heart.

———

Zach

"Well, that solves that. I'm out." Sergio threw his hands up in disgust toward the fading flashlights. "No way am I spending my life chasing demons and protecting the stars. Nope." He turned on his flashlight, and an eerie light show danced along the walls. Sergio ranted as he stormed around the cave. Zach caught snippets: *Diablo, padres locos, ni hablar!*

Zach's feet were planted in his dusty spot while his mind replayed his mom's words.

I did, and you will too.

After tonight, there's no turning back.

Take the vow.

Come forward in trust.

"I don't know what to think." Olivia's words cut through his thoughts. "My dad isn't telling me everything. So, what's an even bigger secret than this destiny bombshell?" She kicked the dusty floor, sending pebbles against the wall. "I don't get it."

Zach listened to his friends rant about their parents and the epiphany.

Guardians...

Demon hunters...

His body was numb and his mind blown by what was being asked of him and his friends. But Zach's heart? It beat a steady rhythm, at peace with the choice he made.

"Hey," Zach called. "We're supposed to be talking to each other, not the hieroglyphics." But he might as well have been speaking to the walls. His shrill whistle got their attention. "Hey! Can both of you stop your tirades and come here?"

"Fine," Sergio grumbled. Disgruntled faces, half hidden by shadows caused by the flashlight, stopped in front of him.

Zach was comfortable in the cave's seclusion. Many nights camping had given him a love for the peace and tranquility found during those nights. He grabbed this peacefulness, hoping it would free his mind on what to suggest next.

"I think it's safe to say that none of us are fired up about this," Zach started.

"Brilliant, Boy Scout." Sergio smirked.

"Hey, I feel like someone has pushed me down the rabbit hole, too. My mom killed a demon in my room. Okay? That's intense stuff." Zach placed his hands on his hips.

"You're right. It's been a stressful few weeks. But none of us thought we'd ever hear anything like that tonight," Olivia said, running her fingers through her hair. "Guardians of the abyss Lucifer fell through and demon hunters? It's unbelievable."

Zach nodded. "It's inconceivable, but we still have to make a choice. We can be cowards and run away from this calling, or stand and fight for something greater than ourselves. Our parents did it, and generations before them did too. We need to step up. It's our turn," Zach argued, crossing his arms.

Sergio leaned forward, his fists clenched at his sides. "Well, her dad said we could say no, so I'm good with that."

Zach saw red. "You're not even going to consider it? Huh... I should have known you'd chicken out. You've been a coward from day one."

So much for peace...

Sergio launched himself at Zach, but he shoved against Sergio's chest, driving him back. Sergio stumbled to the floor, but got back up, standing inches from Zach's face.

"Think you're better than me? That you're so brave?" Sergio snorted, thumping Zach's chest. "Then why did Mommy have to rescue you from the demon?" Sergio's dark eyes narrowed, mocking him. "You couldn't save yourself then. What makes you think you can save the *world* now? We will end up dead!" Sergio's harsh words echoed around the cave.

"Stop it!" Olivia forced herself between them. "You guys fighting isn't helping us. We need to calm down and talk rationally about this, okay?"

Zach stepped back and hung his head, exasperated. He couldn't let Sergio push his buttons. Time was running out.

"I don't like this destiny thing either," Olivia huffed. "But... those times when we were attacked by demons? I never want to face them again without knowing how to kill them." She paused as she scrubbed her face. "Because whether we like it or not, they'll be back. And I don't know about you, but I would rather be the hunter than the prey."

"You don't understand." Sergio started pacing again. "Leaving my family? I don't know, man. Lucia needs me... and Manny," he scoffed. "He'll never let me go."

Olivia grabbed his hand, stopping him. "Hey, your dad didn't leave you. He stayed and has been protecting your family your whole life." She tugged his hand, making him look at her. "And you could never turn away from God."

His face crumbled as he shook his head. "You're right, and that's what scares me." Sergio's voice cracked.

It struck Zach that no matter how scared, mad or unsure they were, they couldn't turn away from God or their families.

"Well, I guess that's what we fight for then. Not for us, but for God... for our families. I can do that," Zach said as he approached them. Olivia slid an arm behind both boys. Zach put his arm around Sergio's neck in a bear hug, smirking at him.

"We're in this together. I promise never to let you down." Zach sent up a silent prayer, hoping that was the case. "Are we good?" Zach asked.

The dusty air was as heavy as the decision they each had to make. Confidence in his choice bolstered Zach as he eagerly awaited their answers.

"Yeah, Boy Scout." Sergio nodded. "We're good."

Olivia clutched the back of their shirts. "I'm not doing this for my dad, but I'll do it for my mom. I'm also doing this because I want to stop being afraid... and because... the only way that will happen is if I earn to fight with you guys." She brought them into a tighter hug. Zach's body relaxed as the tension ebbed away.

"Okay, together it is," Zach said.

They left the safe cocoon of the red cave and hiked back to the campsite. Zach contemplated the ramifications of their decision. As heir three flashlight beams bobbed along the trail, he was thankful he wasn't stepping into the guardianship alone. They had his back, and he had theirs.

CHAPTER THIRTY

OLIVIA

The fire crackled with golden-red-tipped flames dancing inside the circular fire pit enclosed by misshaped red rocks. The warmth from the fire did little to dispel the underlying unease nagging at Olivia. She relished the heat spreading over her front, but her exposed back lay vulnerable to what existed in the dark. The smell of the pine wood burning drifted over to her as sparks flew when Sergio's dad stoked the growing fire. Their makeshift meeting lay in a flattened area below the cave, nestled among the surrounding hills shaped like a crescent moon. The night cloaked the cave from their earlier meeting in darkness, its entrance high above them, their secrets hidden.

Olivia gazed up into the late-night sky. The blanket of stars lay so close, Olivia imagined scooping the bright stars into a jar and having them twinkling in her room. She found Orion, distinct among the stars. She liked the fact that they branded the hunter in the stars on her chest, serving as a link to the evil they'd hunt and destroy.

They had returned to camp quiet but resolved. Their parents gave them space after they told them they'd take the vow. They ate dinner in awkward silence with eyes cast down on their tasteless food, wondering what the night held for them.

Sergio and Zach sat on either side of her. Even though the night effects were peaceful, tension was etched on their faces. Olivia chewed on her bottom lip. The impending ceremony jacked her anxiety level through the roof.

"Are we waiting for someone or can we get started?" All eyes turned to Sergio as his clipped voice bounced off the red hills.

"It is almost time. Paciente," Javier said as he stood back from the fire.

"Come on.... What are we waiting for, Dad? Is God swinging by?" Sergio asked. Olivia reached over and slid her fingers into his hot hand, giving it a gentle squeeze. The tension in the night air was thick. The fear of the unknown grated on their nerves.

Javier chuckled. "No, not tonight, mijo." The parents shared a moment, like an inside joke.

Then who is coming?

Rachel checked her watch. "It's close to midnight. We can start." She gave each parent a nod. "They'll be showing up soon." Her bright green eyes traveled over each of them before settling on Zach.

"Tonight, you will meet your guardian and the angel of your descent. There will be a transfer of knowledge and powers. Your journey will begin." Rachel entwined her fingers with Dad and Javier. "And ours comes to an end."

Olivia's eyes connected with Dad's as her stomach dropped. "Who—"

A sizzling sound behind her broke the hillside's quiet. Olivia jerked around in time to see a circular white web suspended in the dark. It crackled, sending heat and light radiating toward them. Her mind screamed *run*, but she stood, transfixed as the center of the webbing opened, leaving a large, vacant black hole. Electricity snapped through the air as a rush of hot wind whooshed over the fire, sending flames high into the air.

Olivia gasped as a large, muscular man materialized. He stepped out of the webbing, followed by two more men of similar size and shape. When the last one walked through, the webbing closed as quickly as it had arrived, leaving behind the odor of singed air. The three mysterious figures stood cloaked in darkness, ominous and foreboding.

"Demons!" Sergio yelled, yanking Olivia and Zach out of their frozen stupor.

"Wait! They're not demons. This is who we've been waiting for," Dad said. The parents walked out of the firelight and greeted the men. Shadows from the fire played while they exchanged hugs and handshakes along with excited whispers.

"Guess our visitors have arrived," whispered Sergio.

"Wonder who they are and where they come from?" Zach muttered.

"We have many names, but that's not important now," bellowed a deep, rich voice from the dark.

Their parents emerged from the edge followed by three broad-shouldered, lean-hipped men. Golden firelight illuminated the strangers, casting a glow of mystery and authority upon them. The tallest man was dark-skinned and bald with a full beard and serious golden-brown eyes. Behind him appeared a man with rich silver hair pulled back into a stubby bun, exposing his chiseled features and blazing sapphire-blue eyes. The last man, leaner than the others, had caramel skin, thick black wavy hair brushed back from his face, and bright green eyes. They wore black, long-sleeved tunics and loose-fitting pants. Belts hung around their hips, holding menacing swords with golden hilts that glinted in the firelight.

"Are we sure these guys are our friends?" Sergio whispered in Olivia's ear.

The silver-haired man snorted, crossing his arms over his barrel chest. "If we weren't, you'd be dead."

A harsh laugh emanated from the cave above, stretching tight Olivia's already-frayed nerves. A bright white light illuminated the cave's entrance. Shadows played inside the light like the flicker of a movie projector. A glowing figure took flight and landed next to the warriors. The platinum-haired angel stepped forward, his silver armor shining in the darkness. Olivia recognized the majestic white wings ending in cobalt-blue-dipped feathers.

St. Michael.

"Stop scaring the kids," said St. Michael. "They don't think you're funny." A smile spread across his face as he greeted each warrior by clasping forearms and clapping them on the back.

But St. Michael wasn't the only one to exit the cave. Two more magnificent angels landed and exchanged the same familiar greeting. One had shoulder-length copper hair, a sharp face with a pointy chin, and white wings dipped in emerald green. The other had short-cropped brown hair and a square face with a cleft chin. His white wings dripped glittering gold.

I can't believe it!

Olivia pressed a hand to her chest, awestruck by the surreal reality of this humbling moment. They were in the presence of angels. Not fat cherubs with stubby wings, but glorious, fearsome and formidable archangels. A tear slipped down her face as she bit the inside of her cheek, trying to steady her surging emotions.

Zach's hand slipped into hers. "They're spectacular," he whispered.

Sergio dropped to his knees, his eyes wide. "Look at them! Warriors... like..." He waved his arms in front of him, searching for the right word.

"Like something out of a video game?" Zach grinned, squeezing Olivia's hand.

"Exactly, but way cooler!"

Olivia watched, dumbfounded, as their elated parents greeted the archangels like old friends. Olivia stopped trying to figure it out. Instead, she absorbed every chaste word and gracious gesture shared, knowing she might never see something as incredible as this again.

The warriors stayed on the edge of the firelight, but the archangels strode toward them. Olivia took a small step back as their huge presence crowded both space and sky.

St. Michael stopped in front of the trio with the other two flanking him. His bright blue eyes scanned each of their faces. He reached for Sergio, pulling him to his feet.

"Hello, Sergio. There's no need to kneel. We're here to serve you." His warm, deep voice flowed around Olivia. Sergio could only nod.

"I'm Michael." He turned to his right. "This is Raphael." Raphael's green-tipped wings elongated behind him as he nodded in a friendly greeting, but his piercing green eyes gazed intently upon each of them.

"And this is Gabriel." While his golden eyes were peaceful, Gabriel remained in his warrior stance. The gold in his wings glowed molten against the firelight.

"It's an honor to be here tonight." Michael's wings swayed as his large, muscular hand extended in a handshake. Zach's hand shook before Michael's engulfed it.

"I'm Zach. I–I–" Nothing more came out than a nervous laugh. Michael nodded as he smiled.

Michael took Olivia's outstretched hand. A warm current radiated up her arm. "Olivia. Your mother's beauty with your father's strength."

Her empty hand missed Michael's as his fell away. It still tingled, longing for connection with his power and, yes, the peace she felt while in its grasp. He stepped back and held his arms out wide.

"But alas, this ceremony isn't for us. It's for the three of you and these three warriors." Michael's hand pointed to the mysterious men standing silently behind them.

"Come. Let us begin," Michael bellowed.

The warriors approached with powerful, stealthy strides. The three archangels exchanged places at the firelight's edge. Olivia jumped as hands from behind gently squeezed her shoulders. Her pulse drummed when she turned and found her dad there. Michael was right. Dad was powerful, but his secrets made his power untrust-worthy. She pushed those thoughts aside as the three warriors split up, and each took a stance in front Zach, Sergio, and Olivia.

The silver-haired warrior stood in front of Olivia. Even though there was plenty of room between them, his sheer size and power were staggering. His eyes bore into hers, soul-searching and fierce, as if examining a seashell to keep or throw back into the sea. She stood straighter and stared back, wanting to stand up to the scrutiny of this stranger.

Dad cleared his throat and gave her shoulders another squeeze

"We've come here tonight, with the archangels, to transfer our powers and knowledge to Zach, Sergio, and Olivia. These warriors of God, angels on Earth, standing before you are your ancestors." Dad's voice was filled with pride, yet cracked with emotion. "You'll learn how to enhance and harness these angelic gifts as they are awakened inside each of you under their watchful eyes and skilled tutelage."

This man was her family?

Olivia's ears roared. Had she heard her dad correctly? But the roaring wasn't only inside her head. The air stirred around Olivia, kicking up the red dust. It built momentum, lifting her wavy ponytail. She dared not take her eyes off the warrior, who took a step closer. She lost the excited voices of her friends in the rising wind.

Conner stepped beside Olivia and grabbed her hand. "I love you, Livy. You're braver than you'll ever know, and I'll always be right here for you." Dad leaned over and kissed her hard on the forehead. His eyes watered as he smiled at her, his rough hand giving her one last quick squeeze.

"Dad, I don't understand," she said over the swirling wind.

"You will soon."

The wind built up around them, sounding like a far-off train heading their way. Darkness turned a dusty red, aglow with fire. The swirling vortex grew into the night sky, leaving them trapped inside the storm's eye. An unwelcome tremor built inside Olivia, threatening to tear her in two.

Dad took off his shirt. Her eyes found Orion on his chest. "Take off your shirt, Livy. I promise they won't hurt you." For a split second, indecision kept her hands at her sides. She glanced over as Sergio's shirt hit the ground, followed by Zach's. Olivia pulled off her shirt, standing in her sports bra. Goosebumps rose as her heart pounded against her exposed chest.

Tension mounted as the fire's flames snapped and the swirling wind raced around at lightning speed. The warrior placed his wide palm over Dad's mark. He flung his head back and his eyes slammed shut as bright rays of blue shot out between the warrior's fingers. A swirling blue orb emerged as the warrior slowly lifted his hand away from Dad's mark. Olivia ceased comprehending anything around her except the orb hovering in front of his palm. She was mesmerized by the play of electric blue light sizzling with energy. It radiated no heat as his hand moved in front of her. Olivia's body was heavy and unmoving as the orb levitated in front of his hand. A part of her found it hypnotic and exquisite, but another part screamed *no*. Conflict raged within her as she yearned for the orb, yet wanted it swept away with the wind.

"Olivia. Look at me." She heard the voice, yet the warrior's lips didn't move. "Receive this and become one with me." Olivia's eyes were transfixed, her being syncing with his tantalizing, terrifying request.

Olivia shut her eyes, bundled up her fear, and released it with a shuttering breath into the vortex. She opened her eyes, staring at the warrior's strong face and eyes the same color as her own. He waited. The orb's dazzling light danced before her as the moment of decision had arrived.

"Yes," she replied, not moving her lips.

He nodded as a small smile cracked on his magnificent face.

The warrior's hand moved like a cobra strike, slamming the orb against her bare seven black dots. She grunted at the intrusion, at the reality of her choice. Olivia's world exploded into a bright white light, as if struck by lightning. Her every nerve ending was alive with bombarding, extraordinary sensations. Strong arms secured her, but inside she was weightless, tingling as she rode the wave of the orb overtaking her.

Olivia cried out as images flashed before her eyes in a delirious slideshow. People from strange, ancient times mingled with the present in a backdrop of mysterious, unknown places from around the world. Tremendous scenes of grace and love. Mother Nature's exotic landscapes brimming with her untamed animals, a wedding's first kiss, the exquisite joy of holding a newborn child. Love and peace surged through her as she feasted on the tide of images.

But the images lost their beauty, turning dark and horrifying, vivid in exposing man's evil. Slavery, hate, rape, mutilation, murder bombarded her with the violence man inflicted upon one another. It ensnared her heart, shredding and twisting inside barbed wire made of suffering as her soul wept, seared by its evil.

"Please..." she begged, tears leaving streaks down her dusty face. "I can't–"

The images slowed to a final few, stopping on the last picture. Olivia's eyes snapped open.

And peered into the attentive eyes of a man.

A fierce warrior.

A stripped angel.

Her bloodline.

"Melchior," she whispered.

A Magi.

CHAPTER THIRTY-ONE
DELILAH

D elilah lost track of space and time in the wasteland of her tormented, chaotic emotions. Her hate and drive for revenge seethed inside of her like a volcano, bulging with lava seeking release, then destroying everything in its path. It consumed her until the only road, dark and uncharted, lay in front of her.

She must become a Fallen.

If Delilah became a Fallen, she'd be free from serving humans, free from her angelic demands, and free from God's plan. She must walk away to fulfill her ache for freedom and obsession for revenge without remorse or challenge. Her decision was unwavering, her core resolute. She'd cauterize herself from all she ever was, the essence of her being, why she was created. But to carry out this obscene goal, she must do something she had sworn she'd never do.

Descend through the Mar of Sin.

Damned for eternity.

Never to return.

She remembered the indignant howls of fury mingled with persecuted cries of injustice striking out at Heaven as those who chose to deny God's will plunged through the Mar of Sin. Were the Fallen's cries only of anger and defeat, or were they of something vastly deeper? Was it a fall through soul-stripping fire or just a black, hollow void sucking away their heavenly lifeblood, leaving an empty chalice only evil could fill? What maniacal force transformed the Fallen's scorched wings, marble-like skin stretched over their skeletal faces, and eyes of black orbits? Even their vibrant colors, once virtuous in nature, now emblazoned, symbolized their deadly sin. Did this malevolent metamorphosis happen during the scourge of the fall or from life in the hellish shadows of Lucifer?

Delilah could no longer wallow in fear of the pain or the reality of living in Hell. Her time for action was now, lest she retreat a bitter coward.

HER PORTAL CLOSED along with the last of her sabotage-filled thoughts. The brilliant sun dazzled her surroundings, contrasting with the dark serendipity burning inside of her. She relished in her resolution, satisfied it would happen soon. But first, she had to meet with Zar. She settled on the shaded bench facing the hospital. He'd find her—

"Delilah!" Her name broke through her churning thoughts.

Zar filled her vision as he leaned over, nose-to-nose. Smoke filled her nostrils as his blatant anger pinned her, but not before his eyes revealed something different... something surprising.

Is that relief and tenderness you let slip to the surface?

"Where have you been?" he said through clenched teeth. "I've been waiting and looking for you ever since you left Conner's house and—"

"What!" She shoved him away, startling him. "You were following me? Did you overhear my—"

"Yes, I did!" He got back in her face as she jumped off the bench. "I took a chance you'd be there because you stopped meeting me and left me hanging with promises—"

"You don't get to follow me! You don't own me! I'll tell you where I am only if I want to!" Delilah spat.

She turned away, putting distance between them. She refused to go from one she wanted to possess to another who wanted to possess her. This was now about her, and only her.

Zar materialized in front of her, his lip curled back, baring his teeth. His hands splayed out in front of her. Thick green roots entwined around his fingers, extending through the empty area between them. His tentacles of anger lashed out, wrapping around her waist like a greedy vine.

"Don't walk away from me." He jerked her middle. "I'm sick of you walking away from me."

Delilah lurched forward as he tugged again. She punched a burst of electrical energy. It surged over the constricting tentacles, breaking his grip.

"What the−" Zar gripped his singed hands.

"Never try to control me again, or this will be the last time you'll ever see me. I promise you that." Delilah's deadly calm voice held only promise if ignored.

Zar scrutinized her, searching for cracks, but his body deflated. "I'm sorry. The waiting was driving me crazy. You can understand that, right?" His pleading voice dripped with sincerity, but Delilah knew better than to trust him now. Between Conner's stories of demon episodes and this little display, she couldn't afford to give him anything more than enough crumbs to keep him satisfied. It irked her, but she needed him, if only for a while longer.

Till I get to Lucifer...

"Well, I didn't mean to drive you crazy. I needed time to think, that's all." She shrugged, sauntering over to the bench. "When I left Conner's house, I floated, letting my fury and frustrations fly free." She examined her delicate hands folded in her lap, struck, wondering what they would look like after the fall. "I haven't been back to my charge either, if that makes you feel any better. I wanted to weigh my options and plan my next moves."

Zar plopped down beside her, invading her space again.

"And what might that be?" Zar's casual tone didn't disguise his hint of anxiety.

She absorbed every subtle feature on his face. He was a chameleon constantly shifting to fit his needs. Delilah couldn't miss any small reaction.

It's now or never.

"I've decided I don't want to be an angel anymore. I want to become one of you... a Fallen." Her body spiked with dark excitement at having voiced her ambitious plan.

Zar howled with raucous laughter. His mirth irritated her. "That's it? That's what you came up with while you were floating around the clouds?" Zar smirked. "Just how are you going to do that? The Fall already happened, Delilah." He shoved himself off the bench. "Painting your wings black and strutting around in black leather won't make you one of us." Zar faced her as he unfolded his black wings. He raised a tattooed arm, pointing an accusing finger like he was damning her himself. "You'll never be one of us." Zar thrust out his chest, tossing back his platinum hair.

Delilah regarded him, letting him preen in his arrogance.

"Do you remember the Fall?" Delilah asked, cocking her head.

"Why would you ask that?"

Delilah remained silent, rising to her feet.

He huffed. "Of course. Like it was yesterday." Zar crossed his arms, sneering at her. "It was the best day of my life."

Delilah's red hair shifted around her shoulders as she nodded. She raised an eyebrow. "What if I were to tell you that the dark abyss they forced you through was still there... still open, swirling at the edge of Heaven?"

Zar's arms dropped to his sides. His face turned blank. "I'd say you're a liar."

Just as she thought. The Fallen didn't know, but she did, and, oh, so much more.

I hold all the power.

"Well, Zar, once again you'll be proven wrong. I'm going through the abyss. Next time you see me, I'll be a Fallen just like you."

Zar's body froze, his face etched in sublime shock. Delilah consumed the powerful rush, having played him perfectly. Regardless of whether he understood it, she'd entangled him in her deadly web to use at her will.

"You can tell nobody what I'm about to do. It must stay our secret. If you can do that, I'll share all I know on how we can bring down Heaven. You and I... together... and the spoils will be ours to rule." She trailed a long fingernail down the side of his stunned face.

"But if you reveal our secret, I'll destroy you and find myself a new ally." She vibrated in anticipation as her nail continued across his hard lips, tapping them once before stepping back. She kept her cool eyes drilled into his, but Zar hadn't moved a muscle.

"Do we have a deal?" Delilah traced a circle in front of her. She tossed her flowing hair back, tingling with her superiority. "Cat got your tongue?" She giggled as she faded. "I guess not. Goodbye, Zar."

Coming out of his stupor, Zar lunged at her fading form, his arms grabbing nothing but air. "Wait! Yes! Delilah, come back! We have a deal!"

Her roll of laughter mocked him. "See you soon," Delilah said into the void, not caring if he heard her or not.

Zar

Zar dropped to his knees, pounding his fists into the green grass. He unsheathed his dagger, stabbing it into the soft earth. With each slashing stroke, he envisioned Delilah's flawless white flesh, bleeding onto the ground, not the dull brown clumps of soil coming up instead. He loathed her, cursed her treachery. She'd humiliated him and forced him to apologize. His strokes grew more frenzied as his eyes tunneled on her cruel, laughing eyes. How dare she keep treasured secrets from him, binding him to her like a sniveling, weak human! He brutalized the ground, piercing each of her green eyes as she betrayed him with her condescending laughter. Zar was never sorry for anything he did.

Never!

His fury spent, before him lay a hole with brown clumps of shredded grass. Zar rolled over, splaying himself across the cool ground, its damp earthy smell surrounding him. The endless blue sky was too bright and cheery for his dark mood. From behind closed eyelids, he replayed her exquisite face disappearing as her laughter haunted him.

Nobody laughs at me... not even Delilah.

Even after his exhaustive tirade, a simmering madness boiled beneath the surface. His fist slammed the ground as a bitter reality oozed through him that he could no longer deny. His howl of anguish ripped through the air as the truth he tried to keep hidden in his black heart burst open.

Zar loved her as much as he hated her.

And he despised himself for it. It was a self-betrayal of epic proportions. But he knew the wretched roots of his desire had started when they first met. When times were different for them and love consumed all they did. It was the meaning of their whole existence.

But that was then, and this is now.

He sat up and hung his head between his raised knees in complete defeat. As the war inside him settled, he released a cleansing sigh. His unwanted destiny lay before him, precarious and uncharted.

Zar would do Delilah's bidding and keep her secrets, but she must never know his real motive: his love for her. He'd compromise himself in whatever way he needed to keep her close to him. Maybe, if he concocted a perfect plan, her feelings would one day match his.

Fool...

Zar rolled off the ground and wiped his dirty blade against his pant leg before sheathing it. He needed a release. A tortured soul he could abuse until Delilah's return. Zar turned into a shadowy mist, making his way across the parking lot and through the hospital's front doors. People rushed through his form, too absorbed in their pain to notice the darkness passing through them. Some shuddered; most didn't.

He let his senses loose across the waiting room, seeking the despair he craved.

There. In the corner.

A lone woman silently sobbing into her wadded tissues. Vulnerable. Exhausted. Scared.

Mandy never comes home early from school...

The shame of her daughter's accusing words...

The fight...

The pleas...

The tears...

The front door slamming shut...

Why did I let her get in her car...?

And crying out to God, asking forgiveness for her sins. She mumbled promises never to see the man again if God saved her daughter, wiping her puffy eyes with her tattered tissues.

Bargaining with God again... Tsk tsk.

Zar hovered over her, feeding on her desolate misery. His smoky form draped around her like a dank blanket, enveloping her. He whispered words of doubt and self-loathing in her ear, letting them worm their way around her despondent soul, encouraging them to take root.

But it's your fault...

You can never forgive yourself...

You're a horrible person who doesn't deserve her or your husband...

Deep despair and shame rolled off her in delicious waves as her living horror replayed again and again in her head.

Yes, this was the sustenance his black soul coveted, cried out for, demanded.

Mankind living out their deadly sins.

And paying for it.

CHAPTER THIRTY-TWO

DELILAH

D elilah was on a mission.

Her explosive encounter with Zar earlier in the day had solidified her fervor to leave Heaven. Any lingering doubt or fear vanished when she spoke her desire out loud.

I'll become one of you... a Fallen.

The time had come to act. Delilah closed her mind to any errant thoughts and instead concentrated on the Mar of Sin. Her body hummed with this newfound determination and her vision of the future.

She closed her eyes, drew in a deep breath, and watched the film of her existence:

Adorer.

Servant.

Guide.

Protector.

Lover.

Sinner.

Delilah had become a sinner the day she fell in love with Conner. But her forbidden love only brought her a shameful misery, not the joyful bliss she'd imagined of her life with him. Choosing to love

Conner was her unraveling, like tugging on a thread dangling from a sweater. Once the thread unfurled, there was no stopping it until it was cut at the source. She had severed her ties with Conner, and now, she had to do the same with God.

Her eyes flew open as she deleted the old, tired images. Eager to go, she reached out with both hands and parted the blank space in front of her. The world opened, as if a parted curtain, to the heavenly body of stars twinkling in the endless canvas of space. The eternal expanse was breathtaking. She acknowledged its beauty for the last time as she dove into the stars.

With a few quick flaps of her wings, the kaleidoscope of bright stars streaked around her in a spinning motion. A steady, bright light was her beacon, expanding as she approached. She left the twilight of stars behind, embraced by its warmth as she entered Heaven.

She pushed back her apprehension as she landed on an endless, glistening, translucent floor. The edge of Heaven fell off into an iridescent waterfall, flowing over into a boundless pool of reflective stars. Jutting up from the floor at varying heights were an infinite number of sheer columns, glowing with opalescent lights. At the top of each pillar, an angel, unique unto itself just like man, hovered. Their virtue was highlighted by its unique color, which dripped from their shimmering wings and glowed from their eyes. These columns surrounded a lone white mountain. From its peak, glorious bright light blazed in all directions. The angels basked in this loving light with their heads turned up in adoration.

But the light also sought Delilah; she didn't dare let it enchant her. For her, it was too bright and suffocating, probing for her secrets. Delilah's eyes darted away as she turned her back on the majestic stage. She hastily scanned the sea of angels, certain the penetrating light had magnified her intent, captured their interest. But no one paid her any mind... yet. Reunions of families with their guardian angels were the center of attention on the floor before the Heavenly body.

Delilah scoffed at these reunions as an ignorant farce. How could they want to stay here and just exist for Him, when they could have so much more: Their freedom?

She moved past the angels, her eyes seeking the faraway edge, where a murky darkness percolated. The dark mist sullied the purity of the scene, forever churning yet remote enough to deny its dangerous pull. It swirled as a black whirlpool at the end of a peaceful lake, waiting for its prey to drift too close, sucking one into its unbreakable current, lost for eternity. Angels never approached its wispy edges, for its malevolent undercurrent tugged at the purest of beings. But Delilah headed straight for it. There her freedom lay.

The Mar of Sin.

Her obsession pulled at her. She thrust out her wings and flew, focusing on her target. Her eager eyes widened as it grew more prominent, more sinister, calling her like a siren from the jagged cliffs.

His radiant light shone on her back, warning her she wasn't alone. Angels whizzed by her, their vibrant colors leaving streaks, distorting her vision. They barreled closer, growing in number, nudging her as their majestic wings became a frantic, psychedelic roadblock around her. She dodged and weaved a path between them. She shook her head in denial, crying out as another wing batted against her. The closer she got to the chasm, the more congested her path became. Delilah fought against their cries of love, their pleas to turn away, bombarding her with their bodies. She dove for the ground, running as soon as her feet hit the floor.

So close... just a little farther.

The angels landed in front of her, blocking her way. The whirling sound from the chasm thundered behind the angels, its dark tendrils reaching out to her. Delilah battled back, shoving her battered body against the living wall of angels collapsing around her.

"Get out of my way!" Delilah cried. Her path was blocked, but the chasm's churning grew louder, syncing with the roaring in her ears. She beat her fists against her adversaries. "This is my choice!"

Delilah.

Her feverish eyes darted behind her. Panic bubbled in her chest.

God called her name.

Delilah strained against the angels with all her might, ignoring how his deep, gentle voice had awakened her essence, striving to ignite her last vestiges of good. Screams of frustrations tore from her lips. She couldn't stop now, when its depths were within reach....

Delilah.

"NOOOOOO!" Delilah yelled with built-up fury and frustration. She turned back to the iridescent stage she had once adored, fists raised high, her crushed body pulsing with indignation.

"You can't stop me! You said we had free will and could go through the Mar of Sin if we chose." Her chest heaved as she threw her sharp, accusing words back at God and those around her. "I so choose! I'm going through it!"

You'll not find what you're seeking. There's no freedom with Lucifer. His binding chains are heavy. His clever words are hollow promises.

"I won't listen." Delilah covered her ears. Strands of her red hair stuck to her damp face. She shook her head at the radiant figure gliding out of the light toward her. "Stay away! It's my will! It's what I want!"

Delilah turned back toward the chasm. The angels weren't blocking her path anymore, clearing her way as they stepped back. Moonlight-kissed tears streamed down their anguished faces. She wouldn't be distracted by their sadness or become trapped by her guilt. She locked in on the Mar of Sin, hypnotic in its surging call, its roar drowning out everything, and flung herself toward it. Her wings lifted, sucked up by the dark swirling core.

Almost there.

Everything around her stopped. Including her heart.

I love you, Delilah.

His voice thundered in her head, and for a second, she looked back, betraying herself as the words she yearned to hear from another found a chink in her armor.

But the Mar of Sin swallowed Delilah into its mists of cold darkness, those fateful words lost. The heavenly floor no longer touched her feet. She heard herself cry out, vaguely wondering if the angels did too.

She felt weightless. The whirlpool hissed around her, slapping her battered wings. Hot, stifling air whistled, disorienting her swirling descent into the pitch-black, cavernous abyss.

Immense pain racked her body inside and out, as if a molten fireball had struck her. Her agonizing screams echoed in the vortex. Translucent black flames erupted on her body. Where once-flawless skin glowed, cracked black obsidian remained as fire licked up her body. The searing flames fanned out over her wings as another cry of excruciating pain filled the dark void. The white feathers inside her wings burned like wildfire. She inhaled the smoke and the horrifying smell of her burned flesh. The fire spread to her outer feathers. Ravenous sparks sizzled, sliding over her wings, leaving her vane a black mast with pointed black feathers.

Her back arched as the pain twisted inside her. It felt as if lava paved its way through her lifeblood, scalding it into a thick oil. Long black nails erupted from her fingertips, ending in wicked points. Agony tore through her head as sharp horns exploded above her temples and blinding fire shot from her eyes. Her body was devoured by the greedy, malicious flames. A victim of her choice. The raging fire scourged everything pure, transforming her angelic being. She feared she'd be reduced to nothing but ash, inhaled by the relentless whirlpool. Lost and forgotten.

The burning subsided as she continued her aimless descent. Slowly, her tortured body tingled back to life. Delilah's vision returned with charcoal hues, highlighted with emerald green light filling in the lighter shades. Her charred exterior peeled away, revealing hard, marble-white skin. A green swirl appear over the area where her heart thudded, striking a vine-like path across her chest and traveling down her arms, ending at each sharp fingernail. Her once-soft red hair amassed around her like a bed of flames. The lifeblood of fire coursed through her, feeding her transformed body.

Delilah was more alive than ever.

She didn't know how long she'd been trapped in the vortex when she landed on the barren, harsh wasteland. The odor of sulfur surrounded her, but it was no longer offensive. She lay stunned in a

fetal position, ash drifting down around on her like dirty snow. She
wondered if the ash was from her incinerated body or if it was a
permanent part of her new world. She glanced up at the hostile sky
from which she fell; no opening lay inside the dismal clouds, no trail
for her to follow. No matter. She knew the key to its secret.

Conner's daughter.

She feasted upon each new body part, fascinated by her exquisite,
dark transformation. Delilah stood, gloriously naked, on the black
expanse of molten rock shrouded in ominous gray clouds. She
detected no sound, only the thick beating of her black heart. But she
wasn't scared, shamed, or vulnerable. A triumphant, devious smiled
stretched across her hard, tight face.

She was free.

A Fallen.

"Zᴀʀ," Delilah called.

She visualized him, tempted him with her fiery lifeblood.

"Zar, come–"

A green web materialized against the bleak wasteland. Zar stepped
through the portal, and she appreciated him for the first time in his
element. He didn't look human here.

No.

Zar's platinum hair glowed around him, and his features were
honed, more menacing under the marble skin. His arms, free of
tattooed sleeves, were a road map of green veins disappearing inside
his snake-like armor. Fiery green eyes pierced her as he jolted to a
stop.

"Delilah?" he whispered.

She nodded. Her sly smile stretched, exposing her sharp, cat-like
teeth. She lifted her chin and raised her arms wide, not ashamed as his
eyes slowly devoured every inch of her naked body. Her body
hummed under his lust, his desire a validation of her transformation

She ended his hungry gaze by closing her wings of armor around her, leaving only her eyes to appreciate.

My terms, not yours.

"I can't believe it worked.... The chasm is still open." His long stride closed the gap between them. "You took the Fall." He lifted a strand of her flame-colored hair and brought it to his face. Rubbing her hair between his long fingers, he closed his eyes and inhaled deeply. "You're one of us now." Zar's hot breath brushed across her face, fanning her depraved vanity. "I've never seen anything as magnificent as you." His husky voice was thick with need. His tongue flicked across his bottom lip as his face hovered over her. "Tell me everything."

Delilah stepped back, breaking the intensity of his need. Zar reached out and grazed her wing. A green electrical current leaped on his hand and raced up his arm, leaving a singed odor in the air.

Had she done that? What else could she do?

He jumped back, anger flaring across his face. "Why did you do that?"

"I didn't know I could.... Did I hurt you?"

"No," he snarled, scrubbing his hand over his arm. "You'll discover your transformed powers. Just use someone else as your guinea pig."

Delilah bit her bottom lip, thrilled by all the possibilities.

"I still want answers." Zar said as his irritation flashed.

Such an impatient child.

Delilah tried not to roll her eyes. "I think it's better if I tell Lucifer first." She let the comment hang in the air. "My safety depends on what I know and what I tell him. If he suspects you know too, he might kill me before we can put our plan into place. You understand, don't you?"

Rioting emotions ricocheted across his face. "Do you realize who you're dealing with? Lucifer will kill us both if he thinks you're deceiving him." His eyes narrowed; a sneer lifted his upper lip. "I have no interest in getting caught up in your treacherous web."

"Leave it to me. I promise it'll work out as we planned."

"You mean as you've planned. You've tossed nothing but grand ideas and trivial details my way. Don't play me for a fool either, or I'll kill you before Lucifer has a chance." His words hung between them; his vicious threat challenged her brazen bravado.

But Zar didn't intimidate her.

"I'd never play you for a fool. We're a team. I need you." She sauntered to him and unfolded her wings, laying her hand upon his chest. "And you need me to further your own purposes."

Zar inhaled, his breath hissing through his teeth.

"You and me. We'll bring down Heaven and rule over everything and everyone." She inched closer. "Have a little faith, Zar," she whispered into his cold face.

He scoffed. "Fine. But I stay there with you, too."

"I wouldn't have it any other way," Delilah said.

Zar punched out his hand, and a black web crackled open. The intense, smoldering smell of a fiery inferno, pushed by an enigmatic, pulsing heat, teased her with the power and evil waiting on the other side.

Her destiny.

Lucifer.

CHAPTER THIRTY-THREE
OLIVIA

Tremors racked Olivia's body. The blanket draped around her shoulders provided a warm cocoon, but the cool night air wasn't the cause of her body's erratic quivers. These involuntary ripples were her muscles, bones and blood assimilating to the intrusion of the mystical orb Melchior slammed into her Orion mark.

The vortex dissipated as quickly as it had appeared, leaving the desert night to reclaim its calm. The fire's flames no longer roared, now providing heat and a tranquil light illuminating the groups of three sitting around the fire pit. Zach, Rachel, and Caspar sat on her right. Rachel whispered in Zach's ear, but his face was expressionless as he gazed into the fire. Sergio, Javier, and Balthazar completed the circle. Sergio's head rested on his arms, which were crossed over his knees. His dad's hand rubbed Sergio's back in a circle.

Dad's arm lay around Olivia's shoulders, and Melchior sat next to her. He hadn't spoken since he'd shoved the orb into her body. Olivia appreciated his silence, as her mind still reeled from the images and the ceremony. Melchior must have sensed her scrutiny. He turned and looked at her with a smile etched across his handsome face. He leaned over and whispered, "How are you feeling?"

Seriously?

"Like a celestial orb electrocuted me." She smiled back at him. "Um... My mark still tingles and my mind is blown."

"That's normal." Melchior chuckled. He took her hand and squeezed it, sending a rush of warmth zipping up her arm. "You were fantastic tonight. You may not think so right now, but you've got the attributes of a strong guardian."

"Thanks." Her smile was hesitant, intimidated by who he was: a Magi. She still couldn't wrap her mind around that revelation.

"Do you know what today is?" Melchior asked.

Olivia shook her head, wondering what more they could add to tonight.

"It's the Epiphany of our Lord. A star rose in the night sky, more brilliant than the others. This is the star we'd been waiting for since we left Heaven. We followed the star across the desert, leading us to Jesus. We entered and kneeled before him as he was cradled in Mary's arms, humbled to be in his presence, and laid our treasured gifts of gold, frankincense and myrrh at his feet. His light shone bright as an infant." Melchior sighed. "One day this memory will be released in you when you're ready."

"Can I ask"

Balthazar unfolded his large frame, resting his hand on the hilt of his sword. His assessing golden eyes roamed across each face glowing around the fire pit. "This has been a long day for each of you. We understand you have many questions concerning your destinies. You may ask a few, and then we'll leave you to rest."

"The visions from the orb," Zach called out.

"The visions you received are our collective memories, from us and from past guardians. Those memories are a part of you now, and they connect us as one. Most will remain dormant until you become stronger and more equipped to handle them. Your memories from here on will become ingrained in them as well," Caspar answered as he stood.

"The orb–" Sergio asked, his voice hoarse.

Melchior's imposing body rose. "The orb contains a portion of our life force, enhancing you with our angelic gifts. We've passed it on for millenniums, and it's now infused within you. Your brain, senses and body's abilities will be unmatched by any here on Earth. We'll teach you how to harness and wield these abilities."

"Unmatched on Earth?" Olivia asked.

Melchior turned to Olivia. "Man doesn't have these gifts, nor are they in tune to the war waging around them for their souls. The Fallen share in our abilities but use them for evil. We'll teach you how to link and track them. This will help you find and kill them to protect mankind and the Mar of Sin. Your training will start soon. For now, your body needs to assimilate these gifts and recover from tonight."

"But–" Olivia's word dangled in the air.

"We'll be in contact soon. Your parents will also share their knowledge." The white webbing appeared behind the Magi. "Don't worry. Your new guardian angels will watch over you too." Caspar chuckled as he led the way through the portal.

"Until then." Balthazar nodded, walking through the webbing. It closed behind them.

"Great. Just great," Sergio mumbled as his eyes locked with Olivia's. "Don't think I can handle another supernatural meeting." Olivia's frayed nerves agreed.

Javier slapped his son's back. "No need to worry. You've already met them," he said. "The archangels are your guardian angels now. Yours is Gabriel. Zach's is Raphael, and Olivia's is Michael. They'll help you on this mission." He shook his head. "There were many times Gabriel saved my butt, and he'll save yours too."

Michael is my guardian angel....

Just when Olivia thought the crazy was done for the evening, this nugget got lobbed their way. Olivia glanced around the fire pit. "Where did they go?"

"Their presence was complete once they revealed who they were and started the ceremony. They left moments after you received the orb," Rachel said.

"Let's get back to camp. I'm sure your Mom's a hot mess," Javier said, elbowing Sergio.

She's not the only one.

———————

OLIVIA NOTICED two things on the walk back to camp. Where it had been dark outside the flashlight's beam on the hike up, her night vision now captured the landscape outside the beam, and her bum knee felt like a million bucks. It amazed her that these changes happened so quickly.

How else will my body alter? I'll take Wonder Woman, thank you very much.

Zach walked next to her. He hadn't spoken, but she'd caught an errant glance from him. She imagined her eyes reflected the same awe, with an underlying current of excitement.

A trailer's screen door slammed, snapping her back to reality. Two figures stood at the foot of the path, backlit by the campfire glowing behind them. Mom stood under the light of their trailer's screen door with her arms wrapped around herself. Olivia ran the rest of the way to her. She pulled her mom into a hug, holding her tight. Mom released a sob into Olivia's hair.

"Are you okay? I was so worried.... It took so long," Mom said.

"I'm fine, Mom, really." Olivia drew back, offering her a reassuring smile. "The ceremony was intense, to say the least."

Stella's concerned eyes roamed over Olivia's face. "I love you, sweetheart, and am always here–"

"I know. You've always been my rock. But I need you to concentrate on getting better before I can start training. That's what's most important to me. Promise?"

"I promise." She kissed Olivia's cheek.

"Thank you." Olivia's body sagged as the last vestiges of her emotional strength were sapped. "Honestly, I'm so exhausted. I just want to crash."

"And eat. I'm starving," Zach piped up behind her.

"I'll bring out the snacks Olivia's mom put together." Dad

approached the trailer's metal steps. "Get used to being hungry. Your new bodies use up a lot of energy, and training is a butt-kicker too."

Mom and Olivia returned arm-in-arm to the dusty metal bench where they had sat this morning.

Was that this morning?

Olivia's stomach growled when Dad returned with a tray of lunch-meats, cheeses, crackers, and fruit. He placed it on the picnic table next to Sofia's brownies. Matt handed out bottled water while the boys dove into the simple snack. Olivia ate her cheese and crackers while she watched her dad through lowered eyelashes. It was difficult to regard him under this strange new light after spending most of her life despising him. He glanced back at her, but she reached for more cheese instead of acknowledging him. She wasn't ready to unpack all these complicated feelings tonight. Unspoken questions and anxiety crackled around the table, matching her own. But the only thing she could face right now was her pillow. Tomorrow sounded so much better.

Olivia cleared her throat. "I'm going to bed."

She stood up from the picnic table. The boys mumbled in agreement, shoving the last of the brownies into their mouths. Her heart swelled when Zach and Sergio came over to her. After tomorrow's morning light, they'd carve out a new path only they could conquer together. Olivia grabbed Sergio's and Zach's hands and pulled them into a group hug. "I don't know what's in store for us, but I'm so thankful it's with you. We can do anything together. We have to promise right now we'll stay together and have no secrets. It's the only way we'll make it," she whispered. Her tears glistened as she looked at them. "I promise this to both of you."

"I promise, and I'll never let you guys down... even you, Boy Scout," Sergio said, slapping Zach's back. Zach smiled as he rolled his eyes at Sergio.

"I promise, too. I'll always have your backs and fight for both of you," Zach promised.

"Thank you." Olivia closed her eyes, cherishing this moment of trust and commitment, shoring up her weary mind and soul. She turned toward the camper without another word. Opening the door, she found the fold-out bed made for her. As she got ready for bed, the images from the collective memories in her mind shuffled like a deck of cards, not able to focus on a single image. Bone-tired, she crawled into bed. Her eyes closed before her head hit the pillow.

CHAPTER THIRTY-FOUR
CAMILLA

C amilla's eyes darted around her bedroom, searching for what had woken her. The filtered streetlamp light drifted through the wooden blinds, revealing nothing lurking in the shadows. Then why was her heart beating like a jackhammer? She rolled over–

A terrified scream saturated the silent house.

Lucia.

A cold sweat broke out on her brow as she flung off her bedcovers. She yanked open her bedroom door. A familiar smell ambushed her when she lurched across the hallway. She'd never forget the oily, smoky odor or what encompassed it.

It's in Lucia's room.

Need a weapon...

Not enough time.

Panicked for her granddaughter, she threw open Lucia's door as another cry rang out. Camilla scanned the room but found only Lucia in her bed, fisting a wad of blankets up against her chin.

"Abuela!" Lucia's bulging eyes pleaded with Camilla, her mouth sagging open from her spent scream.

"Shh... I'm here now." Camilla rushed inside, heedless of the alarms going off in her head. Pain erupted across her back. Something slammed her to the floor with a crushing thud. She gagged on the stench of her nemesis. Its taloned hand, scraping her scalp, yanked Camilla's head back and stared at her with purple eyes. Rage radiated from the demonic, glowing eyes, but then recognition flashed.

"You," she hissed. The stank breath burned Camilla's nostrils; the black skeletal face was inches from hers.

Lucia's cries became a wheezing shrill, igniting Camilla's struggles to fight back. She grabbed the wrist holding her head, while her other arm pounded against its body.

A silver glint caught the corner of Camilla's eye. The demon brought the curved dagger under her chin. She strained back, but the sharp blade only moved closer. The demon hissed as its forked tongue flicked at Camilla's ear, sending a revolting chill through her.

"Thought you were dead, demon hunter," the demon spat, hot spittle spraying Camilla's face. "Now, I'll get my payback." Its gleeful cackle turned Camilla's blood to ice. "Get the girl...."

Horror struck Camilla as the black choker around the demon's neck uncoiled, thick and shiny. The expanding black snake, with a purple swirl down its back, paid no attention to Camilla. Its large, triangular head turned with its glowing purple eyes stared at Lucia's bed. The snake's hot, scaly body slithered over Camilla's arm. Her sweat-drenched hand lashed out in vain as it taunted her with its purple rattle, shaking as it swished through the carpet.

"NO! Don't hurt her... Lucia!" Camilla gasped as a crazed frenzy burst inside her. She bucked against the clinging demon, thrashed her arms, but it only clamped down harder around Camilla. The knife's tip nicked her neck, and the blade pressed deeper, finding her old, jagged scar. She remembered the blood pulsing through her fingers and spilling around her, sure she would die from that wound. Her fate at this moment seemed no different. Only this time it would drench her granddaughter's carpet instead of the cold cement.

"Too bad she can't move away," the demon snickered in her ear. "You'll watch her die just like I watched you—"

The house boomed as the front door crashed against the entry wall. Thundering footsteps raced down the hallway, careening to a stop at Lucia's doorway.

"Lucia!" Manny yelled into the dark room. But the demon's hiss brought his eyes to the floor, where it straddled Camilla.

"Run, Manuel!" Camilla cried.

The demon leaped off her and lunged in front of Manny, blocking his way.

"Better yet, stay and play!" It licked its lips. Manny stood still as the black-clad demon crouched closer, waving the dagger at Manny.

Camilla scrambled off the floor, her eyes darted between Manny and the deadly snake slithering up Lucia's bedpost. A primal keening sound had taken over Lucia, her eyes glued to the hideous snake.

"No!" Camilla yelled. She lunged for the snake. Desperate to save Lucia, Camilla's hand grabbed its thick, scaly body. Waves of repulsion swamped her. Every fiber screamed for her to throw the creature across the room, but she held on tight. The snake raised its upper body, twisted, and faced Camilla. Its head arched back, mouth wide, needle-sharp fangs slick with deadly venom. She cried out as she slammed the snake down, striking it across the bedpost. Venom sprayed past her, but the stunned snake slowly arched up again.

Camilla heard the demon screech as it launched itself at Manny, its glinting blade raised high. She caught the sight of Manny's right hand thrusting out. A silver streak flashed before embedding into the chest of the demon. Ear-splitting howls echoed in the room as it clawed at its mortal wound. The body exploded into black oil and disappeared, leaving behind a fading trail of smoke and ash. The snake, curved fangs ready to strike, vanished in a puff of smoke inside Camilla's clutched hand.

Camilla lurched over to Lucia's bed, ignoring Manny's torrent of angry Spanish as he hit the light switch. Camilla sat on the bed and brought Lucia into an embrace. She rocked her, crooning words of comfort for herself as much as for Lucia.

"It's all over... never hurt you again," she repeated, stroking Lucia's silky hair. Manny crumbled at Lucia's feet, rubbing her thin legs. He yanked the pink fleece blanket at the end of the bed over Lucia. He was silent, but anger and confusion pulsed off of him like his furious tirade.

"Manuel... I–" Camilla's breathless words stuck in her dry throat when Manny's confused, shaken eyes pinned her.

"I drove by to check the house.... Heard the screams.... My heart stopped. I ran inside to find that thing–" He tucked the blanket around Lucia's legs.

"Que... Abuela..." Lucia moaned.

But Camilla's eyes became vacant, lost in her own world. A time long past swamped her. Memories she'd stowed away now sprang free.

Angels, demons, Balthazar... Gabriel.

Her eyes slipped over Manny, landing on Lucia's pale face. Doll-like eyes lay unblinking, psyche crept back someplace safe deep in her mind. Fearing shock, Camilla adjusted the blanket around Lucia. Her shaking hand stilled over Lucia's exposed shoulder.

There, against Lucia's light-brown skin, glistened seven small black dots.

Orion.

No, no, no... It can't be.

Only Sergio.

"Abuela, talk to me." Manny's anxious voice cut through the panic that had sent her heart into a frenzied pace. Fear clarified her thoughts in an instant.

Manny and Lucia saw it.... He killed it.

Camilla's hand whipped out like a claw, twisting Manny's t-shirt. She pulled him closer, breathing heavily into his face.

"You must never speak of this. Never!" Her shrill voice startled both of her grandchildren. "Your parents must never find out what happened here tonight. Promise me." She felt like a madwoman, wild with fear, seeking the rope that could pull her back to sanity... to her family.

His defiant eyes glared back. "Not until you tell me what that was I just killed and why it was here."

Her shoulders slumped, the weight of her fears too much

"Promise me, Manuel... por favor." A tear escaped, her facade crumbling. He must do this for her. "And I'll tell you what you want to know."

Manny's rough thumb gently wiped her tear away. "Si, Abuela."

She exhaled a shaky breath. "That was a Fallen, but you know them as demons." Her trembling hand released Manny's shirt. "Trained by Astaroth, Prince of the Sloth Realm, one of the Seven Realms in Hell. His realm preys upon the mentally and physically disabled, among others. They consider them weak, easy to manipulate, more amusing to terrorize." Her chin quivered as she found the spot, beyond Manny, where evil had almost won. "That's why they chose Lucia... I thought I had protected her..."

Manny fell back on his heels, his face scrunched. His shoulders shrugged, lifting his brown hands toward her. "Wait. What? How do you even know about that?"

An ironic smile creased the lines on her face as she drew her shoulders back. "Because I was a demon-killer charged with guarding the Fallen's abyss, left open in Heaven, against their return. Just as generations before me, and just like your Papa and..." She swallowed. "...now Sergio. They're transferring powers tonight."

Manny jumped away from her. Confusion mixed with fear played over him as he paced the room like the tattooed tiger on his arm: powerful, stealthy and volatile. He pointed an accusing finger at her. "This is too much!" he exploded. "You're telling me−"

"You killed the demon, Manuel, when you plunged your knife that I gave you into its heart. It is forged from Heavenly steel, made by an angel to kill them. That and beheading are the only ways to kill them. The demon showed itself to terrify Lucia. That's why you saw it."

Manny froze and stared at the empty place in the doorway. He shoved his fists into his jean pockets, his lips set in a grim line. "Your story, Abuela... it's hard to wrap my mind around, but what I killed was evil." He raked his fingers through his thick hair, standing it on end. "Why Sergio? He's just a boy. I'm older−" His fist landed over the top of his heart. "Stronger−"

"It's not for us to understand why one sibling is chosen over another." Camilla's eyes glanced back at Lucia's seven ominous spots. "But we have to accept it, for there is no changing it," she whispered.

"So, there's nothing I can do? No way I can protect our familia? Just sit back while Sergio... my little brother... fights demons?" He waved his arm where evil had struck. "I don't accept that."

"This is difficult—"

"And why can't I tell the familia about tonight?" he mocked. "If they're all demon hunters—"

"I have to take care of something first. The familia can't find out, Manuel. Not yet. It's crucial you do this for me. For Lucia!" Her lips trembled.

Manny's jaw twitched. He put his hands on his hips, exhaling sharply.

"Si, I'll keep your secret." He nodded at her. "For now. But you and I aren't done talking about this. Not by a long shot."

Manny crossed the room. She stared at his approaching chest, too afraid to discover the emotions playing across her noble grandson's face.

What if he—

Manny's warm finger lifted her chin. Onyx eyes, normally guarded and sharp, peered down at her with pride and love.

"I always knew you were a guerrera, Abuela. But now?" He shook his head. "Usted una guerrera feroz." He grinned down at her.

"Te quiero, Manuel."

"Yo tambien te quiero." Manny leaned down and kissed her forehead. His hand fell as he stepped away. A sob of relief escaped her.

"I'm gonna go make some coffee. I need to process all this. You and Lucia go to sleep. I'm not going anywhere." He flipped the light switch off and slipped into the hallway, leaving a void in the room.

A kitchen chair scraped along the kitchen tile. A quick pound on the table signaled Manny had more than thoughts to work out.

Guerrera feroz. Fierce warrior.

No one had called her that since Gabriel.

Camilla looked down at her precious granddaughter. Her eye were closed and her breathing was steady while her hand still clung t

Camilla. Sickening fear threatened again as Camilla tried piecing together what had happened and what it meant for her and Lucia.

They still think I'm dead.

Maybe finding Lucia was just a coincidence.

Have to protect her.

My fault.

Camilla moved Lucia's head onto the pillow. Lucia moaned as Camilla crawled in next to her. Crushing guilt weighed down on Camilla.

You know what you have to do....

"Abuela..." Lucia muttered.

"Shhh. Si, I'm right here." Camilla stroked her hair.

"Is what you said to Manny about the demons, our familia and you... it's all real?" Lucia whispered.

Camilla's wry smile touched Lucia's head, which was tucked under her chin. "Si. You heard everything?"

"Si," Lucia whispered. "I can fight too. I'm sure I can! You could show—"

"This is not one of your books." Camilla spoke more harshly than she'd intended. "We'll talk in the morning, ¿bueno? But just you and me. Promise?"

"I'd never share our secret." Lucia snuggled up against her. "Thank you for grabbing the snake. "Lucia shivered. "You are a brave warrior too." Lucia said giving Camilla a squeeze.

"Gracias." Camilla kissed her forehead and continued stroking her hair.

Camilla's fingers found the cross around her neck. She rubbed the smooth metal, seeking the fuel she needed for fortitude and strength. She'd do it right this time. For her familia, herself, and God.

But would Gabriel help her... after everything she'd done?

His gold-dipped white wings fluttered behind her closed eyelids. She sighed, knowing there would be no sleep for her tonight.

CHAPTER THIRTY-FIVE
LUCIFER

Lucifer swayed to the cries of wretched agony, the hollow moaning, and the piercing screams of pain and horror cascading around him. The damned and their tormented souls cried out, trapped with their sins for perpetuity. The soundtrack of living Hell. A perfect symphony playing for an audience of one. A cacophony created by him, because of him, and for him.

His masterpiece.

His vision.

His Hell.

Long, forceful legs ushered Lucifer, with his arms clasped behind his back, around the enormous dark stone tower. Massive, arched floor-to-ceiling windows allowed him an unobstructed view of his vast, infernal kingdom.

He stopped and chuckled, closing his eyes in pure bliss as the shrill pitch of a new soul rose above the others. He brought his arms up, like a conductor, commanding it to play for him.

"Yes," Lucifer cried.

Its desolate wail, so pure in the horrifying discovery of its damnation, sang to his evil core. His black blood pumped with the raging scream, shocked that there was no escaping the payment for its mortal sins. A whip cracked, silencing the damned at its fevered pitch.

"Welcome." Lucifer lowered his arms, chest heaving with malicious delight.

They deserved every torturous minute of their eternal life with him... in Hell.

And Lucifer was ecstatic to provide it for them.

He strode to the middle of the room, descending the spiral staircase into the darkness. His six massive wings brushed the sides of the stone staircase. Restlessness had plagued him as of late. Nagging at the back of his mind, warning him change was in the air. Lucifer couldn't decipher if it was good or bad. Maybe a visit to one of his Princes would clear his mind.

With renewed excitement, he reached the bottom of the staircase where it opened into the huge circular floor of the Main Hall. A giant open pit lay in the middle. Punishments were doled out to the delight of the crowd. Surrounding the Hall were seven massive arched entrances, each pulsating with its own vibrant color. Like a spoke on a wheel, each entrance led to a long tall bridge with spiked pillars stretching into the slate, nebulous sky. It spanned over the black lava river that swirled around its mighty columns, leading to one of the seven realms.

Which Prince would settle his unrest? He turned to the golden entrance, knowing precisely who to see.

Beelzebub.

Golden light danced on the stone floor of the Realm of Pride entrance. Lucifer smiled, crossing the threshold as the hot golden heat washed over him. Heat came from fire. Fire came from lava. And from the lava, something new arose... his vicious army of damned.

Long strides took him to the edge of the bridge cloaked in the gray mist. Only the colors from the different realms cast any light in this dimension. Now the wails of the damned were thumping through him like a beating drum. His head fell back, eyes closed, as the surrounding chaos brought harmony to his black soul. His eyes flew open in anticipation. He opened his massive ebony wings, lifting himself off the bridge above his wicked kingdom.

His Seven Realms... His kingdom.

Lucifer's eyes scanned each realm: as vivid in color as they were obscene in their missions. Building his army of damned to destroy all of humanity was the only thing that mattered to Lucifer. Crushing man by their own deadly sins was supreme vengeance. The different realms glowed around him in their unique colors, displaying their blood-like life force, thriving in their immorality. Greed pulsed blue, Envy swirled green, Wrath boiled red, Lust churned hot pink, Gluttony whirled orange, Sloth simmered purple. But Lucifer headed toward Pride, surging in gold, where Beelzebub reigned.

The sky was full of Lessors, each bowing as he passed. Lucifer was indifferent to this low hierarchy of Fallen. Lessors understood their place: corrupters of man and escorters of its damned soul. Their constant contact with man gave them a repugnant reek. Lucifer sneered as he passed, abhorrent of their fleshy stench.

Lucifer landed at the end of the stone bridge. Laid out before him, carved out of the black, jagged cliffside, was a series of three tall buildings. A grand series of three stone steps led to each building's wide square landing. They glowed molten gold from arched openings. Rising up from the cliff was a mountain range encircling all the realms. Inside those mountains were endless tunnels and caverns.

He approached the first landing, where a colossal fountain of grotesque human shapes, stacked up on each other's shoulders, spilled molten gold from each mouth in a frozen, macabre scream. Lucifer placed his hand under the golden river. His hand surged with the deadly sin flowing through this golden life force. Pride.

His best customer.

Lucifer cracked a wicked smile, quickening his steps. Lessors perched on top of the buildings like gargoyles as their eyes followed him. The closer he came to the top, the louder the wailing and screeching became, along with the thunderous voices of those causing their agony. He paused at the landing, admiring the gigantic golden pool of lava in the middle surrounded by Lessors and their leaders.

Behind the pool stood Beelzebub. His bare massive back turned away from Lucifer. Beelzebub's long, muscular arm swung down, bringing a black-and-gold braided whip across the chest of a Lessor. The crack of the whip split the air. The Lessor arched his back but didn't cry out in pain. Rivers of black ran down his ravaged chest as he strained against the chains shackled around his wrists.

Beelzebub's hand grabbed the blood-splattered hair and yanked its head back. "Disappoint me again, Rahil, and I'll feed you to my hounds." Two enormous black hounds loomed on each side of Beelzebub. Their large square heads reached his chest, snarling and snapping, their jaws glistening with black saliva. He stroked his hand across each hound's head, running it over the course hair of their raised hackles. "Fala and Nyx won't be happy if I deny them again." His voice held a dark promise.

"Beelzebub," Lucifer called.

He whipped his head around, staring at Lucifer with his golden eyes. Two black horns, twisted with gold, jutted from his bald head. He turned his body around and bowed at the waist. "My Lord, to what do I owe this honor?"

Beelzebub's six wings of ebony feathers turned bat-like as they scaled down to the ends. His upper set of wings had razor-sharp barbs embedded across the top. His broad chest ripped with muscle defined by golden ribbons coursing under his tight brown skin. He wore black armor from the waist down, with deadly hooks protruding from the armor's side of his thighs to his ankles.

"I needed some fresh air." They both smirked. "Walk with me."

The Lessors parted as they strolled by the pool. More Lessors circled overhead, carrying a throbbing black orb in their gnarled hands. Lucifer stopped as one swooped low and released it into the molten pool. The orb flared, absorbing the golden life force. The genesis of a human emerged, growing as it would in the womb. From the torso grew arms and legs along with a head with hair floating around it. Two Lessors, in the pool, pulled the charred form to the steps. A female shape emerged from the pool's steamy mist. Golden fibers hung around her face. Her eyes peered through the strands, exposing gold pupils nestled in black eyes. A scream erupted from her mouth's black chasm as she wildly scanned her surroundings. Her struggles stopped when she saw Lucifer.

"Master," she whispered. Her black lips spread into a wicked grin. The damned stared at Lucifer, straining for last glimpses, as they led her through the building's pillars.

"She seems pleased to be here," Lucifer said as they walked toward the bridge.

"She knew Hell was her destination." Beelzebub glanced back at the pool. Another damned rose from the pool, screams of terror erupting from him. "And others do not," he sneered. "Fala! Nyx!" Beelzebub pointed to the wailing damned.

The hounds sprinted with their jaws open, baring pointed teeth. The Lessors shoved the damned at the charging beasts. Each latched onto a side and pulled the damned in two, cutting the screams short while spraying black oil into the steamy air. They dragged the torn remains away, leaving an oily trail evaporating behind them. The Lessors gave the growling beasts wide birth, not wanting to be their next meal.

Lucifer raised an eyebrow, cocking his head. Beelzebub shrugged. "My hounds were hungry. Besides, it's a good reminder of punishment."

Lucifer smiled, approving of his methods. "Effective indeed." He looked past Beelzebub to the mountains as Lessors buzzed through his vision cradling the black orbs. "How's my army?"

A jeer crossed Beelzebub's brown face, sharpening its skeleton angles. "Your army grows bigger every day. Pride is the human's greatest weakness. More come to my realm than even lust or greed." Beelzebub puffed out his chest as he scanned his realm.

Lucifer studied his closest ally. Beelzebub's hatred for man was as deep and devoted as his own. But Lucifer was the one who stood up to God. Yet, at times, Lucifer sensed Beelzebub's desire to rule as an undercurrent in their relationship.

"Yes, pride is the root of all evil." Lucifer's pointed words had Beelzebub giving him a sidelong glance.

I'm watching you, my old friend.

"All for the glory of you, my Lord." Beelzebub swept his arm wide as he bent in a contrite bow.

Lucifer nodded, walking away from him. "Get my army ready. Change is coming," he said over his shoulder.

Beelzebub nodded. An eager, villainous grin slipped into place. "As you wish."

"I can feel it," Lucifer whispered as he whisked down the steps. The feathers on his wings ruffled, feeling Beelzebub's intrusive stare.

Saxem, one of Lucifer's personal guard, stood waiting at the foot of the bridge. "My Lord, I'm sorry to disturb you, but it's an urgent matter."

"What is it?" he snapped.

"Zar is in the tower. He is requesting an audience with you."

Lucifer couldn't care less about Zar's trivial concerns. "I've no time for him," he said dismissively, waving his hand. "Give it to his Prince, Leviathan." Lucifer walked past Saxem, raising his wings in flight.

"But he said he could only see you. He has a present for you... from Earth." Saxem backed away, out of striking range.

"Did he say what it was?" Lucifer growled as he folded his wings, irritated but intrigued.

"No. Just that it was for you only," Saxem replied.

"Fine. Send him to the Throne Room."

Saxem nodded.

"But if he's wasted my time, see to it personally that his punishment is long and brutal."

"My pleasure." Saxem's red eyes glowed with excitement.

Lucifer slipped into the mist rising above his kingdom. He seethed, growing impatient with watching the legions of his army grow with no battle to fight. He craved more, needed release.

Wanted war.

Revenge against his enemies.

Bloodshed and annihilation of those he hated most...

Humans.

He hated humans with a fury burning eternal.

The fact these prideful, lustful, envious, lazy, greedy, gluttonous, rage-filled human souls comprised his army of the damned disgusted him. But the sweet irony of using them to destroy their own kind was pure justice. War was coming, Lucifer sneered.

But when?

CHAPTER THIRTY-SIX
DELILAH

D elilah would never forget the moment she first laid eyes on Lucifer. He was smug in his all-consuming power, vain in his malevolent beauty, ruthless in his enigmatic evil. She wanted all of him.

He wanted to kill her.

She waited with Zar in a long, dark hallway, facing tall metal double doors, large enough for a giant to walk through. On each door, a carved red-eyed serpent with long spines protruding along its back weaved up the side, and they met in the middle. Flames erupted from each fanged mouth, aimed at each other. Two Fallen guards loomed on each side, staring at her with blatant curiosity.

A Fallen emerged from the opposite side of the winding hallway. He wore sleek black armor with a red slash across his chest, like a lion had clawed him. His bald head, with blunt horns on each side, had the same red slash starting from his forehead over to the back of his neck. His red eyes glowed against his black marble skin. He leered at Delilah, sniffing the surrounding air.

"Zar."

"Saxem."

So much for pleasantries.

"He'll see you in the Throne Room now." Saxem didn't take his eyes off her. Delilah returned his bold look with a raised eyebrow. The long silken robe Zar had given her shifted across her body, accentuating her curves.

"Thank you," Delilah said, sarcasm dripping as she passed him, ignoring his eyes boring into her.

The guards opened the doors, revealing an enormous circular room with a high-vaulted ceiling. Floor-to-ceiling windows encircled the room, creating rioting shocks of color into the misty room. Zar took the lead, crossing a long walkway across the massive room. The air was hot and humid, and alive with something sinister.

Delilah's bare foot touched what she thought was cold, slick metal. Her foot paused, realizing the reflective surface was thick glass walkway hovering over an inky pool. She started across, and a sleek ripple in the water caught her eye. Under her feet, black scales emerged as a row of red spines skimmed across the water. A long spine shot up like a finger, scratching the glass beneath her frozen feet, continuing its fluid pass until it slipped below the surface. Her breathing hitched, imaging what kind of horrid creature ruled the murky pool. She hurried across the walkway, scanning the sinister waters for another ripple.

Delilah raised her eyes as they approached the wide stone landing. A long flight of granite stairs, flanked on each side by a flowing trough of burning black oil, led to a circular landing. A towering onyx dragon overshadowed the room. The majestic, ebony seated throne towered against the scales of the vast upright beast's underbelly. Its hind legs, cradling the throne, ended in vicious claws, while the sweeping wings dominated the back of the chamber. The ferocious head leaned over the throne, red eyes glowing, stalking the approaching prey. Two thick spikes extended up its thick tail, curving under a wing. The mouth hung open in a frozen roar, exposing rows of long, pointed fangs, threatening death for anyone who displeased him or his master. They had carved it from the blackest of stones, and it emanated a malicious energy.

If she'd thought the dragon throne was intimidating, nothing prepared her for who lounged upon it. Her body shuddered as she paused at the base of the stairs in front of her infamous destiny.

Lucifer.

Covered waist-down in tight, scaled black pants, his bare upper body displayed every massive muscle chiseled to white marble perfection. His black hair gleamed around his sharp, angular face. Energy sizzled through her as his black eyes devoured her.

He was as magnificent in his beauty as he was in his evil.

"Zar." His deep voice boomed across the room. "Who's this you've brought me? I don't recognize this ravishing Fallen."

Delilah's heartbeat quickened under his torrid journey over her with indecent accuracy. Her body was alive under the robe, but his abrupt tone set her nerves on edge.

"My Lord, this is Delilah. She is new to us. But you would remember her from before the Fall."

The water broke behind her, splashing over the edge. He remained silent, narrowing his eyes as he cocked his head.

"Delilahhhh—"

Lucifer was upon her before she could move. His hand clamped around her neck, choking off her air. Delilah thrashed at nothing but the air between them as he lifted her off her feet. She grabbed his forearm with both hands, straining for relief, afraid he'd snap her neck with one flick of his wrist. He charged toward the black pool, dangling her over the edge. The serpent broke water, its fin grazed the bottom of her feet, slicing open her heels. Her eyes bulged, frantically searching for the serpent as black blood dripped into the water. Her skin began to weave together, healing the wound, but had the serpent already been enticed by her blood? She panicked, words trapped below the vice grip around her neck.

This can't be the end! He has to listen me.

Zar's frantic cries called out to him, but Lucifer wasn't listening.

"Why are you here, angel? Come to spy on me?" The red around his black pupils churned like lava as his lifeless eyes promised her death. "Answer me!" he sneered.

"She fell through the abyss like us. It's still open!" Zar yelled. "She knows its secrets."

Surprise flickered over his face as the serpent made another pass beneath her. Delilah's struggles weakened. At any moment her head might explode, which would be a better fate than a meal for the repulsive serpent.

"Secrets... I'll be the judge of that."

Lucifer moved away from the edge, dropping her into a heap on the stone floor. Delilah wheezed and coughed, dragging in a breath. Her flaming red hair draped around her, hiding her terror and anger. Her body quivered as she eyed the menacing black boots inches from her face. She dared not move for fear of what he might do next.

"Stand up and look at me." Lucifer's command chilled her.

She pushed herself up and stood on shaky legs. Her head fell back as she raised her eyes to meet his. She didn't know what caused the thin smile tugging at the corner of his lips.

"I remember you, Delilah. One of the weak guardian angels who stayed behind. And look at you now." He raised his large hands and entwined them in her long hair. He stepped closer, inches from her face. Dread surged with his closeness. Her scalp screamed for release as his wicked face filled her vision.

"The most gorgeous Fallen I've ever seen, with your red hair fanning around you like flames, green eyes flashing fear, yet you dare to be angry with me." He chuckled as he held her head tight. "I like that. I'll listen to your words. And then I'll decide if you'll be a meal for me." He paused as he sniffed her neck, then ran his scorching tongue over her pounding artery. "Or my serpent."

Delilah didn't move. Her body crackled with dark primal energy, ignited by his searing tongue, but her mind screamed, *what have you done!*

"So, tell me, Delilah, more about this... secret." He overwhelmed her as she fought to control her chaotic emotions. She closed her eyes, digging deep to find the strength that put her here before this evil.

Freedom, revenge, power.

She opened her eyes and focused on his terrifying, alluring face she tried absorbing power from hands that might crush her skull at any moment. He held the key to everything she wanted, all she'd risked her life—her soul—for. She drew courage from his power, siphoned it from him like an energy source. His wicked smile grew wider as excitement exuded from him.

"All right." She cleared her throat. "After the battle, God left the abyss, a portal from the Fall, open. He wanted the angels to remember their free will when deciding who and where they'd serve." He hissed with a sharp intake of breath. "No one has ever gone through... until me."

Lucifer's face was an unreadable mask, but his black eyes rippled with electric currents. "Tell me more," he whispered, his grip getting tighter.

"I was guardian to a man until he turned eighteen and was taken from me." She grunted in pain, talking faster. "That never happens. It upset me, and no one would tell me why St. Michael was now his guardian."

"St. Michael!" Lucifer spat his name. "What does he have to do with this?"

"They wouldn't tell me! But... I... couldn't get my charge out of my head." She swallowed and looked defiantly up at Lucifer. "I'd fallen in love with him," she whispered.

Lucifer threw his head back in laughter. Its sharp crack echoed over the room. "What a stupid little angel. You broke rule number one." He released her head but grabbed her arm, slamming her against his chest. "You're boring me. Tell me about the portal," he hissed.

Tell him just enough.

She relaxed her body, melting it against him. "There's more..." She cracked a devious grin. "I went back and secretly saw this man over the years. He'd married, but I didn't care. I wanted him for myself... and after some time, he returned my feelings." She let out a ragged breath. "One night, I came to see him, but he wasn't there. So, I channeled him and found him in the fight of his life... with a Fallen."

Lucifer released her arms and stepped away.

"He wielded a beautiful silver sword with blue flames running down the middle. The Fallen was a warrior woman with gold eyes wearing black body armor with the same color slashed across her chest and back. Their battle was intense in the dark alley until he swung the sword across her neck. Her outraged shriek lingered in the air while her body and sword vanished." She took a small step toward him. "When it was over, he realized I was there. He was so angry and told me not to tell anyone what I saw. I told him I wouldn't, but he needed to tell me who he was. He didn't at first. Said it had to remain his secret. But in a moment of weakness, he did." She smiled up at Lucifer.

"I'm losing my patience, Delilah," Lucifer said. A muscle twitched in his jaw as he ground his teeth together.

"He's the guardian of the abyss, named the Mar of Sin. You fell through it. He's also a demon killer sent by God."

"Guardian? Why?" He paced in front of her, his raw anger palpable.

"When God left it open, it stayed open both ways. He knows how to find the portal... and how to close it."

Lucifer paused and turned his fury toward her. "How... how can he do that?"

"I don't know." She rushed out, "He didn't tell me—"

A snarl cut through the steamy air. "Then you are useless to me. Looks like my serpent will—"

"But there's more!" She raised her hands as she backed up. "I gave myself to him that night. But the next day, horrified and ashamed of himself, he said he could never see me again. He loved his wife and had sinned against God. I told him if I couldn't have him, then neither would his wife. He had to leave her or I'd share his secret." She turned from Lucifer. "He left."

"Then why are you now here?"

"He's back." She turned around, squaring her shoulders. "To transfer his powers to his daughter. She'll learn the secrets of the portal. We'll use her and then we can storm Heaven—"

"Quiet!" Spittle sprayed from his mouth. "Did God see you go through this... Mar of Sin?"

"Yes, but He couldn't stop me. He doesn't know my lover told me about the guardian–"

Lucifer's laughter cut at her again. "But He does know all. At least up there."

She heard the restless serpent break the pool's surface. "Michael and the others pushed me aside, didn't give me the time of day. They took who I loved away from me, not caring about how devastated I was! It was only about God's will. Well, I have free will, and I won't be beholden to them anymore. I fell through the Mar of Sin to become a Fallen and serve you, not God. Revenge against Michael, this girl and her family is what I want, and I'll do whatever it takes... whatever you want me to do... to make this war happen." She hurled her hate-filled words at him with a passion she knew he'd understand.

He curled his finger at her. "Come here, my sweet." She obeyed as the hot pool water sloshed over her feet.

"It doesn't matter what He knows. What matters is He knows nothing of what happens in my Kingdom. This may work for my... our... advantage."

Lucifer reached for her hand, bringing it to his face. His thumb mesmerized her as he ran it across her knuckles. His black eyes bore into her dark soul.

"I've decided I won't kill you, for now. Instead, we'll help each other exact our revenge." He brought her knuckles up to his mouth, his lips skimming over the top. "You intrigue me, Delilah."

"Thank you, my Lord," she whispered.

"I appreciate how your mind works. He won't know about this meeting or if you even survived. You help me discover the secrets of the Mar of Sin, and you can have the girl when I'm finished with her. There can be no hint of our plans. Surprise is the only way we'll win. But if you deceive me…" He turned her hand over and bit the end of her palm. Delilah gasped as her dark blood spurted between his teeth. 'Well, you'll wish I'd fed you to my serpent." He licked the blood from her palm. She watched his tongue circle over his lips, gathering in the last of her blood.

Lucifer, devil, Satan, doer of all things evil stood before her. Yet here she was, compelled by his dangerous darkness. Her head spun from the tightrope she was walking. She craved him and yearned for his corrupt power.

And she liked it.

Still holding her hand, Lucifer stepped aside, revealing Zar only a few feet away.

Zar. I'd forgotten about you.

"Thank you for bringing Delilah to me. I'll not forget your loyalty. You, too, will have a place in this, if you can keep silent."

Zar bowed his head, keeping his hooded eyes on the floor. "I serve only you, my Lord."

Lucifer turned away, dismissing him, but she glanced back over her shoulder. Zar's eyes flashed up at her, simmering in resentment. She shrugged, pretending she was helpless. Her wide eyes pleaded for his understanding. She still needed him, if nothing else, for him to keep his mouth shut.

Lucifer led her behind the dragon throne. She glimpsed a door before his broad back blocked it and what lay beyond. Delilah's body hummed under the satin robe. She was exactly where she wanted to be and would do whatever it took to stay there...

One step ahead of evil.

CHAPTER THIRTY-SEVEN
ZAR

I t had been a week since Zar watched Delilah walk away with Lucifer, but it felt like an eternity. He paced in front of the window facing the Wrath Realm. Massive fires of vibrant reds lit up the jagged cliffs. Lessors dropped black orbs into the boiling bright red pools, creating new damned for the Wrath Lord, Berith. Their screams of outrage matched his dark mood, pushing his enraged system toward a breaking point.

Delilah had walked out with Lucifer, pretending she was a victim.

Please.

The only victims were those left in her wake.

And those that loved her.

Zar couldn't stand his room any longer. This festering obsession drove him toward the door. Was Delilah in the Throne Room with him plotting and planning... or worse, still wrapped around Lucifer?

Zar played the scene over and over in his mind. Delilah vs. Lucifer. She played Lucifer like a violin with her beauty, her tears, and her seduction.

And Lucifer never saw it coming.

But was she playing Zar too?

Zar wanted to trust Delilah, believe he was a part of her end game.

Watching her leave with Lucifer left him full of doubts. She played coy, but Zar had seen the triumph in her eyes. Was that how she looked after their meetings in the park?

He punched the wall next to the door, releasing a frustrated growl. Mortar crumbled, clicking on the stone floor. He stared at the gaping hole left by his angry fist.

That felt good.

Zar needed an outlet... maybe go back to a hospital or high school and drum up some action, or battle a Lessor in the Main Hall pit. Killing something sounded satisfying. He yanked open the door—

"Zar." He froze. A familiar voice called from behind him, raising the hair on his neck.

"Close the door." Zar shut it and faced his unplanned visitor.

"Why are you here, my Prince? Have I offended you?" Zar braced himself for an attack he'd never win.

"No. On the contrary. You've pleased me. You and I seem to think alike these days."

Zar cocked his head and relaxed his fists. "I haven't said—"

"Ah. I've been keeping my eye on you since you brought that Fallen trash here."

Zar opened his mouth, but a whip lashed around his neck, lodging the words in his throat.

"Think twice before you defend her. Your feelings for her might get you killed. That would be a shame, since she doesn't share them." Harsh laughter filled the room, a sneer covering the Prince's face. "Where do you think she's been? They haven't left his residence. You can fill in the blanks. She's playing you for a fool, as is Lucifer."

Zar's blood pumped, matching his rising humiliation. The whip fell away, leaving the sound of Zar's raspy breathing.

"But I'll not play you. We can help each other." The Prince moved closer, dominating his small room. Zar braced himself, the sting of the whip still fresh around his neck. The Prince leaned over, his flat eyes full of malice.

"You help me get this... this guardian girl, and I will serve Delilah on a platter for you to do with whatever you please."

The Prince circled Zar. Visions of Delilah whimpering for mercy at his hand spread a vindictive smile across Zar's hard face. His eyes flickered up to the Prince.

Is this a trap or the lifeline I needed?

"How did you know about the girl?" Zar whispered into the charged air.

"Many serve Lucifer in his chambers. They tell me Lucifer and his new whore haven't left his bed. His excitement loosened his lips, made him careless as he plots with his new lover. Ears faithful to me shared their whispered secrets." The Prince's maniacal laughter bounded off the walls. "For my favor, of course."

Damn her! I knew it!

The Prince's depravity fanned Zar's need to destroy the source of his shame and erase his despicable love.

Love is for the weak. She blinded me... used me....

"We don't need Lucifer. He's weak and an imbecile. Now is the time to strike before this... guardian girl... gets stronger and while Lucifer is distracted with his new toy. This girl will spill her secrets when my whip lashes across her fragile human flesh. You and I can then give her a little taste of how we entertain ourselves. She won't last a day, and Lucifer will never know what happened to his precious secret. Then we'll strike and kill Lucifer, wipe out Heaven, and rule Hell for ourselves. Take a few of your trusted Fallen. Be quick and bring the girl to me."

Zar's body vibrated with a vicious need. Delilah dying slowly and painfully at his hands.

"Yes, my Prince." Zar bowed low. "I'll not fail you."

But the Prince was already gone, leaving a trail of swirling smoke.

Zar walked back and stared out the window reflecting his ravaged emotions. This dangerous alliance gave him a new sense of purpose, a path to reclaiming his self-respect. He'd allowed those ancient buried memories to surface from a distant time and place, distracting him from who he'd chosen to be. A Fallen. Killer of humans and usher of their decrepit souls to Hell. He drove his feeble emotion for her deep into a fiery pit until it was nothing but fuel for his hate.

Capturing the girl for the Prince would be easy. She'd spill her secrets like the child she was under his torture. Zar's plan grew more significant and more satisfying, stimulated by the Wrath Realm's malevolent red flames and boiling pool.

It could work.

Zar built his devious plan brick by brick, knowing powerful and deadly eyes were upon him. But they only saw what they wanted to see. His vision—his mantra—was sharpened by the insidious path of being played the fool.

Never trust.

Never hope.

Never love.... Never again.

CHAPTER THIRTY-EIGHT
OLIVIA

Thank God it's Friday!

Olivia slammed her locker shut and laid her scorching forehead against the cold metal. She wasn't sick. Her body had burned with a new level of energy ever since Melchior inserted the orb into her mark. She was growing stronger and more in tune with her surroundings, like tapping into a humming energy force around her. Unfortunately, her preoccupation with the ceremony and her mom were a distraction from school since they'd returned a week ago.

"Hey," Zach whispered. He leaned down and gave her temple a quick peck. He tucked a strand of hair behind her ear. A tingle remained where his fingers had brushed. "Let's get out of here."

Olivia beamed back at him. She wrapped her arms around his waist, placing her ear against his chest. The steady beat of his heart calmed her as she stole some of his steadiness. His handsome face made her heart do a little flip, but it was his gentle understanding and quiet strength that attracted her the most. Zach had been her rock since they'd been back and popped up when she needed him the most... like now. She and Sergio talked every day, but he was more elusive and reluctant than Zach.

"Okay. I need to eat before I go to work." Olivia laughed as she pulled away. "I'm starving!"

Zach entwined his fingers with hers, leading her down the crowded hallway. "Me too. How about a big sub sandwich?" She nodded, and her stomach growled in agreement.

The brisk January air hit Olivia as Zach swung open the door. Dark clouds gathered overhead, signaling a much-needed rain shower for the desert. She sighed in pleasure as the gusty wind lifted her hair, sending a delicious cool shiver across her neck. Zach grinned at her. She hip-checked him.

"Stop! I feel like I'm a thousand degrees!"

"Mom said that's perfectly normal and that our bodies will level out soon."

Olivia jumped into the truck, inhaling the pine scent coming from the cardboard tree. She tugged on her earlobe, running a nervous finger over her dragonfly earring. She darted a quick glance over at Zach.

"What else has she told you?" Olivia wasn't sure he had heard her when he didn't answer.

Zach's hand paused near the ignition. He reached over and turned her chin toward him. He searched her carefully-guarded face.

"You still haven't talked to your dad about this, have you? You said you were going–"

"We've been busy with Mom, and it's just too complicated." She ran her hands down her thighs, turning away. "I can tell he's waiting for me to start the conversation. I guess I'm glad he's not pushing me. But every time I think about approaching him, I just lock up." She shook her head, annoyed with herself. "I'm such a coward, I know. He can answer so many questions. I think a part of me doesn't want to hear what Dad did all those years without us, even if it was fighting demons... which is cool... I guess." She turned back to him. "I lay awake in bed and think this is all a dream. That this can't really be our new life. My mark hasn't hurt since camping... maybe this will go–"

He placed a long finger over her lips. "I've done that too, but it's not a dream. We will train soon with the Magi." A wide smile spread across his face, showing off his dimple. "It sounds wild, but Mom said the time she spent with the Magi were some of the best and toughest times of her life. She understands the dangers out there for us, but learning from the Magi how to harness our angelic powers is the only way we can protect ourselves and the Mar of Sin. She said the archangels take over the responsibility for protecting it for now while they teach us how to use different weapons and the fighting skills to kill demons."

He stopped and took her hand into his. "Liv–"

"Don't stop. Tell me more... please."

He rubbed his thumb over her knuckle, and she sensed his hesitation.

"Just one more thing." She tugged on his hand.

"Okay." Excitement shone in his eyes. "Mom said there's this huge circular room that has every kind of weapon imaginable in different shapes, colors, and sizes. She said we'll learn how to use them all, but the archangels give each of us one special weapon made for us alone. It's enhanced by a power unique in each of us."

"What was your mom's power?" Olivia leaned forward, eager for the answer.

"Mom could..." Zach stopped. He pulled his hand from hers and started the truck.

"She could what?" She nudged his shoulder.

"Let's go eat. Besides, you need to get to work."

Olivia huffed, crossing her arms. He was forcing her hand to talk to her dad by whetting her appetite with stories of powers and weapons.

"I asked Sergio to meet at the coffee shop at closing. It's time we compared notes on what our parents are telling us and pool our knowledge." He glanced at Olivia.

"I like that idea. Maybe he'll open up more tonight. This has been hardest on him to accept," she said.

Zach's face turned serious, gripping the steering wheel. "We'll go to school during the day and train at night. Mom said we have to keep our lives as close to normal as possible. Schools are prime hunting grounds for demons. They look for kids coming and going when they shouldn't be and follow them. Hopefully, we won't get noticed until we are better prepared—"

"Fine, I'll talk to him." She paused, taking in his handsome profile. She'd made promises she was long overdue in keeping. "I promise."

"Good! I'm holding you to that. Try not to think about the father-daughter stuff. Keep it simple and go from there. You've got this." He flashed a bright smile and pulled out of the parking spot.

"Thanks." Her stomach knotted thinking about talking with Dad. Zach was right about keeping her baggage out of it. It was past time to face him. She'd do this for herself, for her friends, for their survival.

But she didn't get the chance...

CHAPTER THIRTY-NINE
SERGIO

S ergio didn't know how long he'd been staring at the same blurry words in the textbook. He sat up straighter against the headboard, trying to get more comfortable, but it didn't matter. He didn't care about chemistry or anything else about school. It wasn't important compared to his newfound destiny. He slammed the book shut and tossed it next to him on the bed.

He glanced up at the mirror over his dresser. His eyes roamed over his dark hair, his golden rimmed-brown eyes, and the cleft in his chin. He appeared different, but the change was inside of him. His body hummed with a new dynamic power, like an electrical current ran through him. It excited yet unnerved him. He leaned his head back against the headboard, drifting back to the ceremony.

The flames danced as tall as he was in the fire ring, Gabriel's golden eyes flashing as he shoved the brilliant golden orb into his mark. Sergio's father held him tight as it overtook his body and mind— becoming one. The beauty and the horrors of mankind, their cries filling his ears, the promises he, Olivia and Zach had made to each other while holding each other tight, his promise—

A knock on his door jerked him out of his memory.

"Mano." Manny peeked through the crack in the door before

opening it when Sergio waved him in. Manny was dressed in his standard attire of black, except for the plain white t-shirt hugging his chest. Manny always looked dangerous, but his eyes were softer when he looked at Sergio. Sergio didn't understand why his brother wasn't chosen as the guardian. He certainly looked the part.

Since they'd been home from camping, Manny had been around more than usual. His quick, clever eyes were always scanning, his body on high alert like he knew something had changed. Sergio wanted to share what happened with him, but Dad said not until training began. Sergio wasn't sure he could wait that long.

Manny closed the door behind him. His chin jerked toward the textbook on Sergio's bed. "Am I interrupting you?"

"Nah. Was just taking a break." Sergio got off his bed, putting his hands in his jean pockets. "I'm meeting Zach and Olivia at the coffee shop. Can you give me a ride?"

"Sure. Are you ready?"

"Yeah." Sergio shrugged on his jacket and followed Manny out of his room. Sergio peeked inside Lucia's room.

"Bye, Abuela... Lucia." He waved as Abuela blew him a quick kiss. Lucia smiled up at him, peeking from under the bedcovers.

"Sweet dreams," Manny called.

Abuela tapped the colorful cover of the book Lucia held in her hand. Lucia's face glowed as she looked at it. Lucia was a voracious reader, escaping into magical worlds where girls discovered hidden powers, fought for their survival, and fell in love with a handsome boy. Sergio smiled as he remembered many times giving her grief about her reading choices. Not anymore.

Have I got a tale for you....

A twinge of guilt hit Sergio. He promised himself to make more time for his twin. Sergio needed his familia's love more than ever even if they didn't understand why.

Dad waited in the entryway. A frown creased his brow as they approached him. Pride spiked through Sergio. His mind still reeled at the hair-raising stories his dad told him about encounters with the Fallen. This quiet, unassuming man was an unselfish brave warrior devoted to his family and the cause he chose to fight. Sergio prayed he would be half the man and warrior his father was.

"Where are you going?" Dad's eyes traveled over each of their faces, searching for clues.

"I'm meeting Zach and Olivia at the coffee shop. Manny's giving me a ride." A current of tension emanated from Manny. Sergio gave him a sidelong glance. Did Sergio miss a fight between them?

"I got him, Papa." Manny shoved Sergio lightly in the arm. "Besides, how much trouble can they get into at a coffee shop?" Sergio shoved back, but Manny snaked his arm around Sergio's neck, pulling him to eye level.

"¿Si?"

"Si." Sergio smirked, hiding the small spike of energy making him feel like, for the first time, he equaled Manny's muscle.

Manny released him and gave him a thump on the chest. Manny's mischievous smile flashed before he opened the front door.

"Zach's giving me a ride home."

Dad pulled Sergio into a quick back-slapping hug. "Sounds good." But Dad leaned in and whispered in his ear, "Stay alert."

Sergio nodded, acutely aware of the seven dots that could flare at any moment. "Night, Papa."

Sergio started down the dark walkway as Manny's car engine roared to life. A rain shower had come through, washing away the desert dust and leaving the air with a fresh rain scent. Sergio glanced up at the clouds that were hiding the moon before jumping into the car.

"Night," Dad called from the doorway.

Sergio looked over his shoulder as the car rumbled around the corner. Dad's back-lit silhouette was still there as they turned out of sight.

A tension ebbed in the car as they made their way to the coffee shop. Sergio shifted in his seat as Manny kept stealing quick glances his way. Sergio turned away and gazed out into night, wondering if something lay in wait for him.

"What's up with Dad?" Manny asked. "He's even more protective than normal." Sergio shrugged, hoping his brother might take the hint.

"And you? Ever since that camping trip, you've been distant from me." He nudged Sergio's shoulder. "Hey, I'm talking to you." Manny's irritation was palpable, as was the fact that he wouldn't let Sergio off the hook.

Sergio closed his eyes, surrendering to his brother's insistence. He gathered himself and faced him, knowing that telling Manny would change their relationship forever. Sergio had never comprehended, until this moment, how vital it was for him to have Manny's support and approval. He couldn't be a guardian without it.

"I learned something about Dad and our family when we went camping last week." Sergio swallowed, but his mouth had gone dry.

Manny glanced at him. The dim dashboard lights cast shadows over Manny's face, giving him an even more forbidding look. The moonless night left little to see except the road flying by in the car's headlights.

"And?" Manny's brow lifted. "What is it? Spit it out."

Here we go...

Sergio exhaled his pent-up breath. "Our family in the past... and Dad... and now me... were, I mean, are, guardians of the chasm from Lucifer's Fall from Heaven... and... are demon killers."

The car remained quiet except for Sergio's excited breathing. He braced himself for Manny's explosive response, but it never came. Manny made the sharp turn into the coffee shop's parking lot. Sergio's heart sank as he pressed his lips together, realizing Manny's silence was a far worse fate.

Manny parked his car and shut off the lights. The parking lot was empty except for Zach's truck parked next to them. Sergio looked through the front windows. Olivia was wiping the counters while Zach played one of the vintage video games. Manny turned, giving Sergio his full attention.

"I need you to tell me everything." He thumped his finger into Sergio's chest. "Don't mess with me... I'm in no mood for it."

"I... I will." Sergio stared at his friends through the windshield as he recalled the events. It helped him to remember he wasn't alone in this twist of fate. They were on the same dizzying road, leading them on a journey bound with an overwhelming burden. But Sergio needed Manny at his side too.

Sergio explained the night with vivid detail. The story of the Magi, the archangels, the golden orb. It flowed from him as Manny remained silent, never interrupting, but his increased body tension spoke volumes.

When he finished, Sergio pulled his shirt down and showed Manny Orion. Manny's hand reached over, grazing his fingertips across the mark. He jerked away like it had shocked him. His eyes narrowed at Sergio, and then he pushed himself back into his seat, slamming his hands on the steering wheel. A string of muffled Spanish broke free from Manny, but Sergio missed most of it. He'd seen Manny's temper many times, sometimes aimed at him. But he'd not seen this face before. Mixed with his anger was a shadow of fear.

"I talk with Zach and Olivia every day. We promised to guard and fight for each other, not just the Mar of Sin and demons. But–" Sergio's voice dropped. "I feel this huge pressure on me. I'm so afraid I'll screw it up and let the family down or get killed–"

Manny reached out and hooked with his arm around Sergio's neck, dragging him close.

"You. Are. Not. Going. To. Die." Manny gave his neck a hard squeeze. "I won't allow it. I'll help you any way I can. You aren't alone."

Manny released him and sat back. "I'm going home to talk to Dad. Promise me you won't do anything stupid, mano. Stay with your friends and never be alone. Promise?"

"Promise." Sergio swallowed past the lump in his throat. "Thank you, Manny, for..." He shrugged. "Believing me. I love you," he whispered.

Manny smirked and hit him in the arm hard enough for Sergio to take that it hurt. Manny snickered until Sergio opened the door.

"Hey," Manny said. Sergio looked back at him. "I love you, too."

Sergio shut the door behind him, telling himself it was the cold air ausing his eyes to water. But he knew it was a lie. Sergio rubbed his eyes, then shoved his hands into his jacket pockets. A huge weight had lifted off his shoulders, telling Manny the truth. Sergio wished he was more like his big brother. Brave, strong, and fearless. Maybe one day, Manny would even be proud of him.

If he didn't mess up first.

CHAPTER FORTY
DARK PRINCE

Blood pounded in the Prince's head, beating like a war drum in sync with the whip cracking the stagnant air. Sinister satisfaction ruled with every slash and scream erupting from the damned, chosen for no other reason than that his new body, raging with unbound malevolence, needed release.

We must get the girl first.... It could ruin everything if Lucifer controls her.

The whip cracked again, this from his other hand, slashing across the damned's ravaged back. Black blood flew at the Prince, painting his heaving chest, feeding his frenzy.

You're the only one worthy to rule. Not Lucifer and his red-headed whore.

The body in front of him blurred as his blows landed on a different back. The back of who he wished bled before him. He sneered, driven by the voice from the ancient, deviant soul from the nun. It spoke often. Sometimes whispers in the night, other times fervent yells of war and blood.

Oh, the tantalizing secrets we must have.... We need.... We cannot let anyone else have the girl.

Demanding.

Constant.

Unrelenting.

Bursting his evil core wide open.

Until he didn't know where the fiendish voice ended and his began.

And he no longer cared.

The soul and his meddled into one, creating an invincible power destined to rule over all.

The Prince landed the last vicious blow. His victim no longer cried out, hanging from the metal chains. His ragged breathing subsided, disappointed that Lucifer's fading back no longer received his wrath.

"Lucifer will one day hang from my chains, helpless at my hands," the Prince growled.

Yes... and he will finally see you for what you are... who we have become.

"And who's that?" the Prince demanded, aching for the answers to his darkest questions, his deepest desires.

You're the future King of Heaven and Hell, Annihilator of Man, Ruler of the Fallen, created from Lucifer's long forgotten nemesis, who was freed from the bondage of humanity and made one with you, a most powerful prince creating an evil even Lucifer will fear until his death.

The Prince closed his eyes, relishing the moment so tantalizingly close. His Fallen form trembled, holding back the evil incarnate consuming his body.

Soon you'll be free.

Zar needed to deliver the girl. It stretched the Prince's patience too tight for any more delay. He pulled out his dagger and thrust it into the heart of the mutilated damned. He pulled it out, wiping the bloodied blade across his tongue. He hissed, returning the dagger to its sheath.

The girl will meet the same death... after she spills her secrets to me while hanging from my chains.

CHAPTER FORTY-ONE
OLIVIA

O livia scrubbed the stainless-steel countertops, contemplating the upcoming conversation with her dad. Every scenario only brought anxiety and angst, each having no good beginning, with horrible endings leading to the inevitable argument about why he left. She wasn't looking forward to it, but she'd do it.

"Those counters make you mad?" Zach asked.

She yelped. "Jeez, Zach! Go sneak up on someone else!" Zack snickered and ducked when she threw the towel at him. He picked it up and tossed it back at her. She cast her eyes to the ceiling when he bent over the counter and grabbed her hands. He pulled her up against the countertop. He scanned her face while his thumbs rubbed back and forth over the top of her hands. A little thrill shot through her, but she kept her squeal of delight to herself.

"What's going on inside that beautiful head of yours?"

He sure knows how to get a girl to spill her guts.

"I'm thinking about my dad and how to talk to him without wanting to slap him again... which I still can't believe I did." She blushed and pulled away, taking out her frustrations out on the counter again. "I don't want to fight anymore, but I think that's where it's headed." Olivia paused. "And I don't want to upset my mom. She's doing so good. Every time she sees Dad, I swear, she melts when she looks at him." She threw the towel down. "I just don't get it! How can she forget how he abandoned us? Well, I guess he only left me. His audacity to waltz back into our lives and pick up right where he left off irritates me! And worse, my parents expect me to just forgive him because he's a demon killer. It's not that easy. I'm not wired that way." She slumped against the counter, rubbing her hands down her face. She glanced at Zach. "I don't even know where to find that kind of forgiveness."

"It'll take time, so give yourself a break. Your mom knows more than she's telling you, as does your dad. Your talk with him may turn ugly, but it has to begin somewhere."

"I know.... You're right. Wow, I'm sick of me." She smiled, shaking her head. "I have a few more things to do. Sergio should be here any minute, but you've got time for another game." She put a token on the counter. He snatched it up, grinning from ear to ear.

"I'm gonna get that frog across the street yet!" Zach skirted around the wooden tables to the Frogger console. Olivia laughed as she put away the cleaning supplies. He had a way of settling her emotions without patronizing her. Her stomach fluttered, aware Zach had peeled away another layer.

But that's good, right?

The front door jingled. Sergio walked in with a big smile, but something deeper glowed.

"Hey." Olivia gave him a hard once-over. She came around the coffee counter, pointing to a table. "Something's up. Spill the beans."

Sergio plopped himself down in a blue wooden chair. He glanced over at Zach, who was banging the console buttons and muttering in frustration.

"I just told Manny everything." Sergio's knee bounced as he looked at her.

"And...?"

Unshed tears enhanced the gold flecks in his brown eyes. "He was awesome. No yelling or threatening to lock me away. I'm still in shock." Sergio smiled. Zach joined them and held out his hand. Sergio accepted the handshake without hesitation.

"Well... that's surprising. What did he say?" Olivia asked.

"That he believed me and was going home to talk with Dad. He didn't say it, but I can tell he's worried and even a little afraid for me... us." Sergio paused. "He said he loved me, for us to stick together, and that he'd watch out for me." Sergio's voice broke, but a smile emerged.

"I wish I had a brother like yours watching out for me." Zach shoved Sergio's shoulder. "He's a bad dude!"

Sergio smirked, shoving him back. "That would be a full-time job, Boy Scout." They laughed until Joe called out from the hallway.

"Let's call it a night." Joe jingled his keys. The chairs scraped against the floor as they got up.

"I think he's got a hot date," Olivia whispered. The boys snickered, pushing their chairs under the table.

"I heard that!" Joe called back. "And that's none of your business." But a blush crept up his neck as he tried holding back his smile. He locked the front door, and Olivia shut off the lights as they headed for the back.

Zach pushed the door open. The sporadic street lights cast the back lot in shadows over her car and Joe's truck. Olivia scanned the lot again, nestling deeper into her jacket. She saw nothing, but that didn't stop her radar from pinging.

Joe hesitated after a few steps. "Where are you guys off too?"

"Gonna grab a pizza," Zach called back. Olivia's stomach rumbled at the thought of a hot, cheesy pizza.

"All right... See you tomorrow." He waved, jogging to his truck.

Sergio nudged Olivia "He *is* in a hurry." They laughed as Joe's tail-lights rounded the corner of the building in record time.

"I think it's great. He's finally loosened up and is an awesome guy. He and Callie were so supportive with Mom, too. I'm lucky. Other places might have fired me with the time I missed. But not Joe."

They headed toward Olivia's car, but Zach stopped short in front of her. "What–"

A sharp twinge hit her chest.

Orion.

Adrenaline shot through Olivia as her eyes scoured the dark parking lot, searching for the source.

Where's the Fallen?

"I can't see it!" Olivia yelled.

"Get to your car–" Zach called. "Come on!"

"Look!" Sergio pointed at the left of the building. A red webbing emerged, illuminating the wall. A sizzling sound cut the air. They turned as two more portals opened: a green web in front of them and an orange web on the right. Two figures emerged from each, blasting them with heat. A lone figure walked out of the web in front of them.

With the building behind them, the five Fallen strutted closer, creating a semicircle around them. Dangerous sets of horns erupted from each of their heads, but it was their striking eye color matching deadly weapons that turned Olivia's blood cold. Menacingly clad in sleek black armor they approached, their huge black wings fanned out, enclosing them in a feathery cage.

Trapped.

Olivia knew they were no match for these demons as she stared at the Fallen facing her with shock-white long hair and neon green eyes. One demon had red eyes with two red-handled battle axes clutched in each of his powerful hands. Another glared at them with gold eyes, holding a long sword swirling with molten gold. The other two demons were female Fallen. One had hot pink eyes with matching short hair, holding a bow with an arrow aimed at Zach. The last Fallen had bright orange eyes with long black hair streaked in fiery orange. Her blazing whip cracked through the air, landing inches from Sergio's feet. He jumped back, pulling Olivia with him. The Fallen broke out in wicked laughter, revealing gaping black holes with sharp teeth. They took another step forward. The red demon snarled swinging his axes at his side.

Olivia shivered at their palpable bloodthirst. The Fallen had found them helpless. Their confidence clear in their lack of urgency while they toyed with the trio. Olivia's heart sank as she realized no one would think them missing until it was too late.

"Olivia." She gasped at the sound of her name. The white-haired Fallen held out his green-veined hand, his long fingers curled toward her.

"Come with me now, and your friends won't be harmed. Fight me and they die, and you'll still be coming with me."

Olivia's pulse pounded as she glanced over her shoulder for the coffee shop door.

Maybe they could get—

"Looking for an escape? I don't think so. Besides, no one can see you. We move among this world unseen if we choose, and so are those who we bring inside our"—he waved his hand around him—"dimension. Man will walk around it, clueless. You know that cold shiver you get for no reason, or how you turn one way when you meant to go the other way? That's us." He cackled, taking a step closer. "But we wanted you to get a good look at us. So we are invisible to the outside world, but visible and very much alive here."

The orange whip snapped at Olivia's feet. "You heard him. Let's go, or I'll drag you over by my whip around your neck."

Olivia's body trembled at the reality that leaving with this Fallen was her only choice to get Zach and Sergio out alive. She took a step forward, but Zach yanked her back.

"You'll never let us go alive! We won't let you take her back to your hellhole." Zach put himself in front of her, while Sergio guarded her from behind.

Hideous laughter mocked them. Zach was right, they'd kill them. A deep anger rose, but her decision was unchanged.

"That's a brave but ludicrous thing to say in front of... what... your girlfriend?" asked the pink-eyed Fallen. She nudged her bow, the arrow still pointed at Zach. "Zar, I want to take him back with me and teach him a few lessons." She licked her lips like she had already tasted him.

Zach's eyes narrowed as he stood his ground. "I'll never—"

"Come now, Kalma. We're not here to find you a new plaything. We're here for the girl." Zar said it like they were picking Olivia up from school.

"How do you know her name?" Sergio called, his hands gripping her upper arms.

"That's none of your concern," Zar sneered. "Let's not waste any more time, shall we?" Zar's voice was laced with his feral threat. Green-spiked fingers beckoned Olivia again. If she touched them, he'd never release her, but she had no choice. She had to save Zach and Sergio. She risked her life going with the Fallen, and they'd do the same for her.

They could run to the door if I distract them....

"I'll come, but promise you won't hurt them." Olivia pushed herself away from the boys. Ruthless laughter drowned out their startled cries. Zar snatched her hand with lightning speed, clamping down and yanking her toward him. She gasped, slamming against his armored body. His long fingers entwined around her ponytail. He pulled down, forcing her to look up at him.

Fear like she'd never known clawed up her spine as she looked into his evil green eyes. She knew in that moment she'd die a terrible death at his hands.

"I won't hurt them. I'll kill them," Zar sneered. "No witnesses..." His evil intent hung in the air, sickening Olivia.

"No!" Olivia howled, struggling against him.

Bright lights swung around the end of the building. For a precious moment, the whole group stood still. All heads turned as the car's high-beam headlights lit up the lot. Olivia, blinded, heard the car gun its engine. Tires squealed. The car sped, aiming at them. She shoved against Zar, but he grabbed her around the waist, leaping into the air, missing the speeding car. The car hit the orange and hot-pink Fallen sending them over the hood, flying into the air and landing in a heap behind the car.

"Manny!" Sergio yelled.

Manny slammed on the brakes, blocking the boys from the other demons with his car.

"Run!" Olivia screamed.

"Get in!" Manny yelled as he jumped out, putting himself between the Fallen and the boys.

"How did–" Sergio cried.

"I was watching you, and then you just disappeared." Manny lunged for Sergio. "Move it!"

Time became jumbled, distorted as it moved in slow motion. Zar trapped Olivia against him, caught in the horror of watching her friends and helpless in their escape. She screamed in fury, fighting harder to find her newly embedded powers to harness.

"Kill them!" Zar screeched as he backed away. A sizzling sound emerged from behind her. She didn't have much time left. She had to do something... fast.

"You'll watch them die, Olivia, and then we'll be gone forever." His excited breathing was hot against her hair, nauseating her.

Michael... Help us.... Michael!

The deafening roar in her ears drowned out her friends' cries, leaving her with only their panicked faces and the wordless movements of their mouths. Olivia's eyes widened as the gold Fallen jumped over the hood, landing in front of Manny. Sergio reached for Manny, but Zach grabbed his arm and pulled him toward the open car door. Sergio strained against him, his face stricken with fear.

The gold demon raised his sword high. Metal glinted in Manny's hand before he plunged it into the Fallen's chest. The Fallen threw his head back in a macabre scream before bursting into oil and ash. For a split second, everything dripped oil as ash fell. The stench of sulfur assaulted Olivia before the oil and ash disappeared like being sucked into a vacuum.

A snarl erupted in her ears. Zar pulled a silver dagger with a green hilt from his belt, and for a moment, Olivia thought he'd plunge the wicked blade into her heart. The evil emanating from him was crushing. Zar laid the sharp edge against her neck. Olivia panted as he pressed it against her flesh.

"Zar!" The red Fallen pointed his axe at the opposite side of the lot. An electric blue light appeared. Manny and the boys paused for a split second, distracted by the light. But the red Fallen took advantage of their hesitation. He ran around the car and charged behind Manny with his axe raised high. He swung the axe, and red flames erupted off its head before he buried it in Manny's back. Manny's body arched at the force of the blow. Blood exploded from his wound, red spreading across his white t-shirt. Shock and pain were carved on Manny's face as he dropped to his knees. He fell face-forward with a sickening thud, the axe's red flames extinguished by Manny's blood.

"Manny!" Olivia screamed.

"No!" Sergio's anguished cry pierced Olivia. He kneeled down next to his brother, wailing his name. Olivia sagged against Zar, hot tears of horror and defeat burning down her face.

He's dead because of me. I shouldn't have fought...

Olivia's eyes locked with Zach's. Pain-riddled, they looked at Sergio and Manny. Engulfed in sorrow, Sergio cradled his lifeless brother in his arms.

"Your turn." The red Fallen pointed at Zach, maliciously laughing as he raised his other flaming axe.

Zach took a step and shoved his hands in the air. Swirling green energy exploded from his palms, slamming against the Fallen's chest. The energy spread, crackling across his armor. The Fallen flew back across the asphalt, landing motionless on his back in a heap of green sparks.

Zach stared at his hands in disbelief, then back at the Fallen. His bewildered eyes flew back to Olivia. A thrill of hope ran through her. She didn't know how he had created the energy, but she wanted him to do it again.

The red Fallen rolled over, getting to his feet. He shook his head, trying to clear the cobwebs from the energy blow. An angry roar erupted as he threw his axe. It flew end over end, aimed for Zach. Before Zach could raise his hands, Sergio, his face streaked with tears, jumped in front of Zach. He stood before the oncoming ax, clothes and hands stained with his brother's blood, heedless of the axe's strike.

Nooooo.

Olivia wasn't sure if she or Zach yelled. All she knew was her best friend was about to die.

Sergio thrust out his hands like he wanted to catch the axe. But i stopped moving, suspended mid-air just a few feet from Sergio. Frozen in place, motion had stopped for each of them.

Kalma released a flurry of hot-pink arrows into the blue webbing, while the orange Fallen crept up from the back of the car. Her whip's orange current ran from handle to tip, slithering through the air encircling Zach's neck. His hands flew around the whip, his face turning red. Zach fell to his knees as she yanked him toward her. His eyes grew wider, clawing at his throat while his face deepened to purple. Her face glowed in evil delight as she pulled hard against the whip, choking him to death.

"Zach!" Olivia strained against Zar's arm, squeezing into her waist. She threw an elbow but hit unyielding armor. Panicked, she wrestled against him even as the knife threatened to cut her wide open.

"You're coming with me," Zar seethed, pulling Olivia toward his portal.

No, I'm not.

A new, buzzing emerged drowning out the surrounding chaos. A pull of powerful energy race through her body. Her senses were like a live wire, one with her surroundings. She felt Zar's hot blood pounding through him, the hate from the orange Fallen for Zach as she choked the life out of him, the engulfing rage radiating from Sergio. She was one with them, stealing their energy and combining it with hers. Olivia didn't understand how to control or stop it, but she didn't care. She let this unknown power take over and course through her body to whatever end would come.

Olivia focused on the axe still suspended in front of Sergio. She imagined it flying through the air, its red flames swirling as it landed in the middle of the orange Fallen's chest, buried in her heart. But it wasn't her imagination when Olivia heard the thud of the axe's impact, the orange Fallen writhing in pain, or the whip unwinding from around Zach's neck. The Fallen exploded in oil and ash and disappeared, taking her filthy grime with her. Zach gasped huge gulps of air, and his surprised face swiveled toward Olivia.

Olivia's chest heaved as the realization of her power unfolded. She hadn't imagined it; she had made it happen and saved her friend. Now she needed to save herself. She stared at Zar's hand, which was holding the knife to her neck. Focusing on it, she wrenched open his hand. Zar snarled as the knife flew from his grip, landing a few feet away. She shoved away, but he grabbed her ponytail and yanked toward him. She fell backward, losing her footing. Desperation drove her struggles even as Zar's grip threatened to rip the hair from her scalp.

Three white-winged angels emerged from the blue portal. They separated as they chased their targets. Their majestic, colored wings gave away who had arrived.

Michael, Raphael, and Gabriel.

Kalma continued shooting arrows at Raphael. He chased her as she flew toward Zar's web. The arrows bounced off his shield, falling to the ground.

The red Fallen also flew for the web. Michael tackled him mid-air, sending them to the ground. The force of the collision separated them. The red Fallen jumped to his feet and unsheathed a black sword, but not in time. Surprise was the final look on his face as Michael's flaming sword sliced across his neck. For a second, the head stayed in place, then wobbled backward off its perch. The demon exploded and disappeared before his head hit the ground.

Olivia had to do something quickly before Zar pulled her inside the portal that was leaching hot, stagnant air. Her body was tiring from using her powers, making it difficult to harness them. They couldn't slip away yet. She focused on the arrows, commanding them to fly toward the escaping Fallen. But only one moved. Its hot-pink tip sliced through the air, heading for her. She moved her head, but the arrow grazed her cheek before piercing Zar's right shoulder. His body jerked back, his hand releasing her hair.

"You little–" Zar yelled at Olivia.

His words were lost as she fell to the ground, panting, numb from the exertion, not even sure if she had the strength to get away if Zar grabbed her again. Her vision narrowed as she looked back at her attackers. Gone was their unbreakable evil; they now showed fear. No longer the predators, now the prey. She willed herself to crawl, to ge up. After all this, she wouldn't let them win. A hard hand snagged her ankle–

"Let her go.... We'll come back!" Kalma yelled as she landed. Zar hesitated, his eyes dark with pain and malice and fixed on Olivia's.

"We're not done," he spat, releasing her ankle.

Kalma pushed him through the portal, but his eyes never left Olivia's, washing her with his hate, disappearing into the dark hole. Kalma passed through the web behind him, her shock of pink hair swallowed up by the closing web that cauterized the cold night air.

Raphael launched his arm inside the closing portal but came out empty-handed. He shot out his fist where the web had been, growling in frustration. Raphael's face turned crestfallen as he absorbed the turmoil behind Olivia. "I'm going to Zach."

Olivia could only nod. Michael kneeled next to her, his hands gently combing over her body.

"Are you hurt?" Michael asked, inches from her.

"No," Olivia muttered.

But my heart is broken.

CHAPTER FORTY-TWO

Manny's Dead

Where once was light,
darkness consumed every pore....

CHAPTER FORTY-THREE

SERGIO

Sergio felt nothing, heard nothing, said nothing. His world was a black, numbing void.

Because of who was draped across his lap.

Manny.... Dead.

Manny's lifeless eyes stared back at him, face pale, mouth slack. The front of Manny's white t-shirt was covered with Sergio's bloody handprints, transferred when he'd grabbed Manny, pleaded with him, begged him not to die.

But he did.

Taken from Sergio by evil... by the Fallen... by Sergio's enemies.

My fault.

The air hung thick with the copper smell of Manny's blood, pooled around them in a dark oil slick. Sergio rubbed the heel of his palm against the pressure on his broken heart. A pain only a brother's love would fill. Only a brother's hug would ease.

The world stopped for Sergio when the Fallen's axe embedded into Manny's back. Life had ceased to matter. Sergio remembered nothing except the exploding pain rocketing through his body, as if he'd also been hit with the flaming axe. His eyes flickered to it, lying under Manny's car, where Sergio had tossed it after pulling it from Manny's back. Dried blood covered the head, the flames doused by Manny's blood. The red handle still glinted in the darkness, hypnotic in its evil. Its mission complete.

Sergio's eyes narrowed, flashes of the Fallen exploding when killed and their weapons disappearing with them.

Why was the axe still here?

Sergio's hand itched as it crept across the asphalt. His hand tightened around the handle, driven by a deep, morbid need to hold the vicious weapon that had killed his brother. His body shook as he brought it closer, Manny's face blurring underneath it.

The axe handle was red, inlaid with large scales. The head was shaped in a half moon, ending in sharp points. Three red claw-like prongs emerged from the handle clutching the head. It was lighter than it looked, but even more deadly close up. Evil vibrations flowed from the axe, snaking their way up Sergio's arm.

He closed his aching eyes. A vision exploded behind them. The axe raised high, the thud of steel splitting bone, blood splattering–

"Sergio!" Olivia's desperate cry broke through his haze. He quickly laid the axe under the car as she came around the hood. Tears fell down her pale face, mixing with an angry cut on her cheekbone. Olivia kneeled next to him, landing in Manny's blood. She pulled him into a hug.

"I'm so sorry," she mumbled as she rocked them back and forth. "This is all my fault."

Her words tore something open inside of him, flooding him like hot lava scorching a path inside, leaving behind a bitter wasteland. What was once quiet, once numb, once deaf, burst open with torturous pain. He shoved himself away from her suffocating grasp.

"This isn't your fault, Olivia! It's not always about you!" Eyes wide with hurt stared back at him, but he didn't care, reckless in his rage. "A Fallen killed him! Not you! Can't you see? It's God's fault!" Hot tears burned; his voice cracked. "We should have said *NO* to their impossible request. Then none of this would've happened. The Fallen wouldn't have come–"

"Sergio," a familiar voice called. Gabriel stood before him, hi golden wings and armor aglow in the dark night. Sergio glared at the face he didn't know well, who had promised to help him... protect him.

"We failed to get here in time to help you... and save your brother," Gabriel said. "I'll forever be sorry for this failure." An iridescent tear slipped from the corner of his eye. Sergio followed its trail down Gabriel's face until it slipped from his jaw, mixing with Manny's blood at his feet. "One day I pray you can forgive me."

Sergio seethed, his rage and pain driving him, blinding him to anyone's pain but his own.

"I will never forgive you... EVER!" Sergio's neck corded, his lip peeled back as his blood pounded in his head.

Gabriel's shoulders sagged against Sergio's condemnation. "Olivia, your dad is on his way to take you all home. Joe will come back here, thinking he'd forgotten to set the alarm. He'll find Manny and call the police. I will stay, unseen, with Manny. He'll not be left alone."

"I'm not going anywhere," Sergio said, lifting his chin.

A set of headlights came around the building. Sergio held Manny tighter. How could he let Manny go? What would he tell to his parents?

"We have to go–" Olivia whispered.

"Just leave me alone!" Sergio yelled at her.

Olivia nodded and stood. She walked into the truck's headlights. Her dad jumped out, hesitating, then scooped her up into his embrace. Olivia sagged against him, her back shaking. Her arms slowly rose and circled his waist. When Zach joined them, her dad laid an arm around his shoulder.

"I have to let you go, Manny." Sergio choked on his bitter words. 'But I promise you... I'll avenge you, big brother. I'll kill as many Fallen as I can in your name."

Sergio's eyes bore into Gabriel's back as Sergio's hand darted under the car to reclaim the axe. Sergio tore off his jacket and wrapped the axe inside. His hand then grabbed Manny's knife that lay next to his dead body. The demon's black blood had disappeared, leaving it clean. Sergio sneered as he snapped the blade closed. He slipped it in his pocket, liking the feel of it close to him.

Sergio kissed Manny's forehead, a harsh sob clawing in his throat. "I love you, Mano."

He eased Manny's head from his lap onto the blood-soaked asphalt. Sergio's heart shattered when he stood, cradling the wrapped axe to his chest with thoughts of hate and revenge consuming him. His eyes returned to Gabriel's back. A small malicious voice whispered:

This is his fault.... He deserves to die.

Gabriel glanced back at Sergio like he'd heard the silent death threat. Sergio returned with a weak smile, hoping to appease him. His smile turned slack when Gabriel turned back to Olivia's dad.

Sergio placed his hand on Manny's car door. Inside, lay Manny's leather jacket on the passenger seat. He opened the door and snatched the jacket. Sergio raised the jacket to his face, inhaling the soft leather entwined with Manny's musky scent. He put it on, placing his coat with the axe against his stomach, and zipped it up. A strong determination enveloped him as he wore Manny's jacket. He gave his brother one last look and made the first devastating step away from him. Sergio didn't glance back again, shutting out the pull to return to Manny and never let go.

Sergio put one foot in front of the other and walked away from his past. He shed the easy-going, naïve Sergio and embraced the hardened, bitter one burning at his core. But no one would know about his change, his motivation. He'd play their games, learn their rules, and master their weapons. All the while growing stronger to carry out his personal destiny.

A killer... an avenger.

Not for him.

Not for his family.

And certainly not for God.

For Manny, because that's what he would have done.

Avenge the ones you love at all costs.

CHAPTER FORTY-FOUR
ZACH

Zach shrugged off his suit jacket, tossing it onto his desk chair. He sat on his bed and ran his fingers through his hair. He sighed, trying to ease the tightness in his chest that hadn't let go since Manny died a few days ago. His head fell forward, still astonished by that horrible night's events. Zach dropped his hands between his knees, flipping them back and forth, looking for changes. But the changes he was searching for weren't on the outside.

The burst of power had come from within him.

Zach jumped up, jolted by a nervous energy crawling through him. He pushed his concerns aside. Sergio was the most important person to worry about, not himself. He stepped out of his dress shoes and pants, needing to get out of his "funeral" clothes. He hated them. The last time he'd wore them was for Cody's funeral. Another senseless death, another person he had tried to save but failed, another memory only half-buried.

Dark water, swirling rapids, blond hair...

He yanked opened his dresser drawer and grabbed his favorite jeans. Manny's funeral had left him spent and anxious. Watching Sergio's family was like a helpless dog getting brutally kicked repeatedly. He slammed his palms against the dresser, frustrated by the waste of both lives. A soft knock interrupted his internal turmoil.

"Zach, can I come in?" his mom asked.

"Yeah, hold on a second."

He pulled a shirt down over his head and opened his door. Mom's too-bright smile greeted him. She held out her hand for him just as she had done when they arrived at the church. She had kept his hand in hers throughout the service. It felt foolish at first, but Zach drew much-needed comfort from her. His eyes never left the front pew, where Sergio and his family grieved for Manny. Javier was stoic, comforting his wife, who sobbed silently on his shoulder. They clung to each other like lifeboats in a storm, trying not to drown in their overwhelming sorrow. Sergio's grandma had her arm resting on the pew around Sergio's shoulders while Lucia clutched her other hand. But Sergio didn't seem to notice. His head never turned away from the polished wood coffin alone on the altar.

"I made a late lunch. Come downstairs and eat, honey."

Zach followed her downstairs, knowing it wasn't a request.

Dad sat at the kitchen counter, dunking his hoagie roll into a small bowl of steaming brown broth. Zach wasn't hungry, but he loved French dips. Mom handed him a plate when he sat next to his dad.

"Thanks."

She smiled at him before she made herself a plate. Silence fell over the family, each wrapped up in their own thoughts, exhausted by today's events. Zach took another bite, the sandwich bland in his dry mouth.

"Olivia will be here soon. We're going over to Sergio's." He placed the half-eaten sandwich on the plate. His stomach knotted, knowing a talk with Sergio would be difficult.

"Olivia and I decided we need to start training right away after what happened." He swallowed the lump in his throat. "We aren't sure Sergio is ready or will even continue." He shoved away from the counter, too antsy to sit. He paced, catching his parents exchanging worried glances.

Zach faced them and slapped a hand against his chest. "I don't even know if I'm ready! Who am I? How can I protect anything or anyone?" His voiced cracked. "I couldn't save Cody, and I couldn't save Manny! I can't..." He shook his head, trying to hold back the tsunami of emotions. "I can't have another friend die." His head fell forward as his shoulders slumped. He looked down, his blurry sneakers against tile.

Arms encircled him, but they weren't the slim arms of his mom. Instead, Dad's broad chest and muscular arms gave Zach the shelter he needed to let go. His forehead fell against his Dad's shoulder. They exchanged no platitudes, just comfort and no judgment. Zach let the bitter tears flow, fisting his Dad's T-shirt. Zach didn't realize how much he had needed the release until it had passed. He took a shaky breath, rubbing the palms of his hands against his scratchy eyes. Dad stepped back but kept a firm grip on each of his shoulders.

"This is a terrible time for you, and it has dredged up memories that need to stay in the past. Cody's death was not your fault." His dad gave his shoulders a reassuring squeeze. "And you may not have been able to help Manny, but you saved Sergio."

"But—"

"Don't do that to yourself. There will always be self-doubt and recriminations after a tragedy happens. I've done it many times to myself after I lost a friend in war. But you"–he shook Zach again–"and this journey... destiny... will have no room for doubt or second-guessing. That will get you killed." His eyes held stern truth.

"What if I fail? There's so much at stake!"

Mom came forward and stepped between them. "I want to show you something." She pushed down the corner of her pants. There lay a jagged red scar above her hipbone.

"A sword."

She turned and lifted her shirt. Pink scars crisscrossed over her back.

"A whip."

She lifted her hair away from the side of her neck. A thin silver line curved behind her ear.

"A knife."

Then she pointed to the bump on the bridge of her nose.

"A punch."

"Most of the battle wounds I received, and that you'll receive, heal because of our angelic powers. But I kept these scars as a reminder to stay tough, stay humble, and stay focused. You need to keep these ideals first and frontmost in your mind."

Zach was stunned and respected her on a completely different level. Why had he never noticed these scars or appreciated her under-stated strength? He'd always saved that sentiment for his dad, the soldier, but before him stood his mom, the warrior.

"I will.... I promise," he whispered.

She cupped his face, demanding Zach look at her. "God isn't looking for you to fail. He's given you exactly what He knows you will need, even when things go bad, for you to be successful. Your self-doubt and worry will only distract you and get you hurt.

"We love you." Mom's face lit up with her dazzling smile. "We have complete confidence in you and will always be here to help you heal when you return." She pointed to his heart. "Your heart"–she tapped his forehead–"and your brain. Use them both wisely."

He grabbed her and engulfed her in a hug. She laughed and squeezed him back.

"Thank you." His eyes landed on each of his parents. "I... I guess I needed that wake-up call."

The doorbell rang, breaking the moment. "I love you." Zach waved goodbye. He walked to the door feeling lighter, with a newfound confidence, because of his parents' encouragement. He opened the door, and there stood Olivia, her long wavy hair framing her beautiful face, still raw from the funeral. Reaching over, he tucked her hair behind her ear, smiling at the four twinkling rhinestone studs running down her earlobe, ending with a silver dragonfly hanging from the bottom loop. Her body stilled at his touch.

"Hi, Liv," Zach said, liking how he'd caught her off guard.

"Hi yourself. You seem better?" Her eyes held questions he didn't want to answer right now.

"Much better now that I see you."

Olivia didn't resist when he brought her in for a hug. "You're s corny," she mumbled against his shirt. He chuckled but didn't let go. "I'm worried about Sergio. I hope he finds the path to peace now that the funeral is done." Olivia bit her lip, looking up at him.

"He will with our help. Let's go. We have lots to discuss with him. I hope he's ready."

CHAPTER FORTY-FIVE

OLIVIA

Q uiet murmuring, discreet sniffles, and a gurgling coffee maker greeted Olivia as she stepped into the Mendes entryway. The kitchen counters and table overflowed with food, their tantalizing aromas of spices she usually found mouthwatering. But not today. There was little solace in food for her or the visitors. The platters were left untouched under the shiny plastic wrap. She and Zach entered the living room hoping to find Sergio. Instead, Javier stepped forward with open arms. His strong embrace did little to hide the devastation stamped on the lines of his face.

"Thank you for coming to the funeral today." His voiced cracked. "And for coming here." His eyes darted down the hallway. "He stays in his room most of the time. We're giving him some space, but the look in his eyes worries me." He shrugged as he stepped away. "Go on back. I'm sure he'll be glad to see you." Olivia nodded, trying to hold the dam of tears threatening to overflow again.

"Hey, Zach. Thanks for what you did for Sergio." Javier's voice lowered as he held out his hand. "Your powers saved him."

Surprise crossed Zach's face as he returned the handshake. "You'r welcome." Zach cleared his throat. "I don't even know how I did it. was so mad and wanted to push the Fallen away, and then he wer flying backward." Olivia remembered the same sensations within her when she used her powers.

"In training, you'll hone your skills and rein in your powers. I hope you start soon... all of you," Javier said, his worried eyes lingering on Sergio's closed bedroom door.

"That's why we're here. We want to talk to Sergio about starting tomorrow, but only if he's ready," Olivia said, but she was determined to get Sergio on board.

"Good luck." A guest tapped Javier on the shoulder, and he turned away.

Olivia reached Sergio's door first. She knocked but got no reply.

"Hey, it's us." Olivia knocked harder.

His steps shuffled across the carpet before the door opened. Sergio turned back to his bed without so much as a hello. Olivia and Zach glanced at each other with raised eyebrows. Olivia walked over to Sergio while Zach stayed back, closing the door.

"Can I sit?" Olivia waved at the space next to him.

"Sure." Sergio's voice was hollow as he stared at the picture he held in his hand.

"Can I see it?" Olivia's request sounded loud in the quiet bedroom.

Sergio handed it over, not looking at her. It was a picture taken at Christmas. Sergio and Manny had their arms slung around each other's shoulders, laughing into the camera.

"That's a great picture of you two." She placed it between them, their beaming faces shining up from a different time.

Sergio nodded with a ragged sigh. "I can't believe he's gone."

Olivia startled when Sergio's normally kind eyes turned to her, holding such tormented rage. Dark shadows under his eyes spoke of sleepless nights; his face had a greenish tint under his brown skin. "I'm so sorry—"

Sergio threw up his hand between them. "Don't. It's not your fault." He glanced up at Zach. "Or yours."

Sergio jumped off the bed and paced with his hands clenched. "But I know whose fault it is." His eyes blazed with a darkness she'd never seen in him. "And I'm gonna kill every single one of them."

Olivia stole another glance at Zach's concerned face.

"Maybe you need more time–" Zach started.

"Don't tell me what I need, Boy Scout," Sergio said. "I know what I need. I need to start training. I can't just sit around here anymore." His body was rigid as he pointed at them. "We need to go to the Magi, learn whatever they'll teach us, and fight!"

Sergio picked up a book on his dresser and launched it at the wall. The book slammed against it, landing in a heap. He kicked over his book bag. He yanked out notebooks, tossing them like Frisbees, bombarding the same wall. Olivia moved toward Sergio, but Zach put his arm out, shaking his head.

Sergio's chest heaved after the last notebook landed with a thud on the floor. He ran his fingers through his hair and fisted the ends. Olivia closed the distance between them, sliding her arms around his waist. She leaned her head on his back, hearing his racing heartbeat. Everything was still, as if the house and its occupants had held their breath while Sergio released his fury.

"I miss him so much." Sergio's ragged whisper cut through her as his body sagged.

Olivia could only nod from behind, wishing she could do more to absorb his pain. She hadn't heard Zach slip in front of Sergio but saw his long fingers clasping his shoulder.

"I can't imagine your pain, but you're not alone in this. We're here and want to help you. We'll learn, train, and fight... together... do whatever it takes to get ready, so nothing like this happens again."

Olivia came around to face Sergio. "We want to start tomorrow. She took his hand. "Do you think you're ready? I mean, really ready to do this. We can hold off till–"

"No!" His intensity lit up. "I need to start now. It'll help me work out my feelings about Manny, and I can release this energy that has no place to go." He blew out a breath.

Olivia nodded. "All right.... You might talk to Balthazar or Gabriel–"

"No. I've got my family and you guys." His quick response

surprised her. "Sorry about the fit, but it kinda felt good." A smirk tugged at the corner of Sergio's mouth.

"It looked like it felt real good!" Zach slapped Sergio's shoulder.

"So, let's meet at my house after school tomorrow," Olivia said. "Dad said the Magi come to us the first time and take us through the portal to their training grounds."

"Awesome. Tomorrow it is," Zach said.

Olivia squeezed Sergio's hand, but he held on tight.

"Thanks, both of you, for coming here. I feel better now knowing we'll start training. I needed that." He released Olivia's hand, smiling. "I better clean up my mess and head to the living room before Abuela pounds on my door."

"Anytime." Zach opened the door, the corner of his lips lifted as he waited.

"See you tomorrow," Olivia said.

"Yeah, tomorrow," Sergio said, closing the door behind them.

The afternoon sun peeked through the gray clouds as Olivia and Zach slipped out the front door. But it only reached skin deep. With Sergio riding the edge of his emotions, combined with her own frayed nerves, uncertainty set in Olivia's bones. What tomorrow or the days following held brought a sense of excitement, but doubt wedged its way in too. Olivia pushed it away, lifting her face to the sunlight. She couldn't sabotage herself with negative thinking. She must focus on the light, not the dark trying to steal it from her.

Her life depended on it.

Sergio

Starting tomorrow....

Good.

Sergio picked up the picture of himself and Manny. He ran his thumb over Manny's smiling face, but his dead face replaced it. A raw ache throbbed in Sergio's chest as he moved to his dresser. He slid the picture between the panels of the dresser mirror's wooden frame, never wanting to forget how his brother had looked before they killed him.

His eyes flickered to the closet reflected in the mirror. He could visualize the axe, still wrapped inside his jacket, tucked inside an old backpack lying on the dark closet floor.

His hands ached to touch it, to caress the steel handle and skim his fingers over the sharp blade. He closed his eyes, imagining himself, body vibrating with excitement, raising the axe at his target.

Zar.

He hurled the flaming axe aimed at Zar's chest, but his face blurred into another. Someone who said he'd protect him.

Gabriel.

Sergio's eyes snap open, seeing himself in the mirror. Hard, golden-rimmed brown eyes looked back, the same as the angel in the vision.

He's the real reason Manny is dead.

Horror snaked up his spine, appalled he even considered such a horrendous thought. It was Zar's fault. He was the one who wanted them dead, not Gabriel.

But it whispered to him, tickled the dark recesses of his mind, which were still tormented by Manny's death. His eyes darted back to the closet. Shame pushed its way through his anger.

You cannot kill an archangel.

You'd be damned to Hell.

Shame your family and friends.

But...

I'd avenge Manny... keeping my promise to him.

He tumbled on the bed and curled up in a fetal position. Sweat broke out on his brow as his fractured emotions raged inside him, hurtling him over a cliff into a dark void of pain, anger and revenge.

CHAPTER FORTY-SIX
DELILAH

The Throne Room was steamy, ripe with uncoiled anticipation. Water lapped against the edge of the dark pool as the serpent skimmed the water. A chill tingled her feet as Delilah remembered its fins slicing her heels as Lucifer dangled her over the pool, wondering if the next time the serpent surfaced, she'd go down with it. But events had taken a different course... just as she had so deviously planned.

Delilah laid a possessive hand on Lucifer's knee. She stood next to him while he lounged on his dragon throne, but looks were deceiving. His evil power and granite hardness radiated in her hand. Delilah's heart jumped when Lucifer's hot hand touched hers. She sent a coy smile over her shoulder, teasing him with a sultry promise. The corners of his lips lifted as his eyes traveled down her body, which was dressed in a tight one-piece body suit.

A thrill of desire sparked inside her. She'd never known such intense passion and had never planned on it happening with Lucifer. But he had unleashed a dark yearning within her. Her body and mind had awakened during her Fall, now greedy to satisfy her dark cravings and thirst for power. This was precisely what she wanted.

Total freedom of mind and body.

Delilah needed to hold Lucifer's undivided attention and complete trust to remain safe. His tastes were depraved, and his determination to destroy mankind was his obsession. Handing out punishment was a playful diversion for him as he plotted out his self-proclaimed destiny for his Seven Realms of Hell. Their Master's demands drove the Princes, knowing the consequences, to please at all costs. She had to be careful, or she'd be Lucifer's next victim.

The whoosh of the massive Throne Room doors opening stirred the still air. Fire flared in Lucifer's eyes, but it wasn't for her. She turned, wondering who had caused this heated reaction. Her hand froze on its trail up Lucifer's leg. Delilah recognized a few of the Fallen, but the middle one stood out. His long white hair fell forward when the guards shoved him from behind. Blazing green eyes locked on her through the strands of his hair, his rage directed at Delilah.

Zar... What have you done?

Sickening dread flushed her nerves. It was an ominous sign for him to be escorted here. Delilah's teeth clenched, returning his hateful gaze with one of her own.

If he's ruined this—

"Leviathan, why have you brought Zar and Kalma before me?" Lucifer asked with a hint of boredom. His thick fingers stroked down her hair, tugging her scalp. What should have delighted her turned her hot blood into ice.

Leviathan moved forward with the same grace and power of a lion. His black dreadlocks rained down around him while his bare black chest glowed green with tribal-like tattoos. His six wings flared, making his presence even more impressive. Leviathan's green eyes flickered at Delilah, seemingly unimpressed by her presence next to Lucifer.

Delilah smirked at the Lord of the Envy Realm but still bowed her head at him. Leviathan couldn't hurt her, nor did she care what he thought of her. Causing friction was part of her plan, and he was playing right into it. But Zar was under Leviathan's realm, which posed a problem for her.

Leviathan... First to go when she has her way.

"My Lord." Leviathan bowed at the waist. "Zar commandeered

few fellow Fallen and went on a hunting mission." He looked back at Zar. "Without permission."

Delilah tried to look bored on the outside, but claws of distress slashed inside her.

He wouldn't have–

"And what was this forbidden mission?" Lucifer lifted Delilah's thick hair off her shoulder, exposing her neck, his breath heating the vulnerable flesh.

The hesitation in Leviathan's voice confirmed her fears. "They went through the portal to kidnap the girl, Olivia."

Zar cried out as an invisible force sent him crashing to the ground. Lucifer soared down the stairs as Zar received a pounding blow to the stomach, and another, snapping his head back. Terror reigned on Kalma's face. She fell to her knees, her eyes riveted to Lucifer's approach. Delilah was livid with these idiots, wanting to throw punches of her own.

Lucifer retracted his wings, landing inches from Zar's face.

"Why would you do such a thing?" Lucifer asked. His voice was deadly calm, but his rigid body vibrated with evil intent.

Zar didn't move, looking up at Lucifer with wary green eyes. "I only wanted to honor you, my Lord. Bring her to you in our cause to destroy man and Heaven–"

"Our cause! It's only my cause unless I tell you otherwise! Don't ever presume to know what I want!" His roar echoed off the walls, cascading down like acid rain. Lucifer glanced at Leviathan. "Bring me the girl."

"They were unsuccessful, my–"

"I had her, but the archangels showed up–" Zar interjected.

"Michael!" Lucifer spat. He picked Zar up and heaved him against a large stone pillar. It cracked on impact, sending dust and stone into the air. Zar landed near the pool's edge. Terror coursed through Delilah; her hand clutched the throne arm so tightly, she thought she might break it.

How could he! What a fool! All my plans...

Lucifer struck with lightning speed. He lifted Kalma by the throat and launched her high over the pool. Her high-pitched scream screeched like nails against glass. Waves rippled in the pool as the serpent tracked his prey. Delilah watched Kalma's hot-pink hair and flailing body fall toward the water. The floor tilted beneath Delilah, who was not able to turn away from her personal nightmare.

The serpent broke surface and launched itself beneath Kalma's flailing body. Water glistened down its wicked red-finned body. Its enormous mouth opened, revealing rows of long teeth ending in sharp, deadly points. Its roar drowned out the hysterical screams of Kalma as their fate met mid-air. The serpent's jaws snapped around her middle like a metal trap. Black blood exploded into the air, raining down on the serpent. The deadly creature slipped back into the pool as quickly as it had surfaced. Kalma's hot-pink hair was the last to sink under the choppy water. A sickening horror washed over Delilah.

She might be next.

All because of the impulsive fool, lying docile on the floor.

Lucifer paced around Zar. "Not a big splash this time." Leviathan chuckled as he leaned against another massive pillar. Delilah sneered at his obvious enjoyment of Lucifer's taunts.

"What to do with you, Zar? Should I throw you over the pool to Tannin as I did Kalma, or tear you limb by limb and let my ravenous serpent play fetch?"

"Master—"

Lucifer's swift kick to Zar's back ended his plea. "I have one question for you first before I decide. Answer wisely, and it might save you. So here it is: You aren't daring enough to have thought of this plot on your own. Who planted this seed of betrayal for you?" He cocked his head.

"No one, my Lord."

"So, first you betray me, and now you lie," Lucifer planted his boot against Zar's chest. "And now Michael knows."

Delilah's breaths came in erratic spurts. The Realm's color exploded through the windows, matching Lucifer's growing rage. But for Delilah, the waves of brilliant color only accented the pure evil dominating the room. Her eyes darted to the door behind the throne

I could slip out... portal away...

But brutal realization halted her rash plan. Delilah didn't know how to raise a portal from down here. She was trapped in her own personal Hell.

Lucifer struck again, tossing Zar closer to the pool's edge. Zar hit the floor hard but caught himself before he rolled into it. He sat up, but Lucifer was upon him.

"Wait! There are more guardians!" Zar yelled, raising his hands in defense. "Two teenage boys... they were with her. All of them used mental powers against us." Zar's chest heaved. "I've seen them before... with Olivia. I'll help you find them."

Delilah froze. Her mind reeled at Zar's revelation. She couldn't believe it! How could she not have known? She racked her memory, licking her lips, finding nothing. She'd been so focused on Conner, she didn't pay attention to Olivia, let alone her friends. Her eyes narrowed at Zar, seeing him in a new, twisted light.

What else are you keeping from me to protect your miserable hide?

Lucifer's head whipped around, pinning her with his dark fury. His foot stayed planted, shoving Zar further against the floor.

"Does he speak the truth, Delilah? Are there more of these guardians?"

The room stank of fear and malice. Her mind raced for a solution, one she needed to answer carefully, or she was the next meal for Tannin.

"Conner only spoke of himself as a guardian. His trite way of trying to protect the knowledge of others from me. Conner is a liar, a sneak. I should have known not to trust his word." She lifted her chin toward Zar. "But if what Zar saw is true, this could benefit us." The weight of the room's eyes bored into her, waiting for her answer: one set desperate, one curious, and one looking for blood.

Be right...

Delilah's heart pounded as she took the first step down the stairs with a false bravado she needed to satisfy their hunger. "These guardians don't know that I've shared their secret with you. So that means the archangels are clueless too. Conner said he'd battled many

Fallen... said they could sense each other when close enough. There's no reason for Michael or the others to think this encounter was any different. The guardians would have known this and prepared for it." Lucifer's body relaxed as she weaved her tale. "So, if Zar has found other guardians, it gives us a better opportunity to watch them and find out what they've learned. We can then pick the weakest one when the time arrives to strike."

The outside wails mixed with her internals cries, waiting for Lucifer's next move. Delilah took a few more steps and glanced at Leviathan. She found him staring at her with renewed interest and a sickening grin.

Lucifer gave Zar a final shove, but not into the pool. "You disappoint me, Zar, but I'll give you a second chance. Find these new guardians, and I might let you live. I'm watching you. And our past ties won't give you consideration for life or death again."

Zar nodded as he raised himself up. Delilah flashed a chilling look to Zar.

Past ties... You owe me.

"Leviathan, punish him for his disobedience." Leviathan walked over to Zar, but Lucifer splayed his large hand across his chest, stopping him. "But if it happens again, you'll be punished next to him."

"Understood. I'll make sure disobedience never crosses his mind again."

Delilah dared not imagine the torture waiting for him, but Zar didn't let his fear show as Leviathan led him down the glass walkway. The massive doors closed along with Delilah's eyes as she sighed in relief.

The backhand was swift and hard, snapping Delilah's head back. Shock struck her as she prepared for another blow. Evil measured her as a trickle of blood rolled down her chin. His hand snaked into her hair. She stumbled as he yanked her to him.

"What else do you *not* know, Delilah?" His fingers pushed into her scalp. "Hm? Or are you keeping secrets from me?"

"Nothing. I've told you everything." She laid a shaking hand on his chest. "I promise."

Lucifer shook her head like a rattle. She was so close to him, she could suffocate in his brutality.

"You please me for now." His wet tongue licked the line of blood from her chin to her bruised lip. "But don't think pleasing me would ever save you."

His hard lips slammed down on her bruised mouth, not interested in her reply. The serpent broke the surface, sending water splashing over the sides like an exclamation point on his promise. Survival kicked as she leaned into the ruthless kiss, raking her hands down his hard, muscular back, hoping to disguise her trembling as wanton desire... not primal fear.

CHAPTER FORTY-SEVEN

ZAR

Z ar remained silent as he followed Leviathan's massive back over the bridge to the Realm of Envy. Black lava below churned and boiled between the jagged rocks. As they passed the green pool, frothing with human souls mutating inside it, two Fallen stepped in stride behind Zar. He unclenched his fists, concentrating on showing no emotion as they entered Envy's dark, malignant mountain's entrance. Zar stumbled, uncertain if it was the change of rocky terrain or from the unknown of what lurked inside the cavernous hole.

One of the Fallen shoved him forward, but Zar ignored their sneers. He searched the dark crevasses of the mountain's tunnel. The air was stifling and smelled of sulfur mixed with the reek of fear and torture. He'd never been inside the mountain, avoiding it at all costs. Punishments happened in the mountain's bowels, and some Fallen or Lessors never returned.

I will... I have vengeance to seek.

As they walked deeper inside, Zar heard them before he saw them. Their wailing.

Their begging.

Their suffering.

The tunnel widened, changing the landscape. The edges of th

opaque rocky walls morphed into a mixture of glowing green streaks and globs. The glow cast an eerie shifting light on the floor and ceiling. The walls moved in undulating waves, but not because of the lighting. His vision sharpened on the tunnel walls, moving as if it were alive.

Because it is alive... with the damned.

Encased inside the walls and around the ceiling, the damned were piled on top of each other like a neon green dumpsite, their naked bodies in constant motion as body parts sought relief from their claustrophobic dog pile. Their hostile eyes watched him. Some hissed while others cried for release. The only thing separating him from them was the thick transparent membrane covering the tunnel like a macabre aquarium. With each step through their prison, the opening at the end of the cavern grew wider and taller. His punishment loomed somewhere beyond it.

Zar stopped when Leviathan moved to the right of the enormous cavern's mouth. Leviathan swept his arm wide, an atrocious smile spanning his black face.

"Welcome to my Realm's pit of the damned, bursting with human souls who spent their lives envious of others." He scoffed as he scanned the shifting mass. "Never satisfied with what they had... always wanting more and hating others who had what they felt was their entitlement." He turned back on Zar. "But you're familiar with this, aren't you?" Not waiting for his reply, Leviathan jumped, his six black wings disappearing over the edge.

Zar cast a wary eye over the side, watching Leviathan circle the edges of the pit. The damned, trapped inside their embryotic membrane, layer by layer, ending at the bottom of the pit, cried out to their Prince. The roars drummed against Zar's body as their cries thundered, shaking the walls of the pit. For a brief second, he thought of fleeing. But they'd kill him, and that wasn't his plan. Whatever Leviathan had in store for him, he had to survive.

"Jump," a Fallen hissed behind him. "Before I cut off a wing and push you."

His anger jettisoned him off the edge. The Fallen guards followed, not allowing him much room to maneuver. The sweltering air grew thin, yet thick with violence on his flight to the bottom. Green blurs rushed by him as their wails and lurid cries assaulted his ears. Leviathan waited for him on a large circular pad, standing between two metal poles with heavy dangling chains.

Maybe I won't make it out alive.

Zar landed and walked with his head held high between the two poles. The pounding malice from the damned nearly broke his control and focus. He zeroed in on Leviathan's face, pushing out the assaulting distractions. Zar set his rage and resentment free inside himself. He needed it pulsing through him while he harnessed his inner strength so he could withstand his torture. The chains rattled, locking around his wrists and ankles. Whatever maniacal persecution was inflicted, Zar would absorb it. Keep it buried deep until he'd return the favor and release this pain upon others.

"Beautiful, isn't it?"

Zar shook his head. Leviathan spoke, but his lips didn't move.

"There's no need for the damned to hear us. They only want your punishment."

Over Leviathan's shoulder, a huge lumbering form emerged from the dark cave. Each step crushed the gravel beneath his misshapen bare feet. The mutilated beast was twice the size of any Fallen. The hideous creature's body was scarred from head to toe with jagged whip marks so thick there was no flesh left unmarked. The damned's roars grew deafening as the beast stalked toward Zar.

Icy dread drenched him. Zar leaned back, but the chains gripped him in place. There was no avoiding the beast. But it wasn't his size that Zar feared. It was the wicked device attached to his forearms. A thick steel rod ran down the front of each arm, held in place by three sets of metal claws buried in his scarred skin. A long, green, electric whip sizzled from the end of each rod. The beast raised his arms and brought the whips down, snapping at Zar's feet. The damned's cries were a frenzy matching their bodies thrashing against the membrane thinning against their force.

"You've shamed the Envy Realm with your deception, your failure. I must remind you of who you are and why you chose to become a Fallen."

The first lick of the whip tore a deep line across Zar's chest. Black blood spilled, but his skin was quick in rejuvenating, closing the wound.

If the beast is slow...

Two green blurs landed at the same time across his neck and thigh. The creature paced around him, landing blows at will. A slice across his face caused Zar to cry out, heightening the pit's madness as his pulverized skin leaked his blood into the pit's black gravel.

"These humans became damned because their sins ruled them with their flesh and passions! We're here because we want to be their masters, not their slaves. To be masters of our own flesh and desires, not ruled by them. To destroy humanity, not serve them! They are nothing! We are everything!"

The blows came faster and harder, shredding Zar's body before he could heal it. His body sagged against the chains, losing his battle of will and healing. The ragged, excited breathing of the beast grew louder as it laid its whip across Zar, leaving no part unscathed.

A green blur flew in front of Zar's face. But it was too late to escape it. The whip snapped across his eyes. His head fell back in agony as a roar of mindless pain tore from him. Zar's eyes were ripped away, remaining flesh burned to nothing. Blood stained his tattered body, his lashed face, his empty eye sockets.

"You are of the Realm of Envy!"

Leviathan's voice railed against him. Zar's chest heaved as visions began in the darkness, his blindness. Man, and their endless, tireless wants of bigger and better things, envious gossip, friend desiring his best friend's life.

"These petty passions feed their weak souls. But you"—Leviathan's voice was thick with malice—*"this is what you want, but you'll never gaze upon her again."*

Delilah's face assailed him. Her as an angel, a Fallen, and her with Lucifer. Visions of the two of them together, laughing, kissing, mating, plotting. A snarl of agony tore across his face while a pit of deep despair took root. His desperate need for her shamed him, feeding his driving desire to kill her. And Lucifer–

"Yes, Lucifer. He's the real problem. He's taken Delilah from you and is so enamored with her, he doesn't see the time for war is now! Destroy Heaven and its angels! Stop the Second Coming before it's too late and make man our slaves, our victims for as long as we want them, trapped in Hell forever."

Zar hung breathless from the chains, destroyed, his body depleted from the agonizing torture. But his mind was renewed by the shared vision, his more profound mission, and Leviathan's persuasive words.

Wrists and ankles freed, Zar crumpled face-first at Leviathan's feet. He lay there until his body healed enough for him to move. He pulled himself up on all fours, then staggered to his feet, blindly facing his Prince. The pit grew quiet, anticipation palpable.

"Zar has survived his punishment from the beast and been reminded of who he is: a Fallen!" Leviathan strutted around the pit, yelling up at the damned. "Are you with us or against us, Zar?"

"I'm with you," Zar rasped.

He heard the crunch of gravel when Leviathan stomped his foot. It came down again, joined by the Fallen around him. The stomps grew faster and rose around the pit, joined by the damned, pounding as one in approval. The beast snarled and lumbered away with footsteps not matching those of the pit.

Zar ignored their praise, for he didn't want or need it. His mangled flesh healed, but his compliance was hollow. He'd play their game...

Until I take my revenge.

CHAPTER FORTY-EIGHT

OLIVIA

O livia made the slow right turn onto her street, but her heart was hammering as if she'd run a race.

Today was the day. This was it.

Training with the Magi.

She passed Zach's house. He'd parked his truck on the curb, but there was no sign of him. He was as anxious as she to begin. Each time they met each other at school, he'd given her hand a reassuring squeeze or sent her a wink. But his eyes mirrored hers: excited, nervous, and mixed with a dose of fear. Olivia pushed her emotions aside. She didn't need the negative clouding her judgment or holding her back. Her ring's glint caught her eye on the steering wheel. Its dragon fire stone reminded her to keep her inner strength burning bright. She must be fearless, or she'd be the next funeral attended.

Olivia parked in the driveway next to her dad's truck and set her jaw, determined not to let him ruffle her feathers. She gathered her gear and headed for her destiny. The house was quiet except for the coffeemaker in the kitchen. It smelled divine, but caffeine was the last thing her revved-up system needed. She put her backpack down and stroked Thunder, who was purring at the foot of the stairs. His light green eyes were half-closed as he arched his back against her strokes.

"Hey." She jumped at her dad's voice behind her. For such a big man, he made little noise. No doubt honed from years of sneaking up on things that went bump in the night. "How was your day?"

Olivia stood as Thunder jumped off the stairs and into the den. She glanced at his somber face as she walked by, shrugging. "Fine. Hard to concentrate with all this taking place. I got called out again for daydreaming by Ms. Thomas. She's my last class, and I'd kinda checked out by then." She poured herself a cup of coffee to occupy her nervous hands. Leaning her hip against the counter, she peeked at Dad above the cup's steamy rim. "Mom upstairs?"

"Yep. Worn out after PT, but she's improving every day. Her balance is better thanks to years of dance and yoga—"

"Thank you," Olivia blurted. "She wouldn't be... uh... where she is without you taking and pushing her."

Why am I rambling?

Dad slipped his hands into his jean pockets. He released a shuddering breath, looking at her with startling blue eyes.

"I love her," Dad said. Olivia bit her lip against her dad's vulnerability. "And you, too." His voice broke.

She cleared her throat and shook her head. "We can't do this—"

"You're not ready to have me back in your life. I get that.... I really do, but I'm here now to help you and build back the trust I broke when I left." His eyes pleaded with her. "You'll never know how truly sorry I am."

Olivia fought back the harsh words she wanted to hurl at him. Not because he didn't deserve it, but because she needed to take a step forward. If she stayed tangled up in her feelings about him, the cost to her would be too high.

"I can't change the past, Olivia. It's done. I want to start now. Whatever you need, or questions, or—"

"What was your first kill?" Olivia interrupted, wanting to change the subject.

Dad's face turned to stone as he sat back on the barstool like he'd had the wind knocked out of him. A range of emotions played across his face before it settled on one: resignation.

"My first kill." His thumbnail picked at a spot on the granite counter. "I haven't thought about that in a long time, kiddo." He sighed, slapping his hands against his thighs.

"It was a succubus, and she was hunting my best friend. I wasn't much older than you." His eyes were distant until they focused back on her. "Anyway, I thought I was somebody with these secret powers and master of weapons... like I was some superhero. But I was so wrong. 'Bout got my butt killed." Dad scratched his beard as he slumped against the barstool. "I learned two valuable lessons that night."

"What's that?"

"I'm not invincible, and evil knows no bounds."

Olivia took another sip, trying to push away the memory of Manny's death.

"What is a succubus?" Olivia asked.

"It's a female Fallen that tries to... uh... have relations with a human male so it can slowly steal his soul."

"Wow. So that's what it's called. That's what must have attacked Zach."

"Yep. Rachel told me. She said she could sense it, but had to lie in wait so Zach wouldn't find out about her. Drove her crazy knowing it was stalking her son." Dad chuckled. "But Rachel is as tenacious and as fearless as they come. It never stood a chance."

"That doesn't match with the fun-loving mom who's always trying to feed me." Olivia's grin matched her dad's.

"When Zach shared with Sergio and me about his attacks, it stunned me. I didn't think *anything* like that existed outside of the movies." Her smile faded as she remembered how freaked out Zach had been.

"Each Fallen is unique in skill and goal in how they undermine us, kill us and steal our souls." He approached her and took her mug, laying it on the counter. He trapped Olivia between him and the counter. Her body tensed as his nearness blocked out the room, demanding her attention. He grabbed for her hands, warm to the touch, holding her in place before she could scoot away.

"They're also master manipulators. They'll do anything to get what they want. You can never let your guard down and never believe what they say, even if it seems to make sense. Their goal is your death so they can have your soul."

"Well, I guess lesson one is complete."

Olivia jumped, but Dad rolled his eyes. Melchior cracked a smile as his large hand slapped Conner's back. A nervous laugh escaped Olivia as Dad stepped away, releasing her hands. She'd only seen Melchior at the ceremony by the firelight. He'd been a frightening, imposing figure, but in the daylight, he wasn't as scary. In fact, he was handsome, and much more at ease, but his cobalt blue eyes studied her. She lifted her chin and returned his stare with one of her own. He wasn't the only one looking to peel away layers. Olivia was putting her life in his hands. She wanted to learn and understand all she could about this Magi. A corner of his mouth lifted, and he gave her a slight nod.

Guess he liked what he saw.

"Caspar and Balthazar are coming." His head turned to the kitchen window. An electric green web appeared in the backyard, widening out from the center. They emerged; the portal closed with lightning speed behind them. They glanced at the inhabitants as they walked through the glass of the sliding door. Olivia gasped, waiting for the glass to shatter. They stopped inside the den; the glass remained intact. The familiar smell of an electrical storm filled the room. Adrenaline hit Olivia. Soon she'd step through the portal, leaving her old life and discovering her new one.

"You know, you should try a door sometime." Conner smirked as he gave each Magi a handshake. They turned to Olivia with the same gaze as Melchior. She tried not to squirm under their intensity. She sensed this was the lens through which they gauged everything and everyone.

The doorbell rang. Olivia rushed to the foyer, thankful to be out from under their collective inspection. Sergio and Zach walked in, as did Javier and Rachel, each giving her a hug as they passed her.

Olivia followed them to the overcrowded den. The boys exchanged handshakes with the Magi. Zach was tense, but excitement emanated from his cocky smile and gleaming eyes. Sergio's excitement was clouded by a darker energy lurking beneath the surface.

Melchior signaled the other Magi. Each of them produced a small disk the size of a quarter. Melchior took Olivia's hand and placed the cool disk on her palm. It was a polished brown stone with black markings. She brought it closer, her heart pounding as she recognized the engraving.

Orion.

She turned the smooth stone over in her palm. It ignited a heat in her already-warm hand. Shiny wisps of black scrolls were written around the edge.

"What does it say?" Olivia asked, marveling at its possibilities.

"It's written in the tongue of angels. *Release what was given,*" Melchior said.

"I don't understand. What does that mean?" Olivia's brow creased.

"Always a curious mind, but it's for you to discover its meaning." He smiled down at her. "Keep this talisman with you at all times. It'll have other uses, but for now, it's your passage through the portal." She stared wide-eyed at the talisman, feeling like she'd plunged down a roller coaster, leaving her stomach at her feet and her heart in her throat. Her mom's voice echoed in her ears.

Your burden and your blessing.

"How does it work?" Sergio asked, his voice higher than usual.

"Let's go outside, and we'll show you." Melchior held out his hand. "Are you ready?"

Olivia could only nod as she took her first step forward. Panic tried to seize her, demanding she deny Melchior's offer, but she accepted. A calmness, like an anchor in a storm, crept up her arm, releasing these anxious thoughts. She passed by Dad, who stood stoically in the kitchen. He'd shoved his fists under his crossed arms, as if he were willing himself not to reach out as she passed.

She floated a confident smile. "I'll be back soon."

"I'll be right here," Dad said, wearing his own brave face.

This time, Caspar opened the sliding glass door. The brisk air was refreshing, clearing up her overwhelmed senses. The pairs spread out to different areas of the backyard, with the three parents watching them through the glass door.

Olivia gazed at Melchior as the disk grew warmer in her sweaty palm. He took her hand into his, engulfing it. Anticipation surged through Olivia as she faced the angel condemned to eternity as a man, tasked to train her as a guardian of the Mar of Sin, a portal jumper, and a weapon-wielding demon killer.

You can do this, Olivia.

She inhaled the fresh afternoon air through her nose and released a cleansing breath.

"See in your mind Orion on the talisman."

Olivia closed her eyes. She concentrated on the stone, seeing the seven dots while attuned to Melchior's voice.

"Now find the power core inside of you. The same energy you used to fight the Fallen."

Olivia's eyes flew open.

"I don't know how to do that." Her breathing hitched.

"I'll help you find it." He gave her hand a quick squeeze. She closed her eyes again, trying to remember how she had felt that night. A seed of tingling bloomed behind her mark as she fed off of the surrounding emotions.

"Don't hold back. Release the energy into the stone."

His voice faded as the tingling grew, spreading warmth. She imagined it flowing through her arm into her palm—

A bright light flashed around her and Melchior. Electric blue energy singed the air and crackled around her. The portal sprang to life behind them. A huge smile spread across Melchior's face. He took a step inside, and she followed, engulfed in a vacuum of swirling lights.

"Here we go!" was the last thing Olivia heard before her body became weightless, her world engulfed in a sea of blazing blue lights

A punch of energy vaulted her into the unknown world of the Magi and the secrets of the guardianship.

Her new life.
Her new burden.
Her new blessing.

Light of Orion
Guardians of Orion Series Book 2

Evil is gathering strength. When she learns the truth, it could cost her life.

Las Vegas. Seventeen-year-old Olivia Drake never asked for the mark of Orion on her chest. Training in secret with her two friends after their hard-won victory over the Fallen, she struggles to master her powers and gain respect as the only woman on the team. But their little band of warriors is more well-known than they think when she's brutally attacked by a demon and left for dead.

Although she escapes, Olivia fears the poison dagger used against her can only mean Lucifer is coming for them. And a horrifying family connection will make her more vulnerable than she knows…

Can Olivia survive the ultimate betrayal with the fate of humanity on the line?

Light of Orion is the second book in the thrilling Guardian of Orion YA Christian Fantasy series. If you like clean-but-gritty stories, jaw-dropping surprises, and age-old battles, you'll love S. L. Richardson's epic adventure.

Buy *Light of Orion* to fight the Damned today!

Click on link below. Available on Amazon and Kindle Unlimited.

https://www.amazon.com/dp/B08DDC4Y1N/

PLEASE WRITE A REVIEW

Thank you so much for reading *Mark of Orion!* I hope you loved reading it as much as I enjoyed writing it! I would like to know what you thought about the book. Reviews breathe life into an author's spirit and help others in the quest to find their next entertaining book. Please write your review on Amazon and/or Goodreads. Thank you so much!

Amazon:
https://www.amazon.com/dp/B07ZN6P1TF/

Goodreads:
https://www.goodreads.com/author/show/
19692005.S_L_Richardson

DON'T MISS OUT!

Never miss any sneak peeks or updates on any of your favorite characters and books or my upcoming books! Go to my website at www.slrichardson.com and sign-up for my weekly newsletter full of fun and intriguing insights about the *Guardian of Orion* series and my writing life. I'd also love it if you'd drop me an email on my *"contact me"* page with questions or what you think about my books. I'll get back with you. You're the best!

Click on the link to get your free copy of Trials of the Guardians, a prequel featuring Conner in his quest to save his best friend from a succubus.

https://dl.bookfunnel.com/g5z3t5d7e0

ACKNOWLEDGMENTS

I never imagined the journey I'd take over the last two years when this story and its characters first burst from my mind while I sat waiting at a traffic light. It wasn't a journey taken on a smooth, easy road where I poured out a perfect first draft effortlessly onto my laptop. Instead, I was riddled with self-doubt, battled with my guilt for taking time away from my family and friends, and overwhelmed by an undertaking of unknown scope and magnitude. All I was sure of was that I was going to write a fantasy trilogy. So, I kept taking bites out of this unruly elephant by placing my butt in the chair and writing words on the screen until the first book was done.

But I *never* would have completed this book without the love and support of family and friends who continue to bless my life.

When I first told the love of my life, my husband, Chris my desire to write this trilogy, he didn't blink an eye. He told me to go for my dream, knock it out of the park and don't give up. He never complained when I'd shotgun blast him with ideas or worries or when I asked him to edit/proofread my drafts. He gave me nothing but his complete love, boundless encouragement, and unending support. He's my rock and this book wouldn't have happened without him. Thank you, my love.

We have four beautiful children that I love with all my heart. Thank you for having faith in me and repeating that it's never too late to chase a dream, and for not complaining when it was *seek and ye shall find night* for dinner. You are my life and I'm so proud and amazed by each of you!

A big hug and thank you to my and Chris's family. My village. Each of you gave me encouragement and love for which I'm so grateful. I love each of you very much! Thank you, Dad, for your loving support. But one special lady was truly the wind beneath my wings… my mom. She is simply the most generous, loving, and unselfish person I know. She'd let me unload all my fears and then prop me back up and tell me to go write. She's my biggest cheerleader. Thank you, Mom. Love you.

I have some amazing friends who inspired me along through this process. Mary R., Teresa, Jen I., Barbara, Lela L., Natalie N., Janet D., and Kristine, I thank you from the bottom of my heart for your unending optimism and undying friendship. Your advice was instrumental in the success of this book. Thank you for also being my beta readers and/or critic advisors. Y'all rock!

And lastly, thank you to God, who is my light when I see darkness and who has forgiven me for my sins. And to my guardian angel, for holding my hand all through life.

Guardian Angel Prayer

Angel of God,
My guardian dear,
To whom God's love
Commits me here.
Ever this day,
Be at my side,
To light and guard
To rule and guide.
Amen

ABOUT THE AUTHOR
S. L. RICHARDSON

When you don't find her reading the latest YA fantasy or thriller or running her high schooler to his various activities, she is at the computer writing the next book in her trilogy, *Guardians of Orion*.

Being an author has been a dream of hers, but like running a marathon, thought it would never happen. After hitting 50, she chased the dream (not running a marathon, but writing), and released her first, *Mark of Orion*.

When she's not writing, she loves cooking, gardening, going to Houston Astros baseball games, and walking her German Shepherd (or maybe he walks her).

She lives in Texas with her incredible and supportive husband and is blessed with four amazing children.

Connect with S. L.!
www.slrichardson.com

facebook.com/authorslrichardson
twitter.com/_slrichardson
instagram.com/authorslrichardson
pinterest.com/authorslrichardson

Made in the USA
Las Vegas, NV
08 August 2024